THE GIRL

IN THE

CASTLE

THE GIRL

IN THE

CASTLE

A Novel

SANTA MONTEFIORE

wm

WILLIAM MORROW
An Imprint of HarperCollins*Publishers*

10-18-16

Originally published as *Songs of Love and War* in Great Britain in 2015 by Simon & Schuster UK Ltd.

FIRST WILLIAM MORROW PAPERBACK PUBLISHED 2016.

Designed by Diahann Sturge

Part title art © Morphart Creation/Shutterstock, Inc.
Chapter opener art © DavidBukach/iStockphoto.

Library of Congress Cataloging-in-Publication Data has been applied for.

ISBN 978-0-06-245685-4 (paperback)
ISBN 978-0-06-249079-7 (library edition)

16 17 18 19 20   OV/RRD   10 9 8 7 6 5 4 3 2 1

To my dear friend, Tim Kelly,
without whose guidance and support
I would never have had
the courage to write this book

Is mise Peig Ni Laoghaire. A Tiarna Deverill, dhein tú éagóir orm agus ar mo shliocht trín ár dtalamh a thógáil agus ár spiorad a bhriseadh. Go dtí go gceartaíonn tú na h-éagóracha siúd, cuirim malacht ort féin agus d-oidhrí, I dtreo is go mbí sibh gan suaimhneas síoraí I ndomhan na n-anmharbh.

I am Maggie O'Leary. Lord Deverill, you have wronged me and my descendants by taking our land and breaking our spirits. Until you right those wrongs I curse you and your heirs to an eternity of unrest and to the world of the undead.

Maggie O'Leary, 1662

Prologue

Co. Cork, Ireland, 1925

The two little boys with grubby faces and scuffed knees reached the rusted iron gate by way of a barely distinguishable track that branched off the main road and cut through the forest in a sleepy curve. On the other side of the gate, forgotten behind trees, were the charred remains of Castle Deverill, home to one of the grandest Anglo-Irish families in the land before it was consumed in a fire three years before. The dry-stone wall around the property had collapsed in places from neglect and harsh winter winds. Moss spread undeterred, weeds seeded themselves indiscriminately, grass grew like tufts of hair along the top of the wall and ivy spread its fingers over the stones, swallowing entire sections completely. The boys were unfazed by the large sign that warned trespassers of prosecution or the dark driveway ahead that was littered with moldy leaves, twigs and mud. The padlock clanked ineffectively against its chain as the boys pushed the gates apart and slipped through.

On the other side, the forest was silent and soggy, for the summer was ended and autumn had blown in with icy gales and cold rain. The drive once had been lined on either side with red rhododendron bushes but now they were obscured by dense nettles, ferns and overgrown laurel. The boys ran past them, oblivious of what the shrubs represented, unaware that that very drive had once witnessed carriages bearing the finest in the county to the magnificent castle over-looking the sea. Now the drive was little more than a dirt track and the castle lay in ruins. Only ravens and pigeons ventured there, and intrepid little boys intent on adventure, confident that no one would discover them in this forgotten place.

The children hurried excitedly through the wild grasses to play among the remnants of the once stately rooms. The sweeping staircase was long gone and the center chimneys had fallen through the roof and formed a mountain of bricks for the boys to scale. In the west wing the surviving part of the roof remained as sturdy beams that straddled two of the enduring walls, like the exposed ribcage of a giant animal left to decay in the open air.

The boys were too distracted to feel the sorrow that hung over the place or to hear the plaintive echo of the past. They were too young to have an awareness of nostalgia and the melancholic sense of mortality it induces. The ghosts who dwelt there, mourning the loss of their home and their brief lives, were as wind blowing in off the water. The boys heard the moaning of the empty windows and the whistling about the remaining chimney stacks and felt only a frisson of exhilaration, for the eeriness served to enhance their pleasure, not diminish it. The ghosts might as well have been alone for the attention the boys paid them.

Over the front door, one of the boys was able to make out some Latin letters, tarnished by soot, half concealed in the blackened lintel. "*Castellum Deverilli est suum regnum 1662*," he read out.

"What does that mean?" asked the smaller boy.

"Everyone around here knows what that means. A Deverill's castle is his kingdom."

The smaller child laughed. "Not much of a kingdom now," he said.

They went from room to room in the fading light like a pair of urchins, excavating hopefully where the ground was soft. Their gentle chatter mingled with the croaking of ravens and the cooing of pigeons, and the ghosts were appeased as they remembered their own boyhoods and the games they had played in the sumptuous gardens of the castle. For once, the castle had been magnificent.

At the turn of the century there had been a walled garden, abundant with every sort of fruit and vegetable to feed the Deverill family and their servants. There had been a rose garden, an arboretum and a maze where the Deverill children had routinely lost themselves and each other among the yew hedges. There had been elaborate glass houses where tomatoes had grown among orchids and figs, and yellow cowslips had reflected the summer sun in the wildflower garden where the ladies of the house had enjoyed picnics and afternoons full of laughter and gossip. Those gardens had once been a paradise but now they smelled of decay. A shadow lingered in spite of the sunshine and year after year bindweed slowly choked the gardens to death. Nothing remained of the castle's former beauty except a savage splendor of sorts, made all the more arresting by its tragedy.

At the rattling sound of a motor car the boys stopped their digging. The noise grew louder as the car advanced up the drive. They looked at each other in bewilderment and crept hastily through the rooms to the front, where they peered out of a glassless window to see a shiny Ford Model T making its way past the castle before halting at the steps leading up to where the front door had once been.

Consumed with curiosity, they elbowed each other in their effort to get a closer look, careful to stay concealed behind the wall. The boys' jaws fell open at the sight of the car with its soft top and smoothly curved lines. The sun bounced off the sleek green bonnet and the silver headlights shone like a frog's eyes. Then the driver's door opened and a man stepped out wearing a brown felt hat and smart camel coat. He swept his eyes over the castle, taking a moment to absorb the dramatic vision. He shook his head and pulled a face as if to acknowledge the sheer scale of the misfortune that had destroyed such a beautiful castle. Then he walked around to the passenger door and opened it.

He held out his hand and a small black glove reached out and took it. The boys were so still that, were it not for their pink faces and black hair, they might have been a pair of cherub statues. With mounting interest they watched the woman step out. She wore an elegant dress of a deep emerald green and a long black coat, with a black cloche hat pulled low over her face. Only her scarlet lips were visible, shocking against her white skin. Glittering beneath her right shoulder was a large diamond star brooch. The boys' eyes widened, for she looked as if she came from another world; the sort of world that had once inhabited this fine castle before it was swept away.

The woman stood at the foot of the darkened walls and lifted her chin. She took the man's hand and turned to face him. "As God is my witness," she said, and the boys had to strain their ears to hear her. "I will rebuild this castle." She paused and the man made no move to hurry her. At length she returned her gaze to the castle and her jaw stiffened. "After all, I have as much right as any of the others."

PART ONE

Chapter One

Co. Cork, Ireland, 1910

Kitty Deverill was nine years old. For other children, born on other days, turning nine was of no great significance. But for Kitty, born on the ninth day of the ninth month in the year 1900, turning nine had been very significant indeed. It wasn't her mother, the beautiful and narcissistic Maud, who had put those ideas into the young child's head; Maud was not interested in Kitty. She had two other daughters who were soon to come of age and a cherished son at Eton who was the light in his mother's eyes. In the five years between Harry and Kitty's births Maud had suffered three miscarriages induced by riding hard over the hills around Ballinakelly; Maud did not want her pleasure halted by an inconvenient pregnancy. However, no amount of reckless galloping managed to unburden her of her fourth child, who, contrary to expectation, was a weak and squeaking girl with red hair and transparent skin, more like a scrawny kitten than a human baby. Maud had turned her face away in disgust and refused to acknowledge her. She had rejected her child, declining to allow her friends to visit, donning her riding habit and setting off with the hunt as if the birth had never happened. For a woman so enraptured with her own beauty an ugly baby was an affront. No, Maud would never have put ideas into Kitty's head that she was in any way special or important.

It was her paternal grandmother, Adeline, Lady Deverill, who told her that the year 1900 was auspicious and that her date of birth was also remarkable, on account of it containing so many nines. Kitty was a child of Mars, Adeline would remind her when they sat together in Adeline's private sitting room on the first floor, one of the few rooms of the castle that was always warm. This meant that her life would be defined by conflict—a testing hand of cards dealt by a God who surely knew that Kitty would rise to the challenge with courage and wisdom. Adeline told her much else, besides, and Kitty far preferred her stories of angels and demons to the dry tales her Scottish governess read her, and even to the kitchen maids' tittle-tattle, mostly local gossip Kitty was too young to understand. Adeline Deverill knew about *things*. Things at which Kitty's grandfather rolled his eyes and dismissed as "blarney," things her father mocked with affection and things that caused Kitty's mother great concern. Maud Deverill was less amused by tales of spirits, stone circles and curses and instructed Miss Grieve, Kitty's Scottish governess, to punish the child if she ever indulged in what she considered to be "ghastly peasant superstition." Miss Grieve, with her tight lips and tight vowels, was only too happy to whack the palms of Kitty's hands with a riding crop. Therefore the child had learned to be secretive. She had grown as furtive as a fox, indulging her interest only with her grandmother, in the warmth of her little den that smelled of turf fire and lilac.

Kitty didn't live in the castle: that was where her grandparents lived and what, one day, her father would inherit, along with the title of Lord Deverill, dating back to the seventeenth century. Kitty lived on the estate in the old Hunting Lodge, positioned by the river, within walking distance of the castle. Overlooked by her mother and too cunning for her governess, the child was able to run wild about the gardens and surrounding countryside and to play with the local Catholic children who took to the fields with their Tommy cans. Had her mother known she would have developed a fever and retired to her room for a week to get over the trauma. As it was, Maud was often so distracted that she seemed to forget entirely that she had a fourth child and was irritated when Miss Grieve reminded her.

Kitty's greatest friend and ally was Bridie, the raven-haired daughter of Lady Deverill's cook, Mrs. Doyle. Kitty believed them to be "spiritual sisters," thrown together at Castle Deverill, where Bridie would help her mother in the kitchen, peeling potatoes and washing up, while Kitty loitered around the big wooden table stealing the odd carrot when Mrs. Doyle wasn't looking. They might have different parents, Kitty told Bridie, but their souls were eternally connected. Beneath their material bodies they were creatures of light and there was very little difference between them. Grateful for Kitty's friendship, Bridie believed her.

Because of her unconventional view of the world, Adeline was happy to turn a blind eye to the girls playing together. She loved her strange little granddaughter who was so much like herself. In Kitty she found an ally in a family who scoffed at the idea of fairies and trembled at the mention of ghosts while claiming not to believe in them. She was certain that souls inhabited physical bodies in order to live on earth and learn important lessons for their spiritual evolution. Thus, a person's position and wealth were merely a costume required for the part they were playing and not a reflection of their worth as a soul. In Adeline's opinion a tramp was as valuable as a king and so she treated everyone with equal respect. What was the harm of Kitty and Bridie enjoying each other's company? she asked herself. Kitty's sisters were too old to play with her, and Celia, her English cousin, only came to visit in the summer, so the poor child was friendless and lonely. Were it not for Bridie, Kitty might be in danger of running off with the leprechauns and goblins and be lost to them forever.

One story in particular fascinated Kitty above all others: the Cursing of Barton Deverill. The whole family knew it, but no one besides Kitty's grandmother, and Kitty herself, believed it. They didn't just believe, they *knew* it to be true. It was that knowing that bonded grandmother and granddaughter firmly and irreversibly, because Adeline had a gift she had never shared with anyone, not even her husband, and little Kitty had inherited it.

"Let me tell you about the Cursing of Barton Deverill," said

Kitty to Bridie one Saturday afternoon in winter, holding the candle steady in their dark lair, an old, disused cupboard beneath the back staircase, in the servants' quarters of the castle. The light illuminated Kitty's white face so that her big gray eyes looked strangely old, like a witch's, and Bridie felt a shiver ripple across her skin, something close to fear. She had heard her mother speak of the Banshee and its shriek that prewarned of death.

"Who was Barton Deverill?" Bridie asked, her musical Irish accent in sharp contrast to Kitty's clipped English vowels.

"He was the first Lord Deverill and he built this castle," Kitty replied, keeping her voice low for dramatic effect. "He was a right brute."

"What did he do?"

"He took land that wasn't his and built on it."

"Who did the land belong to?"

"The O'Learys."

"The O'Learys?" Bridie's black eyes widened and her cheeks flushed. "You don't mean *our* Jack O'Leary?"

"The very same. I can tell you there is no love lost between the Deverills and the O'Learys."

"What happened?"

"Barton Deverill, my ancestor, was a supporter of King Charles I of England. When his armies were defeated by Cromwell, he ran off to France with the King. Later, when King Charles II was crowned, he rewarded Barton for his loyalty with a title and these lands where he built this castle. Hence the family motto: A Deverill's castle is his kingdom. The trouble was those lands didn't belong to the King, they belonged to the O'Learys.

So, when they were made to leave, old Maggie O'Leary, who was a witch . . ."

Bridie laughed nervously. "She wasn't really a witch!"

Kitty was very serious. "She was so. She had a cauldron and a black cat that could turn a person to stone with one look of its big green eyes."

"Just because she had a cauldron and a cat doesn't mean she was a witch," Bridie argued.

"Maggie O'Leary was a witch and everyone knew it. She put a curse on Barton Deverill."

Bridie's laughter caught in her throat. "What was the curse?"

"That Barton Deverill and every male heir after him will never leave Castle Deverill but remain between worlds until an O'Leary returns to live on the land. It's very unfair because Grandpa and Father will have to hang around here as ghosts, possibly forever. Grandma says that it is very unlikely that a Deverill will ever marry an O'Leary!"

"You never know. They've come up in the world since then," Bridie added, thinking of Jack O'Leary, whose father was the local vet.

"No, they are all doomed, even my brother Harry." Kitty sighed. "None of them believes it, but I do. It makes me sad to know their fate."

"So, are you telling me that Barton Deverill is still here?" Bridie asked.

Kitty's eyes widened. "He's still here and he's not very happy about it."

"You don't really believe that, do you?"

"I *know* it," said Kitty emphatically. "I can *see* him." She bit her lip, aware that she might have given too much away.

Now Bridie was more interested. She knew her friend wasn't a liar. "How can you see him if he's a ghost?"

Kitty leaned forward and whispered, "Because I see dead people." The candle flame flickered eerily as if to corroborate her claim and Bridie shivered.

"You can see dead people?"

"I can and I do. All the time."

"You've never told me before."

"That's because I didn't know if I could trust you."

"What are they like, dead people?"

"Transparent. Some are light, some are dark. Some are loving and some aren't." Kitty shrugged. "Barton Deverill is quite dark. I don't think he was a very nice man when he was alive."

"Doesn't it scare you?"

"It used to, until Grandma taught me not to be afraid. She sees them too. It's a gift, she says. But I'm not allowed to tell anyone."

"They'll lock you away," Bridie said and her voice quivered. "They do that, don't you know. They lock people away in the red-brick in Cork City for less and they never come out. Never."

"Then you'd better not tell on me."

"Oh, I wouldn't."

Kitty brightened. "Do you want to see one?"

"A ghost?"

"Barton Deverill."

The blood drained from Bridie's cheeks. "I don't know . . ."

"Come on, I'll introduce you." Kitty blew out the candle and pushed open the door.

The two girls hurried along the passageway. Regardless of the disparity of their coloring, they could have been sisters as they skipped off together for they were similar in height and build. However, there was a marked difference in their clothes and countenance. While Kitty's dress was white, embellished with fine lace and silk, tied at the waist with a pale blue bow, Bridie's was brown and shapeless and made from a coarse, scratchy frieze. Kitty wore black lace-up boots that reached mid-calf, and thick black stockings, while Bridie's feet were bare and dirty. Kitty's governess brushed her hair and pinned it off her face with ribbons; Bridie received no such attention and her hair was tangled and unwashed, reaching almost as far as her waist. The difference was not only marked in their attire but in the way they looked out onto the world. Kitty had the steady, lofty gaze of a child born to privilege and entitlement, while Bridie had the feral stare of a waif who was always hungry, and yet there was an underlying need in Kitty that bridged the gap between them. Were it not for the loving company of her grandparents and the sporadic attention lavished on her by her father when he wasn't out hunting, shooting game or at the races, Kitty would have been starved of love. It was this longing that gave balance to their friendship, for Kitty needed Bridie just as much as Bridie needed her.

While Kitty was unaware of these differences, Bridie, who heard her parents and brothers complaining endlessly about their lot, was very conscious of them. However, she liked Kitty too much to give way to jealousy, and she was too flattered by her friendship to risk losing it. She accepted her position with the passive compliance of a sheep.

The two girls heard Mrs. Doyle grumbling to one of the maids in the kitchen but they scurried on up the back staircase as quiet as kittens, aware that if they were caught their playtime would be over and Bridie summoned to wash up at the sink.

No one ever went up to the western tower. It was chilly and damp at the top of the castle and the spiral staircase was in need of repair. Two of the wooden steps had collapsed and Kitty and Bridie had to jump over the gaps. Bridie breathed easily now because no one would find them there. Kitty pushed open the heavy door at the top of the stairs and peered around it. Then she turned back to her friend. "Come," she whispered. "Don't be frightened. He won't hurt you."

Bridie's heart began to race. Was she really going to see a ghost? Kitty seemed so sure. Tentatively and with high expectations, Bridie followed Kitty into the room. She looked at Kitty. Kitty was smiling at a tatty old armchair as if someone was sitting in it. But Bridie saw nothing besides the faded burgundy silk. However, the room was colder than the rest of the castle and she shivered and hugged herself.

"Well, can't you see him?" Kitty asked.

"I can't see anything," said Bridie, wanting to very much.

"But he's *there*!" Kitty exclaimed, pointing to the chair. "Look *harder*."

Bridie looked as hard as she could until her eyes watered. "I don't doubt you, Kitty, but I can see nothing but the chair."

Kitty was visibly disappointed. She stared at the man scowling in the armchair, his feet propped up on a stool, his hands folded over his big belly, and wondered how it was possible for her to see someone so clearly when Bridie couldn't. "But he's right in front of your nose. This is my friend, Bridie," Kitty said to Barton Deverill. "She can't see you."

Barton shook his head and rolled his eyes. That didn't surprise him. He'd been stuck in this tower for over two hundred years and in all that time only the very few had seen him—most unintentionally. At first it had been quite amusing being a ghost but now he was bored of observing the many generations of Deverills who came and went, and even more disenchanted by the ones, like him, who remained stuck in the castle as spirits. He wasn't keen on company and there were now too many furious Lord Deverills floating about the corridors to be easily avoided. This tower was the only place he could be free of them, and their wrath at discovering suddenly, upon dying, that the Cursing of Barton Deverill was not simply a family legend but an immutable truth. With the benefit of hindsight, they would have gladly taken an O'Leary for a bride and subsequently ensured their eternal rest as a free soul in Paradise. As it was they were too late. They were stuck and there was nothing they could do about it except rant at *him* for having built the castle on O'Leary land in the first place.

Now Barton turned his jaded eyes onto the eerie little girl whose face had turned red with indignation, as if it were somehow *his* fault that her plain friend was unable to see him. He folded his arms and sighed. He wasn't in the mood for conversation. The fact that she sought him out from time to time did not make her his friend and did not give her permission to show him off like an exotic animal in a menagerie.

Kitty watched him stand up and walk through the wall. "He's gone," she said, dropping her shoulders in defeat.

"Where?"

"I don't know. He's quite bad-tempered, but so would *I* be if I were stuck between worlds."

"Shall we leave now?" Bridie's teeth were chattering.

Kitty sighed. "I suppose we must." They made their way back down the spiral staircase. "You won't tell anyone, will you?"

"I cross my heart and hope to die," Bridie replied solemnly, wondering suddenly whether her friend wasn't a little over-imaginative.

IN THE BOWELS of the castle Mrs. Doyle was expertly making butterballs between two ridged wooden paddles, while the scrawny kitchen maids were busy beating eggs and plucking fowl for that evening's dinner party, to which Lady Deverill had invited her two spinster sisters, Laurel and Hazel, known affectionately as the Shrubs; Kitty's parents, Bertie and Maud; and the Rector and his wife. Once a month Lady Deverill invited the Rector for dinner, which was an obligation and a great trial because he was greedy and pompous and prone to spouting unsolicited sermons from his seat at her table. Lady Deverill didn't think much of him, but it was her duty as Doyenne of Ballinakelly and a member of the Church of Ireland, so she instructed the cook, brought in flowers from the greenhouses and somewhat mischievously invited her sisters to divert him with their tedious and incessant chatter.

When Mrs. Doyle saw Bridie she pursed her lips. "Bridie,

what are you doing loitering in the corridor when I have a banquet to cook? Come and make yourself useful and pluck this partridge." She held up the bird by its neck. Bridie pulled a face at Kitty and went to join the kitchen maids at the long oak table. Mrs. Doyle glanced at Kitty, who was standing in the doorway with her long white face and secretive mouth that always curled at the corners, and wondered what she was thinking. There was something in that child's eyes that put the heart crossways in her. She couldn't explain what it was and she didn't resent the girls playing together, but Bridie's mother didn't think any good would come of their friendship. As they grew older, their lives would inevitably take them down different paths and Bridie would be left feeling the coldness and anguish of Kitty's rejection. She went back to her butter. When she looked up again Kitty had gone.

Chapter 2

Kitty's attention had been diverted by the loud crack of gunfire. She remained for a moment frozen on the back stairs. It sounded as if it had come from inside the castle. There followed an eruption of barking. Kitty hurried into the hall to see her grandfather's three brown wolfhounds bursting out of the library and up the staircase at a gallop. Without hesitation she ran after them, jumping two steps at a time to reach the landing. The dogs raced down the corridor, skidding on the carpet as they charged around the corner, narrowly missing the wall.

Kitty found her grandfather in his habitual faded tweed breeches and jacket at the window of his dressing room, pointing a rifle into the garden. He gleefully fired another shot. It was lost in the damp winter mist that was gathering over the lawn. "Bloody papists!" he bellowed. "That'll teach you to trespass on my land. Now make off with you before I aim properly and send you to an early grave!"

Kitty watched him in horror. The sight of Hubert Deverill shooting at Catholics was not a surprise. He often clashed with the poachers and knackers creeping about his land in search of game and she had eavesdropped enough at the library door to know exactly what he thought of *them*. She didn't understand how her grandfather could loathe people simply for being Catholic—all Kitty's friends were Irish Catholics. Hubert's dogs panted at his heels as he brought the gun inside and patted them fondly. When he saw his granddaughter standing in the doorway, like a miniature version of his wife, with her eyebrows knitted in disapproval, he grinned mischievously. "Hello, Kitty my dear. Fancy some cake?"

"Porter cake?"

"Laced with brandy. It'll do you good. Put some color in those pale cheeks of yours." He pressed the bell for his valet, which in turn rang a little bell on a board down in the servants' quarters above the name "Lord Deverill."

"I was born pale, Grandpa," Kitty replied, watching him open his gun and fold it over his arm like her grandmother held her handbag when they went into Ballinakelly.

"How's the Battle of the Boyne?" he asked.

She sighed. "That was last year, Grandpa. I'm learning about the Great Fire of London."

"Good good," he muttered, his mind now on other things.

"Grandpa?"

"Yes."

"Do you love this castle?"

"Minus point for a silly question," Hubert replied gruffly.

"I mean, would you mind if you were stuck here for all eternity?"

"If you're referring to the Cursing of Barton Deverill, your governess should be teaching you proper history, not folklore."

"Miss Grieve doesn't teach me folklore, Grandma does."

"Yes, well . . ." he mumbled. "Poppycock."

"But you would be happy here, wouldn't you? Grandma says you love the castle more than any Deverill ever has."

"You know your grandmother is always right."

"I wonder whether you'd mind terribly living on—"

He stopped her before she could continue. "Where the devil is Skiddy? Let's go and have some cake before the mice eat it, shall we? Skiddy!"

As they made their way down the cold corridor to the staircase they were met by a wheezing Mr. Skiddy. At sixty-eight, Frank Skiddy had worked at Castle Deverill for over fifty years, originally in the employ of the previous Lord Deverill. He was very thin and frail on account of an allergy to wheat and lungs scarred by a chest infection suffered in early childhood, but the idea of retirement was anathema to the old guard, who worked on in spite of their failing bodies. "My lord," he said when he saw Lord Deverill striding toward him over the rug, followed by his granddaughter and a trio of dogs.

"You're slowing down, Skiddy." Hubert handed the valet his gun. "Needs a good clean. Too many rabbits in the gardens."

"Yes, my lord," Mr. Skiddy replied, accustomed to his master's eccentric behavior and unmoved by it.

Lord Deverill strode on down the front stairs. "Fancy a game of chess with your cake, young lady?"

"Yes, please," Kitty replied happily. "I'll set up the board and we can play after tea."

"Trouble is you spend too much time in your imagination. Dangerous place to be, one's imagination. Your governess should be keeping you busy."

"I don't like Miss Grieve," said Kitty.

"Governesses aren't there to be liked," her grandfather told her sternly, as if liking one's governess was as odd an idea as liking a Catholic. "They're to be tolerated."

"When will I be rid of her, Grandpa?"

"When you find yourself a decent husband. You'll have to tolerate him, too!"

Kitty loved her grandparents more than she loved her parents or her siblings because in their company she felt valued. Unlike her mama and papa, they gave her their time and attention. When Hubert wasn't hunting, fishing, picking off snipe around the estate with his dogs or in Dublin at the Kildare Street Club or attending meetings at the Royal Dublin Society, he taught her chess, bridge and whist with surprising patience for a man generally intolerant of children. Adeline let her help in the gardens. Although they had plenty of gardeners, Adeline would toil away for hours in the greenhouses, with their pretty blancmange-shaped roofs. In the warm, earthy air of those glass buildings she grew carnations, grapes and peaches, and nurtured a wide variety of potted plants with long Latin names. She grew herbs and flowers for medicinal purposes, taking the trouble to pass on her knowledge to her little granddaughter. Juniper for rheumatoid arthritis, aniseed for coughs and indigestion, parsley for bloating, red clover for sores and hawthorn for the heart. Her two favorites were cannabis for tension and milk thistle for the liver.

When Hubert and Kitty reached the library, Adeline looked up from the picture of the orchid she was painting at the table in front of the bay window, taking advantage of the fading light. "I suppose that was you, dear, at your dressing room window," she said, giving her husband a reproachful look over her spectacles.

"Damn rabbits," Hubert replied, sinking into the armchair beside the turf fire that was burning cheerfully in the grate, and disappearing behind the *Irish Times*.

Adeline shook her head indulgently and resumed her painting. "If you go on so, Hubert, you'll just make them all the more furious," said Adeline.

"They're not furious," Hubert answered.

"Of course they are. They've been furious for hundreds of years . . ."

"What? Rabbits?"

Adeline suspended her brush and sighed. "You're impossible, Hubert!"

Kitty perched on the sofa and stared hungrily at the cake that had been placed with the teapot and china cups on the table in front of her. The dogs settled down before the fire with heavy sighs. There'd be no cake for them.

"Go on, my dear, help yourself," said Adeline to her granddaughter. "Don't they feed you over there?" she asked, frowning at the child's skinny arms and tiny waist.

"Mrs. Doyle is a better cook," said Kitty, picturing Miss Gibbons's fatty meat and soggy cabbage.

"That's because I've taught her that food not only has to fill one's belly, but has to taste good at the same time. You'd be surprised how many people eat for satisfaction and not for pleasure. I'll tell your mama to send your cook up for some training. I'm sure Mrs. Doyle would be delighted."

Kitty helped herself to a slice of cake and tried to think of Mrs. Doyle being delighted by anything; a sourer woman was hard to find. A moment later the light was gone and Adeline joined her granddaughter on the sofa. O'Flynn, the doddering old butler, poured her a cup of tea with an unsteady hand and a young maid silently padded around the room lighting the oil lamps. Soon the library glowed with a soft, golden radiance. "I understand that Victoria will be leaving us soon to stay with Cousin Beatrice in London," said Adeline.

"I don't want to go to London when I come of age," said Kitty.

"Oh, you will when you're eighteen. You'll be weary of all the hunt balls and the Irish boys. You'll want excitement and new faces. London is thrilling and you like Cousin Beatrice, don't you?"

"Yes, she's perfectly nice and Celia is funny, but I love being here with *you* best of all."

Her grandmother's face softened into a tender smile. "You know it's all very well playing with Bridie here at the castle, but it's important to have friends of your own sort. Celia is your age exactly and your cousin, so it is natural that you should both come out together."

"Surely, there's a Season in Dublin?"

"Of course there is, but you're Anglo-Irish, my dear."

"No, I'm Irish, Grandma. I don't care for England at all."

"You will when you get to know it."

"I doubt it's as lovely as Ireland."

"Nowhere is as lovely as here, but it comes very close."

"*I* wouldn't mind if I were cursed to remain here for all eternity."

Adeline lowered her voice. "Oh, I think you would. Between worlds is not a nice place to be, Kitty. It's very lonely."

"I'm used to being on my own. I'd be very happy to be stuck in the castle forever, even if I had to pass my time with grumpy old Barton. I shouldn't mind at all."

After playing chess with her grandfather Kitty walked home in the dark. The air smelled of turf smoke and winter and a barn owl screeched. There was a bright sickle moon to light her way and she skipped happily through the gardens, along a well-trodden path.

When she reached the Hunting Lodge she crept in through the kitchen where Miss Gibbons was sweating over a tasteless stew. Kitty could hear the sound of the piano coming from the drawing room and recognized the hesitant rendition as sixteen-year-old Elspeth's, and smiled at the thought of her mother, on the sofa with a cup of tea in her thin white hand, subjecting some poor unfortunate guest to this excruciating performance. Kitty tiptoed into the hall and hid behind a large fern. The playing suddenly stopped without any sensitivity of tempo. There was a flurry of light clapping, then she heard her mother's voice enthusiastically praising Elspeth, followed by the equally enthusiastic voice of her mother's closest friend, Lady Rowan-Hampton, who was also Elspeth's godmother. Kitty felt a momentary stab of longing. Lady

Rowan-Hampton, whom her parents called Grace, was the most beautiful woman she had ever seen and the only grown-up, besides her grandparents, who made her feel special. Knowing she wasn't allowed downstairs unless summoned, Kitty retreated up the servants' staircase.

The Hunting Lodge was not as large and imposing as the castle, but it was suitably palatial for the eldest son of Lord Deverill, and much larger than its modest name suggested. It was a rambling gray-stone house partly covered by ivy, as if it had made a halfhearted attempt to protect itself from the harsh winter winds. Unlike the castle, whose soft, weathered stone gave the building a certain warmth, the Hunting Lodge looked cold and austere. It was icy and damp inside, even in summer, and turf fires were lit only in the rooms that were going to be used. The many that weren't smelled of mildew and mold.

Kitty's bedroom was on the top floor at the back, with a view of the stables. It was the part of the house referred to as the nursery wing. Victoria, Elspeth and Harry had long since moved into the elegant side near the hall and had large bedrooms overlooking the gardens. Left alone with Miss Grieve, Kitty felt isolated and forgotten.

As she made her way down the narrow corridor to her bedroom she saw the glow of light beneath the door of Miss Grieve's room. She walked on the tips of her toes so as not to draw attention to herself. But as she passed her governess's room she heard the soft sound of weeping. It didn't sound like Miss Grieve at all. She didn't think Miss Grieve had it in her to cry. She stopped outside and pressed her ear to the door. For a moment it occurred to her that Miss Grieve might have a visitor, but Miss Grieve would never break the rules; Kitty's mother did not permit visitors upstairs. Kitty didn't think Miss Grieve had friends anyway. She never spoke of anyone other than her mother, who lived in Edinburgh.

Kitty knelt down and put her eye to the keyhole. There, sitting on the bed with a letter lying open in her lap, was Miss Grieve. Kitty was astonished to see her with her brown hair falling in thick curls over her shoulders and down her back. Her face was pale in the lamplight, but her features had softened. She didn't look wooden as she did when she scraped her hair back and drew her lips into a thin line until they almost disappeared. She looked like a sensitive young woman and surprisingly pretty.

Kitty longed to know what the letter said. Had someone died, perhaps Miss Grieve's mother? Her heart swelled with compassion so that she almost turned the knob and let herself in. But Miss Grieve looked so different Kitty felt it might embarrass her to be caught with her guard down. She remained transfixed a while by the trembling mouth, wet with tears, and the dewy skin that seemed to relax away from the bones which usually held it so taut and hard. She was fascinated by Miss Grieve's apparent youth and wondered how old she really was. She had always assumed her to be ancient, but now she wasn't so sure. It was quite possible that she was the same age as Kitty's mother.

After a while Kitty retreated to her bedroom. Nora, one of the housemaids, had lit her small fire and the room smelled pleasantly of smoke. An oil lamp glowed on the chest of drawers against the wall, beneath a picture of garden fairies her grandmother had painted for her. Kitty opened the curtains wide and sat on the window seat to stare out at the moon and stars.

Kitty did not recognize loneliness because it was so much part of her soul as to blend in seamlessly with the rest of her nature. She felt the familiar tug of something deep and stirring at the bottom of her heart. Even though she was aware of a sense of longing she didn't know it for what it was—a yearning for love. It was so familiar she had mistaken it for something pleasant and those hours staring into the stars had become as habitual to Kitty as howling at the moon to a craving wolf.

At length Miss Grieve appeared in the doorway, stiff and severe with her hair pulled back into a tight bun, as if she had beaten her emotions into submission and restrained them within her corset. There was no evidence of tears on her rigid cheeks or about her slate-gray eyes and Kitty wondered for a moment whether she had imagined them. What was it that had made Miss Grieve so bitter? "It's time for your supper, young lady," she said to Kitty. "Have you washed your hands?" Kitty dutifully presented her palms to her governess, who sniffed her disapproval. "I didn't think so. Go and wash them at once. I don't think it's right for a young lady to be running about the countryside like a stray dog. I'll have a word with your mother. Perhaps piano lessons will be a good discipline for you and keep you out of trouble."

"Piano lessons have done little for Elspeth," Kitty replied boldly. "And when she sings she sounds like a strangled cat."

"Don't be insolent, Kitty."

"Victoria sounds even worse when she plays the violin.

More like a chorus of strangled cats. I should like to sing." Kitty poured cold water from the jug into the water bowl and washed her hands with carbolic soap. So far there had been no piano or violin lessons for her, because music was her mother's department and Kitty was invisible to Maud Deverill. The only reason she had enjoyed riding lessons since the age of two was due to her father's passion for hunting and racing. As long as he lived no child of his would be incompetent in the saddle.

"You're nine now, Kitty, it's about time you learned to make yourself appealing. I don't see why music lessons can't be afforded to you as they are to your sisters. I will speak to your mother tomorrow and see that it is arranged. The less free time you have, the better. The Devil makes work for idle hands."

Kitty followed Miss Grieve into the nursery where dinner for two was laid up at the table otherwise used for lessons. They stood behind their chairs to say grace and then Miss Grieve sat down while Kitty brought the dish of stew and baked potatoes to the table from the dumbwaiter which had been sent up from the kitchen. "What is it about you that your parents don't wish to see you at mealtimes?" Miss Grieve asked as Kitty sat down. "I understand from Miss Gibbons that luncheon was always a family affair when your siblings were small." She helped herself to stew. "Perhaps it's because you don't yet know how to behave. In my previous position for Lady Billow I always joined the family for luncheon, but I ate my dinner alone, which was a blessed relief. Are we to share this table until you come of age?"

Kitty was used to Miss Grieve's mean jibes and tried not to be riled by them. Wit was her only defense. "It must be for your pleasure, Miss Grieve, because otherwise you might get lonely."

Miss Grieve laughed bitterly. "And I suppose you consider yourself good company, do you?"

"I must be better company than loneliness."

"I wouldn't be so sure. For a nine-year-old you have an inappropriate tongue. It's no wonder your parents don't wish for the sight of you. Victoria and Elspeth are young ladies, but you, Kitty, are a young ragamuffin in need of taming. That the task should fall to me is a great trial, but I do the best I can out of the goodness of my heart. We've a long way to go before you're in any fit state to find a husband."

"I don't want a husband," said Kitty, forking a piece of meat into her mouth. It was cold in the center.

"Of course you don't want one now. You're a child."

"Did you ever want a husband, Miss Grieve?"

The governess's eyes shifted a moment uncertainly, revealing more to the sharp little girl than she meant to. "That's none of your business, Kitty. Sit up straight; you're not a sack of potatoes."

"Are governesses allowed to marry?" Kitty continued, knowing the answer but enjoying the pained look in Miss Grieve's eyes.

The governess pursed her lips. "Of course they're allowed to marry. Whatever gave you the idea that they weren't?"

"None of them ever are." Kitty chewed valiantly on the stringy piece of beef.

"Enough of that lip, my girl, or you can go to bed without any supper." But Miss Grieve had suddenly gone very pink in the face and Kitty saw a fleeting glimpse of the young woman who had been crying over a letter in her bedroom. She blinked and the image was gone. Miss Grieve was staring into her plate, as if trying hard to control her emotions. Kitty wished she hadn't been so mean but took the opportunity to spit her beef into her napkin and fold it onto her lap without being seen. She tried to think of something nice to say, but nothing came to mind. They sat awhile in silence.

"Do you play the piano, Miss Grieve?" Kitty asked at last.

"I did, once," she replied tightly.

"Why do you never play?"

The woman glared at Kitty as if she had touched an invisible nerve. "I've had enough of your questions, young lady. We'll eat the rest of the meal in silence." Kitty was astonished. She hadn't expected such a harsh reaction to what she felt had been a simple and kind turn of conversation. "One word and I'll drag you by your red hair and throw you into your bedroom."

"It's Titian, not red," Kitty mumbled recklessly.

"You can use all the fancy words you can find, my girl, but red is red and if you ask me, it's very unbecoming."

Kitty struggled through the rest of dinner in silence. Miss Grieve's face had hardened to granite. Kitty regretted trying to be nice and resolved that she would never be so foolish as to give in to compassion again. When they had finished, Kitty obediently loaded the plates onto the dumbwaiter and pressed the bell to send it down to the kitchen.

She washed with cold water because Sean Doyle, Bridie's brother, only carried hot water to the nursery wing every *other* night. Miss Grieve watched over her as she said her prayers. Kitty prayed dutifully for her mama and papa, her siblings and grand-parents. Then she added one for Miss Grieve: "Please, God, take her away. She's horrid and unkind and I hate her. If I knew how to curse like Maggie O'Leary, I'd put one on her so that unhappiness would follow her all the days of her life and never let her go."

Chapter 3

Maud Deverill sat in the carriage beside her husband in silence. Her gloved hands were folded in the blanket draped over her lap, a fur coat warmed her chest and back but still she shivered. The night was clear and cold with a dampness brought inland on the salty sea breeze, assertive enough to penetrate bones. Bertie had returned in the early evening as was his custom, smelling of horse dust and sweat. He had greeted Lady Rowan-Hampton warmly but Maud wasn't fooled by their veneer of respectability. She had often smelled Grace's perfume on his collar and caught the mischievous glances between them. Why, one might ask, did she foster such a close relationship with her husband's mistress? Because she believed, perhaps misguidedly, that it was important to keep one's friends close and one's enemies even closer. So it was with Grace, the most dangerous of all enemies, who she simply couldn't have brought any closer.

The carriage lurched along the farm track that circled the estate, over puddles and holes, until it reached the castle, its passengers quite shaken up. The footman opened the door and offered his hand to Mrs. Deverill, who accepted it and put out one uncertain foot, feeling in the dark for the top step. She descended at last and took her husband's arm. Bertie was flaxen-haired and handsome with a wide, well-proportioned face and gray eyes as pale as duck's eggs. He had a dry sense of humor and a penchant for pretty women. Indeed, he was celebrated across Co. Cork for his quiet charm and gentle geniality and was every lady's favorite gentleman, except for Maud's, of course, who resented the fact that he had never really belonged exclusively to her.

Flares had been lit on either side of the castle door to light the way. Bertie and Maud Deverill were the closest neighbors but always the last to arrive on account of Maud's procrastination. She subconsciously hoped that if she dithered and dallied and took her time her husband might go without her.

"If I'm sitting next to the Rector again I shall shoot myself," she hissed, her scarlet lips black in the darkness.

"My dear, you always sit next to the Rector and you never shoot yourself," Bertie replied patiently.

"Your mother does it on purpose to spite me."

"Now why would she do that?"

"Because she despises me."

"Nonsense. Mama despises no one. The two of you are simply very different. I don't see why you can't get along."

"I have a headache. I should not have come at all."

"Since you are here, you might as well enjoy yourself."

"It's all right for you, Bertie. You're always the life and soul of the party. Everyone loves *you*. I'm just here to facilitate your pleasure."

"Don't be absurd, Maud. Come along, you'll catch your death out here. I need a drink." They stepped into the hall and Maud reluctantly peeled off her fur coat and gloves and handed them to O'Flynn.

Maud was a beautiful, if severe-looking, woman. She was blessed with high cheekbones, a symmetrical heart-shaped face, large blue eyes and a straight nose. Her mouth was full-lipped and her blond hair thick and lustrous, pinned up in the typical Edwardian style with curls and waves in all the right places. Her skin was milky white, her hands and feet dainty. She was like a lovely marble statue, carved by a benevolent creator, yet cold and hard and lacking in all sensuality. The only quality that gave her an ounce of character was her inability to see beyond herself.

Tonight she wore a pale blue dress that reached the floor and showed off her slender figure, a pearl choker about her neck with a diamond clasp glittering at her throat. When she entered the drawing room there was a collective gasp of admiration, which cheered her up enormously. She glided in, feeling much better about the evening, and found herself accosted at once by Adeline's eccentric spinster sisters Hazel and Laurel.

"My dear Maud, you look lovely," gushed Hazel. "Don't you think, Laurel? Maud looks lovely."

Laurel, who was rarely far from her sister's side, smiled into her chubby crimson cheeks. "She does, Hazel. She truly does. Simply lovely." Maud looked down her nose at the two round faces grinning eagerly up at her and smiled politely. Then she extricated herself as quickly as possible with the excuse of going to greet the Rector. "Poor Mrs. Daunt has taken a turn," said Hazel of the Rector's wife.

"We shall ask Mary to bake a cake tomorrow and take it round," suggested Laurel, referring to their maid.

"Splendid idea, Hazel. A little brandy in it should restore her to health, don't you think?"

"Oh, it will indeed!" exclaimed the ever-exuberant Laurel, clapping her small hands excitedly.

The Rector was a portly, self-important man with a long prickly mustache and bloated, ruddy cheeks, who enjoyed life's pleasures as if the obligation to do so was one of God's lesser-known Commandments. He hunted with gusto, was a fine shot and a keen fisherman. Often seen waddling among his flock at the races, he never missed the opportunity to preach, as if his constant moralizing justified his presence there in that den of iniquity. Maud was a religious woman, when it suited her, and she abhorred the Rector for his flamboyance. The vicar in her hometown in England had been a man of austere and simple pleasures, which was how she believed all religious men should be. But she held out her hand and greeted him, disguising her true feelings behind a veneer of cool politeness. "Well, if it isn't the lovely Mrs. Deverill," he said, taking her slender hand in his spongy one and giving it a hearty shake. "Did Victoria get the reading for tomorrow's service?" he asked.

"Yes, she did," Maud replied. "I've practiced with her but you know young people, they read much too quickly."

"I understand she will soon be leaving us for London."

"I don't know how I shall make do without her," said Maud,

who always managed to swing every conversation around to herself. "I shall be quite bereft with only Elspeth for company."

"You will soon have Harry back for the holidays and of course you still have—" He was about to mention Kitty but Maud cut him off briskly.

"One pays a heavy price for a good education," she said solemnly. "But it is the way of the world and Harry is happy at Eton so I shouldn't complain. I miss him terribly. He is worth ten of my daughters. God didn't see fit to give me more sons," she added reproachfully, as if the Rector were somehow responsible.

"Your daughters will look after you in old age," said the Rector helpfully, draining his glass of sherry.

"Harry will look after me in my old age. My daughters will be much too busy with their own children to think about me."

At that moment Adeline joined them, her sweet smile and twinkling eyes giving the Rector a warm feeling of relief. "We were just saying, Lady Deverill, how daughters are great comforts to their mothers in old age."

"I wouldn't know, my daughter having crossed the Atlantic without a backward glance," said Adeline, not unkindly. "But I'm sure you're right. Maud is quite spoiled with three daughters." Maud averted her eyes. Adeline had an unsettling way of looking right through her as if she recognized her shortcomings for what they were and was even slightly amused by them.

"There's a good chance Victoria and Elspeth will marry Englishmen and leave Ireland altogether. My hope lies with Harry for, whomever he weds, he will live here."

Adeline looked steadily at Maud. "You're forgetting Kitty, my dear."

The Rector grinned broadly, for he was very fond of the youngest Deverill. "Now *she* won't be leaving Ireland, not Kitty. I'd put a lot of money on her marrying an Irishman." Maud tried to smile but her crimson lips could only manage a grimace.

Adeline shook her head, her special affection for Kitty undisguised. "She's quite fearless. She'll do something surprising, for certain. I'd put good money on *that*." Maud felt she was expected to add something to the conversation, but she didn't really know what her daughter was like. Only that she had the same flame-red hair as Adeline and the same unsettling knowing in her eyes.

At last O'Flynn appeared in the doorway to announce that dinner was now ready. Maud found her husband discussing the next hunt meeting with his father, who was already on his third glass of sherry. Lord Deverill always managed to look moth-eaten. His gray hair was wild, as if he had just arrived at a gallop, and his dinner jacket looked as if it had been nibbled at the elbows by mice. As hard as Skiddy tried to keep his master's clothes clean and pressed, they still appeared to have been pulled out of the bottom of a drawer—and he refused, doggedly, to buy new clothes, ever. "May I have the pleasure of escorting you in to dinner, Maud?" Hubert asked, taking pleasure from her beautiful face. Maud, who could always rely on her father-in-law's support, slipped her hand under his arm and allowed him to lead her into the dining room.

Bertie escorted the Shrubs on either arm, allowing their excited chatter to rise above him like the unobtrusive twittering of birds. The Rector walked in with Adeline, their conversation having been reduced to a one-sided lecture by him on women's suffrage, to which Adeline listened with half an ear and even less interest.

They stood to say grace, Hubert at the head, Adeline at the foot, with the Rector on Adeline's right side, next to a furious Maud. They bowed their heads and the Rector spoke in the low, portentous voice of the pulpit. The moment it was over the door burst open and Rupert, Bertie's younger brother, stood, disheveled and obviously drunk, with his hands on the doorframe. "Is there a place for me?" he asked, appealing to his mother.

Adeline didn't look at all surprised to see her middle child, who lived in the house previously occupied by her late mother-in-law, the Dowager Lady Deverill, a mile or so across the fields, overlooking the sea. "Why don't you sit between your aunts," she said, sinking into her chair.

Hubert, who had less patience for his hopeless son and believed he would have done better to have joined his younger sister in America, found a wife and perhaps made something of his life, gave a loud "Harrumph" and said, "Cook's day off, is it?"

Rupert smiled with all his charm. "I heard my dear aunts Hazel and Laurel were coming for dinner, Papa, and I couldn't resist." The Shrubs blushed with pleasure, unaware of his slightly mocking tone, and moved apart so O'Flynn could slip a chair between them.

"What a delightful evening this has turned out to be," gushed Laurel. "Don't you think, Hazel?"

"Oh, I most certainly do, Laurel. Come and sit down, Rupert, my dear, and tell us what you have been up to. You lead such an exciting life, doesn't he? In fact, we were only saying yesterday what it must be to be young, weren't we, Laurel?"

"Oh yes, we were. We're so old, Hazel and I, that all we can do is enjoy the little titbits you give us, Rupert, like crumbs from the rich man's table."

Rupert sat down and unfolded his napkin. "What has Mrs. Doyle cooked up for us this evening?" he said.

IT WAS PAST midnight when Bertie and Maud drove back to the Hunting Lodge. Maud vented her fury to her weary and pleasantly tipsy husband. "Rupert is a disgrace, turning up uninvited like that. He was smashed, too, and poorly dressed. You'd have thought he'd have the decency to dress properly for dinner, considering the amount of money your father lavishes on him." She fell forward as the carriage went over a pothole.

"Mama and Papa don't care about that sort of thing," he replied with a yawn.

"They should care. Civilization is about standards. This country would descend into barbarism if it wasn't for people like us keeping the standards up. Appearances matter, Bertie. Your parents should set an example."

"Are you suggesting they're poorly dressed, Maud?"

"Your father's eaten by moths. What harm would it do to go to London and visit his tailor once in a while?"

"He's got more important things to think about."

"Like hunting, shooting and fishing, I suppose?"

"Quite so. He is old. Leave him to his pleasure."

"As for your aunts, they're ridiculous."

"They're happy and good and kind. You're a harsh judge of people, Maud. Is there no one you like?"

"Rupert needs a wife," she added, changing the subject.

"Then find him one."

"He should go to London and look for a nice English girl with good manners and a firm hand to smack him into shape."

"You're bitter, Maud. Was tonight really so bad?"

"Oh, you had a splendid time in the dining room, drinking port and smoking cigars, while we languished in the drawing room. Do you know, your mother and her sisters are going to hold a séance here at the castle? They're a trio of witches. It's absurd."

"Oh, leave them to their fun, my dear. How does it affect you if they want to communicate with the dead?"

Maud realized her argument was weak. "It's ungodly," she added tartly. "I don't imagine the Rector would think much of their game—no good will come of it, mark my words."

"I still don't see how it affects *you*, Maud."

"Your mother is a bad influence on Kitty," she rejoined, knowing that Kitty's name would carry more weight.

Bertie frowned and rubbed his bristly chin. "Ah Kitty," he sighed, feeling a stab of guilt.

"She spends much too much time talking nonsense with her grandmother."

"Might that be because *you* don't spend any time with her at all?"

Maud sat in silence affronted. Bertie had never complained before about her obvious lack of interest in their youngest. Besides, it was customary that young children should be kept out of sight and in the nursery with their governesses. Then it came to her in a sudden flood of pain: Grace Rowan-Hampton must have mentioned it to him. By keeping her enemy close she had allowed a spy into her home.

The carriage drew up in front of the Hunting Lodge and stopped outside the front door. It was lightly drizzling, what the locals called "soft rain." A strong wind swept over the land, moaning eerily as it dashed through the bare branches of the horse chestnut trees. The butler was waiting for them in the hall with an oil lamp to light their way upstairs. Feeling more discontented than ever, Maud followed her husband up to the landing, hoping he would notice her silence and ask what was troubling her. "Good night, my dear," he said, without so much as a glance. She watched him disappear into his room and close the door behind him. Furiously she went into hers, where her lady's maid was waiting to unhook her dress. Without a word she turned her back expectantly.

THE FOLLOWING MORNING Kitty breakfasted with Miss Grieve in the nursery, then dressed for church. The Sunday service, in the church of St. Patrick in Ballinakelly, was the only time the family all gathered together. The only time Kitty really saw her parents. Miss Grieve had put out a fresh white pinafore and polished black boots and spent much longer than necessary combing the knots out of her hair without any consideration for the pain she caused. But Kitty fixed her stare on the gray clouds scudding across the sky outside the window and willed herself not to shed a single tear.

While her parents and grandparents rode in carriages, Kitty and her sisters sat in the pony and trap with Miss Grieve in the front beside Mr. Mills, who held the reins. Victoria was pretty like her mother with a wide, heart-shaped face, a long straight nose and shrewish blue eyes. Her blond hair fell down to her waist in lustrous curls as she sat with her back straight and her chin up, much too aware of her own beauty and the admiring looks it aroused. Elspeth was more modest and less attractive than her elder sister. Her hair was mouse-brown, her nose a fleshy button, her expression as submissive and dim-witted as a lap dog's. The older girls ignored Kitty completely, preferring to talk to each other. But Kitty didn't mind: she was much too busy looking around at the fields of cows and sheep. "Mother says I have to have new dresses made for London," said Victoria happily, holding her hat so it didn't fly off in the wind. "She has already sent my measurements to Cousin Beatrice. I can hardly wait. They'll be the most fashionable designs for sure."

"You're so lucky," said Elspeth, who had a tendency to elongate her vowels so that her voice sounded like a whine. "I wish I were coming with you. Instead I'm going to be all alone with no one to talk to but Mama. It's going to be frightfully dull without you."

"You had better get used to it, Elspeth," said her sister sharply. "I fully intend to find a husband."

"That's what it's all for, I suppose."

"Mama told me that if one doesn't find a husband it is because one is ugly, dull or both."

"You are neither ugly nor dull," said Elspeth. "Fortunately neither of us inherited Grandma's ginger hair."

"It's not ginger," interrupted Kitty from beneath her bonnet. "It's Titian red."

Her sisters giggled. "Mama says it's ginger," said Victoria meanly.

"It's very unlucky to have red hair," Elspeth added. "Fishermen will head for home if they see a red-haired woman on the way to their boats. Clodagh told me," she said, referring to one of the maids.

"You'd better keep it under that bonnet of yours then," said Victoria. She looked down at her youngest sister and Kitty lifted her gray eyes and stared at her boldly. Victoria stopped laughing and grew suddenly afraid. There was something scary in her sister's gaze, as if she could cast a spell just by looking at someone. "Let's not be unkind," she said uneasily, not wanting to incite Kitty's wrath in case she somehow jinxed her first London season. "Red hair is all right if it's combined with a pretty face, isn't that so, Elspeth?" She dug her elbow into her sister's ribs.

"Yes, it is," Elspeth agreed dutifully. But Kitty was no longer listening. She was watching the local Catholic children walking back from Mass, looking for Bridie and Jack O'Leary.

Chapter 4

Ballinakelly was a quaint town of pretty white houses that clustered on the hillside like mussels on a rock, all the way down to the sea. There was a small harbor, three churches (St. Patrick's, Church of Ireland, the Methodist church and the Catholic church of All Saints), a high street of little shops and four public houses, which were always full. The local children attended the school, which was run by the Catholic church, and gathered at the shrine to the Virgin Mary most evenings to witness the statue swaying, which it very often did, apparently all on its own. Built into the hillside in 1828 to commemorate a young girl's vision, it had become something of a tourist attraction in the summer months as pilgrims traveled from far and wide to see it, falling to their knees in the mud and crossing themselves devoutly when it duly rattled. The children were greatly amused by the spectacle, running off in their pack of scruffy scamps, hiding their fear beneath peals of nervous laughter. It was whispered that horses sometimes balked when passing it, foretelling a tragedy.

The pony and trap made its way slowly through the town. Kitty eagerly searched the rabble of Catholic children walking toward her. They were pale with hunger, having fasted from the evening before, and dazed with boredom from the service. At last she saw Bridie, treading heavily up the street with her family. Her face, half hidden behind a tangle of knotted hair, was grim. Kitty knew she didn't like going to Mass. Father Quinn was a severe and unforgiving priest, prone to outbursts of indignation in the pulpit and quite often reproachful finger-wagging as he picked on members of the congregation whom he felt had, in some way, transgressed. The poorest among them received the worst of his tongue-lashing.

Kitty focused hard on her friend until Bridie raised her eyes and saw her, just as the pony and trap clip-clopped past. Bridie's face lit up and she smiled. Kitty smiled back. A little behind Bridie, Liam O'Leary, the vet, walked beside his twelve-year-old son, Jack. Kitty smiled at him, too. Jack was more discreet. His blue eyes twinkled beneath his thick brown fringe and the corners of his mouth gave a tiny twitch. The pony walked on. When Kitty looked back she caught eyes with him again as he tossed her another furtive glance over his shoulder.

The church of St. Patrick was almost full. Here the aristocracy came together with the ordinary working-class Protestants—shopkeepers, cattle jobbers, dressmakers and the Castle Deverill estate manager and bookkeeper, all descended from the Huguenots. Lord and Lady Deverill sat in the front pew with Bertie, Maud, Victoria and Elspeth. Miss Grieve sat in the row behind with Kitty. Much to Kitty's delight she found herself sitting next to Lady Rowan-Hampton, wrapped snugly in a warm coat and fur stole. Her husband, the portly and red-faced Sir Ronald, had to sit on the aisle side in order to get out to read the lesson. "My dear Kitty," whispered Lady Rowan-Hampton happily, placing her prayer book on the ledge in front of her. "I haven't seen you for such a long time. Haven't you grown into a pretty girl? I must say, you've inherited your grandmother's good looks. You know, as a young woman her beauty was the talk of Dublin. Now, how are we to get through the service? I know, let's play a game. Find an animal that matches each member of your family, and Reverend Daunt, of course, let's not forget him. If you were an animal, Kitty, you'd be . . ." She narrowed her soft brown eyes and Kitty was transfixed by her rosy cheeks, slightly on the plump side, her smooth powdery skin and full, expressive mouth. Kitty thought that, if people were cakes, Lady Rowan-Hampton would be a juicy Victoria sponge cake, whereas her mother would be a dry and bitter porter cake. "Of course, my dear, you'd be a fox!" Lady Rowan-Hampton continued. "You'd be a very cunning and charming little fox."

The service began with the first hymn and Kitty stood tall and sang as prettily as she could in order to impress Lady Rowan-Hampton. Miss Grieve just mouthed the words, Kitty supposed, because her voice was inaudible. Mrs. Daunt, the Rector's wife, usually played the organ, almost as badly as Elspeth played the piano, but today, as Mrs. Daunt was indisposed, their neighbor, the porcine Mr. Rowe, played the violin beautifully. Kitty could smell Lady Rowan-Hampton's perfume, which was floral and very sweet, like tuberose, and Kitty decided that when she was grown-up she wanted to be just like her. Of course, she didn't want a fat old husband like

Sir Ronald, who was master of the local hunt, a loud bore and contrary when drunk—Kitty had often heard him holding forth in the dining room after dinner when the women had gone through to the drawing room. Lady Rowan-Hampton always wore glittering diamonds about her neck and wrists and long dresses that swished as she walked. She was the closest thing to a princess that Kitty had ever seen. Now that she was sitting beside her, Kitty was more enthralled than ever.

Sir Ronald read the first lesson. His booming voice rebounded off the walls as he threw each syllable into the congregation as if he were a colonel lobbing grenades. Victoria read the second, softly and a little too fast, swallowing the ends of the sentences so their meaning was almost entirely lost. As Reverend Daunt warmed to his sermon, Lady Rowan-Hampton leaned down and whispered a word into Kitty's ear. "Walrus." Kitty stifled a giggle, because *that* was the very animal Kitty had thought of when Sir Ronald had read the lesson.

During the final hymn the collection plate was passed around. Lady Rowan-Hampton handed Kitty a coin so that, when the plate reached her, she was able to drop it in among the others with a light clink. At the end of the service Mr. Rowe took up his violin and played a jig, which made most people smile in amusement, except for Maud whose tight lips pursed even tighter with disapproval. "So, what animal do you think your father would be?" Lady Rowan-Hampton asked Kitty.

"A lion," said Kitty.

"Very good," said Lady Rowan-Hampton approvingly. "I think you're right. He's fair and handsome, just like a lion. And your mama?"

"A white weasel."

Lady Rowan-Hampton was shocked. "My dear, are you sure you know what a weasel looks like?"

"Of course. Don't you think she looks just like one?"

Lady Rowan-Hampton hesitated and flushed. "Not really. I think she's more like a lovely snow leopard." Kitty crinkled her nose and thought of the dry porter cake. "Your sisters?" Lady Rowan-Hampton asked.

"*Little* weasels," said Kitty with a grin.

"Oh dear, a very weaselly lot," said Lady Rowan-Hampton, smiling too. "I think we should keep this game to ourselves, don't you think?" Kitty nodded and watched the weasels get up and file down the aisle toward the door.

Once out in the sunshine, the congregation took the opportunity to mingle. The Anglo-Irish, being such a small community, had known one another for generations and cleaved to each other for comfort and safety. They hunted together, met at the races and enjoyed an endless circuit of hunt balls and dinner parties. They were united by a love of sport and entertainment, a loyalty to the Crown, a wary respect for the Irish and a subliminal determination to keep going in a changing world as if their decline as a people were not inevitable.

Kitty found a spider's web studded with raindrops on the grass not far from where her father was now talking to Lady Rowan-Hampton. Sensing they were discussing *her*, she turned her attention away from the spider to see if she could work out what they were saying. Once or twice her father glanced in her direction and she had to pretend she was looking elsewhere. Lady Rowan-Hampton was gesticulating in a persuasive manner, and quite crossly too, by the way she vigorously moved her hands.

Kitty was surprised to see her father so contrite, as if he was being told off. Then Kitty was diverted by another pair of eyes that watched the couple from the opposite end of the yard. They belonged to her mother and they were colder than ever.

Sunday lunch was always held up at the castle. The family gathered in the drawing room by a boisterous fire, to warm up after the freezing-cold church and blustery ride back with glasses of sherry and large tumblers of Jameson's whiskey. The Shrubs were always included, arriving in a trap with the ribbons of their hats flapping madly in the wind and their heads pressed together, deep in conversation. Rupert always came alone, already tipsy, and charmed his parents' other guests who often increased the number around the table to as many as twenty. Today, it was just the family, however, and Kitty sat at the very end of the table, beside her sisters, who ignored her. To her surprise, her father addressed her.

"Kitty, my dear, come and ride with me this afternoon. I'd like to see how you're coming along." Elspeth turned and glared at her in surprise. It was a rare treat to be asked to ride with their father. "It's about time you rode with the grown-ups, eh? No more languishing in the nursery for you, my girl. How old are you now, eight?"

"Nine," said Kitty.

"Nine, eh? Where's the time gone? When I was nearly half your age I was hunting with the Ballinakelly Foxhounds."

"What fun!" exclaimed Hazel.

"Yes, indeed," agreed Laurel. "Do take care to find her a gentle pony, Bertie. When I was a girl I barely escaped with my life after being thrown into a ditch by my naughty little pony, Teasel. Do you remember, Hazel?"

"Do I ever!" laughed her sister. Hubert immediately launched into his favorite hunting anecdote and Kitty was quite lost again in the sudden swell of conversation. But her heart began to thump excitedly at the thought of riding out with her father. She wondered whether her mother would come too, but decided not. After all, this impromptu arrangement was clearly Lady Rowan-Hampton's idea and her mother rarely rode. When she did she cut a dash in her black riding habit and hat with its diaphanous black veil reaching down to her chin.

KITTY LOVED TO ride. She adored the wild and rugged hills, the birds of prey that hovered overhead, the gurgling streams and swelling sea. She was curious about the world outside her own isolated existence and liked nothing more than to escape whenever the opportunity arose. Now she set off with her father at a gentle pace, he on his tall chestnut horse, she on a small gray pony called Thruppence. "Where are we going?" she asked, as they walked up the long avenue of tall, leafless trees.

"Where would you like to go?" her father replied, looking down at her with kind, smiling eyes.

"To the Fairy Ring," Kitty replied.

Bertie arched an eyebrow. He knew it well but the place held no interest for him. "If that's what you want."

"I ride there with Grandma."

"I bet you do." He laughed. "Do you dance among the stones when there's a full moon?"

"Of course," she replied seriously. "We turn into wolves and howl."

Bertie stared at her in astonishment. His daughter held his

gaze for a long moment with her unsettling gray eyes, then her face broke into a grin and Bertie realized, to his relief, that she was joking. "What a sense of humor you have for an eight-year-old."

"Nine," Kitty said emphatically.

He shook his head and thought how irregular it was for such a young child to be so unnaturally grown-up. Grace had been right to berate him. It wasn't fitting for his youngest to languish alone in the nursery with her austere Scottish governess. He knew full well that Maud had no interest in the child, but he hadn't bothered to find out the extent of her neglect. Now he felt guilty. He should have intervened earlier. "You're a weak man," Grace had scolded him, and her words had stung. "Your aversion to confrontation has meant that Maud has been allowed to do as she pleases. Now take charge, Bertie, and *do* something about it."

"Then let's go to the Fairy Ring and you can show me what you and Mother get up to when you're alone together," he said, and the smile Kitty gave him made him wonder why he didn't seek her company more often.

The Fairy Ring was an ancient and mystical formation of seventeen large gray rocks positioned on the summit of a hill, overlooking the patchwork of fields that stretched all the way to the ocean. From up there they could see cottages shivering in the dusk, thin ribbons of smoke rising from their chimneys as the farmers' families huddled by their turf fires to keep warm.

"All this is Deverill land," said Bertie, sweeping his eyes over the vast acres of farmland. "We had ten times as much before the Wyndham Act enabled tenants to buy their own land. We've lived well for over two hundred years, but life as we know it will one day come to an end as our diminishing estates will no longer be able to support our lifestyle. I don't suppose Miss Grieve has taught you anything about *that*." Kitty shook her head. Her father had no idea how to talk to a nine-year-old. "No, I didn't think so," said Bertie dolefully. "What does she teach you?"

"The Great Fire of London and the Plague."

"It's time you learned about your own heritage."

"Barton Deverill?" she said eagerly.

Her father smiled. "You already know about him. Of course you should know about your ancestors, but you should also know about the Irish nationalists' struggle for independence, Kitty. The Irish people don't want to be ruled by the British. They want to govern themselves."

"I know about that," she said, remembering what Bridie had told her. "They hate that the British have all the power and the taxes are too high."

He raised his eyebrows in surprise. "So you know something already?"

She knew not to reveal that she played with the Catholic children and listened to their patriotic chatter. "I know that the Irish don't like us, even though we are Irish too."

"We're *Anglo*-Irish, Kitty."

"I'm not," she said defiantly, folding her arms. "I don't like England."

"It's England that enabled you to live here. If it wasn't for Charles II Barton Deverill would never have been given these lands in the first place."

"They belonged to the O'Learys," she said boldly.

Bertie narrowed his eyes and thought a moment before replying, as if working out the best way to be tactful. "The land he built the castle on was indeed O'Leary land."

"Do they want it back?"

"I'm sure they did at the time, Kitty. But that all happened over two hundred years ago. Liam O'Leary is a vet, as was his father before him. They haven't been farmers for generations."

"So, there's no fighting then?"

"No fighting, no."

"Then you're friends?"

He shuffled uneasily on his horse, thinking of Liam's resentful wife. "Quite friendly, yes."

"Then there's the possibility that a Deverill might one day marry an O'Leary, after all?"

"I think that's highly unlikely," Bertie replied tightly. "You've been listening to your grandmother, haven't you? Her stories are great fun, Kitty, but it's important that you understand that they are just fun and not real. They're like Greek myths and Irish legends like 'The Children of Lir,' to be enjoyed but not taken literally. So, what do you and Grandma do here?" He pointed his riding crop at the rocks.

"This was an ancient place of worship for pagans," said Kitty confidently. "Each one of these stones is a person cursed to live as stone by day. When the sun sets they come alive."

"Very interesting," said Bertie, not in the least interested in magic. He turned his mind to the bottle of gin and the cheery fire that awaited him on his return.

"Don't you want to see it?" Kitty turned her face to the sun. It was already melting into the sea on the horizon and setting the sky aflame with rich reds and golds.

"Another time," he replied patiently, realizing that even

Maud had a point when she complained that Kitty was spending too much time talking nonsense with her grandmother.

They set off back down the hill. The evening was cold, but rich smells of heather rose up from the ground to infuse the February air with the promise of spring. Occasionally a partridge or a hare bolted out of the gorse as they passed, and a herd of cows came close to watch them with their big brown eyes and placid mooing. Kitty delighted in them all, wishing she could stay out for longer and not have to return to the dull nursery wing to dine alone with Miss Grieve. But when she got back to her room Miss Grieve was there, in her stiff dress that left only her pale face and hands exposed, to inform her that she was expected at the dinner table tonight.

"I can't imagine why they want you all of a sudden," said Miss Grieve reproachfully. "After all, up until now they've barely noticed your existence."

"It's because I'm nine and Papa thought I was eight," Kitty replied. "Silly Papa."

"I hope you mind your manners. I won't be there to prod you."

"I don't need any prodding, Miss Grieve. I shall behave like a young lady."

"Don't get above yourself, my girl. You're not a young lady yet. So, where did you go with your father?"

Kitty knew not to mention the Fairy Ring. Once, on a wave of enthusiasm, she had told Miss Grieve that she had seen the stones come to life, only to receive a good walloping on the palms of her hands with the riding crop. She wouldn't forget herself so quickly again. "We rode up on the hills. It was delightful."

"Well, don't get too used to it. I don't suppose he'll ask you again. I think he must prefer the company of Miss Victoria; after all, she's a young woman now. Oh, she'll be off to London in the spring and that'll be the last we'll see of her, I don't doubt. She'll find herself a nice husband, a pretty girl like her. Then it'll be Miss Elspeth's turn and she'll be away like the wind. As for you . . ." Miss Grieve looked down her long nose at Kitty. "A poor little thing like you. You'll be lucky to be as fortunate as your sisters with all your disadvantages. Don't look at me like that. Screwing your face up makes you even less attractive."

Kitty stepped into her best dress and clenched her fists as Miss Grieve pulled the knots out of her hair. "If I had my say I'd cut it off altogether," she said, tugging on a particularly sensitive tendril of hair at Kitty's temple. "The lengths we go to when the simplest solution would be a pair of scissors!"

When Kitty was ready she ran downstairs, leaving Miss Grieve to eat alone in the nursery with only her sourness for company. She stopped in front of the mirror on the landing and stared at her reflection. Was she really so ugly? Had Lady Rowan-Hampton simply been kind when she had complimented her looks? And, if she was so unattractive, did it really matter? Then she thought of her grandmother and smiled. She was a beautiful soul of God; Miss Grieve was just too blind to see it.

Chapter 5

It was Sunday night. Old Mrs. Nagle's turf fire was smoking heavily as she puffed on a clay pipe and fingered her rosary. A big black bastible full of parsnip and potato stew was suspended above it, throwing out steam into the already smoggy atmosphere. She sat in her usual chair beside the fire, a hunched and emaciated figure dressed in black, chewing on her gums for her teeth had fallen out long ago. Her granddaughter, Bridie, dutifully stirred the stew with a wooden spoon as her stomach groaned like a hungry dog at the rich, salty smell. Mrs. Doyle sat in her rocking chair opposite her mother, half listening to her husband and sons, the rest of her attention focused on her basket of darning. Bridie's two elder brothers, Michael and Sean, sat with their father around the wooden table talking in low voices, their serious faces distorted in the flickering candlelight that burned through the gloom, their rough laborers' hands clutching pewter tumblers of Beamish stout. Every now and then Bridie caught something of what they were saying. But she'd heard it many times before. Talk of Fenian uprisings against the British, worry about working for the aristocracy, always the concern that they might be seen as spies or traitors, and then what?

Bridie had long been aware of the Irish struggle for independence, and the resentment of the British. She had heard talk of it wafting up through the floorboards with the scent of porter and tobacco as she drifted off to sleep, her father and his friends discussing it long into the night, their voices loud and unguarded as they drank and played cards. She had seen copies of the Sinn Féin newspaper lying hidden beneath Michael's bed but struggled to read them. Her father, Tomas Doyle, was a wise man when sober. He would argue that Lord Deverill was a beneficent landlord, unlike many, and Sean as well as Mrs. Doyle were employed up at the castle and treated kindly. Wasn't it true that during the great potato famine the previous Lady Deverill had set up a soup kitchen in one of the hay barns and saved many from starvation? It was well known that not one of the Deverill tenants had died of hunger during the famine, or taken the coffin ship to Amerikey, thanks be to God. But Michael, Bridie's oldest brother, who was nearly nineteen now and worked with his father on the land, wanted the British Protestants out, whoever they were and however good they were to their tenants. It was a matter of principle and honor: Ireland should belong to the Irish, he maintained passionately, and the British "Prods" should go back to England where they belonged. "A privilege to buy our land? What privilege is it to buy back land that was stolen from us in the first place?" he would maintain, banging his fist on the table, his long black hair falling over his forehead. "They've stolen more than land. They've stolen our culture, our history, our language and our way of life." Bridie would hear their voices grow louder as they each tried to persuade the other and she would feel anxious for Kitty and for their secret friendship, which she so treasured. She hoped that if ever there was trouble in Ballinakelly, the Deverills would not suffer at the hands of the rebels on account of their well-known generosity and kindness toward the local people.

Bridie was disappointed Kitty hadn't come to see her today. Usually she'd find Kitty sitting on the wall surrounding the castle grounds and they'd run off together and play pikki with the local children. Kitty called it hopscotch but she played it all the same. Kitty was like that; if it was fun she'd throw herself into the game with all her heart and not give a thought to whether she should or should not mix with the Catholic children. She didn't care either whether one of those children was an O'Leary.

When Bridie thought of Jack O'Leary, with his idle gaze and his pet hawk on his arm, something tickled her belly, like the soft fluttering of butterfly wings. Jack was lofty and handsome with thick brown hair and eyes like an Irish sky in winter. An arrogant smirk played about his lips as he watched the girls at their childish play. But Jack had a sensitive side too. He loved all God's creatures, from the secretive spider to the docile donkey, and spent most of his time among them. He'd lie on his stomach in the early evening and wait for badgers, leave out food for stray dogs and bird-watch down on the beach in Smuggler's Bay. He'd taken Kitty and Bridie along one afternoon in January to watch a family of mice in the garden shed behind his house. They'd stayed for over an hour, as still as statues, as the mice had scampered about the wooden floor as if on tiny wheels, eating the seed Jack had put out for them. That small episode had bonded them like plotters in a conspiracy, and from that moment on they had set out together for more adventures in the wild. Kitty was bold and unafraid, curious about all the creatures Jack showed them, but Bridie was scared of creepy-crawlies and hairy mollies and sometimes needed coaxing. Jack would laugh at her apprehension and say, "All animals are the goodies if you see life from their point of view, even the smelly rat. Indeed they all have a God-given right to be on this earth." And Jack would tell them about life from the rat's point of view and Bridie would try hard to be sympathetic.

Today Jack hadn't come out either. His father, Liam O'Leary the vet, had begun to take him along when he went to examine colicky horses, lame sheep, and dogs wounded in fights. There was plenty of work for a vet in a place full of animals. So Bridie had spent the day with the other children whom she didn't like as much as Kitty nor admire as much as Jack.

Bridie loved Kitty like the sister she had never had, but she did wonder sometimes if the girl wasn't a bit "quare" with her talk of ghosts. Perhaps she was driven to make-believe because she was so lonely hidden away in the nursery with only the grim Miss Grieve for company. Bridie shuddered to think that those ghosts might be real. "Don't ye be forgetting to stir, Bridie," said her mother sharply, looking up from her sewing. Bridie hadn't noticed her hand had stopped and sat up with a jolt.

"She's away with the fairies," Old Mrs. Nagle tutted, shaking her head. Bridie didn't think her grandmother would say that about *her* if she knew some of the things Kitty said.

After tea Mrs. Doyle announced it was time for prayer and Bridie knelt on the floor with her father and brothers, as she did every evening, elbows on the chair, fingers knitted, head bowed. Old Mrs. Nagle remained seated in her chair and mumbled the words of the prayer through toothless gums. "Thou, oh Lord, will open my lips," said Mrs. Doyle solemnly.

"And my tongue shall announce thy praise," they all responded. Then Mrs. Doyle recited the prayer she knew so well it might have been embossed on her heart. The tail ends were short: a hasty prayer for friends and family and for Lord and Lady Deverill, who were both benevolent and fair.

After prayers the neighbors descended on the cottage, as they always did, with their fiddles and Old Badger Hanratty's illegal poteen, distilled from potatoes in a disguised hay rick. It wasn't long before the singing began. Bridie loved to sit with her buttermilk, listening to the Irish folk songs and watching the sentimental old men wallowing in nostalgia. Sometimes they'd dance the "Siege of Ennis" and her mother would shout, "Off ye go, lads, twice round the kitchen, and for God's sake mind the dresser." Or her father would grab her mother and they'd dance to the foot-stamping and table-banging, around and around, until Mrs. Doyle's red face glowed with pleasure and she looked like a young girl being courted by an overzealous suitor.

Bridie's father was rough with coarse black hair and a thick black beard and she doubted she would recognize him if he returned home one day clean-shaven. He was short and strong as a bull, and woe betide anyone who dared take him on in a fight. He'd won many a pub brawl and broken countless jaws and teeth in the process. He was quick to temper but just as quick to repent, and the few times he'd struck his sons he'd fallen to his knees in a heap of regret, crossing himself profusely and promising the Holy Virgin Mary not to do it again. Drink was his curse but a good heart his blessing; it was simply a matter of finding a balance between the two.

Suddenly her father weaved his way across the room toward her. She expected him to send her up to bed, but instead he took her hand and said, "Indeed and I'll be dancing with my Bridie tonight." And he pulled her to her feet. Everyone was watching and she blushed the color of a berry. But she needn't have worried about the steps; she had seen the older girls dancing often enough. Her father swung her around and around the kitchen just like he did Mrs. Doyle, and as she was swung she saw a sea of smiles and among them was her mother's, a tender look softening the work-weary contours of her face. After that her brothers took turns and Bridie, so often the spectator, became the focus of their attention and her heart swelled with pleasure.

That night Bridie could barely sleep for excitement. Her mind had drifted during the recital of the rosary because it had been such a joyous evening. She didn't imagine Kitty had evenings like that, dancing with her father. She rarely saw her brother who was at school in England. For a moment Bridie gave in to the superior feeling. She bathed in it, allowing her envy to be eclipsed by a warm sense of supremacy. She tried not to compare her life with Kitty's, but recently Bridie had grown more aware of their differences. Perhaps it was due to her brother Michael's resentful comments or maybe a result of the increasing amount of time they were now spending together; whichever the case, Bridie was being given a bigger window into Kitty's life and a greater perspective, causing her to wonder why it was that Kitty had so much when *she* had so little.

She could hear voices downstairs; her father and brothers playing cards, Mr. Hanratty, drunk on his own poteen, snoring loudly from her mother's rocking chair, and the longing in the lyrics of "Eileen a Roon" sung to the haunting tones of a lone fiddle. It was a comforting and familiar lullaby, and Bridie soon drifted off to sleep.

SHE AWOKE ABRUPTLY at dawn to the sound of loud knocking on the front door. It was still dark, but for a streak of red bleeding into the eastern sky. She sat up and wondered who would come calling at this time of the morning. She heard her father's heavy tread on the stairs and felt a cold sliver of wind, like one of the snakes St. Patrick banished from Ireland, winding its way around her door and slipping into the room. She shivered and pulled the blanket tightly around her. A moment later the door slammed and the footsteps went back up the stairs. The house was silent again but for the chewing of a mouse beneath the floorboards under her bed, and the moaning of the wind outside.

"Da, who was at the door this morning?" she asked her father when she came down for breakfast.

"No one," he replied, taking a loud slurp of tea.

Old Mrs. Nagle crossed herself. "'Tis the auld Banshee with the first of three knocks, God save us," she said darkly. Mrs. Doyle blanched and crossed herself as well, sprinkling drops of holy water around the room from the little Norah Lemonade bottle by the door.

"'T'was a tinker, more like," said Sean with a chuckle.

"Whoever it was, he was off before I got to the door," Tomas Doyle continued. Bridie cut herself a hunk of soda bread upon which she spread a thick layer of butter. She didn't like the frightened expression on her mother's face and tried not to look at it.

"'T'was the Banshee," said Old Mrs. Nagle, crossing herself again.

"Lord preserve us from the Banshee!" muttered Mrs. Doyle.

"I tell you, woman, there was no one at the door. Sean's right. It must have been a tinker in search of a warm hearth. Come, let's not be late for Mass." Her father stood up.

Bridie dismissed dark thoughts of the Banshee. As legend had it she was a fairy woman heard wailing when someone was about to die. There had been no wailing, as far as she had heard, so her mother and grandmother were over-reacting. As she walked down the street on the way to the schoolhouse she saw, to her relief, an old shabby horse pulling a cart full of grubby-faced children. There were skinny goats tethered to the back and one or two young ones inside the cart. The ragged children watched her with wary black eyes as she passed, the mother busy shouting at her husband. Tinkers, her father had been right. They'd probably spent half the night knocking on doors in search of a warm place to sleep. Bridie quickened her step. Her father had told her never to trust a tinker and never to look one in the eye.

The school of Our Lady in Ballinakelly was run by the

church but fortunately Father Quinn had little to do with the day-to-day teaching. Bridie's teacher was a nun from Cork City called Sister Hannah, who was softly spoken and kind. "It is through education that we better ourselves," she had once told Bridie's class. "The only way out of poverty is through learning, so listen hard to what I'm teaching you. They can take everything you own but no one can take your heart or your mind or your love of God. They're the only things that really matter." Bridie concentrated hard, but Jack O'Leary, who was in the boys' class next door, just gazed out of the window and watched the birds.

At the end of the day Bridie and Jack found Kitty in her usual place on the wall. However, this time she was standing on one leg, very still, like a heron. "What are you doing?" Jack asked.

"Balancing," she replied.

"Why?"

"No reason. For fun, I suppose. It's a challenge. What are you doing?"

"Jack has to give a lesson about birds tomorrow in school," said Bridie. "A punishment for gazing out of the window during class."

"There's no challenge in that," said Kitty. "There's nothing Jack doesn't know about plovers and cormorants!"

"Indeed, and I'll give Sister Margaret a lesson she'll never forget." Jack laughed.

"Doesn't she know you're an expert?" Kitty asked.

"She will tomorrow," said Bridie, flushing with admiration for Jack.

"Come and balance with me," Kitty exclaimed. "It's much harder than it looks. Come on!" Jack scaled the wall like a monkey while Bridie struggled to find her footing. After a while Jack put out his hand and hauled her onto the top.

"Don't you go falling off now," he said to her, and Bridie looked down anxiously.

"I'm not sure I can do it," she said.

"Course you can. Like this." And he lifted one foot. "Easy," he crowed. "Now *you* do it." But just as Bridie was about to raise her leg they heard voices in the trees behind them. Hastily they jumped down, even Bridie who was afraid of heights, and crouched out of sight.

"Who is it?" Jack hissed. "Did you see anyone?"

Kitty and Jack raised themselves up so they could just see over the wall. There, sneaking in among the trees, was a ragged group of people trespassing on Lord Deverill's land. Jack pulled Kitty down with him. "Tinkers," he snarled. "They were in town this morning."

"I saw them too," said Bridie, pleased to be able to add something to the conversation. "What do they want here?"

"Game," said Kitty darkly. "They're after anything they can eat."

"I'd say they're after more than that. We have to warn Lord Deverill," said Jack excitedly.

"Follow me," said Kitty. "I know a quick way to the castle."

The three children crept around the edge of the wall until they reached a farm entrance, which was easy to scale. They scampered eagerly up the dirt track until they reached the stables at the back of the Hunting Lodge.

"What's the matter with you three? Running from the

Devil, are you?" asked Mr. Mills, who was busy in the stable yard with the horse and trap Lady Deverill had just brought back from her trip into town.

"There are tinkers in the trees," gasped Kitty, catching her breath.

"They're up to no good, Mr. Mills," Jack added.

"We've come to tell Lord Deverill," Bridie joined in eagerly.

"Slow down now. Tinkers in the trees, you say?"

"Yes, we must tell Grandpa," Kitty insisted, hoping her grandfather would get his gun out and fire at them from his dressing-room window.

"No need to bother Lord Deverill," said Mr. Mills. "I'll get some of the lads and we'll deal with them ourselves. Now where are they?"

"We'll show you," said Kitty, hopping from foot to foot with excitement. "Hurry before they get away!"

"Miss Kitty, you'd better stay here. It might be dangerous," said Mr. Mills.

"Then I *must* come!" Kitty exclaimed. "I'm not afraid of a few tinkers."

"Your grandfather would not thank me if you came to harm."

Kitty pouted crossly. "But I *want* to come."

"You're safer here," said Mr. Mills firmly and Kitty was left with no alternative but to watch Jack, Bridie and Mr. Mills set off toward the wood with Sean Doyle, Bridie's brother, and some of the grooms and beaters, armed with sticks and hurleys.

BRIDIE FELT MORE courageous with her big brother by her side. Like her father, Sean wasn't tall but he was strong and fearless and deeply loyal to the Deverills. If there was a thief on Lord Deverill's land he'd be sure to see him off and give the man such a fright he'd be unlikely ever to come back. Now they walked through the walled vegetable garden, past Lady Deverill's greenhouses and on out the other side to the paddock where some of the horses grazed lazily in the waning light. This way they came to the wood from the eastern side and worked their way toward where the children had seen the tinkers. It was dark among the trees and the air had turned cold and moist. They crept, quietly as cats, alert to every sound.

Suddenly they came upon the ragged, unwashed, wild-looking wanderers. The woman carried two pheasants and a partridge by the neck while the men were standing staring into a bush, presumably having spotted something worth poaching. Bridie noticed that one of the pheasants in the woman's grasp looked like it was still alive, twitching every now and then in a vain attempt to escape. She glanced at Jack and saw his face contort with outrage. When the tinkers noticed Mr. Mills and his men they swung around and froze to the spot like animals trapped with nowhere to run. There was no point hiding their spoils; they knew they'd been caught red-handed. Two skinny men and one woman were no match for Mr. Mills and his burly boys. "You're trespassing on Lord Deverill's land," said Mr. Mills sternly.

"Lord Deverill's land. Well, we didn't know," said one of the men, grinning toothlessly.

"I'll kindly ask you to put down those birds and leave at once." The men narrowed their eyes and looked Mr. Mills up and down as if calculating the risks involved in a fight. Sean held up his pitchfork and the look on his face left them in no doubt that they'd be the worse off. They scowled and ordered the woman to drop the birds.

"Curse you!" she screeched at Mr. Mills, but he wasn't alarmed by the feeble words of a tinker woman.

"Be off with you now before we call the constabulary and have the three of you locked up," he said with the authority of a man who has the full weight of Lord Deverill behind him. The woman reluctantly threw the birds to the ground and the three of them slowly walked away.

Mr. Mills patted Jack on the head. "Good stuff, lad," he said. "And Bridie, where would she be got to?" Mr. Mills searched through the semi-dark for Bridie. When he saw her cowering behind her brother he nodded his appreciation. "You too, Bridie. I will tell Lord Deverill. I'm sure he will want to reward you." Bridie's eyes widened and she caught Jack's eye. "Now be off with you, too, before it gets too dark to see the end of your nose."

THE NIGHT WAS drawing in. Jack and Bridie made their way back to Ballinakelly with a skip in their step. They had had quite an adventure and looked forward to a generous reward from Lord Deverill. When they reached the town they were horrified to find themselves face-to-face with the tinkers, preparing their horses for departure. Glancing about them they saw the street was quiet, except for the golden light inside O'Donovan's public house opposite. Seeing the children the tinker woman pointed at them accusingly and shouted something in a dialect that neither Jack nor Bridie understood. Before Jack could register what was happening he felt a blow to his jaw and fell backward in the mud as one of the men dealt him the full might of his fist. Bridie let out a scream, so loud and piercing that the pub door opened, throwing light across the place where Jack lay inert. A moment later Bridie's father Tomas hurled himself into the street. Just as one of the tinkers pulled back his arm to give Bridie a similar blow, Tomas grabbed him by the shoulder and thumped him on the nose. Blood spouted from the tinker's face and he recoiled, landing on his backside in the mud. But the other man came at Tomas from behind and he had a knife. With one thrust he dug the blade through Tomas's ribs.

Somewhere deep in the woods came the distant shriek of the Banshee, carried on the fairy wind that had suddenly risen.

Chapter 6

Ballinakelly was shaken to its foundations by the foul killing of Tomas Doyle. Mrs. Doyle wailed so loudly she might easily have outdone the Banshee herself. "When I was a young girl at a regatta in Bantry," she said, pressing her handkerchief to her nose, "an old tinker woman told me my fortune and she said that my life would be a vale of tears. Never a truer word spoken, God help us." Bridie was devastated. Not only had she lost her darling da, but she believed *she* was to blame. If she hadn't gone with Mr. Mills and the boys the tinkers would never have seen her. If she hadn't screamed so loudly her father might not have come out of O'Donovan's. Oh, if only she hadn't gone to find Kitty at the wall none of it would have happened and her father would still be alive. Sean comforted her as best he could, but she was inconsolable.

Michael accused them both of recklessness. "You're a pair of shoneens, the two of you! A few of Lord Deverill's pheasants for the life of your da!" he shouted, his dark face purple with rage. "Was it worth it? Didn't he say never to look a tinker in the eye?" Old Mrs. Nagle's eyes were dry for she had witnessed the deaths of so many during the potato famine that her tears had all been used up. However, beneath her scrawny chest her heart bled for her daughter and her loss. She wanted to know if anyone had said the Act of Contrition in Tomas's ear before he went cold to ensure that he bypassed Purgatory on his way to Heaven, but there was no one to reassure her.

The tinker responsible for the murder had been arrested at the scene of the crime and was likely to be sentenced to hang. But that was of little consolation to Mrs. Doyle. "Hanging is too good for the likes of him," she said in a deep and quivering voice. "May the Devil take his soul and burn it in Hell for all eternity, God save us."

Tomas Doyle was laid out on the kitchen table for two days. Mrs. Doyle had flung open the window to let out his spirit. Two old women known as the two Nellies, Miss Nellie Clifford and Miss Nellie Moxley, arrived in their white dresses and blue veils to wash the body clean and Father Quinn was called to do the anointing. He arrived in his thick robes, his face red with indignation that one of his flock should be taken by an inebriated thief. Being so tall he had to bend his head as he strode into the cottage. "He was a good man," he said to Mrs. Doyle, kneeling by her side as she sat sniveling on her rocking chair beside the hearth, clutching her rosary beads. "He's with the Lord now, Mariah. Indeed and the man who did this will rot for all eternity in the fires of Hell." His voice was surprisingly soft and tender and Bridie stopped crying with the shock of it. She watched her mother look up at the priest with big, shiny eyes and her face relaxed into a beatific smile, as if his words had literally lifted her grief out of her heart and replaced it with the certainty that her dear Tomas was with Mary and the Angels. If Father Quinn had said it, it must be true, for Father Quinn knew the mind of God.

"Michael," said Father Quinn, standing up and towering over Tomas's sons. "You're head of the family now. Sean, you must help him on the land. You're needed here. And, Bridie?" He settled his powerful gaze on the child, who felt herself tremble beneath it. "You will help your grandmother in the home until you are old enough to work at the castle with your mother."

"Yes, Father," she replied quietly.

He put a heavy hand on her shoulder. "And it wasn't your fault. Do you understand?"

"Yes, Father," she answered, unable to stop the tears from spilling over onto her cheeks.

"You must be strong for your mother. And, Michael?" he said and his voice had once more taken on its habitual severe and uncaring tone.

"Yes, Father?"

"Don't go casting blame. Every action has a consequence and we can never know what that consequence might be. However, it is God's will and we mustn't question it."

"Yes, Father," Michael replied obediently, disguising the craving for vengeance behind dark impenetrable eyes.

Lady Deverill visited with a basket of food. She paid her respects to Tomas Doyle and sat with Mrs. Doyle and Old Mrs.

Nagle, giving comfort as best she could. "You know, Mrs. Doyle," she began, looking kindly at the widow through the smoke coming from Old Mrs. Nagle's clay pipe. "We're not human beings having a spiritual experience, but spirits having a human experience. Your Tomas will always be with you. Just because you can't see him doesn't mean he's not here. He's made of light now, like a rainbow, and he's in a far better place."

"Indeed, Tomas is with the Lord, Lady Deverill, and I am at peace," Mrs. Doyle replied.

Adeline handed Bridie a shoebox. "And this is from Lord Deverill. It's a reward for you, Bridie, for your bravery. I know it won't bring your father back, but I hope it will give you some consolation." When she had gone Bridie opened the box to find a pair of shiny black patent-leather dancing shoes with big silver buckles. She gasped in wonder. Bridie had never worn shoes before and the soles of her feet were as tough as hide. With her breath caught in her chest she put them on at once. "They're a fine pair of shoes, Bridie," Sean said softly, hoping Michael wouldn't spoil the moment by accusing her of profiting from an incident that had led directly to their father's death. But Michael had heeded Father Quinn's words and sat solemnly on a chair, biting his tongue.

The shoes were slightly too big, which was fortunate because that meant they'd last longer. She walked clumsily around the kitchen like a cart horse, trying to get used to the heaviness of the leather after the lightness of her bare feet, and the feeling of having something hard against her skin. But she couldn't take her eyes off them: they were the most magnificent things she had ever owned.

Soon neighbors and friends arrived to pay their respects and

Mrs. Doyle offered them snuff, whiskey and Lord and Lady Deverill's generous basket of food. Liam O'Leary came with his wife, Julia, and Jack, nursing a shiny purple bruise on his cheek. He took off his cap and shook his head dolefully at the sight of poor Tomas Doyle. Julia, who believed herself much too grand to enter such a humble abode, put a handkerchief to her nose and grimaced at the sight of the corpse, waxy in the candlelight.

Liam O'Leary didn't stay long, just enough time to have a drink and pay his respects. As he left, he blessed himself with the bottle of holy water Mrs. Doyle always kept by the door, along with the sprig of palm from Palm Sunday. Julia ignored the water: she was eager to be as far away as possible from the miserable cottage and the corpse inside it.

Bridie was pleased to see Jack and gave him more sympathy for his bruise than his mother had done. He noticed her shoes at once. "Lord Deverill gave me a beagle," he told her. "Mother wanted me to give it back."

"Why?" Bridie asked in astonishment.

"I don't know, but she doesn't like the Deverills."

"Will you give it back?"

He grinned raffishly. "Not on your life, Bridie. A reward's a reward and I earned it." He ran rough fingers over his jaw.

"Does it hurt?" Bridie asked.

"It sure does." He glanced at Tomas lying on the table and shook his head. "But I'm lucky to be alive, Bridie. Your poor da, God rest his soul."

THE FOLLOWING DAY the entire town came out for the funeral and the sun shone down as if Tomas himself had made it so.

"Happy is the corpse that the sun shines on," they all said as they made their way into All Saints Church. Every chair was taken and barely an inch of stone floor was left free for an extra pair of feet. Mrs. Doyle sat in the front with her family, dignified in her black shawl and dress, between her two sons with Bridie beside Sean in her new polished shoes. Father Quinn gave a rousing sermon, praising Tomas for his hard work and kind heart and holding him up as an example to the rest of the community, omitting his temper and his love of whiskey. "God always takes the good ones," said Miss Nellie Moxley under her breath.

"Sure, I'm only waiting for the call now meself," Miss Nellie Clifford whispered back. "It can't be long. I've one foot in the grave and the other on a bar of soap."

Tomas was buried in the churchyard alongside those of the community who had gone before. Bridie found it hard to believe that her father was in the ground, never to appear again with his kind eyes and reassuring presence. Even though Michael was a man now and more than capable of doing his father's work, she still felt as if the once solid foundation of her existence had turned to marshland. She would miss the comforting certainty of her father's love. Her eyes watered as she remembered the times she had ridden beside him in the cart to take the butter to the Cork Butter Exchange. *Irish butter*, her father would proudly tell her, *to feed the Empire*. She could hear his voice as if he were whispering in her ear: *Don't mind the thunder, Bridie. 'Tis only barrels rolling across the sky.* Quietly she began to cry.

WHEN ADELINE TOLD Kitty the sad news about Tomas Doyle she gasped in horror and pressed her hand to her open mouth.

"I have given her a pair of shoes as a reward for alerting us to the poachers, but it'll be a bittersweet present considering the tragedy it brought," said Lady Deverill. Kitty sat beside her on the sofa in her grandmother's warm sitting room and thought of her friend Bridie. "The funeral was today," Adeline continued. "I gather the whole of Ballinakelly turned out for it. He was well loved," she reflected.

"I'd like to have gone to the funeral," said Kitty.

"My dear, that would not have been possible. One has to be tactful."

"But Bridie is my friend."

"She *is* your friend, but there are many who would think ill of her for mixing with the likes of us."

"Why is that so, Grandma?"

"Because there is a lot of resentment, Kitty. A conquered people always resent the conquerors. That's only natural, isn't it? Many Irish Catholics had their lands taken away from them and given to the English—"

"Like the O'Learys," interjected Kitty.

"Quite so, my dear, just like the O'Learys." She sighed, weary of the acrimony. "So, they want their land back, the English out and they want independence. Naturally they are suspicious of anyone who associates with the English. That's us, Kitty. Bridie would not want her family and friends to think her disloyal, would she?"

"*I* would want my land back if someone had taken it."

"Of course you would." Adeline smiled indulgently at her granddaughter, and a little proudly, too, because of her sharp intelligence. "But if the O'Learys were to have their land back we wouldn't have Castle Deverill and all that goes with it.

What is done cannot be undone now without terrible consequences. It is better that we all live in the present moment and not think too much about the atrocities of the past. After all, we have to live together and get along."

"Poor Bridie." Kitty sighed.

"I know, her life is hard. Losing people we love is bad enough but intolerable if one doesn't realize that they never really leave, they just fade out of sight."

"You will never leave me, will you, Grandma?" Kitty asked sincerely.

Adeline put her arm around Kitty's shoulder and pulled her close. "You know I won't, my darling. And what's more, you'll know I'm still with you because you will be able to see me. That's a rare and wonderful gift."

Kitty ran into the garden, her thoughts with Bridie. The sun was warm upon her skin and the air scented with the sweet, creamy smells of sweet box and *Daphne bholua*. She knew every inch of her grandmother's gardens and fell upon a witch hazel bush, whose yellow flowers gave off a soothing, medicinal fragrance. She picked enough to make a small posy, which she tied with string from one of the greenhouses. When she had finished she went to the stables to find Mr. Mills.

"Mr. Mills, Mr. Mills!" she shouted across the stable yard.

Mr. Mills appeared beneath the stone arch of the stable block, carrying a rag in one hand and leather polish in the other. "What can I do for you, Miss Kitty?"

She ran over the cobbles and held out her posy. "I want you to give this to Bridie. Mrs. Doyle and Sean aren't here and she *must* get it today."

Mr. Mills shook his head gravely. "A terrible business. Poor little Bridie, losing her father so young." He went back inside and Kitty followed him. The stables smelled of horses, hay and manure. A couple of lads were sitting on stools, polishing tack, their sleeves rolled up to reveal strong arms as they vigorously rubbed the leather. They stopped working a moment to watch. If Kitty had been Lady Deverill, or any of the other women of the family, they would have jumped to their feet, but Kitty was a child and usually running about the grounds with Bridie Doyle so they remained on their stools.

Mr. Mills put down his rag and polish and found a dusty jar in the tack room. He plunged it into a barrel of water and took the flowers from Kitty. "I'll pass by their house and pay my respects later this afternoon. They'll keep like this. I'm sure she'll be grateful for your thoughtfulness, Miss Kitty."

"It's the least I can do. She's my friend, Mr. Mills," said Kitty boldly, affronted that he should be surprised by her gift. "My *best* friend."

Since her afternoon riding with her father, Kitty had been released from the nursery and included in the family meals. Maud watched her suspiciously from the end of the table. There was something troubling about the audacious look in the child's eyes that made Maud feel guilty. They were much too large, an unusual shade of gray, like a wolf's or some other wild animal's that Maud couldn't think of, and somehow terribly impertinent. It was as if Kitty, like Adeline, could see into the hidden recesses of her soul and knew all her secrets. Maud felt defensive even though Kitty was too young to understand her mother's coldness. She tried to talk to her youngest daughter as she would talk to Victoria and Elspeth, but those eyes seemed to mock her attempts at conversation, as if Kitty was amused by how hard her mother struggled to find a meeting of minds when there clearly wasn't even a scrap of understanding between them.

"Miss Grieve, I would like you to teach Kitty a little humility," Maud instructed the governess after one particularly uncomfortable luncheon. "She has a very brazen way of staring at people. Frankly, it's rude. A girl of her age should learn to lower her eyes and not look at one so directly."

"I will see to it, Mrs. Deverill," said Miss Grieve.

"Please see that you do or Kitty will have to have her meals in the nursery again." It was a relief for Maud when Kitty sat through the following luncheon with her eyes on her food. Kitty, much too wily to allow herself to be cowed, soon learned that she could look at anyone else directly; it was only her mother who flinched when she caught her daughter's eye. Wily she might be, and resilient too, but Kitty wasn't so hardy as to be unaffected by her mother's hostility. It cut her deeply.

MR. MILLS LEANED his bicycle against the whitewashed wall of the Doyles' cottage and pushed open the door. Old Mrs. Nagle was sitting in her usual chair, keeping the bastible hot with burning twigs while fish hung in the chimney to smoke. Mrs. Doyle was in her rocking chair, sewing a black diamond to denote mourning into the elbow of Michael's jacket. The cottage was dimly lit but warm and the smell of cooking made Mr. Mills's stomach groan.

"Good day to you, Mrs. Nagle and Mrs. Doyle," he said, taking off his cap and nodding formally.

"Would you like some tea?" Mrs. Doyle asked. "Bridie will pour you some. The pot is still hot."

Mr. Mills turned to see Bridie's pale face appear out of the gloom. Her big dark eyes made her face look small and miserable. The buckles on her dancing shoes caught the light of the fire and glinted. "What a grand pair of shoes, Bridie," he said and for a moment the child's face regained its color and she smiled, gazing lovingly down at them.

"A gift from Lady Deverill," she replied quietly.

"A gift well earned." He held out the posy. "These are for you, from Miss Kitty." Bridie took them gratefully and pressed them to her nose. Her eyes welled with tears at this small kindness and she lost her voice for a moment. "She said it was important that I give it to you today." Mr. Mills's heart caved in at the sight of the wretched child. "She said you're her best friend."

Bridie smiled tentatively and she nodded. Mr. Mills saw the effort in her straining neck as she tried to suppress her emotions. "Why don't you make me a cup of tea?" he asked gently, allowing her time to compose herself. She nodded briskly and set about pouring it into a basin.

"Life goes on," said Mrs. Doyle from the hearth. "Mr. Doyle is with our Lord now and we have to continue as before. He wouldn't want us to fall apart now, would he?"

"He most certainly wouldn't, Mrs. Doyle," said Mr. Mills.

"Well, there'll be no more tears shed then." She pursed her lips and went back to her sewing.

Kitty gave Mr. Mills his tea and walked over to give her grandmother another. "I have my Bridie for comfort and my boys," said Mrs. Doyle, smiling at her daughter with a fondness Mr. Mills had never seen before. "Mr. Doyle was very proud of his children, Mr. Mills. Michael and Sean are hard-working lads and Bridie here will soon be old enough to work for Lady Deverill. We'll get by, won't we, Bridie? We have much to be thankful for. We have a roof over our heads and a kindhearted landlord. Few can claim as much."

Bridie sat at the table and put the jar of witch hazel in the center. She thought of Kitty and pictured her face as though she were sitting right opposite her, her eyes bright and eerie in the candlelight, and she could hear her voice in her head as if she were really speaking. *Your father is still with you, Bridie. You have to believe he's beside you. Those we love and lose are always with us.* And Bridie, once doubtful that Barton Deverill was really in the armchair in the tower of the castle, now wanted to believe more than anything that her dear father had simply faded out of sight. She wished she had Kitty's certainty and her gift of seeing the dead; more than ever she wished she could turn back the clock and bring her father home.

MICHAEL WAS NOT a man to sit quietly with his prayers. He wanted revenge and his lust for vengeance consumed him. The hanging of the murderer was not enough for the life of Tomas Doyle. The whole settlement would pay for the crime, he decided, knocking back a cup of Hanratty's poteen that burned a trail down his gullet. *An eye for an eye, a tooth for a tooth*, he thought darkly, hate and grief no longer two separate emotions, but one potent force of malevolence, fueled by alcohol. As he crept through the undergrowth toward the shabby caravans and carts parked together in the middle of a field he was glad that clouds covered the eye of the moon for perhaps even God had turned away, leaving *him* to see that justice was done.

He reached the cluster of simple dwellings, glad that the tinkers hadn't yet moved on. Perhaps they stayed in the hope of a last-minute reprieve for the man sentenced to be hanged. Michael didn't care. Quietly he untied the horses. The docile beasts neighed quietly but remained where they stood. He lit his torch and with the flame lit the other four he had brought with him. Sneaking up on the caravans he thrust the torches anywhere there was a gap. The fire spread quickly and efficiently, catching light on the straw bedding and devouring the thick fabric covering the roofs. Then screams rose above the noise of cracking and burning and people poured out of the blaze like rats. That'll teach them, Michael thought with satisfaction. As he stole into the darkness he turned to see the devastation, a great bonfire in the center of the field, throwing golden light onto the surrounding grass and hedges. But as he walked away the cry of a woman reached his ears and turned his heart to ice. "Help! Help! My little Noreen! My little Noreen!"

THERE WAS NO doubt in anyone's mind that Michael Doyle was responsible for the fire that killed the tinker child, but no one in Ballinakelly dared mention his name when questioned by the constabulary. Michael Doyle was wild and menacing, capable of reducing a person to pulp with one look of his hard black eyes, and there was not a man in Ballinakelly who wanted to incite his wrath. Indeed, the town closed ranks around him and Mrs. Doyle, Old Mrs. Nagle and Badger Hanratty vouched for his presence that night beside the hearth. Yet Michael's torment was only just beginning. Noreen was a whisper in his nightmares and a stain upon his conscience, and his guilt blackened ever deeper his calcifying heart.

Chapter 7

The second week of August, after the Dublin Horse Show, which took place during the *first* week of August and was an immutable fixture on the Irish calendar, Cousin Digby Deverill and his family left Deverill Rising, their Wiltshire estate, and descended on Castle Deverill with enough luggage to last an entire year. Sir Digby and his wife, the flamboyant Beatrice, stayed with Maud and Bertie in the Hunting Lodge with their four very spoiled and insufferable children for four weeks. Celia was Kitty's age exactly, twins Leona and Vivien contemporaries of Elspeth, and their son George a little younger than Harry and in the same house at Eton. Digby's parents, Stoke Deverill, who was descended from Barton Deverill's younger brother, and his wife, Augusta, stayed in the castle with Hubert and Adeline. They all left England, as they did every year, with heavy trunks full of tennis rackets, riding habits, evening dresses, day dresses and dancing shoes, ready for the tennis parties, summer balls, dinner parties and lunch parties for which the Anglo-Irish were famous. In attendance was a retinue of lady's maids, valets and Celia's governess, Miss Springer.

This was Kitty's favorite time of the year. Not only did she enjoy wriggling out of her governess's clutches but she, Bridie and Celia formed a secret club to spy on the adults. Kitty's sharp powers of observation meant she missed nothing and their game kept them entertained for the entire holiday. The highlight was the Summer Ball at Castle Deverill, to which the whole of West Cork came in their fine carriages and silk ball gowns and danced until sunrise. Kitty and Celia were allowed to stay up. Due to the excessive amount of alcohol consumed by the adults they were left to wander, infiltrate and observe. The small girls, going about the rooms unnoticed, often witnessed things the adults would have preferred they didn't.

Maud tolerated Beatrice, who was a large soufflé of a woman, with big breasts and a big heart and a collection of the finest diamonds given to her by her entrepreneur husband who had made a fortune in the South African diamond mines. Indeed, Digby had been knighted by Queen Victoria for his services to the Crown, which infuriated Maud all the more because Beatrice was not only rich but titled as well. In Maud's opinion Beatrice was brash and lacked breeding, but Kitty's father enjoyed Digby because he was a great enthusiast. He could barely ride a horse, but galloped over the hills all the same, roaring with laughter every time he fell off. He couldn't cast a fishing line but spent hours trying his luck in the sea and never minded if the only thing he caught was an old bottle of rum from a sunken pirate ship. He brought with him the finest Cuban cigars, and whiskey and wine in large crates, and Beatrice gifted the girls silks and lace in the most luxurious colors. As a couple they were extravagant, affectionate and very grand but Kitty loved them for the laughter they brought into her home.

George, Leona, Vivien and Celia were spoiled, with an unsavory air of entitlement lingering beneath their pert little noses. The girls always arrived in thick coats and hats, with woolen shawls wrapped tightly around their shoulders, complaining loudly of the cold, racing to huddle in front of the fire as if they'd arrived from the tropics. Beatrice brought extra blankets for the beds and soft bed socks for chilly feet. "This is an adventure," she would exclaim to her daughters as they grumbled about the damp linen and the faint but unmistakable smell of mice in their bedrooms. But they soon got swept along by the Irish way of life, dancing all night, playing croquet on the immaculately cut lawn, tennis on the grass court, picnicking on the beach in fine weather, dining up at the castle with the local gentry, giggling behind their hands at the eccentric behavior of their cousins and their cranky friends. It wasn't long before Leona and Vivien were pursued by the Irish boys, for not only were they blond and beautiful, but rich as well. For a declining society like the Anglo-Irish, the attraction of English money was irresistible. Celia loved nothing more than excitement and Castle Deverill provided all the intrigue and escapades she could dream of. She found the perfect partner in crime in Kitty. For a child who bored easily and was prone to sulking, her cousin Kitty was a tireless source of activity and fun.

Victoria had enjoyed a successful London Season staying with her cousins in their palatial Italianate home Deverill

House on Kensington Palace Gardens. She returned to Co. Cork with an air of sophistication, as if she had grown out of Ireland and all that went with it and belonged instead in the ballrooms of London, among the landed gentry and aristocracy. She sighed at the drizzle and the damp as much as Leona and Vivien did and started most of her sentences with "In London . . ." in a tone that implied everything was better there. She received letters from suitors and read them out loud to her mother and Beatrice, who pondered with indefatigable enthusiasm which earl or lord might make the best match for her. Kitty rolled her eyes and wondered why liking the man never came into consideration.

Kitty enjoyed Celia in spite of her petulance. Her cousin had her father's sense of fun and her mother's sense of mischief and she didn't mind playing with Bridie, whom she considered something of a curiosity with her funny accent and foreign vocabulary. Soon after the cousins arrived, Kitty, Bridie and Celia gathered among the tomatoes and grapes in one of Kitty's grandmother's greenhouses.

"Victoria is very pleased with herself since she came back from London," said Kitty, chewing on a piece of wild sorrel.

"I heard her telling Mama that she doesn't want to live in Ireland anymore," said Celia. She pulled a fig off its branch and examined it for insects.

"I'd be very happy for her *and* Elspeth to go and live in London. I don't like them at all. Mama doesn't really like them much, either. She only likes Harry." Kitty lowered her voice and added darkly, "Do you know, I was meant to be a boy?"

"How do you know?" asked Celia.

"I overheard Mama talking to Lady Rowan-Hampton in the drawing room. She said, 'If only Kitty had been a boy . . .'"

"So she didn't want you at all?" Celia gasped, her open mouth full of fig.

"I'm sure she did," interrupted Bridie, who tended to say less when Celia was present.

"No, she didn't. I was a disappointment. One day when I have a baby girl I will love her very much." Kitty grinned, for she wasn't one for self-pity. "Let's do something really wicked."

"Oh let's!" Celia clapped her hands. With Kitty life was always full of excitement and mischief.

"Perhaps, if we find a frog, Victoria might kiss it in the hope that it turns into a prince. What do you think?" Kitty laughed. "Shall we see if we can find one?"

"Where would we find a frog?"

"Down by the river. If we go to the lily pond we'll risk being seen," Kitty replied. "What do you think, Bridie?"

"As long as I don't have to touch it," she replied anxiously. "Frogs give you warts."

"That's an old wives' tale, Bridie," said Kitty. "Come on. Last one at the river is a rotten egg!"

The three girls ran through the garden. When they reached the wall Celia complained that she'd dirty her dress on the stones. "Isn't there a gate?"

"Not if we want to go unnoticed," said Kitty.

Celia sighed and watched Kitty scale it like a lizard, followed closely by Bridie, whose dress was already dirty so it didn't matter. Celia clenched her fists and stuck out her bottom lip. "I can't," she exclaimed. "I'll have to use the gate and risk being caught."

"No, you must climb it. It's not difficult," Kitty insisted.

But Celia didn't move. She folded her arms and went red in the face with indignation. "You can't make me!"

At that moment there came the sound of footsteps on the leafy ground behind them. Kitty swung around, half expecting to find the three tinkers poaching again. She was relieved to see Jack's freckly face grinning at her from beneath his cap, his beagle trotting along beside him. "So, there you are!" he exclaimed. "I've been looking for you."

"I thought you were a tinker," said Kitty.

"No tinker would dare enter these woods after . . ." He hesitated, his eyes flicking to Bridie who stood camouflaged against the wall in her brown dress like a scrawny partridge. Bridie's face lit up when she saw him, and she swept back her knotted hair with a grubby hand.

"Celia won't climb the wall," said Kitty.

"Come on, Celia. I'll give you a hand," said Jack. He jumped easily onto the wall and reached down. Celia reluctantly accepted his aid and let him pull her up. She smoothed down her dress and checked for signs of dirt. Jack laughed. "What are you girls up to?"

"We're going to find a frog," said Bridie.

"We want to give it to Victoria to see if it turns into a prince with a kiss," said Kitty with a giggle.

"You'll be kind to it now, won't you?" Jack asked, concerned.

"We'll put it back where we found it, I promise."

"Then I'll show you where to find one. Follow me." At that moment Jack's pet hawk swooped out of the sky and landed onto his thick, protective glove. "He's been hunting for rabbits and mice," said Jack. "So far, he hasn't found anything."

"That's because Papa is out with Cousin Digby and the boys and they're killing everything that moves," said Kitty.

Jack led the way through the long grasses into the crevice of the hillside where the water trickled down to the sea. It was dark among the ferns and moss. Bridie stood behind Kitty as she crouched down. She didn't fancy getting too close if one hopped into view. Jack stood in the middle of the stream, hands on hips, gazing about him, more interested in his hawk than in the search for frogs. Celia kept shouting from the bridge, "Have you found one yet?"

At last Kitty spotted a small olive-brown frog among the stones at the water's edge. With a gasp of excitement, she gently picked it up and cupped it in her hands. "Jack!" she hissed. "I've found one!" Jack peered between her fingers.

"Have you got one?" Celia was jumping up and down with excitement.

"It's a small one," said Jack. "Do you know it can change its color to blend in with its surroundings?"

"Will it go pink then, to match my skin?" she asked.

"No, it takes two hours to change. It might go a yellow color if you give it time. You should carry it on a bed of leaves, not on your skin. You might harm it." He bent down and started looking about for suitable foliage.

Bridie peered gingerly into Kitty's hand. "Is it cold and slimy?" she asked.

"It feels soft and damp," Kitty replied happily. Jack helped her arrange the frog onto the leaves. "You have to help me up, Jack. I can't use my hands."

Jack laughed and swept Kitty into his arms. "You're like a sack of potatoes, you are," he said, striding back up the bank. Bridie looked on enviously. She wished Jack would carry *her* up the bank too. But she scrambled out by herself and watched Kitty showing the frog to Celia. As she observed the two cousins with their heads together, one red and one blond, but both so similar in attire and language, she felt a swell of pride that at least Jack was from *her* world and not theirs. *They* were united by a common culture, whereas Kitty and Celia were so very different, being English and aristocratic. Jack might be fond of Kitty, but he would never be allowed to think of her as his equal.

"Bridie, will you find us something to put it in?" Kitty asked when they got back to the castle, trying not to look guilty as one of the footmen walked past. She knew they were expected for lunch and their sisters and mothers would probably be in the drawing room already with Adeline, and Celia's grandmother Augusta.

Bridie disappeared, returning a moment later with the box of Fry's assorted chocolates that Beatrice had bought in Harrods and which the family had polished off the night before. "Where are you going to put it?" she asked.

"I don't know," said Kitty, arranging the frog on its bed of leaves inside. "I'll think about that when we're up there."

"Leona and Vivien will die of fright," said Celia excitedly. "I can't wait to see their faces."

"I can't wait to see Victoria's and Elspeth's. And Mama's. Let's not forget Mama." Kitty giggled. "She hates creepy-crawlies more than anyone. Let's catch a mouse next time and put it in her bed!"

Kitty and Celia washed their hands and faces and tidied their hair before sneaking up the servants' staircase and through the green baize door into the hall. Kitty put the chocolate box on the table behind a large display of lilies. "It'll be safe there for a while," she said confidently, taking Celia's hand.

They walked innocently into the drawing room where the women sat chatting over glasses of sherry on sofas and armchairs, the girls huddled in the corner talking quietly among themselves, while the men stood smoking beside the fireplace.

"Ah, here are the little devils," said Hubert, watching with pride as his granddaughter walked in with the hem of her dress smeared with mud and her untamable red hair coming away from the ribbons that swept it off her face. "What have you two been up to?"

Kitty stood before him. "Nothing, Grandpa. We've been in the greenhouse," she replied.

"Plotting, no doubt," added Cousin Digby with a chuckle. Maud glanced over from her seat on the sofa and a shadow of irritation darkened her face as she noticed Kitty's dirty dress, but before she could say a word Adeline reached out her hand.

"Kitty, my dear. Come over here and tell me what you've been doing all morning. You look like you've been digging a hole in the garden." Kitty walked up to her grandmother, glancing down at her dirty shoes, aware of her mother's disapproval.

"Miss Grieve has been neglecting her duty," said Maud frostily, noticing how pristine Celia looked.

Adeline laughed. "I don't think it's poor Miss Grieve's fault. I would imagine Miss Grieve has a hard time keeping track of this child's whereabouts! How did you manage to get so grubby while Celia remained so clean?"

"I don't know," Kitty replied, glancing at Celia in a silent plea not to tell.

"You take after your grandfather," said Adeline. "He can never stay out of the mud either!"

Cousin Beatrice joined in with exuberance. "Celia turns into a savage the moment she sets foot in Castle Deverill. I'm surprised *her* dress is clean. Perhaps it's in the air, but every summer here in Ireland is a great adventure, isn't it, Celia? An adventure we all look forward to with enormous anticipation."

"I suspect this year will be my last," interrupted Augusta grimly. Celia's grandmother was a handsome woman with thick gray hair swept up onto the top of her head, large drooping breasts contained behind reams of black lace and emeralds, and wide arthritic hips. She was tall and broad and dwarfed her husband, who was diminutive in stature as well as build, with a small face dominated by a sweeping white mustache. Her favorite subject was death and no one's fascinated her more than her own. "I spent my whole life thinking of everyone else but myself and here I am now with a lifetime of regrets and broken dreams. Oh to be young again." She sighed. "When I was a girl I thought old age would never arrive, but here I am, one breath away from the grave." She didn't notice Leona and Vivien rolling their eyes. "If you hear noises in the middle of the night, do not worry, it is only me, talking to God."

"Nonsense, Augusta. You'll outlive us all," said Adeline, who seemed to find extra reserves of patience when it came to Cousin Augusta.

"I've told Stoke that I don't want any fuss when the time comes. Just a little church service with close family and friends."

"I don't think you'll care, Augusta," said Adeline. "You'll be far away."

"My dear Adeline." Augusta placed a hand on Adeline's and squeezed it. "I trust *you* to make sure that Stoke doesn't spend money unnecessarily. You know how he is. I am a humble woman who does not need pomp and ceremony. I will leave the world quietly and peacefully as I have lived my life."

At last lunch was announced and the family began to move from the drawing room. Elspeth and Victoria led the way into the hall, followed closely by Leona and Vivien. Stoke dutifully assisted his wife as she heaved herself up. Kitty grabbed Celia and hurried into the hall to retrieve the chocolate box. But when they got to the table they discovered, to their horror, that it had gone. "What are we going to do?" hissed Celia. "It could be anywhere!"

"One of the servants must have removed it." Kitty sighed.

"Do you think they've thrown it away?"

"I don't know. Oh dear! This is very inconvenient."

"Shall we go and ask someone?"

"Come along, girls," said Beatrice, striding into the hall. "I bet you're both hungry, or have you been eating your way through the greenhouses?"

"No, Mama. We're very hungry," said Celia.

Kitty reluctantly walked into the dining room with Celia and Cousin Beatrice, trying not to worry about the fate of the poor frog and her promise to Jack.

The adults sat down at one end of the table, presided over by Hubert, whose place was always at the head, while his grandson Harry sat at the foot, surrounded by his young sisters and cousins. Bored by female company, he talked across them to George about their plans for the afternoon. Kitty pushed her food around her plate. All she could think about was the frog. Victoria and Elspeth kept looking at her and smiling, as if they knew something she didn't. Then suddenly Kitty saw the box. It was placed directly in front of her mother. The blood drained from her face as she realized her two sisters had discovered it on their way through the hall. She caught Elspeth's eye, but Elspeth looked away before she could ensnare her with her furious gaze.

It wasn't until dessert that Maud picked up the chocolate box. Kitty blanched as her mother looked at it quizzically. "Really, Beatrice, you spoil us with all these delicious chocolates." And then she opened it. Kitty's breath caught in her throat. Elspeth and Victoria smirked triumphantly. Celia, who had only just noticed the box, blushed scarlet. There was a moment when time seemed to hang suspended over the table, as Maud saw the frog and took a second to register what it was. Then she gasped and cried out in terror, "A frog!"

Elspeth and Victoria pretended to look surprised and stared accusingly at Kitty. Harry tried to suppress his smile—he couldn't help but find his little sister's mischievousness amusing. Maud snapped the box shut and swallowed hard in an attempt to control her outburst.

Bertie was on his feet. He strode around the table and picked up the box. "What is the meaning of this?" he barked, glaring at the children. Kitty's eyes began to brim with tears. She knew she was about to be rumbled, for Victoria and Elspeth would only too happily betray her. She clenched her fists, anticipating the pain of Miss Grieve's riding crop.

And then Adeline laughed. "Silly me!" she exclaimed. "Really, O'Flynn must have thought it was full of chocolates. I found the dear little frog in the morning room and thought I'd keep him for a while. Isn't he lovely?"

Maud stared at her mother-in-law. "It's *your* frog?" she asked in disbelief.

"I'm terribly sorry, Maud, my dear, if it gave you a fright. Give it to me, Bertie. I'll ask one of the children to put it back in the garden." Adeline looked down the table, as if deciding whom to ask. Then her pale eyes settled on Kitty, who stared at her grandmother with love and gratitude. "My darling Kitty, you like animals. Why don't you find a nice damp place to put him. I really shouldn't have kept him in a box. It's awfully cruel of me. Celia, why don't you go with her? Now, who would like some more dessert?"

Chapter 8

There is nothing in the world like an Irish summer. The air is damp with gentle rain, alive with the sounds of the seabirds that live off the rich fruit of the ocean and the abundant fodder of this fertile land. But when the sun shines it is surprisingly warm. The skies clear, bright and clean, the clouds disperse, revealing a canopy of indigo blue. The sun sets with a grand display of fiery crimson, and in that moment, when the dying day melts into the horizon, turning the water to liquid gold, one might believe there is nothing more beautiful on earth or in Heaven.

Kitty, Celia and Bridie stood at the very top of the castle and gazed out of the window across the sea. The spectacle rendered them speechless. Their tender hearts were touched by the otherworldly magnificence and a sense of something so much greater than themselves, but of which, in some incomprehensible way, they were part. Bridie thought of her father and wondered if he was out there somewhere, in that magical light. Her heart ached for him in an intense and urgent longing, but the melting sun sinking into the ocean filled her soul with something soothing but unidentifiable. Celia was too young to know what it was in the sunset that resonated deep within her but she was captivated by the wild mystery of Ireland. She recalled Kitty's Fairy Ring and wished with a sudden rush of passion that she could leave England altogether and live here in this enchanted place. Kitty, whose senses were so much in advance of her years, was overcome with love for her home. She knew for sure that, whatever happened in her future, wherever she was made to go, she would always carry Castle Deverill inside her—and there was nothing anyone could do to take that away from her.

It was the beginning of September and the night of the Castle Deverill Summer Ball. Grand carriages rattled up the drive, pulled by fine horses driven by men in livery. On either side of the track flares illuminated the way. The castle, a proud and majestic symbol of British ascendancy, stood in the light of the full moon. The girls raced to the other side and stood over the front door to watch the ladies in ball gowns and gentlemen in tailcoats climb the steps to be graciously received by their hosts, Lord and Lady Deverill.

Kitty and Celia wore their very best dresses with wide sashes at their small waists and patent-leather shoes on their delicate feet. Their hair had been brushed so vigorously by their governesses that it shone like spun copper and gold. Bridie looked at them with a mixture of admiration and envy. She would have to return to the kitchen belowstairs to help her mother. It was all very well being persuaded to accompany Kitty and Celia upstairs, but her mother would be wondering where she was and, if anyone caught her there, in the private side of the castle, she'd be in grave trouble.

"Will you tell me all about it in the morning?" Bridie asked the cousins.

"We wish you could come and spy with us," said Kitty truthfully. "Don't we, Celia?"

"We do, Bridie. You're like Cinderella, having to work in the cellar while her sisters are allowed to go to the ball."

"If only I had a fairy godmother to wave a wand for me," Bridie replied with a sorry smile. She shrugged. "But I don't."

"You have a fine pair of dancing shoes," said Kitty. Bridie's cheeks flushed scarlet as she remembered with a stab of pain the moment two girls at school had mocked her: "Oh, here comes Lady Deverill," one had said, her voice full of scorn. To which the other had replied with equal derision, "Oh no, it's only Bridie wearing her charity shoes, just like a tinker!" Bridie hadn't worn them since but had put them back in their box for safekeeping, like a priceless treasure.

"I need more than fine shoes, Kitty," she said quietly.

Bridie hurried to the end of the corridor and slipped through the door to the basement. The kitchen was like an ants' nest with maids and footmen coming and going, and in the middle of the room was Mrs. Doyle, the ant queen, shouting orders as she made the final touches to her dishes. Bridie's brother Sean was back for the night, going through the castle rooms to check the fires were blazing, but Bridie was too young to help in the private side. She took her place by the kitchen sink and began to dry the dishes.

From the stairs Kitty and Celia watched the grown-ups coming into the hall. They awarded points for beautiful dresses and jewelery and minus points for the ladies who, in their opinion, had not made enough effort. In came the couples, one after the other, greeting Lord and Lady Deverill and moving on into the growing throng of guests. Lady Rowan-Hampton arrived on the arm of her portly husband Sir Ronald, in a dazzling silk dress of the palest blue. Kitty awarded her ten points for her dress and another ten for the diamonds and sapphires that glittered against her creamy décolletage. Grace raised her eyes, sensing that she was being watched, and smiled at the two little spies hiding behind the banisters on the landing halfway up the grand staircase. "We had better keep ourselves in check tonight," she said to her husband. "Look at those two monkeys."

Sir Ronald turned his rheumy eyes to the stairs and waved up at Kitty. "My dear, *I* always keep myself in check. *You're* the one who throws caution to the wind. Perhaps tonight you'll be more careful not to embarrass me."

"Look, there are Adeline's hilarious sisters, the Shrubs. Come, let's say hello."

"Two sillier women I have yet to meet," said Sir Ronald rudely. "They should be pulled out by the roots. You go and give them a good weed. I will find entertainment elsewhere." And the two parted, Lady Rowan-Hampton into the drawing room, Sir Ronald into the library where Bertie was holding court by the fireplace, smoking a cigar and drinking whiskey with Cousin Digby and his racing friends.

"Isn't this a lovely ball, Grace," said Laurel, as Lady Rowan-Hampton joined them.

"The castle looks beautiful with all the candles," said Grace.

"Beautiful, simply beautiful," echoed Hazel enthusiastically.

"Have you seen the ballroom? They've had a fire in there for the last three days to get rid of the damp," Laurel told her. "It took O'Flynn and an army of boys three weeks to take down the chandeliers and polish the pieces. Imagine all those candles, but the effect is quite magical."

"Then I shall dance until dawn," said Grace happily. "Ah, my dear Maud, you look lovely," she gushed as Maud glided through the crowd to join them. Grace kissed her cheek. "Goodness, you're cold. You should go and stand by the fire."

"Yes, you really should, Maud," Hazel agreed.

"Are you quite well?" asked Laurel, her round face shining with sweat. "It's almost too warm in here for me. It's enough to make me wilt."

"I'm perfectly fine," Maud replied.

"Where are the girls?" Hazel inquired. "We haven't seen Victoria since she went to London but we hear that she created quite a sensation. It won't be long before there's a wedding, no doubt."

"Ooh, I love weddings!" exclaimed Laurel gleefully. "I expect she'll win the heart of an English aristocrat."

Maud sighed melodramatically. "And leave Ireland, as they all do. I shall end up alone, see if I don't."

"She might marry an Irishman," said Grace optimistically. "You never know, there are some very handsome ones here tonight."

"But they're poor," said Maud, casting her eye about the room and catching sight of the DeCourcey brothers, both high-born and good-looking, but lacking in the one thing that would enable them to marry girls like Victoria and Elspeth: money.

"Tom and William DeCourcey," said Grace, following Maud's gaze. "There, two of the finest huntsmen in Ireland with a castle to boot."

"But precious little land," said Maud disparagingly. "And no money to last through to the next generation. Tom will inherit Dunashee Castle, William will flee to America or Australia, and Tom's children will be left with nothing but a shell to live in when Tom's inheritance runs out, which it surely will. No, I'd rather rich Englishmen for my daughters."

"But *you* married an Irishman," said Grace softly. "And you haven't done half badly."

"We are the last generation to enjoy *this*." Maud swept her long fingers through the air. "Harry will one day be Lord Deverill, but our lands are shrinking, the tenants we have left rarely pay the rent and Hubert is much too lenient—they take him for a fool. It is only a matter of time before they all rebel—"

Grace laughed. "Oh, they are much too lazy for that!"

"Bertie will be just as incompetent as his father. He's more interested in hunting and fishing than pawing over the accounts. He thinks there's a limitless pot of gold at the bottom of his rainbow and that the sun is always shining. He's considering buying a new hunter, for goodness' sake, but he already has a dozen. Harry will have nothing to live on and I will sit back in my threadbare sofa and say 'I told you so.' But by then it will be too late. Yes, I hope my daughters marry Englishmen because there will be nothing left for them here." Laurel and Hazel, usually so bright and jolly, looked at Maud in confusion. Neither knew what to say or what to make of her bitter outburst.

"Well, that's not very jolly," said Grace, trying to make light of Maud's grim soliloquy. "I hope my girls marry Irishmen, because Ireland is the most beautiful place on earth. I wouldn't leave it for all the money in the world."

The Shrubs smiled again. "Neither would we," they trilled in unison.

"Come, Maud, let's go and talk to Roddy Fitzgerald. I hear he's over for the summer, staying with the Claremonts, and he is such a charming fellow." Grace and Maud disappeared into the party.

"What was that all about?" Laurel asked.

"She's not very happy," said Hazel.

"She was born unhappy, that one," said Laurel. "I've always found her cold."

"Yes, indeed. *Very* cold." Hazel sighed. "Poor Bertie. I hope he finds comfort elsewhere."

"My dear, that's just the problem. If he found comfort at home his wife would have no reason to be bitter at all."

KITTY AND CELIA were having a delightful time wandering around the rooms. The grown-ups found them as charming as pretty dolls and made a fuss of them. Dinner was served in the long gallery upstairs, where a table for two hundred guests had been laid up among large gilt-framed paintings of ancestors going back to Barton Deverill, the first Lord Deverill of Balli-nakelly. The children were put together at the very end, because Adeline had never subscribed to the notion that children should be kept out of sight. Victoria was seated between two boys her own age whom she had known since childhood. But they strug-gled to make conversation with a girl who had lost interest in Ireland and set her sights on the stately homes and castles of England. Her cousins, Vivien and Leona, were only too happy to have the dashing DeCourcey brothers to entertain them with stories of hunting and had agreed by the main course to ride out with them the following morning. Elspeth had always found Peter MacCartain incredibly handsome. He was a stunning tennis player and masterful on a horse, but her mother had told her often enough that she would never consent to an Irishman unless he was the Marquess of Waterford. George and Harry found friends from school who had also returned to Ireland for the holidays and spent most of dinner discussing cricket.

Dinner was long and the children were restless by the end. The candles had burned down and the plates been taken away. O'Flynn had clearly been at the bottles of wine for he was weaving around the room as if it were a ship in a storm. At last the sound of music wafted up from the ballroom downstairs and one by one the adults were lured away from the table. The DeCourcey brothers disappeared with Vivien and Leona, and Elspeth agreed to dance with Peter MacCartain, but Victoria refused all offers with a graceless yawn. Kitty and Celia hurried downstairs to watch the dancing. The ballroom was magnifi-cent, lit up with hundreds of candles, flames reflected in the mirrored panels along the walls. The crystal chandeliers glittered. A small orchestra had been set up on a raised platform. Couples took to the dance floor and began to glide around the room in a glorious kaleidoscope of color. Kitty and Celia watched in wonder, longing to be old enough to be swung around the room. "Elspeth has flat feet," said Kitty with a laugh as her sister plodded a clumsy waltz.

"Vivien is no better," Celia added.

"But look at the Shrubs!" Kitty exclaimed, pointing at her two great-aunts who were dancing with Kitty's uncle Rupert and a reluctant Sir Ronald. "They dance better than everyone!"

The girls watched for a long while. Kitty noticed Peter Mac-Cartain's hand drop dangerously close to Elspeth's bottom. She also saw that the adults had grown unsteady on their feet. The women's faces flushed with the effects of champagne while the men had become ruddy and disheveled, puffing on their cigars, filling the air with the sweet scent of tobacco. No one noticed the children now; they might as well have been invisible as they wandered around listening to snippets of conversation, giggling when they heard something inappropriate.

It was well after midnight when Kitty and Celia, weary of spying on grown-ups, decided to wander the corridors upstairs. Candles in hand, they crept through the rooms like a pair of mice. Suddenly Kitty saw a shady figure at the end of the corridor. Curious, she strode on, her cousin following after. The music got fainter as they made their way further into the depths of the castle. Every time Kitty felt they were getting nearer the ghost, it disappeared again. "Come on, walk faster."

"Why the hurry?" Celia whined.

Just as Celia was about to lose courage, Kitty stopped walking. The ghost, whom she could now see clearly, was Egerton Deverill, Barton's son. Of all the Deverills stuck in Limbo, Egerton was her least favorite. He had a mean and menacing energy. He was staring at her with dark eyes and a scowling face, standing by a door beneath which there spread a shallow puddle of light.

Celia put a hand on Kitty's arm. "There's someone in there."

Kitty grinned at her. "Aren't you even a little curious?" she asked.

"I'm frightened!"

Just then Barton Deverill loomed out of the dark. Kitty caught her breath. Barton began to remonstrate with his son but Kitty couldn't hear; she could just feel the anger in the atmosphere and the chill that now enveloped them. She knew Barton didn't want her to go in.

Kitty was too courageous for her own good. While Celia backed away, Kitty, unable to surmount her curiosity, turned the knob and pushed open the door an inch. What she saw inside was so terrible it smothered her daring as surely as peat on fire. Her father was on the four-poster bed with his trousers pulled down, thrusting into Grace, whose legs were wrapped around his waist and hooked at the ankles. She hadn't even taken her shoes off. Kitty was disgusted. Barton slipped through the wall. In a moment he was by the mantelpiece. With one swipe of his hand he swept a decorative ceramic shepherdess onto the floor. It landed with a loud crash and shattered into many pieces.

Kitty didn't wait to see what happened next. She backed away and hurried down the corridor with her cousin following close behind. She didn't look back. She was sick to her stomach. She wanted to be as far away from there as possible.

BRIDIE SAT ON the edge of her bed and gazed out of the window at the moon. It was so round and fat it looked as if it were pregnant with lots of little moons. She watched it for a moment, hypnotized by its mystery. High in the sky it could surely see half the world below it. Countries that Bridie would never visit, people she would never meet, seas she would never sail. Was her life to be always here, in Ballinakelly, following her mother's path? Was there another future out there for her if only she could find the key to unlock the secret door? Was it simply a question of searching for it?

Was she to leave school and work for the Deverills as her mother did, until she was old and worn out just like her? Would she find a husband among her people, here in Ballinakelly, raise a family and watch her daughters live the same life of drudgery as she did? Was there nothing else? Bridie blinked and a tear trailed down her cheek. Kitty had given her a glimpse of a world to which she could never belong, and with that glimpse something of the attraction had been taken from *her* world, and a seed of discontent planted in its place. Kitty would leave, as Victoria had done. She claimed to love Ireland, but one day she would go to London with Celia and marry an Englishman. Little by little the gulf between them would grow bigger until Kitty would become out of reach altogether. She, Bridie and Celia were all born in the year 1900 but no amount of nines could change *her* destiny.

Bridie opened the shoebox and took out the black patent-leather dancing shoes with their large silver buckles that Lady

Deverill had given her. Holding them to her chest she made a vow. *One day when I am grown, I will leave Ballinakelly and make something of my life. I will find the key and I will go. And when I return I will put on my dancing shoes and no one will call me a tinker. As God is my witness, no one will look down on me, for I will be a lady.*

PART TWO

PART TWO

Chapter Nine

Co. Cork, Ireland, November 1914

At the outbreak of the war Maud had taken to her bed, complaining of a mysterious malaise, from which she did not emerge for weeks. Bereft of her husband and precious son, who were fighting the Germans in France, she found herself alone in the Hunting Lodge with only Elspeth, now twenty-one and still unmarried in spite of a marginally successful London Season, and Kitty, fourteen years old and almost entirely unbiddable. Victoria was now Countess of Elmrod, married to Eric, a dull and chinless aristocrat eighteen years her senior with a minor stately home in Kent and a white stucco town house in Belgravia, living the life Maud had once envisaged for herself. She could not deny that she envied her daughter, even though Victoria, too, was bereft of her husband and fearful of losing him and all the material comforts that went with him. As yet, she remained childless, which, for the wife of an earl, was a very great worry indeed.

On top of her anxiety about war with Germany, Maud felt insecure in a country whose people were waging their own war against their English oppressors. Small attacks here and there by radical Irish nationalists in defiance of the British state gave the country an air of unrest and instability, which made her want to dive deeper beneath her quilt and recall the good old days when the great British Empire had ruled supreme. She hoped this mad fever for Home Rule would peter out; after all, the Irish were an uncivilized lot in dire need of a firm hand. Didn't they know what was good for them? How she wished Bertie were home to reassure her. Her father-in-law was no use at all with his irrational rants about the "bloody papists" and his growing paranoia that they were lurking in the woods, awaiting their moment to scale the castle walls and do away with the lot of them. The sound of his gunshots echoing through the estate did not make Maud feel any safer. If anything, it made her feel even more desperate.

Then there was Kitty. For all Miss Grieve's efforts Kitty had not been broken into submission. Try as she might, Maud had not managed to overcome the fear that gripped her whenever Kitty stared at her with those large and eerie eyes—the eyes of a stranger—and the guilt that came with knowing that her lack of affection for her child was unnatural. The fact that Kitty had long been aware of her mother's feelings, albeit not the reason why, had only compounded her shame. As she lay in bed, tossing and turning in misery, Maud began to grow feverish and delusional. She cried out for "Eddie." This bewildered the servants who didn't know who Eddie was. "I don't want the baby!" she cried, which only fueled the gossip downstairs. She told herself that if she hadn't experienced the pain and discomfort of the child leaving her body she would have sworn Kitty did not belong to her. Kitty was Adeline's, to be sure, she reasoned, and in her confused state of mind it seemed perfectly logical: one way or another, her mother-in-law had surely used sorcery to replicate herself.

When she recovered sufficiently to travel Maud took Elspeth to England to stay with Victoria, leaving Kitty to live with her grandparents in the castle she loved and with the dreaded Miss Grieve. Kitty was delighted. With her mother out of the way life could continue without restraint. There would be no tiptoeing around the house for fear of disturbing her, no talking in hushed voices, no tension in the air as the servants hurried up and down the stairs with boiling tea, hot water, compresses, extra blankets, night-burning oil, smelling salts and always the anxiety that their efforts would somehow fall short and merit a sharp lashing from her tongue, which, in her frayed condition, was more poisonous than usual.

The castle was run at a slow and stately pace. The servants were ancient and doddery. Kitty's grandparents had grown thick and inflexible over the years. The regular ticking of the grandfather clock in the hall was a soothing beat. The invisible presence of ghosts gave the castle an air of timelessness, somehow set apart from the rest of the world, and Kitty settled into it with pleasure.

She missed her father, but her grandfather was a reassuring male presence around the castle and his obvious affection for her, and indulgence of her, made Bertie's absence easier to bear. Hubert and Adeline were very sociable and the house was filled most evenings with the Shrubs, who came to sit around the green baize table to drink sherry and play whist, and neighbors whose husbands were old enough to have fought in the Boer War. The men discussed the fighting, puffing on their cigars and sipping whiskey, and all agreed that the war would be over by Christmas, if not then certainly by spring. As for Home Rule, the House of Lords would never let the bill through, they concurred; therefore if the war didn't bury it, the Lords would and hopefully forever. Two hundred Irishmen had joined up in Irish regiments to serve Great Britain. Most Irish people supported the war in the same way the English did, and the Shrubs had been convinced by Reverend Daunt's opinion that, as dreadful as war was, the silver lining would be the unification of Ireland and England and the melting away of the dream of Home Rule, which, in his opinion, had always been an impossible dream to begin with.

Kitty enjoyed playing whist. She was formidable at the bridge table and was close to beating her grandfather at chess. She painted with her grandmother, who with patience and humor taught her to play the piano, pottered about in the greenhouses and joined the Ballinakelly hunt, riding out as often as twice a week with as courageous a heart and the same disregard for inclement weather as any young man. Miss Grieve continued to tutor her, but had relinquished control long ago on account of Kitty's willful character. The child had grown into a fearless young woman and Miss Grieve could no more wield her riding crop than persuade her that she was English.

Kitty was defiantly Irish. As much as she loved her grandfather, his loathing for Catholics was something she could neither understand nor condone. She had spent too much time with Bridie and Jack to be ignorant of the true state of Ireland's poor and the perfectly understandable reasons the nationalists had for wanting to govern themselves.

Kitty was not alone in her defense of the Irish. The trouble was her ally was now a woman she despised, having found her in flagrante with her father the night of the Summer Ball. Grace Rowan-Hampton had once been the woman Kitty admired above all others, after her grandmother Adeline. She had marveled at her beauty, been dazzled by her charm and flattered by her attention. When she had peered through the bedroom door and seen her in such an uncompromising, not to mention undignified, position, she had been irrevocably wounded. The disappointment had been tremendous. Even though she knew nothing of sexual relations between a man and a woman she had witnessed the mating of animals often enough to know what they were doing, and it had repelled and frightened her. Not once did she blame her father, however; the fault lay in its entirety with Grace. She had seduced him, lured him into the shady recesses of the castle and had her wicked way.

Not only had Grace seduced her father but she had betrayed her mother, who was meant to be her friend—and Kitty knew all about friendship. Even though Kitty felt little affection for Maud, she was conditioned to be loyal; after all, like it or not, she belonged to her. Too young to understand the complicated tangle of her mother's bitterness, she did understand betrayal. It had a strong scent like onions and she had smelled it whenever Lady Rowan-Hampton had come to visit, which, before her mother had sunk into depression and taken to her bed, had been as much as three times a week. Now that Bertie was in Flanders and Maud recuperating in England, Grace didn't come so often but Kitty saw her out hunting and somehow managed to slip away whenever she came close. Sir Ronald had also gone off to war along with their sons and Grace wore her unhappiness well. Her black riding habit set off her pale skin and pink cheeks to her advantage and the black veil reached just below her nose, where her wide and sensual mouth smiled valiantly in the face of despair.

Kitty was now used to swallowing the tender memories of Grace like regurgitated food drenched in bile. She questioned whether her kindness had simply been part of her ploy to win the affections of her father. Had she felt any real warmth for Kitty at all? Since the Summer Ball four years before Kitty had given her a wide berth, which wasn't difficult considering her mother's desire to keep her out of sight. When they *had* met, at family dinners, hunt meets and the various tennis and croquet parties, Kitty had greeted her politely and extricated herself as quickly as possible. Whether Grace had sensed her remoteness she couldn't tell. But on this frosty, late-November morning as the Ballinakelly Foxhounds met outside the castle for a glass of sloe gin or port, she found herself positioned next to Grace before she had time to kick her horse into motion.

"My dear, how you are growing," Grace exclaimed, her soft brown eyes searching Kitty's face with a fondness Kitty dismissed as disingenuous. "Tell me, have you news of Harry?"

Kitty lifted her chin. "Harry doesn't write, which infuriates Mama, but Papa writes warmly of home. He misses Mama," she lied, hoping to torment Grace, but the older woman's features betrayed nothing.

"I miss Ronald and my boys dreadfully. They say that it will be over by Christmas but I'm not so sure. I sense it will go on for a lot longer than we think. I pray for them and try to live as normally as possible. The trick is to keep busy." Kitty noticed how thin she was looking behind the veil. Her cheekbones were more prominent, the flesh thinner: she had lost some of her gloss. "Tell me, how is your dear mama?"

"She is better, thank you," Kitty replied tightly.

"That's good. I miss her too." She smiled. "Do you remember that day in church when you said she looked like a weasel?"

Kitty stiffened at her attempt to break through her frostiness. "Well, I suppose I've grown up since then," she retorted bluntly. She hated herself for her rudeness. There was a part of her, deep down, that still craved Grace's affection.

The older woman frowned. "This beastly war!" she exclaimed suddenly, turning her face away. "It's taking its toll on all of us. What is more important than the people we love?" She sighed and when she looked back her brown eyes blazed with an intensity that took Kitty by surprise. "Love for our country, that's what! Yes, Ireland. We come and go and leave nothing but memories in the minds of our children, but they fade too and eventually we're gone, as if we never lived. But Ireland remains with all its beauty and all its tragedy. I hope we win the war, but let's not forget we have an enduring war on our own soil that must not be cast aside. I know you agree, Kitty. In that we are sisters, are we not?"

Kitty was so taken aback by Grace's sudden outburst that she didn't know what to say. Usually so quick-witted, she was lost for words. "You are cold toward me, my dear, and I don't know what I have done to offend you."

Now Kitty looked at her steadily, her wit returning like the crack of a whip. "And how might you know that I agree with your politics, Lady Rowan-Hampton?"

"Your dear father has told me of them, in despair of course, for he is loyal to king and country." She laughed indulgently, giving away her clear and enduring fondness for Bertie.

"In which case you should know exactly how you have offended me." Kitty gave a little sniff. "I hope you enjoy the hunt, Lady Rowan-Hampton. The weather is cold enough for the hounds to find a line but the ground is hard so we must take care not to fall off."

"Please, Kitty, call me Grace—" But Kitty had given her horse a gentle kick and moved away.

Later she sat in her father's library in the Hunting Lodge, which had been locked up and covered in dust sheets since her mother's departure a couple of months before. It still smelled of cigar smoke and damp. She had lit the fire, which crackled weakly against the cold, and wrapped a blanket around her shoulders while she waited for Bridie and Jack to come and meet her, as they promised they would, after tea. No one would find them there.

She felt despondent. Her confrontation with Grace Rowan-Hampton had pained her and she had to keep reminding herself of the scene in the bedroom at the Summer Ball to keep her heart from softening. She wasn't lonely; she had Bridie and Jack and letters from Celia were frequent enough to keep their friendship alive and strong. She wasn't bored, either. But something was missing. Her days were full but at night, especially when the stars were bright, she craved something that she couldn't identify. This curious longing made her morose and restless.

The door opened and Jack and Bridie entered, bringing in a draft of icy air. They took their usual places, Jack in Bertie's leather armchair, Bridie on the sofa beside Kitty, neatly clad in a black dress and white apron, her hair combed and pinned onto the top of her head now that she worked up at the castle as scullery maid. Jack smoked languidly from the fireside. He was sixteen now, tall and handsome with a feisty, rebellious energy, inflamed by patriotic talk he heard from the older boys in O'Donovan's. Even though he was too young to fight in the war, he would have resisted enlisting and resented his father for joining the Royal Irish Fusiliers.

"Fancy a swig of sloe gin?" Kitty asked, handing Jack the hip flask her father took out hunting.

"Don't mind if I do," said Jack with a smile. He looked at the silver flask and admired the Deverill crest engraved on the front with Bertie Deverill's initials. "Nice," he said with an appreciative nod.

"It's even nicer inside," Kitty joked, watching Jack take a swig.

He then held it out for Bridie, who vigorously shook her head. "Go on! Just a little. It's very sweet," he cajoled.

Bridie was unable to refuse Jack, who she admired above all others. She took the flask and put it to her lips, where only a moment ago Jack's lips had been. She swallowed the gin and gave a cough. "That really burns!" she said, turning red. Kitty and Jack laughed.

"You'll get used to it," said Jack, taking it back and having another swig. "So, tell me, how's the charming Miss Grieve?" he asked Kitty.

"As charming as ever, thank you, Jack!"

"Why don't you get rid of her? How long do you have to have a governess anyway?"

"Until I come of age."

"That's a long way away."

"It is, but I can manage her. I think she's a little afraid of me."

"Well, you're a bold girl now," said Jack, his light eyes twinkling at her.

"If the castle is haunted, as they say it is," said Bridie, proud to be party to Kitty's secret, "why hasn't she been scared away? I know *I* would be if I saw a ghost."

Kitty frowned at her friend, remembering how it had been Barton's son, Egerton, who had led her to that bedroom the night of the Summer Ball. She hadn't told Bridie, she hadn't even told Celia, what she had seen in there. Since then she hadn't been very keen to mingle with spirits. But Bridie had a point. It was the least Barton could do to make up for his son's cruel joke. "Because she sleeps like an old sow," said Kitty meanly. "Nothing would wake her, not even a noisy ghost."

"I'll climb the wall and scare her if you like," said Jack, blowing a stream of smoke out of the corner of his mouth. "Just tell me which is her bedroom window and I'll do the rest."

Kitty narrowed her eyes. Jack's idea was inspired. "All right," she said with a smile. "So long as you don't do something silly." She described the window overlooking the box garden. "If Grandpa sees you he'll shoot you and I'm not joking."

Bridie blanched. "I'm sure it's not a good idea, Jack."

"It's good training," he replied.

"For what?" Kitty asked.

"I'm going to join the Volunteers and fight for our liberty."

Kitty's eyes widened.

Bridie looked startled. "You've been listening to Michael, haven't you?" she said. "I imagine that's what they all talk about in O'Donovan's every night. Freedom from British rule. I hear nothing else when I'm at home."

"You're too young to join the Volunteers, surely," said Kitty.

"I can help."

"What'll your father say?" asked Bridie.

"He won't know. Right now he's on the Western Front fighting for England." Jack shook his head disdainfully. "He shouldn't be cannon fodder for the British. He should be fighting for Ireland."

"He *is* fighting for Ireland, Jack," Kitty interrupted. "England's war against the Germans is Ireland's war too. They're our common enemy. That's what Grandpa says."

"Your grandpa would say that, wouldn't he! Well, I'm not going to sit back and let the English stamp away our identity." He had clearly heard that from someone else, Kitty thought. "I'm going to stand with my brothers and fight for our freedom. For Home Rule."

"Grandpa says the bill will never make its way past the House of Lords."

"Then we'll have to force them to pass it, won't we!" Jack leaned forward, elbows on his knees, eyes blazing in the candlelight. "We have to make them listen."

"With violence," said Kitty.

"If that's the only way to make them listen."

"We have to get through this war first," said Bridie.

"You're missing the point, Bridie. While the English are distracted fighting the Germans we can seize the opportunity over here."

"What'll happen to Kitty?" Bridie asked anxiously, thinking also of herself and her mother who worked for the Deverills.

"We'll look out for her. After all, she's one of us, aren't you, Kitty?" He grinned at her and Kitty grinned back and the two of them radiated a confidence that only made Bridie feel more uneasy.

"Ballinakelly has a high regard for Lord Deverill," said Bridie hopefully. "He's always been good to the people here. There's no reason for anyone to harm him, is there, Jack?"

Jack nodded, wanting the girls to think him important. "No reason," he agreed, but the truth was he wasn't sure. As far as the nationalists were concerned Lord Deverill was an English usurper, loyal to the wrong side. If Michael had his way the whole family would be deported to England where they belonged and the castle razed to the ground.

THAT EVENING KITTY climbed the wooden staircase to the western tower of the castle. She found Barton in his usual chair, feet up on the stool, staring ponderously into the half distance as if dreaming of his life long gone. When she entered he looked up, surprise. "I know, it's been a while," Kitty said, wrapping her shawl around her shoulders. She hadn't spoken to him in four years but for Barton time meant nothing.

"I tried to stop you," he said grudgingly. "But you wouldn't listen."

"I was curious and I have paid the price for my curiosity," she replied solemnly. "I need your help."

"Again?"

"I'll take it this time."

"I'm not in a position to help anyone, least of all myself."

"Oh, but you are. I saw you sweep an ornament off a mantelpiece. If you put your mind to it, I'm sure you can terrify my governess out of the castle."

Barton grinned. The idea pleased him. "If that is what you want."

"I'm surprised Egerton hasn't scared her away already."

"Egerton is a lazy man, Kitty. He was useless in life and he's even more useless in death. It takes effort to be evil."

"Then I thank you in advance for your effort."

All Barton's meanness and frustration went into his grin. "Consider it done, my little friend."

Chapter 10

Kitty watched Miss Grieve like a leopard stalking its prey. The woman looked old now. Her pale lips had thinned to almost nothing, her cheekbones protruded, her complexion had become sallow. Gone forever was the young woman Kitty had spied through the crack in the door crying over a letter. She wondered why women like her mother and Lady Rowan-Hampton seemed to benefit from the soft Irish rain while it coarsened Miss Grieve's skin until it resembled old leather. At one point she had thought her the same age as her mother; now she looked even older than Kitty's grandmother, whose lively face was still fine and youthful.

Miss Grieve looked up from her book to find Kitty staring at her. "Kitty, you're not going to find the answers in my face."

"How old are you, Miss Grieve?" Kitty asked boldly.

Miss Grieve stiffened. "That's very rude."

"Come now, Miss Grieve, we've known each other for many years and I'm not a child anymore. Can't we be friends?"

"I don't know why you think the status of friend would warrant knowledge of my years," she replied, her tight Scottish accent squeezing the life out of the vowels.

Kitty grinned. Age had made Miss Grieve smaller too and somehow vulnerable and Kitty found herself feeling sorry for the woman who had once made her life so miserable. She narrowed her eyes. "I think you're fifty," she said, believing she had given Miss Grieve a great compliment.

Two red spots spread on Miss Grieve's cheeks like ink on a blotter. "You think I'm fifty?" She blinked at Kitty incredulously. "I'm thirty-eight," she stated in a strangled voice. Kitty didn't know what to say. She watched, horrified, as Miss Grieve pushed her chair out and stood up. The governess turned her back on Kitty but the shudder that seized her shoulders left Kitty in no doubt that she had deeply offended her. "Finish the comprehension. I will be in my room where I do not wish to be disturbed."

Kitty finished the comprehension, which had hardly posed a challenge, and wandered downstairs to find her grandmother. The sound of piano playing came from the drawing room. When Kitty entered, her grandmother stopped playing. "Kitty, my dear, has Miss Grieve finished with you already?"

"I'm afraid I offended her," said Kitty with a sigh, running her fingers over the shiny surface of the piano. "I told her I thought she was fifty, but she's thirty-eight. She doesn't look thirty-eight, does she?"

"An easy mistake," her grandmother replied. "Though I

wouldn't think it prudent to discuss a woman's age in any circumstance."

"We've never liked one another," Kitty said. "She's the most humorless person I've ever met."

"I don't recall liking my governess much. They're an odd breed."

"Why are they so odd?"

"Because they're well-educated women who for some reason or other never married. The only option open to them is earning a living as a governess or companion. I feel sorry for them. It must be very unsatisfactory never to be mistress of one's own home."

"Miss Grieve is the meanest woman I've ever met," Kitty grumbled.

Adeline looked at her granddaughter wisely. "My dear, you must have compassion for her. Unkind people are unhappy people and I believe Miss Grieve is deeply unhappy."

"I don't think unhappiness justifies cruelty, Grandma."

"It doesn't, but it certainly explains it. Miss Grieve must have suffered terrible disappointments in her life. I imagine your happiness, Kitty, served only to remind her of her own unhappiness. As hard as it is to find it in one's heart to understand and forgive, I believe one must try."

At that moment O'Flynn shuffled in bearing a letter on a silver tray. "Your ladyship," he said.

Adeline took the letter and looked at the handwriting. "It's from Rupert. How lovely!" She opened it with the silver knife placed beside the letter. She read a moment in silence, then smiled wistfully, holding it against her chest. "Darling Rupert, he's not cut out for war. Hubert thinks he's not cut out for any-thing, but I think it'll be the making of him."

"Does he have any news of Papa?" Kitty asked eagerly.

"Yes, he says he's peeved your father wears his uniform better than he does." She laughed. "Really, that's so typical of Rupert, always seeing the funny side of everything." She sighed. "Oh, I do hope we'll have them home for Christmas."

WHEN KITTY RETIRED to bed that night she had forgotten all about asking Barton to scare Miss Grieve away. She had dined with her grandparents and the Shrubs, who seemed to be a permanent fixture at the dining table ever since Rupert and Bertie had gone to fight. They twittered like sparrows and talked of every sort of nonsense in the hope of distracting their sister, as well as themselves, from the telegrams now trickling into Ireland with news of the missing, the wounded and the dead. The reality of war was beginning to bleed through the veneer of bravado.

On her way to her bedroom Kitty passed Miss Grieve's door. She noticed that it was closed and that there was no light seep-ing out from beneath. Kitty hadn't seen her since she had left the room in tears. She paused a moment outside, suddenly feel-ing a wave of regret. The corridor was quiet and still; only the sound of the gale, blowing in off the sea, could be heard whip-ping around the chimney stacks. Kitty crept into her room, which was next to her governess's, and opened the curtains a little to gaze out onto the crisp winter night. Clouds as thick as porridge scudded across the sky, parting every now and then to give a tantalizing glimpse of the moon. It cast a maze of box hedges below in an eerie silver light. She thought of Miss Grieve and her heart flooded with compassion. She was a woman old before her time with no prospects besides tutoring girls like Kitty. She wondered whether her unhappiness really had made her cruel. If Miss Grieve had married a man who made her happy would she have been kind?

Kitty stood for a long time staring out of the window until her head began to feel heavy with sleep. At last she closed the curtains and undressed, laying her frock across the chair. She liked her bedroom in the castle. The four-poster bed was large and she could draw the curtains around it to keep out the cold. The remains of the fire smoldered in the grate and the rattling of the wind against the glass was a soothing lullaby that sent her off to sleep.

She was awoken abruptly by a loud scream. It took her a moment to realize that she wasn't dreaming and that the scream had come from Miss Grieve's bedroom next door. She climbed out of bed and fumbled for the matches to light her bedside lamp. Blinking in the glow, she threw on her woolen robe and slid her feet into her slippers. The corridor was dark and silent but Miss Grieve's bedroom door was open. Kitty hurried inside. She expected to find her governess sitting up in bed, but the quilt was pulled back and Miss Grieve was nowhere to be seen. Then something caught her eye and she turned to see a ghostly figure at the window, but she blinked and he was gone. Kitty's heart went cold. She walked across the floor as if wading through water. She held her breath, fearing the worst, and looked down onto the garden below. The wind tore a hole in the clouds and the moon shone a spotlight onto the writhing figure of her friend Jack, stuck in the box hedge beneath the ladder customarily used for cutting back the roses. "Jesus!" she hissed, relieved that it was Jack and not Miss Grieve who had fallen from the window. "What's he gone and done?"

Kitty ran down the stairs and hurried out through the kitchen door. She plunged into the darkness, pulling her robe around her as the wind tried to whip it away. It took her hair instead, releasing it from the ribbons and tossing it about gruffly, but she strode on around the corner of the castle toward the box garden, head down, bracing herself against the cold. Frost was already crystallizing the grass beneath her slippers and she shivered as the wet seeped through. When she reached the hedge, Jack had managed to disentangle himself. He saw her and his features flooded with relief. "Sacred heart of Jaysus, Kitty, I saw a ghost at the window, I swear to ya!" He stumbled on his words, his face as white as ash, his pale eyes wide with fright. "God save us all . . ."

"It's OK, Jack. It's only a ghost," Kitty said, placing her hands on his trembling shoulders. She noticed him lift a foot off the ground, leaning heavily on the other one. "Are you hurt?"

"All I wanted to do was to frighten her but 'twas myself was nearly frightened to death instead."

Suddenly a screech sliced through the wind with a sharp and ragged edge. They both turned toward the woods. "The Banshee!" Jack whispered darkly.

Kitty heard a thud, like a sack of potatoes fallen from a great height. "That wasn't the Banshee, Jack." Now it was her turn to blanch. "Oh God!" She reeled slightly and Jack put out a hand to steady her.

"What is it?"

"You must go, Jack. Now!" She pushed him urgently. "Please."

"But . . ."

She stared at him with terrified eyes. "Just go, Jack. Before anyone knows you were here. Go!"

Jack limped into the darkness and disappeared. Kitty slowly walked around to the back of the castle, the sense of foreboding growing inside her. Her heart pounded against her ribs and her throat constricted because she already knew what she was going to find. She sensed it in the pit of her belly, in the bile that had begun to rise. And she wasn't wrong. There, lying in a heap on the frosty ground, was Miss Grieve.

Kitty fell to her knees beside the body. With a shaking hand she pressed the woman's wrist to feel for a pulse. There was nothing. She was like a doll, broken and discarded on the nursery floor. Tears burned Kitty's cheeks. She wanted to throw her arms around her, but she couldn't because they had never been friends, so she threw her arms around herself instead and sobbed. In that brief time, before she cried for help, she remembered nothing of Miss Grieve's cruelty, only her youthful face and gentle tears as she had poured out her sorrow over the letter lying open on her knee.

The following morning the Royal Irish Constabulary arrived at the castle and Miss Grieve was taken away in an ambulance. Kitty was comforted by her grandmother in the library. The ladder was found lying against the box hedge and the hole Jack had made was scrutinized intensely and cordoned off as a crime scene. Kitty explained to Constable O'Duggan that she had heard a scream but, when she reached Miss Grieve's bedroom, her governess wasn't there. She went to the window and saw a man's face. She must have terrified him because the ladder wobbled and fell backward, sending the man flying into the hedge. She ran into the garden but when she got there he had gone. That was when she heard the cry and thud of Miss Grieve.

"Did you get a good look at the face, Miss Deverill?" the constable asked.

"I did not," replied Kitty. "I was so shocked to see someone there. Before I had time to look at him, he was gone. All I can tell you is that he was a man. Otherwise it was too dark for details."

"I'm afraid it appears that Miss Grieve threw herself from the roof."

"How on earth did she get out there?" Adeline asked.

"She found her way into the attic, Lady Deverill, and through a small window."

"Goodness, she must have wanted to kill herself very badly to go to all that trouble."

"Why didn't she just holler for help, I ask you?" said Hubert, hands on hips. "I always have my shotgun at the ready. Would have given me a lot of pleasure to have had a go at him. Goddamn shame he didn't choose *my* bedroom window instead!"

"Will you find him?" Kitty asked anxiously.

Constable O'Duggan shook his head. "Unlikely, I'm afraid. There's no evidence and no one's going to talk in Ballinakelly. But we'll do our best."

"Thank you, Constable," said Adeline.

The constable scratched his whiskers and looked perplexed.

"The thing is, Lord Deverill, I'm not sure what the motive was. You see, if he was intending to rob you, why would he enter through a bedroom window on the first floor, requiring the use of a ladder? If he wanted to do harm, why *that* particular window? It wasn't left open or ajar. And why did Miss Grieve run all the way up to the attic to throw herself off the roof? Did she have a suitor perhaps? Was she being harassed by anyone?"

Adeline looked surprised. "I hadn't thought of that," she said, turning to her granddaughter. "Kitty would know."

"Miss Grieve had no one in the world but her mother," Kitty replied, making the decision in that moment not to speak of the letter she had managed to steal from Miss Grieve's bedroom before the police arrived to go through it with a fine-tooth comb. "She never talked to anyone in Ballinakelly and no one talked to her. She was very private and very solemn."

Constable O'Duggan nodded gravely. "Well, thank you for your time. One other thing, Miss Deverill . . ."

"Yes?" Kitty felt a nervous heat crawl over her skin.

"Don't go after chasing these people. They're armed and dangerous. It's not safe."

"I won't do it again, Constable. I wasn't thinking." She lowered her eyes and sighed heavily. "I won't be so impulsive in future."

WHEN KITTY WAS at last alone she closed her bedroom door and took out the letter from where she had hidden it beneath her pillow. Then she sat on the bed to read it.

18th January 1910

Dearest Lottie

I know you told me not to write until I was in a position to make good my promise, and I fully intended to do just that. Honest to God, that's the truth. I can't stop thinking about you, my dear Lottie. Your face is engraved on my heart and your voice, your beautiful singing voice, is forever ringing in my ears and I hear it on waking in the morning and drifting off to sleep at night and my dreams are tormented because I hold you then, only to lose you at dawn. Every time I play the piano I think of you and I feel such a great sorrow I can barely go on.

Why fate had such cruel designs I cannot fathom.

Why we couldn't have met a few years before, when I was unattached, is a question that runs around my head in a never-ending circle.

"If only" the saddest words ever written.

But I'm writing with my heart full of sorrow. I am an honorable man, but I fear I cannot honor my promise, even though you have waited so many years for me. I know why you ran to Ireland, because you were exasperated by my endless promises and believed them false. But I swear, my love, they were not false, the time was never right. You know I would have left Edwina if I had been able to. I truly believed the time would come. But now it never will. I can only assume that God does not have plans for us.

My joy at becoming a father is only marred by the knowledge that you are not the mother.

My darling Lottie. My heart bleeds for you but you must let me go now as I have to let you go.

I have failed you and I have failed myself. I will forever live with my regret.

Your loving friend,
Jonnie

Kitty folded the letter and put it back in the envelope. Then she wiped her eyes and took it to the fire. She watched it burn in the flames until it was finally reduced to ash and was gone.

She gazed into the blaze until her eyes watered. Did Miss Grieve kill herself because she faced a life without love? It didn't seem probable considering she had received the letter four years before. Did she do it because Kitty had told her she looked fifty and she suddenly realized she had turned into an old woman before her time? Was it her fault? She sat trembling even though it was warm in front of the fire.

THE POLICE SEARCHED Miss Grieve's bedroom and the ground directly beneath her window, but concluded that it was a simple case of suicide as the result of an attempted robbery. No one had any faith in them finding the culprit. If anyone had the slightest knowledge Constable O'Duggan knew he'd be the last to hear of it.

Kitty rode into Ballinakelly that afternoon to find Jack. He lived in a small but tidy white house with a view of the harbor. With his father away at the front it had fallen on Jack's shoulders to take over his duties as vet. She hoped he'd be home. She dismounted and knocked on his door. A moment later Jack's mother opened it. When she saw Kitty she looked none too delighted. "Miss Deverill, to what do I owe the pleasure?"

"I'm after Jack," Kitty replied smoothly. "I have a problem with my horse."

Mrs. O'Leary called for her son. Then she looked past Kitty at the gray mare that was tied to a post. "Is she all right?" she asked.

"Yes, she is. It's just a small matter. Nothing serious." Kitty felt foolish: she didn't imagine there was a fitter horse in the whole of Ballinakelly.

"Jack!" his mother called again. A minute later Jack appeared.

"Miss Deverill," he said, as surprised as his mother to see her.

"I hope I haven't disturbed your dinner."

"No, you haven't. I twisted my ankle on the stair last night and have been laid up all day." He shook his head and pulled a sorry face. "'Tis a right pity." Jack's mother withdrew back inside the house and Jack stepped outside, closing the door behind him.

"I had to see you," she said quietly.

Jack limped to Kitty's mare and pretended to look it over. "I heard what happened."

"It's dreadful, Jack. She's dead because of me," she hissed, eyes filling with tears again.

"Because of *us*," he emphasized.

"They think it's an attempted robbery."

"So much the better."

"But I know and I'll never forgive myself."

"We're in it together," Jack said solemnly. "I'll take it to the grave, Kitty. Don't fret about that."

"I never thought you'd do it."

Jack looked up and down the street furtively, patting the horse's flank. "I wanted to impress you," he replied dolefully. "I didn't expect to see a face staring at me in the window." He straightened and looked at her steadily. "What's this about ghosts then?"

"I can see them," she whispered. "I've always seen them. It's a gift."

He stared down at her a moment. "Well, I can't say I don't believe you, can I?"

"Not now."

"Scared me half to death."

"You were lucky. If you hadn't had that hedge beneath you there might have been two bodies to grieve over."

Jack lifted the horse's hooves, one by one, as Kitty followed him. "Why didn't you tell me?"

"Grandma told me never to tell a soul. But I told Bridie. She said people are locked away for less."

"So, Lady Deverill sees them too, does she?"

"Yes."

"And they don't scare you?"

"No."

He grinned up at her and Kitty was grateful for his humor. "You're a quare one, Kitty Deverill."

She smiled back. "I know. But you'll still be my friend, won't you?"

"I'll always be your friend," he said, dropping a hoof and

standing up. "We're bound by our secret now, forever. Indeed and we'll take it to the grave."

"To the grave."

"There's nothing wrong with your mare." Jack gave it a hard pat on the neck. "She's a fine horse altogether."

"I'd better go." She mounted with ease. "Is your ankle going to mend?"

"It'll mend. Will you get a new governess?"

"Not if I have anything to do with it," said Kitty, riding off.

THAT NIGHT KITTY found Barton in his usual place, in the silk chair with his feet up on the footstool. "Well, hello, little Kitty," he said. She was surprised to see him in good humor, but perhaps other people's misery appealed to his dark character.

"I came to talk about Miss Grieve," said Kitty. "I'm sorry I asked you. I never will again as long as I live. It was a terrible mistake and one I regret bitterly."

Barton frowned. "You think *I* had something to do with that?" he asked.

Kitty was confused. "Well, didn't you?"

"I did not," he said. "But you got what you wanted all the same."

"I did not want Miss Grieve to die!" She rounded on him furiously. She bit her lip and lowered her voice. "I did not want her scared to death."

"Oh, she wasn't scared to death. Quite the opposite."

"What are you talking about?"

"The man who appeared in her bedroom, nice fellow though a little too sentimental for my taste . . ."

"Who was he?"

"A soldier, killed in the war, poor sod." Kitty felt cold tentacles creeping across her skin. "He'd been trying to get her attention for some time. Can be very frustrating for us dead people."

"What was his name, Barton?"

He scratched his beard. "Let me see if I recall."

"Try," said Kitty.

"Jonnie Wilson. That was it. Jonnie Wilson."

Chapter 11

After the tragic death of Miss Grieve, Lady Deverill received word from Maud that Kitty's governess should be replaced at once. She did not want her daughter spending her days in idleness and mischief. Maud turned to Cousin Beatrice for advice. Celia no longer had a governess, it transpired, but a tutor, which seemed more fitting for a young lady of fourteen. So Cousin Beatrice came back swiftly, recommending a twenty-four-year-old Cambridge scholar called Robert Trench, who was the middle son of great friends of theirs in London. He was an intelligent, sensible man who would certainly give Kitty a fine education as well as imposing important boundaries. He was exempt from fighting in the war because of an infection suffered in childhood that had resulted in the stiffening of his leg, so the post at Castle Deverill would be a most welcome one indeed. Maud agreed without further ado—she didn't really care what he was like, only that he was suitable—and sent word to her mother-in-law that he would arrive after Christmas.

Another change in Kitty's life was the surprise promotion of her friend Bridie, who exchanged her job at the kitchen sink for one in the private side of the castle, as Kitty's lady's maid. This, of course, had nothing to do with Kitty's mother and everything to do with her grandmother, who felt sorry for Kitty after the loss of Miss Grieve. With Bridie as her personal maid at least she'd have a girl her own age to talk to—and she wouldn't have to skulk about the castle corridors concealing their friendship.

The new position meant that Bridie shared a small bedroom at the top of the castle in the servants' quarters with a young maid from Bandon, called Molly Seymour. Bridie was relieved she wasn't on her own. The wind moaned around the turrets at night and the ancient floorboards creaked as if Kitty's ghosts were restlessly walking up and down. At first Bridie missed her bed in the farmhouse. She missed the familiar smells of cooking, her brothers' tobacco, the scent of turf fire and cows. She missed the sound of Michael and Sean playing cards at the table with friends: the castle was so quiet and eerie. Then she worried her mother wouldn't be able to do without her. But Michael was head of the family now and he had told her she couldn't refuse a job that paid her thirty pounds a year. It didn't take her long to adapt to her new surroundings; it was adapting to the rules of the upper household that she found confusing, having been friends with Kitty for so long and previously confined to the kitchen.

Servants were never to let their voices be heard by the ladies and gentlemen of the castle. They were always to "give room" if they met one of the family or betters on the stairs. They were to stand still when spoken to by a lady or gentleman and never to begin a conversation or offer an opinion, nor even say good night. They must be as specters, going about their duty without being seen, like silent leprechauns. This, of course, was all very well for the servants who had no relationship with the family but not for Bridie, who had to master a life of deception. In Kitty's bedroom she could be herself. She could lie on Kitty's bed and tell her the gossip from Downstairs. In Kitty's bedroom they could be friends. But in the rest of the castle she had to follow the rules like the other servants. O'Flynn, the butler, was above all of them, for he was the link between Lord and Lady Deverill and Downstairs, and, having worked for the previous Lord Deverill, he had a more superior status than most butlers.

Bridie had much to learn and Miss Lindsay, Lady Deverill's lady's maid, was keen to instruct her, believing strongly that standards should be upheld, even though many of the old guard were too doddery to do their jobs properly. As a lady's maid, Bridie began her day rising early to bring her mistress a morning cup of tea. She prepared the bath, the water for which was brought up in cans, and laid in readiness everything Kitty needed for dressing. Then she would have her own breakfast in the housekeeper's room and wait for the bell to summon her, which, as it was her friend Kitty ringing it, was almost immediately. Bridie had to understand hairdressing, dressmaking, packing, the care of dresses, boots, shoes, gloves, hats, bonnets, riding habits, ball gowns, and the art of mending. She learned to wash lace and fine linen, mend buttons on boots and replace feathers on Kitty's riding hats. Miss

Lindsay prided herself on her high standards, but Bridie discovered that she, too, could be meticulous. Her stitches were so small and neat Miss Lindsay was rendered speechless, her care of Kitty's clothes impressive for a fourteen-year-old with no experience of expensive fabrics. She was obedient, dutiful, conscientious and able.

While Kitty was inclined to disorder and ill discipline, in spite of a severe upbringing by the late Miss Grieve, Bridie was naturally tidy and well organized. She was surprisingly quick to learn, regretful of her mistakes and always intent on doing better. Miss Lindsay interpreted her enthusiasm as a reaction to having labored in the kitchen as a scullery maid, but in truth her eagerness was fired by ambition. She watched Kitty and her privileged world Upstairs and knew for certain that she wanted more than her poor upbringing in Ballinakelly could offer her. Perhaps Kitty would take her to London when she left at eighteen. Once in London the opportunities would be endless, for sure. Kitty might marry a great man, a duke or even a prince, and then Bridie would rise as high as a domestic servant could rise. Kitty was her friend but also her ticket to a better life—she observed and she copied, for Kitty was as fine an example of a lady as ever there was.

AFTER CHRISTMAS KITTY'S new tutor arrived. He was tall, with flaxen hair, a long, expressive face and intelligent brown eyes looking out solemnly through a pair of round-rimmed spectacles. Serious and perhaps a little shy, he did not smile when introduced to Kitty, but shook her hand and gave a small bow. "It's a pleasure to meet you, Miss Deverill. I look forward to tutoring you to the best of my ability."

Kitty wanted to giggle at his formality but, as she was in the presence of her grandparents, and not wanting to embarrass him, she simply replied that she was delighted to meet him, too, and asked him, somewhat tactlessly, if he hunted, to which the poor man responded that he didn't. She tried not to look at his left leg, which didn't bend at the knee, but gave in to her curiosity when he was shown upstairs by O'Flynn.

"My dear, you will see worse afflictions than that before the war ends," said Adeline sadly.

"They said it would end by Christmas," Kitty replied, thinking of her father and suffering a sudden pang of anxiety.

"And they were wrong."

"But it will end soon, surely?"

"I hope so," said Adeline, but the cloud that darkened her face told Kitty her hope was optimistic.

"I wish Papa had a stiff leg."

"Kitty!"

"Then he wouldn't have to fight either."

"Your father wants to fight, my dear." Adeline turned her eyes to the stairs. "I'm sure Mr. Trench would like to fight too."

Mr. Trench was indeed a serious man. Kitty tried all sorts of shenanigans to make him smile, but nothing seemed to work. She tried jokes, flattery, self-deprecation and wit, all to no avail. "He's so very grave," she complained to Bridie one evening as they lay on her bed after Kitty had returned cold and wet from a hard day's hunting. "He finds nothing amusing at all. What do you think he does in his free time?"

"He reads," Bridie informed her.

"What sort of books does he read?"

"Long ones, apparently!" The two girls fell about laughing.

"Well, he *is* very clever, isn't he?" said Kitty. "It's a shame he's so dull. What's the point of being clever if one has no wit?"

"At least he's not unkind," Bridie reminded her.

"No, he's not unkind."

"Poor Miss Grieve."

Kitty changed the subject. The mention of Miss Grieve's name made her decidedly uncomfortable. "Cousin Beatrice should have sent someone who could ride, not a cripple. What's the point of coming to Ireland if one can't hunt?"

"He hasn't come to hunt, Kitty, he's come to teach."

"Yes, and I've asked him to teach me Irish history. I want to know the history of the country I live in and love, not that of a country which is foreign to me and for which I have no affection."

"You should talk to my brother Michael. He's against fighting for England. He says the Irish should rule themselves. He gets very angry about it."

"Jack tells me everything I need to know about *that*," Kitty retorted. "It's Jack who reminds me where my loyalties lie."

"Well, is Mr. Trench going to teach you Irish history or not?" Bridie asked.

"He has no choice. I folded my arms and started singing the moment he started going on about Oliver Cromwell from the British point of view. He didn't even smile at that. In the end he relented. I'm learning about the history of this country from Irish patriots like Robert Emmet, who strove to end British conquest. For seven hundred years the Irish have suffered at the hands of the British. My family are ancestors of the first conquerors. They drove the natives into the marshlands and the woods across the Shannon and into the Connaught and took the best land for themselves. I was so ignorant of my own history, Bridie. Ignorant of what happened right here at Castle Deverill." She sighed heavily as if her new knowledge were a burden weighing on her conscience. "He told me not to tell my grandfather." She laughed. "Everyone's afraid of Grandpa. Perhaps it's because he's got a shotgun and he's not shy about of using it!"

As 1915 PROGRESSED there seemed little hope that the war would end. People learned to dread the sight of the boy in navy uniform with red livery delivering telegrams. The bereaved wore black bands around their arms and grief etched forever on their faces. Prayers of hope were said in all the churches of Ireland and Catholics and Protestants mourned with equal heartache.

Bertie, Uncle Rupert and Harry came home on leave and put on a good show of bravado, but Kitty heard Harry crying in his room in the middle of the night and saw the glow of light beneath his door because he had grown fearful of the dark. Maud returned with Victoria and Elspeth and stayed in the castle for it was too much bother to open the Hunting Lodge for just a few weeks. Kitty found her sisters intolerable with their incessant talk of London and their complaints about the damp in Ireland. They sounded like their English cousins, which is exactly how they *wanted* to sound. But Kitty was a bold girl and bit back with remarks that hurt. "Didn't Victoria say that if one doesn't find a husband during one's coming-out season it is because one is ugly, dull or both? Oh sorry, Elspeth, it was Mama." And to Victoria: "Shouldn't you have produced an heir and spare by now? I've heard it on good authority that a wife of an earl loses her head if she doesn't produce a son." So her sisters avoided her as best they could, which suited her well.

They were shallow, ignorant girls whose conversation was full of nonsense, and neither had the wit to retaliate. Kitty preferred to talk to Jack and Bridie; at least they were interested in Irish history and the progress (or lack of, at present) of the Home Rule bill.

Maud had hoped a taste of war might have given Bertie an appreciation of home; after all, didn't absence make the heart grow fonder? Perhaps it did and his heart hadn't grown fonder of *her*, but of Grace. He disappeared every morning on horseback and returned after dark. She knew he was spending time with Grace. His departure every morning was full of enthusiasm and vigor and his return full of reluctance and regret. If her perfume on his collar wasn't enough, he had a faraway look in his eyes. Maud demanded his attention but he was deaf to her whining.

When Maud first laid eyes on Kitty she was astonished to find her daughter was flowering into a beauty. She had grown taller in the six months her mother had been in England, her face had thinned and she had acquired a certain poise she hadn't had before. Her contribution at the dinner table reflected the astonishing progress of her education. She debated the Irish Question with her grandfather and her argument was sound. Even Bertie and Uncle Rupert were surprised by the eloquence of her speech and the confidence with which she delivered it. Those eyes of hers had attained an intelligence that made her more formidable. It seemed that, while Maud had been away, Kitty had grown beyond her control.

It wasn't until she was introduced to Mr. Trench that Maud realized the reason for her intellectual flowering, and that the damage had already been done; he had unleashed in Kitty a power that was quite beguiling and there was precious little she could do about it. Comparing her to Victoria and Elspeth with their poor education, she resented her youngest for having benefited, in such a short time, from Mr. Trench's tutoring. This child, whom she had done her best to keep out of sight, was now in full view of everyone and, to add insult to injury, a great success. If one more person told her how brilliant Kitty was she would scream. Kitty was a dazzling card player, Laurel had told her. Kitty was a fearless horsewoman, Hubert had raved. Kitty was a beautiful dancer, Hazel had admitted, after confessing to have taught her herself. Maud had responded by ignoring their comments and pushing her other daughters forward. Elspeth was celebrated in London, she told anyone who would listen, and with so many suitors she couldn't count them. The fact that the only young man to have shown interest was the third son of a meager baronet who was now at the front, with all the other eligible young men in the country, was not mentioned.

Kitty worried about Harry. He was withdrawn, as pale as porridge and fidgety. He couldn't sit still. It was as if his nerves were frayed and the slightest movement made him jump. Maud, who had never disguised the fact that she loved her son the most, fussed around him, making his nerves even more ragged. She second-guessed his wishes, asked him if he was all right twenty times a day and pressed him for details about the war. She unwittingly drove him out with the hunt, which he hated on account of his lack of courage, but anything was better than sitting at home with his mother. If he confided in his father, Maud never knew, because the two of them walked out with their guns and the dogs, putting up snipe and shooting hares, and Bertie never shared their conversations with his wife. It infuriated Maud to think he might share them with Grace. It hurt to think that Grace might know more about her beloved son than she did.

Then the night before Harry was to be sent back to the front Kitty decided to talk to him. She couldn't bear to lie awake thinking of him sobbing into his pillow with no one to comfort him. Who looked after him out there in France? Might he die as so many had? Would she perhaps never see him again? She put on her robe and picked up her candle and tiptoed down the corridor. It was cold out there but she hurried on, determined to give comfort where she could.

At last she reached his bedroom door. It was firmly shut but a faint light glowed beneath it. She pressed her ear to the wood and she heard a muffled sob. Needing no further confirmation of his misery she turned the knob and quietly pushed open the door. The curtains were closed around his bed. The embers were dying in the fire. Outside, the wind howled like a pack of wolves. She crept to the bed and pulled back the curtain. Not one, but two faces stared back at her in horror and surprise. Kitty's jaw dropped. Harry sat up abruptly. "Kitty," he hissed. "What the hell are you doing here?"

Kitty looked from her brother to Joseph, the first footman. Both were young, naked and handsome—and looking guilty. Scattered on the bed were loose sheets of poetry written in Harry's hand.

"I heard crying. I thought you needed comfort." She grinned, shock making her want to laugh out loud. "I see Joseph got to you first."

Harry's face reddened, the fear in his eyes exposed. "You

won't tell," he said.

"Of course I won't tell. I've got more secrets than you can imagine, Harry."

"You promise me. Even if I die in France, you swear you won't tell?"

"I cross my heart and hope to die."

"Now go and we won't ever speak of this again. Do you understand?"

"I understand." She dropped the curtain and rushed out of the room. When she reached her bedroom she sank onto her bed, trembling. She knew what her father had been doing to Lady Rowan-Hampton at the Summer Ball all right, but was it possible Harry was doing that to Joseph? She thought not. They were simply cuddling—and why shouldn't Harry be comforted by a loyal servant? But, as she climbed beneath the blankets and blew out her candle, she instinctively knew that what Harry and Joseph were doing was wrong; after all neither had had any clothes on and the terror in their eyes had told her as much. But Kitty was a master at keeping secrets. She'd guard this one closely in the same way she guarded the others. It gave her a feeling of power to know so much.

The following day Harry went back to the war. He gave her a hug, which was out of character, and a look that silently begged her to honor her word. Bertie left a few days later. He didn't know the secret she kept for *him* but he embraced her all the same. Uncle Rupert went off to the front as if he were going to a party. He waved extravagantly and threw his head back with laughter and only *he* knew how much of a brave face he put on in order to conceal the crippling fear inside.

Before Maud left for England she managed to take Mr.

Trench to one side under the pretext of discussing her youngest daughter's education. Once they were alone she spoke directly. "Mr. Trench, I see you are giving Kitty a wonderful education and my husband and I are very grateful to you. However, I feel you might be happier in England. Ireland is very damp and cold and this old castle is terribly creaky." She looked down at his leg. "And I can't imagine what you get out of a country that is obsessed with horses. Might it not appeal to you, Mr. Trench, to come and tutor my daughter, Elspeth, instead? She's a bright girl and I'm sure it won't be long before she marries, but every young woman should be in possession of a good education, don't you think?" Maud was quite satisfied that Mr. Trench would leap at the chance to leave Ireland. However, he replied with equal directness, for he belonged to the same social class as Mrs. Deverill and was by no means afraid of her.

"Mrs. Deverill, I am flattered that you should offer me a position in England but I fear I must disappoint you. Kitty is a very rewarding student and I am enjoying tutoring her immensely. As for Ireland and this castle, I have grown very fond of them indeed. It would take more than you could offer to lure me back to England."

Maud was enraged. She tried another tack. "Life is terribly unfair," she said, pulling a pitiful face. "Kitty has every advantage and my poor Elspeth—"

"I am not unique, Mrs. Deverill," Mr. Trench replied. "In fact, I'm sure there are many like me in London who would be grateful for a job."

"There aren't any like you in London," Maud replied tightly. "They are all away fighting the war. Well, if I can't persuade you now, I leave my offer open. When Ireland gets too much, and I assure you it *will* get too much, you may change your mind."

Maud left for England with Victoria and Elspeth. The castle was Kitty's once again. She resumed her lessons with Mr. Trench and the more she learned about Ireland's history, the more her patriotic fire was fanned. She saw a great deal of Jack, for with his father away fighting on the Western Front, he was the only vet in Ballinakelly and Castle Deverill had many animals. When he didn't ride up to the castle, she rode to find *him,* and sometimes they arranged to meet on the hills. They would canter over the heather, their laughter carrying on the wind with the mournful cries of gulls. They would lie on the grass and talk as the days grew longer and the little purple flowers of mountain thyme opened in the sun. Often they would meet at the Fairy Ring to watch the sun set behind it, elongating the shadows until the stones were brought to life.

It was in that spring of 1915 that Jack began to look at Kitty with different eyes and Kitty, drawn close to Jack because of the secret they shared and their mutual love of Ireland, began to feel a budding tenderness in return. She began to look forward to their meetings with impatience, and the heaviness in his gaze when he looked at her wielded an irresistible power that turned her stomach to jelly. When she wasn't with him she found herself staring out of the window thinking of him, and the idea of their shared patriotism grew ever more romantic.

Chapter 12

By 1916 all hope of an imminent end to the war disintegrated. Battles were fought in Europe and the Middle East at devastating human cost on both sides. Soldiers dug themselves into trenches like rodents and there seemed little in the way of advancements, only death. As the black bands on the arms of grieving mothers and wives grew in their number in Ballinakelly, the shadow of death had not yet reached Castle Deverill. The Deverills prayed for the continued safety of their loved ones and tried to live their lives in the normal way, for what else could they do?

The year before, their English cousins had come to stay for the summer as usual, but Digby and George were absent, as were Bertie, Harry and Rupert, leaving old Hubert and Stoke to entertain the ladies. Victoria was still not pregnant in spite of Eric returning on leave and Elspeth was yet to find herself a husband. Kitty wasted no time in telling Elspeth that she should find a nice Irishman as there were plenty about who had not gone to war, to which Elspeth replied that only Kitty would do such a thing and send their dear mama to an early grave.

There had been picnics on the beach, croquet and tennis, dinner parties and grand lunches, but beneath the gaiety was a desperate anxiety as news filtered through in the newspapers of the horrors of battle and the thousands dead. One night Beatrice got particularly tipsy and broke down in tears as she described the shocking sight of the wounded soldiers in London who were too crippled to rejoin their regiments. "They're like the walking dead," she sniffed. "And all I can think of is George and Digby and our boys." Augusta tried everyone's patience by declaring that she would welcome her own death in order to avoid the terrible suffering her son and grandson were putting her through.

But in the week of Easter 1916 Ireland suffered her own tragedy. An uprising by Irish Republicans intent on ending British rule in Ireland brought the clatter of gunfire to the streets of Dublin. "Bloody knackers," boomed Hubert furiously, throwing down the *Irish Times*. "Isn't there enough bloodshed in the world!" But Kitty was secretly excited. The Irish rebel forces had seized key locations in Dublin and proclaimed the Irish Republic independent of the United Kingdom. For a glorious six days it looked as if they were going to win but then the British Army suppressed them with their artillery and felled them like ears of barley.

"In the name of God and of the dead generations from which she receives her old tradition of nationhood, Ireland, through us, summons her children to her flag and strikes for her freedom," Kitty read from the proclamation that Jack had given her, signed by the seven

leaders of the Easter Rising at the General Post Office, Dublin, having declared themselves the provisional government of the Republic of Ireland.

"They've shot three of them," he told her solemnly, picking a sprig of heather and twiddling it between his thumb and finger.

"I'm sorry," Kitty replied truthfully. "Do you think they'll shoot them all?"

"All the leaders who signed that bit of paper and more, I suppose. Maybe they'll shoot the lot of 'em."

"Must be horrid to die like that," said Kitty quietly.

"I'd rather die in battle than be blindfolded and shot by a firing squad, a little white rag pinned to my chest to show them where my heart is."

Kitty winced. "Is that what they do?"

"The Irish Citizen Army was no match for the British Army, Kitty. There were only two thousand of them, against twenty thousand soldiers. Jaysus, they didn't stand a pup's chance in hell!"

"But if the Germans had helped, they might have had a chance?"

"If the German supply of arms had reached them, perhaps. But it didn't."

"What's going to happen now?"

Jack looked at her steadily. "We rally, we train, we keep up the pressure. We don't give up."

"Jack—"

"You think shooting hundreds of rebels by firing squad or sending them to the hangman is going to stamp out the desire for independence? No, Kitty, it's just going to make us all stronger. There's not a single man, woman or child in the whole of Ireland now who doesn't want to be free of British rule. The Rising has made sure of that."

"What are you going to do?"

"I've joined the Volunteers, Kitty. We're about fifty of us in Ballinakelly, but as Napoleon said, *In war, it is not the men who count, it is the man*."

"How do you know what Napoleon said?" Kitty asked with a smile.

"I heard it," he retorted defensively. "They're not all as poorly educated as I am."

"I want to be part of it."

Jack stared at Kitty in amazement. "You're English, Kitty. You're one of them."

Kitty rounded on him furiously. "I'm Irish, Jack, and you know it. Do you think I'd be your friend if I were one of them? Do you?"

"You're too young."

"I'll be sixteen in September."

"You're a child."

Kitty sat up and stared out to sea. "I'm old for my years and you know better than anyone how good I am at keeping secrets."

"This isn't a game, Kitty. Look what's happened to Countess Markievicz. Well, she's one of you, don't you know, and she's going to be shot like all the rest."

Kitty was appalled. "They won't shoot a woman, surely."

"She renounced her status as a woman by joining the rebels, wouldn't you say? They'll court-martial her like all the rest, see if they don't." Jack smiled fondly at Kitty. "You want independence for Ireland, same as us. You want an end to poverty and exploitation of the Irish people by the British same as us. But you haven't thought about what comes after, have you? What'll happen to Castle Deverill and your grandparents? You'll have to leave, all of you. It'll be too dangerous for English people to carry on living here. Have you thought about that? Are you prepared to give it all up for your cause?"

"I won't give it up. The Deverills are Irish. We've lived here since 1661 . . ."

"On *our* land," said Jack with a grin.

Kitty lowered her eyes. "I can't help what happened over two hundred years ago, Jack."

"But that's the point, isn't it? You Anglo-Irish can never shake off the fact that you're part of the conquering power, given land that wasn't yours."

"What do you want me to do, Jack? Give it back?"

"There's no chance of that now."

"There, you see? Nothing can be done about that."

"They'll want you out all the same, Kitty."

"Not if I fight for the rebels."

Jack laughed at her naïveté. "You're not going to fight for anyone," he said softly.

Kitty stared at him with her gray eyes full of knowing. "You're going to need me one day, Jack O'Leary, and, when you do, I'll remind you that you laughed at me."

"Out of the hundreds arrested, only fourteen rebels executed," Hubert complained over breakfast, slamming down the newspaper. "I ask you! Bloody Shinners! They should have shot the bally lot of 'em." Hubert huffed furiously and left the dining room. He folded his shotgun over his arm and strode out of the castle with his dogs. As he walked onto the gravel he saw a boy in navy uniform cycling toward him. Hubert stopped. The dogs at his heels sat down as the boy approached.

He had a brown parcel tied with string on the back of his bicycle. Hubert's mouth went dry. His bravado evaporated. "Top of the morning to ye, Lord Deverill," said the boy. Hubert couldn't speak. He stood there and waited. It seemed a long time before the parcel was placed in his hands along with a telegram edged in black. The boy cycled away. He had delivered bad news too many times to be affected by it now. Hubert remained outside on the gravel, unable to move. One of the dogs whined and looked up at him in a silent plea. There were snipe in the marshes and hares in the heather but Hubert felt the weight of the parcel and wept.

Adeline, drawn by a sense of foreboding, reached him as the heavy clouds above them released a light drizzle. She looked at the parcel in his hands, at his ashen face and white lips, and read the telegram through a blur of tears. Rupert had been killed at Gallipoli.

She slipped her arm through her husband's and led him slowly back into the castle. O'Flynn's weary old eyes flicked from their faces to the parcel and his shoulders stooped a little lower. Once in the library O'Flynn poured his master a strong whiskey, then, noticing Lady Deverill's distress, poured her one too. They gulped it back gratefully, but nothing could dull the pain of losing a son.

With a deep breath Adeline opened the parcel. Inside was Rupert's uniform, his Soldiers' Small Book, a packet of letters tied with ribbon and a silver hip flask his father had given him on his eighteenth birthday. She wiped her wet cheeks with trembling fingers. Now she was no different from the other mourning mothers in Ballinakelly, for there is no discrimination in death.

Kitty was called out of her lesson with Mr. Trench and given the news. For some inexplicable reason she had believed her family exempt from death on the battlefield. She had told herself that Deverills didn't fight on the front lines. They had always been special; but no one was special in war.

She ran up to her bedroom and rang for Bridie. "Uncle Rupert's dead," she sobbed as Bridie entered. "He's been killed. Will it be Papa next?" Bridie put her arms around her friend and felt her tears seeping into her uniform. "I know you understand because you lost your father."

"I do understand," said Bridie gently.

"When will it end? When will Papa and Harry come home? It's beastly, just beastly!"

"The war will end and Master Harry and your father will come home. They will. It can't go on forever, can it?"

"I don't know. Can it?" Kitty took Bridie's hands. "You must miss your papa."

"I do. Not a day goes by when I don't think of him, God rest his soul."

"It makes little difference that I know Uncle Rupert is in Heaven now because he's not here, where he should be. Grandma was crying her heart out even though she knows he's in Heaven too and not dead on that battlefield. A ghost is not the same as a living person. You can't touch a ghost and a ghost can't hold *you*." Kitty squeezed her eyes shut. "Oh God, please don't take Papa."

The hardest part about Rupert's death was the fact that there was no body to bury. His home was boarded up like a tomb because it was part of the Deverill estate and Adeline couldn't bear to clear out his things, or for anyone else to live there. She organized a small service in his memory in the church of St. Patrick in Ballinakelly, outside of which many of the locals and tenants gathered to pay their respects. It was there that Adeline noticed how hungry they all looked. She gazed in horror at the scrawny bodies and gaunt faces of the children and wondered why she hadn't noticed before. The sight hauled her out of her grief and galvanized her into action. She arranged for herself and Kitty to drive into town the following morning with a cart full of food baskets for the tenants. With the help of the gardeners they raided the greenhouses for vegetables and instructed Mrs. Doyle to set about baking loaves of soda bread.

Their charity was so gratefully received that Adeline made it her mission to care for the poor. It was a way of suppressing her grief; she buried it beneath the distraction of activity and purpose. The gardens were large enough to grow plenty more produce, she said, giving orders for more seeds to be sown and nurtured and harvested. "It's wrong of us to keep it all for ourselves." Hubert huffed and puffed like an old engine, complaining that his wife's undertaking to save the poor would only end in bankruptcy.

When the family reunited for the summer she put the women to work. Gone were the days of croquet and tennis, dinner parties and lunch parties, and languid afternoons in the sunshine playing cards beneath parasols. The people needed them and they would rise to their need and save them from starvation, just like Adeline's mother-in-law had done during the famine with her soup kitchen.

Maud complained that Adeline had gone mad with sorrow. Beatrice rolled up her sleeves and set to work with relish, for it was like Marie Antoinette's Petit Trianon, was it not? A delightful game that she could play all summer before returning to the civilization of Deverill Rising, their country estate in Wiltshire, where she wasn't required to dig up potatoes and drive them around to the poor. Victoria, Elspeth and the twins complained bitterly while they podded the broad beans and picked endless baskets of raspberries but Kitty and Celia enjoyed the task, probably because their sisters so loathed it.

At the end of the summer there was no ball at the castle. There were no young men to invite and it didn't seem appropriate to hold a party when half the guests were risking their lives at the front. After the cousins returned to Wiltshire and Maud to Kent with Victoria and Elspeth the castle was quiet once more and the shroud of mourning that had been temporarily lifted during the summer months now fell over the family again.

Adeline sank into a torpor. It was as if she had exhausted her energies with all the planting and harvesting. The usual casual laborers arrived in September to pick the fruits. There were apples, figs, pears and plums, loganberries, strawberries, and currants and Adeline turned a blind eye to the ones they surreptitiously ate along the way and to the stones they added to their bags when it was time to weigh them for their pay.

She sat in her little sitting room on the first floor and listened to music on the gramophone, drinking herbal tea made with the cannabis she grew to calm her nerves. It was there that Kitty would find her in the evenings while Hubert was still out. She looked frail and older now, curled up in the big armchair, gazing into the flames as if hoping to find answers there. The sweet smell of turf smoke and herb tea gave the room a comforting air and Kitty liked to sit in there with her and read. She enjoyed the soothing sounds of classical music and her grandmother's familiar presence. It was a cozy, restful room, detached from the uncertainty disrupting the world at war.

"Rupert was a troubled soul," said Adeline quietly, staring into the fire. "He put on a show of being this wild and glamorous man to hide the inadequate boy he was inside. He was always like that, even as a child, showing off to hide his insecurities. Bertie, on the other hand, was born sure of himself. I suppose that comes with being the eldest son. He knows where he's going. If he survives the war he will inherit Castle Deverill when Hubert goes and after him Harry. It's all mapped out, all very predictable."

"But what will happen if Ireland wins independence?" Kitty asked. "Will we have to leave and go and live in England?"

"Of course not. Just because there's a revolution doesn't mean we won't be able to continue living here. Wild horses wouldn't drag us away from our home. We belong here and Lord knows we deserve to stay. We look after our tenants and we respect those who want to break free . . ."

"Grandpa doesn't."

Adeline slid her eyes to where Kitty was sitting on the sofa and put her teacup in its saucer with a clink. "Grandpa," she chuckled sleepily. "Hubert thinks by saying it won't happen he will somehow prevent it from happening. Of course, saying it doesn't make it so. He grew up believing in the might and power of the Crown. It's what his parents believed." She shrugged. "Loyal to king and country he simply can't see it from any other point of view. Mind you, Rupert's death has woken him up to the fallibility of the British Army. The Deverills aren't any different from anyone else. They can cut us down as surely as the next man. I fear Ireland will descend into violence, Kitty. The Irish people will never forgive the English for executing those men after the Easter Rising. They will be treated as martyrs in the eyes of the Irish people and there is nothing more dangerous than a martyr. They live in Tir na nÓg—the Land of the Forever Young. It'll come back in the form of reprisals, I know it."

"When will there be an end to this war?" Kitty sighed. "It's been two years now. Surely someone has to win?"

"Not until they've all killed each other first," said Adeline with uncharacteristic pessimism. "The root of all evil in the world is man's ego. If only they could rise above their bloody egos the world would be a peaceful place. But they can't. They're no better than beasts."

Kitty watched her grandmother's eyes droop and her head fall onto her chest. She got up and walked over to the chair, catching the cup and saucer before they dropped onto the rug at Adeline's feet. Curious about this sweet-smelling herb that intoxicated her grandmother, she poured the last drops out of the pot and took a sip. It tasted benign, sugary even, and Kitty wondered whether her grandmother had added honey to improve the flavor. Soon her head began to spin and she only just made it back to the sofa before collapsing into the cushions. In a moment she felt better about the world. Nothing mattered. Not independence, nor Jack, nor Ireland. She took another swig and smiled. Her grandmother really was a witch and this was her brew.

IN THE SPRING of 1917 Harry returned home from the war, wounded by a gunshot to the shoulder. But he didn't come to Castle Deverill. Maud felt it was too dangerous for him as a British soldier to be seen in a country growing increasingly violent toward the English there and summoned him to Kent. She had no such concerns for Kitty and had no intention of calling for her to join them. She wouldn't know what to do with the girl once she got there—and she knew in her heart that Kitty was flowering into a beautiful and articulate young woman who would easily eclipse Elspeth. There weren't enough eligible men to go around as it was, so she certainly wasn't going to narrow Elspeth's chances of finding a husband by inviting Kitty onto the playing field.

Hubert lifted his spirits by purchasing a shiny red Daimler motor car. It arrived from England and caused a sensation when he drove Adeline and Kitty to Ballinakelly and back. Hordes of children ran after it, old women stared as if they were seeing something otherworldly and grown men laughed, shaking their heads at the flamboyance of Lord Deverill who didn't care a hoot what anyone thought. At the castle the servants spilled out onto the gravel to look at it. Bridie had never seen anything so magical in all her life. Mrs. Doyle shook her head, believing it to be the Devil's work, but O'Flynn ran his fingers over the hood and remembered with affection the toy train he had been given as a boy, which had been painted the same red. When

Hubert offered to take him for a drive around the estate O'Flynn became that boy again, springing into the front seat as if he wasn't eighty years old and decrepit.

They passed Jack O'Leary on the drive, riding his horse toward the castle to see to a lame mare. Jack doffed his cap and watched the motor car speed over the mud. Lord Deverill waved as he passed and Jack wondered what the point was of wasting money on such an expensive toy.

At the castle he saw to the mare. It was nothing more serious than a pulled muscle and required only a few days' rest in the stable. As he was closing the stable door, Kitty appeared in her riding habit. "I'll ride you home," she said, but he knew that meant riding to the Fairy Ring to talk politics, war and their own brand of nonsense.

Kitty rode sidesaddle. In her black habit she looked poised and stylish. Beneath her black hat her red hair was tied in a thick plait that reached down to her waist. Against the black dress and white collar her skin was as flawless as the smooth surface of cream. Her full lips curled mischievously while her gray eyes couldn't help but look intelligent and serious. Jack admired her in the saddle. She rode with a confidence that came from years of practice as well as a courageous heart. He mounted his horse and they set off up the drive beneath the avenue of budding trees.

Once out on the hills they cantered side by side over the heather, laughing at the sheer pleasure of being in the wind with a magnificent view of the sea. They reached the Fairy Ring and dismounted, leaving their horses untethered. "I remember telling my father that these stones come to life after sunset," said

Kitty, walking among them. "Of course he thought I was mad. I remember the look in his eyes. I never got the chance to explain that it's only at sunset, when the shadows lengthen, that they *appear* to move. I imagine growing up with my grandmother meant he'd heard all sorts of stories about the supernatural and thought perhaps this was just another. Poor Papa. He's so patient." She looked out across the ocean where the waves rolled in over the wide expanse of white sand. "I pray for him, Jack. I pray that he comes back to us, not wounded like Harry, but as he was when he left."

Jack stood beside her and turned his gaze to the horizon. "You seeing spirits and all that, what happens when we die then?"

"We leave our bodies and float away, to a place where there's no war and no violence and no poverty."

"You really believe that, don't you?"

"I know it, Jack. You know it, too, remember?"

"That face I saw in the window was a ghost. That's different."

"No, it isn't. It's the same. That was Jonnie Wilson who'd been killed in the war and had come back to find the woman he loved. It's romantic, don't you think?"

"Aye, 'tis romantic," he agreed. "And you think Miss Grieve killed herself to be with him?"

"I think so."

Jack turned to face her. The sun was beginning to set, bathing her features in a warm amber gold. "If I died I'd come back to be with the woman I loved. If I could."

Kitty smiled. "Who would you come back for, Jack?" But as she said it her words caught in her throat because she saw the tender way he was looking at her. Her cheeks flushed suddenly and her lips parted in surprise.

Jack looked quite serious and a little anxious. He held her gaze but her eyes were wide and guarded and he couldn't keep it, nor could he read what was in it. He breathed deeply, as if about to take a great risk. Then he reached down for her gloved hand. He squeezed it gently. "I'd come back for you, I would," he said softly.

Kitty's eyes shone. "Do you love me, Jack?" she asked.

"I do, Kitty, with all my heart."

Kitty felt something warm and sweet flow into the aching hole in her heart, the one that hurt with longing whenever she gazed out at the starry night and full moon. "I think I love you, too, Jack," she replied hoarsely.

Jack took her in his arms and pressed his lips to hers. She let him part them and kiss her deeply. She inhaled the horse dust on his skin and the turf smoke in his hair and wanted to weep at the familiar smell that was home to her. Wrapping her arms around his neck and sinking into him, she closed her eyes and let down her guard, allowing herself to take pleasure from the unfamiliar feelings that were now taking hold of her. As the shadows lengthened and the stones began to move Kitty knew she belonged to Jack O'Leary as surely as she belonged to Ireland.

Chapter 13

Bridie noticed a change in Kitty. She was distracted and pensive and uncharacteristically placid. Her sharp eyes had softened, more often turned to the window now where she'd stand and stare, her gaze lost among the turning leaves and tempestuous sea. She didn't lie on the bed with Bridie and laugh about Mr. Trench, but lay staring into the gathered silk of the canopy above, sighing heavily but contentedly, like a romantic heroine in the magazines Bridie read. Bridie could only assume that she had fallen in love with her tutor, for who else could have turned this feisty, defiant young woman to sap?

Mr. Trench was certainly handsome. Behind his spectacles his eyes were a soft chestnut-brown. Although serious, his features were regular and pleasing, his nose straight, his chin angular, his jaw and cheekbones well defined. Bridie considered him gentlemanly. He always said good morning and acknowledged her politely, which was more than most Deverill guests did. Most never even looked at the servants unless they wanted something, and a "please" or a "thank you" seemed not to be part of their vocabulary. Bridie wasn't privy to what went on in the classroom and unlike Kitty she wasn't a natural spy, so peeping through keyholes was not an option. She could only wait until Kitty confided in her, which she was sure she would; after all, she shared everything else.

The war burned on like an uncontrollable forest fire, consuming men indiscriminately. George Deverill, Digby and Beatrice's son who used to play with Harry every summer, was killed at sea and Digby himself was left for dead on the battlefield, beneath a pile of bodies, only to be discovered a day later, wounded in the leg but alive. He returned to England to recover, but nothing could heal the damage done to his heart at the loss of his only son. Kitty mourned George and prayed ever more fervently for her father. Bridie comforted her as best she could.

Bridie's wages were gratefully received at home. Michael and Sean worked hard on the land to pay the rent and feed themselves. Mrs. Doyle toiled in the castle kitchen, Old Mrs. Nagle cooked for the family and none of them were ever late for Mass. Wherever they stood they would take off their caps, bow their heads and pray twice a day at the sound of the Angelus. Twice a day Bridie would remember her father and however much she told herself that time would heal, it never did. She missed him as acutely now as she had the day he was taken from her. *"Angelus Domini nuntiavit Mariæ . . ."* and she would squeeze back tears as she remembered Tomas, larger now in memory than he had been in life, and silently she would promise him that she would make something of her life and give him reason to be proud.

Bridie saw Jack at Mass every Sunday morning. His raffish grin and intense gaze would make her heart flip over and her whole being would expand with light. He'd walk her home and she'd entertain him with stories from the castle. He loved stories of Kitty best, throwing his head back and laughing at her antics.

"Kitty's in love, don't you know," she told him one Sunday in October as they ambled slowly up the road.

"What makes you think that?" Jack asked.

"She's dreamy."

"She's *always* dreamy," said Jack, smiling fondly.

"It's a different kind of dreamy altogether. She's all sighs and soft looks."

"Who's she in love with, then?"

"I believe it's Mr. Trench."

For a moment Jack's face darkened. "Mr. Trench?" he exclaimed.

"Her tutor." She shrugged. "Who else could it be?"

"Have you been earwigging, Bridie?"

Bridie was affronted. "I don't go putting my nose through cracks in doors, Jack, and you know it. She spends all morning with him and indeed he's a fine-looking fella."

"I don't doubt you, Bridie." Jack sighed. "I'm just surprised."

"I'm not. Why shouldn't she fall in love with Mr. Trench? His stiff leg only makes him more romantic."

"Sounds like you've taken a shine to him yourself."

"I have not," Bridie retorted, flushing. She wished she could be honest and confess how much she shone for *him*.

"I do believe you're blushing, Bridie Doyle!" He laughed. When she didn't reply he nudged her gently. "I'm only codding ya!"

"Well, don't. It's not a laughing matter."

"You sound hoity-toity these days, Bridie. You've been mixing too much with them up at the castle."

"I have to talk proper up there," said Bridie, pleased that he'd noticed. "I'm a lady's maid."

"It's grand, Bridie."

She looked at his profile and wondered where the boy had gone, for he was surely a man now. "Michael doesn't want me and Mam working for the Deverills but he can't deny my wages."

"They're generous, I give them that."

"And you, Jack? How are you? We don't see much of you these days."

He sighed heavily, the sigh of a man whose days were burdened with toil and uncertainty. "It's all work and no play, Bridie. With Dad fighting—"

"I pray for him, Jack."

"So do I," he said quietly.

As they parted at the end of the road, where the town stopped and the countryside began, Bridie turned. "You won't tell Kitty now, will you, Jack?"

"May the Devil carry me if I ever do," he replied, taking off his cap and waving it at her. "Tell her I say hello."

Bridie laughed. "For all the good it will do! Kitty has eyes only for Mr. Trench!" and she walked back to the castle with a bouncing stride.

KITTY HURRIED THROUGH the garden, holding tightly onto her shawl so it didn't blow away. She looked around once or twice to make sure that she wasn't being followed, or watched. Brown leaves were heaped into piles, discarded by the wind and left to rot with the summer foliage. The borders, once bright with flowers, were now bare and decomposing, for the old gardeners didn't have the time or the energy to cut back and clear away. Kitty hurried on, her breath coming out in puffs of smoke, her red hair loose and wild, curled into thick waves by the damp.

When she reached the wall she stopped. Glancing around like a vixen about to steal a hen, she made sure that she was quite alone. She crouched down and removed a loose stone, clothed in a soft covering of green moss. Behind it, in the dry hole, was a white piece of paper folded neatly into a square. Jack always folded his paper in the same way, doubling it over, tucking it in, so that once opened it was impossible to fold again. She pulled out of her skirt pocket the note she had written and placed it in the hole, securing it safely behind the stone.

She hurried excitedly to one of the greenhouses and sat on the iron bench where she used to sit with Celia and Bridie in the summertime, hatching their plots. She took a deep breath and opened the note.

> *Beautiful Kitty of mine, I saw a fox today as I was*
> *riding to Morgan's Point. She had a bright, wary gaze.*
> *I thought of you and I thought of us and my heart filled*
> *with gladness. Whatever happens I will always thank*
> *God for you, Kitty, my own little fox. I am the luckiest*
> *man in all of Ireland. As I write the word I realize now*

that I was wrong to accuse you of being English. To me you are Ireland, Kitty, in every way. I will meet you at the Fairy Ring at sunset, if you can get away. I hope you can. I miss your kisses. Your loving Jack.

Kitty read it again then pressed it to her heart with a long, satisfied sigh. It never occurred to her that her future with Jack was by no means assured. They were from opposite sides of the social and religious divide and she was well aware that she was expected to marry an Englishman. But Kitty loved Jack and to her their love was strong enough to smash through every barrier. She knew in her heart that nothing would keep them apart, not her mother nor her father, and she could count on her grandmother to fight for her.

She didn't waste time changing into her riding habit but hurried to the stables to saddle her mare, mounting in her black buttoned boots, dress and shawl. Mr. Mills was nowhere to be seen, but one of the stable lads watched her curiously from beneath his black fringe, wiping his dirty hands on an old rag.

Kitty felt a sense of defiance and freedom. No one could tell her what to do or when to do it. She was seventeen now and the stable boys stood for her when she stepped into their midst. Her mother was in England, her father at the front, her grandfather in Dublin, where he seemed to now spend a great deal of his time. If her grandmother saw her riding out in her dress she would smile to herself and shake her head, for Adeline admired her granddaughter's spirit. As for Mr. Trench, he was her tutor, not her nanny, and was in no position to question her whereabouts. But as Kitty galloped up the avenue of trees he was returning from a long walk around the estate. She didn't see him crossing the lawn where they played croquet in the summer months, his footsteps darkening the wet grass as he went, and she didn't see the wistful expression on his face as he removed his glasses and gazed after her. She was too busy looking at the setting sun.

Once at the Fairy Ring she dismounted and flung herself into Jack's embrace. The wind blew in salty and cold and he wrapped his arms around her tightly to shelter her. His lips found hers through her tangle of hair that flew about her head in long red tendrils like a mermaid's in the sea. She pressed herself against him so that not even the wind could slip between them. He was warm and solid and familiar and she inhaled his scent like a drunkard smelling whiskey after a day of sobriety. Jack kissed her icy cheeks and her soft neck then held her face in his hands to look at her. "You're a beautiful woman, Kitty Deverill."

"And you're a handsome man, Jack O'Leary." She laughed, gazing into his eyes which were old and wise beyond his years.

"I love the bones of ya."

"And I love the bones of you too. Every one."

"Do you love me more than Mr. Trench?" His tone was light but his eyes betrayed his anxiety.

Kitty frowned. "What's brought that on? I don't love Mr. Trench at all."

"That's good."

"Whatever gave you that idea, Jack?"

"I'm a jealous man, Kitty."

"You have no need to be jealous. I'm yours, body and soul. Don't ever doubt that." He kissed her again, deeply and fiercely, as if he knew in his heart that one of these days he'd kiss her for the last time; that Kitty would never belong to him. And Kitty, unaware of his deep fear, laughed at his fervor and lifted her chin so he could bury his face in her throat.

MAUD RETURNED TO Castle Deverill with Victoria, Elspeth and Harry for Christmas. Harry had insisted on coming. He was still recovering from the wound to his shoulder. When Kitty saw him she was immediately struck by how different he looked. Gone was the carefree boy and in his place a man, haunted by what he had lived through, haunted by what he had seen. Maud fussed over him more than ever and instead of tolerating her he lost his temper, stunning her into silence with his uncharacteristic outbursts. He insisted on having Joseph as his valet and only Kitty knew why. She didn't dare enter his room in case she found them in bed together again, but something told her that Harry wouldn't mind. The fact that she knew his secret seemed not to bother him anymore. If anything it brought them closer. He sought her company on long walks up and down the beach and rowing out to sea in their father's fishing boat, and, although it was never mentioned or even alluded to, he was more at ease in her company than in anyone else's.

Bridie listened to the chitchat in the kitchen. Molly, the maid with whom she shared a room, was an avid gossip. Assigned to look after Kitty's mother and sisters, she revealed that Maud was prone to shouting at her daughters, who were clearly afraid of her even though the eldest was a countess. She was particularly impatient with Elspeth, reminding her at every opportunity that she was getting old and if she didn't find a husband soon she would be left gathering dust on the shelf. Elspeth had replied, in her defense, that there were precious few men around, to which

Maud had snapped, "If you can't find a duke, find a *crippled* duke, but for goodness' sake don't humiliate me. I don't want to be the mother of a spinster." Bridie was shocked by that revelation. She couldn't imagine a mother being so heartless, but Maud was a vain and self-centered woman. Only Harry drew her out of herself. "He'll find a suitable bride," Molly reported her saying to her daughters. "He's handsome and heroic and heir to a great estate. He'll have to fight them off. It's a great shame you weren't all born boys."

Kitty spoke to her mother only when she had to. She was always polite, kept her sentences short and made sure she asked her about herself. "There won't be a London Season next spring," her mother told her over lunch the day before Christmas. "So you might as well stay here."

"How will Kitty find a husband then?" asked Victoria smugly. "Poor Elspeth hasn't had much luck."

"Is that the only thing that concerns you, Victoria? Marriage?" said Kitty.

"What else is there?" her sister replied.

"If that's the only option for a woman I rather wish I'd been born a man," Kitty retorted.

Elspeth rolled her eyes. "You sound like a suffragette."

"Suffragettes don't want to be men, Elspeth, they just want equality," Kitty said, bored by her sisters' ignorance.

"A woman's place is in the home," Hubert interrupted. "Politics is no place for the fairer sex."

"I do feel for young women these days," said Adeline. "The war is wiping out an entire generation."

"Then we'll all have to marry Irishmen," said Kitty provocatively. Her words got the reaction she hoped for.

Maud's lips pursed furiously. "That's a ridiculous idea, Kitty," she exclaimed.

"Beggars can't be choosers," Elspeth rejoined, thinking of Peter MacCartain, whom she had always found handsome.

"Deverill girls are no beggars," said Hubert. "My grand-daughters will marry the finest England has to offer."

"The finest are being shot in their thousands," said Harry suddenly. "Mother, I think it's disgusting that all you can think about is marrying your daughters off. Men are dying over there and those who aren't will never be the same again. Excuse me if I don't sympathize with your predicament."

Maud paled. Hubert wiped his mouth with his napkin. O'Flynn stood to attention as if he hadn't heard. "That's enough, Harry," said his grandfather sternly. "The war is indeed robbing the nation of its young men, but life must go on and your sisters must marry. It is a natural concern for a mother."

"Don't think I don't worry about your father, Harry," said Maud stiffly, her jaw tightening as if in a vise. "Don't think I don't grieve for Rupert and George and all the other boys we know who have lost their lives in the war. Don't think I don't grieve for you and ask myself where the gentle boy I raised has gone."

Harry looked at her steadily. "He died on the battlefield, Mother. It is no place for a boy." Maud's eyes glittered.

Adeline gestured to O'Flynn to take the plates away. "Let's raise our glasses to Bertie," she said. "Let's pray for his safe return and an end to this beastly war." They all lifted their wineglasses and in that, at least, they were united.

THE FOLLOWING DAY the family went to church. Hubert drove Adeline, Harry, Maud and Victoria in the Daimler while the others went in the pony and trap with Mr. Mills. Kitty and Elspeth sat side by side beneath a blanket and for a while neither spoke. They looked out under their hats at the bleak countryside and the gulls wheeling like gliders in the ice-cold sky, each alone with her thoughts. Then, finally, Elspeth spoke. "I loathe Mama," she said.

Kitty was stunned. She turned to face her sister and noticed how pale and thin she looked. "Are you unwell?"

"I'm sick of *her*," she said bitterly. "I envy you, Kitty. You're here with Grandma and Grandpa and you can do what you like. Why do I have to live with her in Kent? It's like being imprisoned."

"Surely it's not that bad."

"Eric's a bore." Elspeth laughed guiltily. "He's the dullest man in England."

Kitty put her glove to her mouth. "Elspeth, Victoria would kill you if she heard you denouncing her husband."

"She doesn't love him. I'm not even sure she likes him. But he's rich and that's all that matters." She looked at her sister forlornly. "Isn't there more than that? Isn't it possible to feel something for one's husband?"

"Grandma loves Grandpa, I'm certain of it," said Kitty, thinking of Jack and feeling the familiar warmth envelop her heart like a fur glove.

"Do you think Mama loves Papa?" Elspeth asked.

"In her own way," Kitty replied truthfully. "I don't think Mama truly loves anyone other than herself."

Elspeth turned away and sighed. "She never liked you. Why?"

Kitty shrugged. Even though she didn't like her mother, her rejection still hurt. "I don't know."

"She's frightened of you, I think. I can see it in her eyes. She can't control you. That's why. You have spirit. I wish I had spirit like you."

"I'm not like her," said Kitty.

"You're not like Papa either. You're like Grandma. Really, the two of you are like mother and daughter."

"Grandma's been more of a mother to me than Mama could ever be."

Elspeth took her hand suddenly and squeezed it. "I want us to be friends, Kitty," she said with passion. "I'm sorry I was ever horrid to you. I bitterly regret it. I was a beast."

"I'd like us to be friends too," said Kitty. She smiled at her sister and realized that a person isn't all bad or all good but a complicated mixture of the two. "But I'm afraid I can't save you from Mother."

"Then who can?" she asked pitifully.

"A man," Kitty replied. "You have to fall in love and marry and then, at least, you will belong to someone else."

"Exchanging one master for another," said Elspeth dully.

"No, exchanging a master for an equal partner. You don't have to marry an Eric, Elspeth. You can marry whoever you want to." Kitty folded her hands in her lap and sat up straight. "I can assure you, that's exactly what I am going to do."

Chapter 14

Maud stayed until New Year, when she departed with Victoria, Elspeth and Harry on the boat for England, wrapped warmly in an exquisite fur coat. Out of all of them Harry was the most sorry to leave. Kitty recognized love, for that's what it was. It wasn't conventional, but she knew that in his own way Harry loved Joseph like she loved Jack and her heart went out to him. She hugged him tightly and watched him go, his eyes full of regret. Due back at the front in January he wondered whether he'd live to see his inheritance.

Kitty worried constantly about her father and brother but she took great consolation from Jack, knowing that whatever happened he wouldn't go off to war. That was until David Lloyd-George, the British Prime Minister, decided to extend conscription to Ireland. "Bloody good idea!" said Hubert, puffing on his cigar and raising his eyes over his playing cards. "Ireland is part of Great Britain and we have to fight together."

Kitty's heart froze. "That will mean all young men in Ireland will have to fight?" she whispered.

"Absolutely."

The Shrubs, who had come for dinner and a game of whist, weren't so sure. "I can't bear to think of more young men being sent out to die," said Hazel. "Don't you agree, Laurel?"

"I think we should surrender at once and stop the killing," said Laurel.

"Good God, woman, what have you got inside that head of yours? Sawdust?" Hubert spluttered.

"If we surrender, those young men would have died for nothing," said Adeline from the armchair, where she was sipping cannabis tea.

"But they can't make the Irish fight, surely?" said Kitty with forced calmness.

"Of course they can, and they will," said Hubert. "Goddamn it, we have to win the war. Right now we're on the back foot. We need more men. There are plenty here. They can turn their violent intentions in the right direction. Do them good to know who the real enemy is." He turned his attention to his cards again. "Now where were we?"

Kitty felt faint. "I think I need some air," she said, pushing out her chair.

"Oh," said Hubert, let down. "I was enjoying myself. Don't be long."

Kitty went outside where she sat on the steps leading up to the front door and hugged her knees. She didn't think she'd survive if Jack went to war. She gazed up at the stars, bright and twinkling, and wondered what God thought of the mess human beings had made of the world. Her heart ached for

Jack. She longed for him to hold her and reassure her that he'd never go to war. That in spite of the conscription law, he'd refuse. Surely they couldn't make him? She put her head in her hands and squeezed back tears. Somewhere in the distance an owl hooted and she wondered whether Jack heard him too in his house in Ballinakelly, and whether he was thinking of her.

A while later, when she had composed herself, she returned to the library. At first she thought they were all drunk, but then she realized that it was her grandmother's cannabis, which she was generously sharing with her sisters. The Shrubs had flopped onto the sofa and were lying back against the cushions giggling inanely. "Oh, he was a looker!" Laurel was saying, barely able to get her sluggish tongue around the words. "Hazel, tell Adeline what you said to me."

"I can't," Hazel replied before bursting into a fit of laughter. "I truly can't. Our dear mother would turn in her grave."

"You must. We're all family here." Laurel put her hand to her head. "I do feel dizzy."

"Why doesn't he come and shoot anymore?" Hazel asked. "Hubert used to invite him. He was so dashing and brave, like an old-fashioned knight."

"Who?" Kitty asked from the doorway.

"The Duke of Rothmeade," said Hazel. "He was here all the time in the old days. As permanent as this sofa."

"A fine-looking young man he was too," said Laurel. "But he suddenly stopped coming. Now, why was that?"

"Didn't he have a thing for Maud?" Hazel asked, giggling again. "I remember the two of them being joined at the hip and the look on Maud's face—"

"Now you're going too far," said Adeline quickly, cutting her sister off mid-sentence.

"What is it we're drinking, Adeline? It's very strong."

"Cannabis," Adeline replied sleepily. "It's a herb I grow for my nerves."

"She's a witch," said Hubert from the card table, where he was now getting tipsy on a third glass of whiskey. Kitty looked around in astonishment. They were all intoxicated, every one of them.

"Oh, we know she's a witch," said Laurel. "The three of us are witches, aren't we, girls?"

"Why aren't you named after a shrub, Adeline?" Hubert asked.

"I don't know," Adeline replied. "Our mother wasn't a very keen gardener. Perhaps she couldn't think of one." The three sisters dissolved into laughter again.

Adeline filled her teacup, then handed the silver pot to Laurel, who poured greedily before passing it to her sister.

"Kitty, why don't you have some? It's frightfully nice," said Hazel.

Kitty sighed resignedly. If Jack went off to war there'd be no point in living, she thought. "Oh all right, I might as well," she surrendered, recalling the delightful feeling of carelessness it had given her.

"What about our game?" said Hubert from the card table. Kitty took a sip and looked at the Shrubs. They looked back at her, and then, as the herb took over Kitty's senses, they all burst into a fit of uninhibited, delicious laughter.

THE FOLLOWING MORNING Kitty refused to get out of bed. She sent Bridie up to Mr. Trench with the message that she was unwell. Bridie wondered whether they'd had a fight, but Mr. Trench only looked concerned and not at all like a man spurned. "I hope she feels better later," he told Bridie. "If she feels like a gentle walk around the gardens this afternoon, I am at her disposal." Bridie thought him most gentlemanly and envied Kitty the attentions of such a handsome and charming man.

"They say the Irish are going to have to fight," said Kitty dolefully from the bed when Bridie returned. "That means your brothers will have to fight."

"Michael would rather die than fight for the British," said Bridie briskly.

"So would Jack, I'm sure."

At the thought of Jack going off to fight, Bridie was alarmed. "Jack won't fight. None of them will. The British will have another war on their hands; here in Ireland."

"They already do," said Kitty, sitting up and sipping the cup of tea Bridie had brought her. She looked out of the window. The spring sun shone brightly and birdsong wafted on a sugar-scented breeze. "Do you think Jack knows about this?"

"Of course he does. They all do. They're talking of nothing else."

"What are they saying?"

"That they won't fight. They'll have to imprison the entire male population of the country." Bridie sat on the bed. "Michael says the British are playing into their hands. It's good for the cause, is it not?"

"Oh it is. I hadn't thought of it like that," said Kitty, cheering up. She climbed out of bed and began to dress.

"I thought you were sick," said Bridie in surprise.

"I'm feeling a lot better now," Kitty replied cheerfully. "Must be something you put in the tea."

"I put nothing in the tea," said Bridie innocently. "Shall I tell Mr. Trench you're better now?"

"Goodness, no!" said Kitty, laughing.

"He says if you're feeling better he'll walk with you in the gardens."

Kitty smiled. "Oh, I'm not up to that. Anyway I don't want to give him the terrible bug that I have. No, I'll walk alone."

Bridie watched her in confusion. That wasn't the behavior of a woman in love, nor was it the behavior of a sick woman.

When Kitty reached the dining room for breakfast she was surprised to see her grandmother and the Shrubs sitting around the table. "We stayed the night," said Hazel with a smile. "We weren't in any state to go home, were we, Laurel?"

"No we weren't. I don't know what came over us, but it was delightful."

"Your grandfather's gone fishing," said Adeline. "I don't think he could take any more of us."

"We never finished our game," said Hazel.

"I do believe we were winning, Kitty. Tell me, why on earth did we stop?"

Kitty sat down and poured herself a cup of tea. O'Flynn shuffled around the table. "Would you like some eggs, Miss Kitty?" he asked.

"Why not, O'Flynn. It's a lovely day. I might go out for a ride."

"What about Mr. Trench?" said Adeline.

Kitty sighed. "I have a headache," she lied. "I couldn't possibly concentrate today."

Adeline smiled. "I must say Mr. Trench is a saint. I'm sure he'd find more diversion in England."

"I don't think he'd find a prettier pupil than Kitty," said Laurel.

"He certainly wouldn't," Hazel agreed. "I'm sure he's more than a little in love with you."

"Nonsense," said Kitty. "He's the most serious man I've ever come across."

"Not dull though," said Adeline. "He's a very intelligent young man."

"What does he do all day when he's not tutoring you?" Laurel asked. "He can't ride with that leg."

"He reads," Kitty told her. "Reads and reads and reads and when he's done reading, he reads some more." She grinned over her teacup. "I've tried to make him laugh. Oh, how I've tried. But he barely even smiles."

"Well if *you* can't make him smile, Kitty, no one can," said Adeline.

"Give him a taste of your cannabis and I'm sure you'll find he opens up like a boiled mussel," said Laurel.

Hazel laughed in agreement. "Like a boiled mussel," she repeated.

KITTY RAN TO the wall. She retrieved Jack's letter and wandered into the greenhouse to read it. Just as she sat down on the bench she heard quiet and secretive voices. Kitty stood up and slipped the letter down the front of her dress. Hiding behind a large fern, she strained her ears but she couldn't make out what they were saying. Their words came in rushed, sporadic whispers. Careful not to be seen she peered through the leaves.

There, chewing on radishes, were two scruffy children. Kitty was astonished. She hadn't expected to see children. They weren't tinkers but urchins from Ballinakelly. Their hair was matted and dirty, their clothes ragged and frayed, their feet bare. Kitty stood in silence as they munched through lettuce, carrots and raw parsnip. She wanted to tell them that they'd have the most terrible stomach ache if they didn't cook the parsnip first. But she waited until they had had their fill and run off before she returned to the iron bench and her letter.

After she had read Jack's message she decided to put out some food for the children in case they returned the following day. Some bread and butter and slices of ham would satisfy them more than vegetables. It wasn't right that children should go hungry, she reasoned, when they had so much at Castle Deverill. Mrs. Doyle didn't question her when she asked for the food, nor did she look surprised when Kitty took it into the garden. She was used to Lady Deverill making up baskets of provisions for the poor. Kitty arranged the food beneath a fly net on the table where she had spotted the children. Evidence of their snacking could be seen in the radish heads lying scattered at her feet.

As she came in from the garden she bumped into Mr. Trench on his way out. "Ah, Kitty, I'm pleased to see that you're feeling better," he said. Though Kitty wondered why his face did not break into a smile to show her *how* pleased.

"I am, thank you," she replied, trying not to look guilty.

"I'm taking the trap into Ballinakelly. It's the fair today. Why don't you join me? The fresh air is clearly doing you good."

She couldn't think of a suitable excuse and was left with no alternative but to accept. "I would like that very much," she replied politely, thinking that perhaps she'd be lucky and bump into Jack. "Let me get my hat."

As she set off toward the stables she raised her eyes to one of the bedroom windows and saw Bridie's face peering at her through the glass. Her friend waved and watched as Kitty disappeared out of sight. Bridie smiled knowingly. It was plainly obvious that Kitty had arranged the whole diversion so that she could spend time in the garden with Mr. Trench. But why hadn't she confided in her?

It was a warm day. Spring filled the air with birdsong and the fertile scent of renewal. Buds were turning green and beginning to open in the sunshine and the countryside was no longer looking bleak. It was hard to believe, on such a lovely day, that there was disharmony anywhere in the world.

Mr. Mills had got the pony and trap ready and was standing waiting in the stable yard. When he saw Kitty he doffed his cap. "Top of the morning to you, Miss Kitty."

"Good morning, Mr. Mills. Isn't it a fine morning?" she replied.

"It is indeed, Miss Kitty." He looked gravely at Mr. Trench. "Be careful out there," he warned. "There are people who are none too happy at present."

"I will, Mr. Mills," Mr. Trench replied, climbing into the trap and taking the reins. Mr. Mills gave Kitty his hand and helped her up so that she could sit beside her tutor. Mr. Trench shook the reins and the pony set off at a gentle trot.

For a while neither spoke. Kitty wasn't used to being with her tutor outside the classroom and she didn't know what to talk to him about. Mr. Trench kept his eyes on the track ahead.

A gust of wind nearly blew Kitty's hat off, which gave her the opportunity to break the awkward silence. "That was close," she said, holding it down with her hand.

"The wind is an unpredictable thing," said Mr. Trench.

"Oh, it is," Kitty agreed. "Is it so windy in England?"

"Depends on where you are. On the coast it can be very blustery. In the winter there are winds that fell trees."

"What did Mr. Mills mean by unhappy people? Are they hungry?" she asked, thinking of the children she had seen that morning in the greenhouse.

"No one wants to be forced to fight, Kitty."

"Conscription." She sighed. "I know and they shouldn't have to."

"Ireland is part of the United Kingdom, like Wales and Scotland. It's only right that the Irish should play their part as well."

"Many already *are* playing their part, God help them."

"Not enough."

"Do you wish *you* were fighting, Mr. Trench?" Kitty asked.

Mr. Trench was used to Kitty's bluntness. "Yes, I do," he replied, equally blunt.

"I wish Papa had a stiff leg so he didn't have to."

"No you don't. You wouldn't wish it on anybody. One feels a failure."

She looked at him and frowned. That was the first piece of personal information he had ever volunteered. "You're not a failure, Mr. Trench. You might find you're the last man standing. All the young women will throw themselves at you. Your leg might make you the luckiest man in England."

"I doubt that," he replied, embarrassed.

Kitty smiled. "When God takes with one hand He gives with the other."

"Is that so?"

"According to my grandmother and you know that she's right about everything."

At last they reached Ballinakelly. As it was fair day there was no school. Some of the children looked after animals for a few pence while the farmers went to O'Donovan's to get drunk. Others played chase up and down the street like a pack of stray dogs. Groups of women wearing their Bandon cloaks and carrying wicker baskets stood chatting and gossiping. The square was heaving with chickens and sheep, pigs and horses as it did the first Friday of every month. The townspeople mingled tightly with those who had come from neighboring towns and villages, and tinker women weaved among them selling holy pictures and begging. It was a noisy affair and Kitty could hear the sound of music playing over the drone of voices as a trio of violinists busked at the far corner of the square.

Kitty enjoyed the fair. She lifted her chin and searched the faces for Jack. Where there were animals he was sure to be. Mr. Trench tied the pony to a post and went around to help Kitty down, but she had already jumped into the mud and was striding into the crowd.

"Kitty!" he called, running after her. He found her looking at a stall of hanging rabbits, yet to be skinned.

"Poor little things," she said, peering at them. "One minute grazing happily, the next hanging up here by their hind legs, destined for the pot." She sighed. "I suppose people have to eat, but still."

"Well hello, Kitty," said a voice Kitty recognized. She lifted her eyes to see Lady Rowan-Hampton smiling at her beneath a bright blue hat.

"Hello, Lady Rowan-Hampton," said Kitty coolly. Then remembering her manners she added, "I don't think you've met Mr. Trench."

Grace extended her gloved hand. Mr. Trench shook it and bowed politely. "It's a pleasure to meet you," she said with her usual cheeriness.

"He's my tutor," Kitty said.

"Yes, your father mentioned the fine education this young man is giving you."

Kitty frowned. "What else did he tell you?" she asked frostily.

"How proud he is to have such an articulate and opinionated daughter."

"I don't think I can take all the credit for that," said Mr. Trench.

"No, I don't suppose you can. Kitty's always had a mind of her own." Grace laughed. "I imagine you'll be leaving for London at any moment."

"Certainly not," Kitty retorted. "I'm staying here where I belong."

"Well, that's something you and I have in common," said Grace. "Our unwavering love of Ireland."

"As well as a few other things," said Kitty pointedly. Grace frowned. "Good day to you, Lady Rowan-Hampton."

Mr. Trench hurried after her. "Was it really necessary to be rude?" he asked.

Kitty turned to see his face red with indignation. "Why, Mr. Trench, I think you're showing emotion for once."

He ignored her comment. "She seemed a perfectly charming lady."

"Oh she is, perfectly charming. But you don't know the half of it."

"Good reason or not, one should always try to be polite."

Kitty rounded on him fiercely. "Why? Because, if we're not all polite, our true feelings might be revealed and then what? God forbid we show our feelings."

"Now you're being unreasonable."

"Mr. Trench, you're my tutor. You're to teach me history and maths and geography and French. You're not employed to teach me manners. Miss Grieve taught me those and by God did she hammer them home. I was rude to Lady Rowan-Hampton because she has done something unforgivable that I will never forget as long as I live. I don't expect you to understand but the least you can do is remain silent on the matter. Now, I'm going to look at the horses. I shall return to the trap in half an hour. Does that give you enough time to do what *you* want to do?"

Mr. Trench sighed. "It does."

"Good." Kitty marched off and was swallowed into the sea of people.

She went in search of Jack but to her disappointment he was nowhere to be found. She saw his mother talking to Robin Nash, who ran the best dealing yard in Ireland, but she didn't dare ask where Jack was. She sensed Mrs. O'Leary didn't much like her, although she couldn't think why. Among the people were members of the Royal Irish Constabulary in their black uniforms and forage hats, Father Quinn in his long black robes and the Rector, Reverend Daunt, in a tweed suit and bright white clerical collar. Kitty managed to avoid the Rector and Mr. Trench, whom she saw ambling aimlessly among the sheep, looking lost.

After half an hour she walked back to the trap, feeling dissatis-
fied. Mr. Trench was waiting for her, being watched by a surly
bunch of young men in caps and jackets, smoking in the road
outside O'Donovan's. He offered her his hand and she took it,
lifting her skirt and climbing into the trap. Just as they were about
to depart something came flying toward Kitty and struck her in
the eye. She gave a howl of pain and slumped forward, putting
her hand to her eye. Mr. Trench began to shout at the offending
young man, but it was Jack who appeared suddenly and put his
arm around Kitty. When she saw him she cried all the more,
afraid to peel back her hand. With a little gentle coaxing he lifted
her trembling fingers and she realized to her relief that she wasn't
blinded after all, just bruised.

Jack leaped down to punch the man who had thrown the
potato but a constable pushed through the crowd and stood
between them. After a brief discussion it came out that a Mr.
Murphy had thrown the potato because Kitty was a symbol of
England and Mr. Murphy was cross about the pending threat
to send him off to the front against his will. "Will you be pressing charges, Miss Deverill?" asked the constable, holding a defiant Mr. Murphy by the arm.

Kitty would have liked to have seen the man thrown into
prison for his malice, but she looked at Jack and realized that if
he didn't know her and love her as he did he might very well
have thrown the potato himself. "No, I won't," she replied.
"Just realize this, Mr. Murphy. I am as against conscription as
you are, make no mistake. Throwing potatoes at defenseless
young women won't change Mr. Lloyd-George's mind." The
constable let the man go and he slunk back into the throng and
disappeared into O'Donovan's with his band of friends.

"Are you all right?" Jack whispered, perching on the step for a quiet word with her.

"I'm going to have a horrid black eye," she replied, giving him a small smile.

"At least you still have an eye."

She laughed. "Would you still love me if I didn't?"

"You know I would."

"When can we meet?"

"Tomorrow? Down on Smuggler's Bay at four?"

"I'll be there."

He caressed her wounded face with his eyes. "You look after yourself now. Things are going to get rough."

"Tell that Mr. Murphy he has a good aim," she said loudly, remembering that Mr. Trench was seated beside her. "Why doesn't he put it to good use?"

Jack stepped down. "I'm sure he will. Off you go now."

Mr. Trench shook the reins and Kitty tore her eyes away from Jack, who put his hands in his pockets and watched the pony and trap trot off down the road. As they drove to the castle Mr. Trench was very talkative. The drama had injected him with excitement. He gave Kitty his handkerchief with which to wipe her tear-stained face and nurse her bruised eye and he discussed the band of men who were clearly up to no good. "I saw them watching me," he told her, "and I just knew something was going to happen."

But Kitty wanted to explain to Mr. Trench that she was on *their* side. That they had her sympathy and her support, but all she could say was, "What a silly lot. Potato throwing won't get them anywhere."

The following morning her left eye had swollen to the size

of a golf ball. When her grandparents saw it, her grandfather threatened to deal with the potato thrower himself until her grandmother convinced him that *that* sort of bullish behavior would only make matters worse. She told Kitty to rest and applied a cool poultice of comfrey to the bruise. Nonetheless Kitty crept out of the castle to retrieve Jack's note from the wall. He had placed a posy of wild woodbine there too, tied with a piece of string. She brought it to her nostrils and inhaled the sweet perfume and her heart swelled with happiness that Jack belonged to her. When she entered the greenhouse to read his letter she noticed the empty plates at once. The children had returned and they had eaten all the food. She smiled at the thought of those satisfied bellies. But what if word got out and they brought their friends with them tomorrow? She would end up feeding the entire population of children in Ballinakelly.

Chapter 15

In the summer of 1918 the conscription crisis was over but the fighting continued on the Continent and the number of dead grew. The cousins descended once more on Castle Deverill, but a sadness hung over their usually glorious arrival. Beatrice, once so spirited, had expanded in her grief as if armoring herself in fat would defend her beleaguered heart. She now moved around the castle grounds in a stately fashion, like a rudderless galleon with black sails. Augusta lamented that God had not taken *her* in George's place. "He had his whole life ahead of him," she declared. "Whereas I am used up and spent. I only hope God preserves our darling Digby and takes me instead of him. I am ready for the call whenever it may come."

Digby's father Stoke and Hubert went out fishing as usual but they stayed away much longer, finding the company of sad women too emotional for their tastes. They preferred not to talk about their sorrows, but to chew on them in private like dogs with bitter bones.

Maud returned with Victoria and Elspeth, but she quarrelled with Elspeth and tormented Vivien and Leona, who were both engaged to marry Army officers once the war was over. Her jealous remarks were wasted on Beatrice, whose emotions were numbed by a mixture of heartbreak and Adeline's cannabis, but not lost on Elspeth, who confided in Kitty that she was thinking about entering a convent: "The only place on earth I can be free of our mother and the beastly convention of marriage."

Kitty, Celia and Bridie met in Barton's tower, which was the only place in the castle where they were safe from intrusion. Kitty and Celia complained about their sisters and Bridie told them the gossip from the kitchen and how her mother had reported that Victoria had asked her if she knew of a wise woman in Ballinakelly who could help her conceive—Bridie giggled that she'd happily play the part for a sixpence. Barton Deverill listened from his chair and his face shook off its habitual grimace and the corners of his mouth twitched as he inserted comments into their conversation that only Kitty could hear.

In November the war finally came to an end. The fighting ceased. The guns fell silent. But the tremor would vibrate on in the earth the artillery had violated and in the minds of those who had walked through Hell and survived. The euphoria of victory was soon replaced by the sobering realization that almost an entire generation had been killed. Every family had suffered losses. No one had been spared the anguish of mourning. The British Empire had won, but something of the old world had been broken forever.

Bertie, Digby and Harry returned home to their families,

who gratefully received them. Outwardly they looked the same as the men who had left four years before, albeit thinner and a little older, but inwardly they had been irrevocably altered. In the tradition of all Deverill men they drank to blot out the images and they smiled to hide the truth that they never shared, for putting it into words would only breathe life into the memories they wanted so badly to forget.

In December the Irish voted in the general election, the result of which was a landslide victory for the radical Sinn Féin Party, defeating the nationalist Irish Parliamentary Party that had dominated Irish politics since the 1880s. Of the one hundred and five MPs elected, most had fought in the Easter Rising. "By Jove! Who would have predicted the bloody Shinners winning like that, eh?" Hubert huffed over his newspaper.

"I think it was entirely predictable, my dear," said Adeline patiently. "If it hadn't been for the clumsy way the British dealt with the rebels after the Rising, Sinn Féin wouldn't have won the country's support. I suspect the tide is going to turn now and the British will be swept away on the current."

MAUD RETURNED TO Cork for Christmas and the Hunting Lodge was inhabited once again. The dust sheets were lifted, the windows opened and the servants reinstalled to scrub and polish, dust and clean. Maud dismissed Mr. Trench. Kitty was eighteen now, she explained, and required a husband, not a tutor, although she didn't think the former would be so easily found considering that the majority of eligible young men had been slaughtered on the battlefield. Mr. Trench's face darkened with regret and for a moment he looked as if he might break down. Maud was appalled. She couldn't imagine how the young man had grown fond of such a willful and rude child as Kitty. But before he could offer himself Maud added that there were bound to be suitably aristocratic men in London who hadn't been lost on the front lines. "We'll be returning to London soon and I'm sure the matter will be resolved very quickly."

When Mr. Trench said good-bye to Kitty he looked defeated. Kitty thanked him politely for everything he had taught her. "You are a very intelligent young woman," he told her. "I hope you don't waste your fine intellect but put it to good use."

"Oh, I will, Mr. Trench. I hope you have a safe journey back to England."

Mr. Trench let down his guard for a moment. His lips paled, his cheeks drained of color and his brown eyes seemed to darken like damp suede. "Be safe," he said, and his voice, usually so clear and strong, broke. "Ireland is a dangerous place, Kitty, and I'd hate you to come to harm."

"I will be safe," Kitty reassured him firmly. "I am Irish. No one is going to harm *me*."

"That's not what Mr. Murphy thought when he threw his potato."

Kitty gave a sigh. She really couldn't be bothered to explain and wished he'd get on and finish saying good-bye. "Perhaps the potato was meant for *you*, Mr. Trench. Did you not think of that?" Mr. Trench didn't know how to respond. "Well, it doesn't matter now, does it, seeing as you're leaving us. I do hope to see you again someday. You'd better hurry or you'll miss your train." She gave him her hand and he took it, surrendering to her. Unhappily he climbed into the Daimler, now driven by a chauffeur, and allowed himself to be parted from the woman he had grown to love.

BERTIE AND HARRY returned to their old ways, chasing hares and shooting snipe, fishing on the sea and hunting with the Ballinakelly Foxhounds. Harry, who had never much liked hunting, now rode as often as possible because it was the only time he was liberated from his thoughts. And then there was his valet Joseph, who crept into his bed to hold him when the night terrors rose out of the dark to grab him by the throat.

Bertie disappeared for hours, returning late, his skin reeking of Grace's tuberose perfume he no longer bothered to disguise. He rarely spoke to his wife and so she created little dramas to force his attention. Bertie drank more to drown out the noise she made and little by little Grace began to grow weary of her lover's descent into intoxication. Sir Ronald had tolerated her affairs in the past, so long as they were conducted with discretion—after all, he had mistresses of his own in both Dublin *and* London—but now Bertie was becoming increasingly reckless and threatening to tarnish their reputation. "If he can't control his drink," Sir Ronald told his wife, "you will have to find another man to amuse you for I will not have our good name sullied." Grace gave Bertie an ultimatum. He had to choose between her and the bottle. But Bertie didn't think he could live without either.

After Christmas there were the usual hunt meets and hunt balls, point-to-points and social gatherings that gave structure and meaning to the lives of the Anglo-Irish. The country was in a fine state of celebration, and those to whom their sons, brothers and fathers were returned had much to be grateful for. However, while Castle Deverill reverberated with music and laughter the Irish fight for freedom went on beyond its border.

On January 22, 1919, Hubert was reading the *Irish Times* over breakfast when his mustache began to twitch with indignation. "*The Assembly gave the British Government a formal notice to quit and proclaimed this country's complete independence*," Hubert read in disbelief. "It's a bloody disgrace," he gasped. "They won't get away with it, y'know."

"I fear they will do terrible things to get their way," said Adeline calmly.

"One would have thought they had learned their lesson after the Rising," said Hubert. "The British won't accept it."

"My darling," said Adeline. "The Volunteers are growing in numbers thanks to the foolish attempt by the British government to conscript them into the war. They're gaining support all over Ireland. Right here in Ballinakelly too. I fear there will be civil war—"

Hubert cut her off. "I'll deal with the traitors myself if I hear a whiff of support from anyone in *my* employ. I demand loyalty to our king and country." His face had now turned the color of a beetroot.

"You can raise your fist and stamp your foot all you like, my dear, but you won't stop the Irish wanting to govern themselves."

"They're Bolshevists," he continued with a grunt. "Can't they see what the bloody idiots have done in Russia? That's no way to run a country. It's the way to *ruin* a country."

"They're idealists, Hubert."

"Immature dreamers, more like. Any fool can see what Ireland will become if they get their way. They'll destroy agriculture, industry, religion, law and order. We'll be living in a quagmire of lawlessness and papism. It's a disgrace. A bloody disgrace!"

Adeline wandered into the garden. She had had enough of her husband's huffing and puffing. It was icy cold but the sky was a clear, watery blue. She inhaled the fresh sea air and watched a robin perch on the bird table to eat the seed she put out. Thrusting her hands into her pockets she wandered across the grass, her footsteps crunching on the frost, her keen eye taking in the yew hedges and shrubs that looked like they were sprinkled with a thin dusting of confectioners' sugar. She loved Ireland with all her heart and it pained her to think of the violence breaking out across the country in the name of nationalism. She understood Ireland's desire for independence, but why did they have to resort to bloodshed to achieve it? Sometimes she thought it would be safer to leave but that would be defeatist. They belonged at Castle Deverill. Love would always bind them to it.

As she made her way to one of the greenhouses, she noticed a group of ragged children at the door. They were stuffing things into their mouths in great haste. At first she thought they were consuming plants, for what else was there at this time of the year? But then she saw the hunks of bread in their fingers. She quickened her pace, fearing those tinkers and re-membering what had happened to poor Tomas Doyle. As she approached, one of them saw her and nudged his friends. In a moment they had run off like frightened rabbits, disappearing over the vegetable-garden wall. With her heart beating franti-cally she peered around the door frame. Evidence of their feast was plain to see in the row of empty plates. Barely a crumb remained. But who was putting food out for them? It didn't take her long to work it out. There was only one other person in the family who cared for the poor as much as she did.

"Kitty, I believe you have been feeding children in the greenhouse," she said later when her granddaughter came to the castle for tea.

Kitty looked momentarily guilty. "I have," she confessed. "I didn't think you'd mind. The poor mites are so hungry. I can't bear to see a hungry child."

Adeline smiled indulgently. "You should have said. Why don't we organize something in one of the farm barns, rather than encouraging the children to trespass on the castle grounds? You know what your grandfather is like. If he gets wind of it I can't guarantee he won't fire at them like rats and we wouldn't want *that* on our consciences!"

"We could talk to the school. Perhaps we can organize hot-soup lunches once or twice a week?"

"We could get the Shrubs involved. It would give them something to do," Adeline suggested.

"That's a capital idea, Grandma."

"And Grace Rowan-Hampton. She's already giving children free English lessons. I think we should rally the ladies of Ballinakelly. It's our responsibility to look after those who don't have the means to feed themselves. Grace is a life-force. We need women like her. Women who get things done."

Kitty stiffened. She hadn't seen Grace since the fair the previous spring. "Yes, Grandma," she said. "She's certainly a woman who gets what she wants." Her remark was lost on Adeline, who was already thinking of the other ladies she could approach. "We must make ourselves useful," she said with deliberation. "And be seen doing it," she added craftily.

Kitty wandered back to the Hunting Lodge with a heavy heart. She really didn't want Grace involved in their soup kitchen. Her grandmother was the most perceptive of women; why hadn't she noticed how devious Grace was? That beneath her sugary coating she was a manipulative, conniving seductress? When she reached the house she went upstairs and threw herself onto her bed with a sigh. A moment later there came a light knocking on the door. She knew from habit that it was Bridie. "Come in," she called.

Bridie opened the door. She didn't have much time to gossip with Kitty now that Elspeth had returned to Cork, for she had to look after the two of them. "I have news," she said in a low voice, hurrying over to the bed.

"What news?" Kitty asked, propping herself up on her elbow.

"It's Miss Elspeth. She's being courted by Mr. MacCartain."

"Peter MacCartain?"

"Yes, that's him."

Kitty sat up. "Goodness. How did you find out?"

Bridie flushed. "Because he just came to the back door asking for her."

"The *back* door?"

"Miss Elspeth winked at me and put her finger over her lips."

"Mama will kill her if she finds out." Kitty grinned. "Well, I'm happy for her. I didn't think she was cut out for a convent."

"I think she's in love, Kitty. Her face was all pink and smiling. I don't think I've ever seen her so happy."

"I'm astonished she's managed to hide it from Mama." Kitty lay down on the bed again and sighed heavily.

"What's the matter, Kitty?" Bridie asked, perching on the end. "You're not missing Mr. Trench, are you now?"

"Mr. Trench? Goodness, Bridie, whatever gave you that idea?"

"So, you're not in love with him?"

"In love with him? With Mr. Trench?" Kitty sat up again. "I couldn't be less in love with him. He's the dullest man I've ever met."

Bridie frowned. "Then what's all the sighing for?"

Kitty laughed. "You thought I was sighing over Mr. Trench?"

"Well, you've been sighing a lot recently."

"I think I'd have to be desperate to want to marry Mr. Trench."

Bridie looked at her seriously. "Do you ever think of marriage, Kitty?"

"Sometimes," Kitty said dismissively as if it was of no importance. "Do you?"

Bridie smiled shyly. "Sometimes."

"Who would you like to marry, Bridie?" Bridie looked down at her fingers nervously. Kitty narrowed her eyes. "There is someone, isn't there?" She was appalled that she hadn't noticed. "Tell me, who is he? Does he love you back?"

Bridie's forehead creased into a frown. "I don't think he loves me back, Kitty. But I know he likes me, which is a start, isn't it?"

"Is it one of the servants? Is it John McGivern?" she asked, referring to the second footman.

"No!" Bridie screwed up her nose. "It's Jack."

Kitty stared at Bridie. So deft was she at keeping secrets that her face gave away nothing of the horror she felt at Bridie's confession. "Jack O'Leary?" she said.

"The very same."

"How long have you loved him?"

"Years and years," Bridie replied, and her face flowered into a faraway smile. "I've been wanting to tell you, but I thought you'd laugh."

"Why would I laugh?"

"Because I'm not good enough for the likes of him. His mother would want better for Jack."

"Has he given you any encouragement?" Kitty asked, averting her eyes because she felt bad for asking when she already knew the answer.

"No." Bridie lowered her eyes. "But we're friends, so . . ." She gave a helpless shrug.

"Oh Bridie." Kitty sighed, sitting up again. "Do you think it's wise to pin your hopes on someone you might not be able to have?"

"There's no one else, Kitty. No one else like Jack." Bridie's eyes brimmed with tears. "I'd follow him to the ends of the earth, I would."

"Does he know?"

"He does not."

"Does anyone else know?"

"No."

Kitty took a deep breath, trying to think what advice she would give were she not in love with Jack herself. "Surely there must be someone else in Ballinakelly?"

Bridie shook her head. "Jack's not like the others."

"No, I don't suppose he is," said Kitty.

Bridie put her hand on Kitty's knee. "One day you'll know what it is to love a man like I love Jack. I hope you'll be luckier than me, Kitty."

When Bridie left, Kitty flopped back onto her pillows again, in despair. She put her hand to her forehead and groaned. What a mess! The irony was that neither of them could have Jack. Bridie was too low born, Kitty too high. If her mother balked at the idea of Elspeth marrying Peter MacCartain how would she feel about Kitty marrying Jack O'Leary? Maud had no interest in her daughters for themselves but for how they reflected on *her*. Victoria, Countess of Elmrod, enabled her to hold up her head in London society. Elspeth MacCartain would bring her shame. Kitty O'Leary would finish her off completely. The thought made Kitty laugh out loud. But it was a hollow, miserable laugh. And what of her father? She stopped laughing. He was too busy drinking himself into oblivion in the arms of Lady Rowan-Hampton to notice what his daughters got up to.

IT WAS A few days before Kitty was able to see Jack again. They hid in the greenhouse, sheltering from the rain. He took her hands. "It's going to get nasty, Kitty," he warned. "They've declared war on the British. There's going to be violence, as the British aren't going to give over so easily. I don't think it's safe for you to remain in Ireland."

"I'm Irish," Kitty protested defiantly.

"Saying it doesn't make it so, Kitty. You're Anglo-Irish and that's different. You're the enemy in their eyes and you're not safe. I'm not going to let you stay when you could just as easily sit it out in London until it blows over."

"I'm not going anywhere!" she retorted. "I'm not leaving you and I'm not leaving Castle Deverill. It's my home and I love it. And I love you, Jack O'Leary, to the marrow of your bones." She gave him a winning smile.

Jack took her face in his hands. "And I love *you*, Kitty, which is why I want you safe where I don't have to worry about you." He kissed her.

She closed her eyes and savored it. "I want to help."

"Kitty . . ."

"I *can* help," she insisted. "There must be a way for me to be useful."

"I'm not letting you get involved."

She folded her arms. "Well, I'm not going anywhere and that's the end of it."

"You're as stubborn as a mule."

"But a great deal prettier," she added with a grin.

"You worry me, Kitty."

"That's not *my* problem," she replied tartly.

"It will be when you discover it's not even safe to leave the castle gate."

His anxious expression unnerved her. "But *you* could get into trouble, Jack." She took his hand and pressed it to her cheek. "Please be careful."

"We'll have the British on their knees, see if we don't," he replied, but somehow that didn't release the grip that had suddenly taken hold of her belly and was squeezing it hard.

IT WAS DARK when Michael and Sean Doyle, Jack O'Leary and six other men from the Third West Cork Brigade of the Irish Republican Army set out toward the Royal Irish Constabulary barracks in Ballinakelly. Black clouds rolled across the sky and the wind whipped in off the sea. They hugged the walls as they edged noiselessly down the back streets of the town, their faces hidden behind masks, their caps pulled low, their breath shallow and full of tension. They had trained for this sort of attack in one of Hanratty's barns hidden in the hills, along with map-reading, ambushes and street-fighting, and were bristling with patriotic zeal and a heightened sense of camaraderie as they came together for their cause, knowing that most of Co. Cork was on their side. Only Michael had a gun and very little ammunition at that. His plan was not to waste any precious bullets.

They stopped when the austere gray building of the police barracks came into view. It was small and unimpressive, having once been a mediocre hotel. The bigger British garrisons were stationed in Bandon, Clonakilty, Dunmanway, Skibbereen, Bantry and Castletownbere, but intelligence had been gleaned that here in this insignificant barracks was a disproportionate amount of artillery hidden in the cellar, if only the rebels could break their way in to steal it.

Michael signaled to the men and two members of the group broke away and scurried down to the square where the fair took place on the first Friday of every month. It was quiet and still now in the dead of night, the mud frozen on the ground, the only movement the wind blowing swiftly across it. A moment later the sound of an exploding grenade shattered the tranquillity and set the blood racing at Jack's temples. He braced himself for what was to follow. If it wasn't for the adrenaline coursing through his veins he would have surely felt the icy hand of fear squeeze his heart. There was an ominous pause, as if the town held its breath, before light suddenly glowed in the windows of the barracks and men spilled out into the cold, buttoning up their shirts and belting their trousers, then pointing their guns at the unseen enemy. Their confusion was palpable.

Michael held up his hand as the police ran down to the square, leaving the barracks sparsely guarded. His men trembled like racehorses in their starting blocks, eager to commence, waiting for the hand to drop and for the action to begin. At last Michael gave the command and they ran forward, hurrying into the building where startled constables reached for their guns only to be met with fists and bayonets as the rebels ruthlessly beat them to the ground.

Suddenly the room was ablaze. Jack kept guard at the top of the stairs as the men ran down to steal the guns. A moment later their feet were heard clattering on the steps and they emerged triumphant with revolvers, rifles and ammunition. With the building now in flames, consuming the files of papers and wooden furniture as if they were kindling, the rebels exited through the back window and, as planned, dispersed in different directions, confusing the enemy still further.

Jack took a back street, but soon realized he was being pursued. He glanced over his shoulder to see two constables chasing after him. He jumped over a garden gate, across a patch of grass, which glittered in the moonlight with frost, and over a fence into a neighboring yard. With his heart beating like a military drum he ran for his life.

At length he came to a large pink house set back from the street with an iron gate and a neatly kept garden. Noticing the ground-floor window was ajar, he leaped over the wall, lifted the window and threw himself inside. He landed with a thump but managed to reach up and close the window just as the two policemen came running around the corner. "Where did he go?" asked one.

"I dunno," replied the other. Jack cowered on the floorboards.

Upstairs Hazel was awoken by the sound of the thud and subsequently the voices outside. Frightened, she lit her candle and tiptoed into Laurel's bedroom next door.

"Laurel, wake up!" she hissed, shaking her sister by the shoulder.

"What is it?" asked Laurel in alarm.

"Did you hear a noise? A thud. Downstairs."

"No, I didn't."

"There are voices outside." Hazel hastened to the window and pulled back the curtain. The two policemen were still looking up and down the street in bewilderment.

"What do you see?" Laurel asked.

"Policemen."

"What are they doing?"

"Looking for something."

"At this time of night?"

"It appears so. They're walking away now. I don't think they've found it."

"Good."

"They don't look very happy."

"We can ask them what it was tomorrow and offer our help. We're rather good at finding things."

"Do you remember Hubert's reading glasses?" said Hazel, dropping the curtain.

"Of course I do. They were down the back of the sofa. And Adeline's necklace?"

"We didn't find Adeline's necklace," Hazel corrected her.

"No, we didn't. I quite forgot." She sighed. "We must have another look."

"Good night, Laurel," said Hazel.

"Good night, Hazel," said Laurel.

Jack waited for the policemen to leave, then very quietly so as not to disturb the person sleeping upstairs he lifted the window and squeezed out like a burglar. When he was sure it was safe, he left by the gate and headed for home.

Chapter 16

Toward the end of 1919 the anti-British feeling was spreading across the country like a stain, and the Shrubs, busy in Ballinakelly with the soup kitchen they had set up with Adeline in the schoolhouse, were the first to notice the slights. The locals who failed to doff their caps, the schoolboys who sneered, the farmers who refused to give way at the gate, the shop girl who declined to serve. Every snub was sharply perceived and eagerly reported over tea in the castle.

"I swore a young lad threw a stone at me this morning as I walked out of the butcher's," said Laurel indignantly, holding her teacup in a trembling hand. "I don't think I imagined it. When I had words with him he sneered. Yes, that's the word, sneer. He looked perfectly pleased with himself."

"The audacity of the boy!" Hazel exclaimed. "He knows he won't be beaten for it. You see, it filters down from the parents. They think it's all right to insult an old lady . . ."

"An *English* old lady," added Laurel, inhaling through dilated nostrils.

"A stone today, a rock tomorrow," said Hazel darkly.

"But it was the look in his eye that caught my attention. It
was the look of a rebel. Give that child a few years and he'll be
firing a gun, mark my words."

Adeline, who was quietly painting at the window, looked up.
"Extraordinary, considering we're feeding their children."

"Feeding their children or not, we're the enemy, Adeline,"
said Laurel. "Eaten bread is soon forgotten."

"They'd be pleased to see the back of us," Hazel agreed,
pursing her lips.

"Do you know, now I come to think of it, Mr. O'Callaghan
did not say good morning to me when I walked into his shop,"
Laurel added, dropping her teacup into its saucer. "He ignored
me until I said good morning to *him*. Then he simply nodded."

"Nodded?" Hazel asked.

"Nodded." Laurel narrowed her eyes and her mouth hardened at the perceived offense. "Oh, the insolence, Hazel. I'm
afraid the situation is very bad indeed."

As the months passed, the slights became more offensive
until a stone was thrown through the Shrubs' window, causing
them great distress. Adeline invited them to move into the
castle at once. "We have plenty of rooms here," she said happily. "And if anyone dares throw a stone at one of *our* windows
he shall be met with a bullet in his backside before he can
shout, 'Jesus, help us.'"

However, when news reached them of their friends the
Goodes' house being burned down in Bandon, their anxiety
turned to real fear. "It'll be us next," Laurel warned, reaching

for her glass of sherry and taking a loud slurp. "Those Shinners will stop at nothing."

"Poor Arthur and Lizzie only escaped with their lives. The whole house was reduced to ash in one night. It went up like straw apparently," said Adeline.

"How can we protect ourselves from men like that?" Hazel asked in distress. "We're no longer safe in our own homes. Do you not think we should all pack up and leave? So many have."

Adeline shot her a fierce look. "We're not leaving!" she exclaimed. "We have nothing to fear from the Shinners. It is well known that we are good to our tenants and always have been. Hubert is held in great affection by the people of Ballinakelly. No one would dare lay a finger on him or his home." This seemed to satisfy the Shrubs.

Laurel wandered over to the card table and ran her fingers over the velvet surface. "At least we're all here together," she said. "There's strength in numbers. And a rubber of bridge will surely take our minds off our woes."

SINCE KITTY HAD turned nineteen in September Maud had begun to focus her attention, so sorely lacking in the past, on her youngest daughter. It was time she got married, but to whom? There were no suitable young men in Ireland; they were all too poor or too low born. No, there was only one place to go, and that was London. But when she brought up the subject one evening at supper, Kitty did not respond in the way she had hoped. "I'm not going to London," Kitty said calmly, regarding her mother with the coolness of someone who knows she will win the argument.

Maud turned to Bertie for support. "We are not going to

find her a suitable match here in Cork," she said. "Cousin Beatrice would be very happy to have us if Victoria is at Broadmere. Kitty never had a London Season because of the war, but there is still time."

Bertie's rheumy eyes swam a moment as he looked from his wife to his daughter, then back again. "Does Kitty want to find a husband?"

"It's not a question of want, but must. If she leaves it too late she will be left on the shelf like Elspeth." Elspeth's lips tightened around her secret. Harry looked down at his food. He hated confrontation.

"I don't want to go to London," Kitty said. "I'm staying here at Castle Deverill. If you want me to leave, you will have to drag me away by my hair."

"Kitty, how dare you speak to me like that!" Maud exclaimed, flushing pink.

"How, Mother? Directly?"

"Don't be insolent. I thought Miss Grieve taught you manners."

Kitty held out her palms and glared at her mother with such bitterness Maud froze. "Miss Grieve was a tyrant and a bully. She taught me to be strong."

Maud looked away. It was easier to ignore than to take responsibility for unpleasant things that happened in the past. She appealed to Bertie. "Say something, for goodness' sake. How can you sit there and listen to her rudeness and do nothing about it?"

Bertie took a swig of wine. "If she doesn't want to go, my dear, I'm not going to force her. That would *not* be very seemly."

Maud stiffened like a threatened cat. "I am always alone. No one ever backs me up. I'm the only one thinking of our daughters' futures. I could sit pretty and let them all get on with it, but you won't thank me when they marry unsuitable men who drag the family name into the mud."

"Is Victoria happy?" Bertie asked.

"What's happiness got to do with it?" said Maud.

"You see, that's the flaw in your plan, my dear. If you put their happiness and not your ambition first I doubt they'd be so reluctant to consent to your plans."

"Marriage has got nothing to do with happiness. You should know that better than anyone." She turned to Kitty. "Then you won't come with me and Elspeth?"

Elspeth slowly put down her knife and fork. "I'm not coming either," she said, not quite as boldly as her sister. The two girls caught eyes in silent camaraderie. Harry's jaw dropped in astonishment; Elspeth had always been a meek girl.

Maud's ears turned scarlet. "Elspeth?"

Elspeth's eyes flicked to Kitty for encouragement. "I'm sorry, Mama. But I don't want to go to London."

Maud smiled as if she had just worked out who was behind Elspeth's subversion. "Very well," she replied quietly. "I'm not going to fight you. God forbid I put your happiness above my own! In any case, there's no point if I don't have your father's support. But don't think you'll find suitable husbands here."

"Will *you* be staying, my dear?" Bertie asked his wife.

"I will stay for Harry," she replied, lifting her chin. Harry looked embarrassed as the weight of her gaze fell on *him*. "When it's no longer safe I will persuade you to come to London. You're not going to find an heiress in Cork and you'll need an heiress if you're to inherit the castle. God only knows where the money will come from otherwise." She turned to her daughters. "If you silly girls want to sit it out, you're welcome to do so, but don't snivel with remorse and regret when I tell you I told you so." With that she placed her napkin on the table and left the room. Kitty grinned at Elspeth, who began to tremble.

Their father waited for the door to slam, then acted as if nothing had happened. "Tell me, Harry, how do you like your new hunter? She goes well, doesn't she?"

THE FOLLOWING WEEK Peter MacCartain made an appointment to meet with Kitty's father. They talked for a whole hour in the library while Kitty and Elspeth tried to listen at the door, but the men's voices were so low they could hear nothing but mumbling. When at last the door opened Peter walked into the hall to find Elspeth waiting for him. "What did he say?" she hissed, accompanying him outside.

"He has to talk it over with your mother."

Elspeth's face fell. "She'll never agree."

Peter squeezed her hand. "Perhaps not, but your father prizes your happiness."

"Then there's hope?"

Peter grinned. "Plenty of hope, my darling," and he kissed her briskly on the cheek.

There ensued the most terrible row between Bertie and Maud. Kitty and Elspeth eavesdropped in the room above the library through a glass pressed to the floorboards. Maud was screaming at Bertie, her voice rising and falling, the word "I" punctuating every phrase as she turned each argument around to herself. "I've had a terrible year," she wailed. "And now this! How much more do I have to endure?" A moment later she added, "After all I've done for that child! A mother's life is nothing but self-sacrifice. The least you can all do is appreciate what I do for you!" Elspeth wondered whether there was, in fact, any hope at all, and tears welled in her doe eyes as she declared resolutely that if she couldn't marry Peter she'd marry Jesus and become a nun.

The house fell silent and Elspeth was duly summoned to the library. Kitty remained in the room above, her ear glued to the glass. The voices were soft but she could hear her father's every word. He would give his consent if it was what Elspeth wanted. "If the war has taught me anything, Elspeth," he said solemnly, "it is the value of love. Love for one's fellow soldiers, love for one's children, love for life. When I was at the front it was all that mattered. So, if you think Peter can make you happy, you have my blessing."

"Oh Papa!" Elspeth cried and Kitty imagined them embracing. Her mother remained silent: her objections had been loud enough. Kitty knew he would never give his consent to her marrying Jack, even if Jack would make her happy. There was a limit to his beneficence. Not only was Jack a different class and a different religion, but he was an Irishman. Her father would never stand for a Sinn Féiner as a son-in-law.

A while later Elspeth ran up the stairs two at a time and burst into the room where Kitty was waiting for her. "He said yes!" she exclaimed, throwing her arms around her sister. "If it wasn't for you I'd never have had the strength to defy Mama." Elspeth was trembling. "But I did it and Papa says I can marry Peter if he makes me happy."

"And Mama?" Kitty asked.

"She left the room as white as a sheet."

MAUD LOCKED HER bedroom door and sank into the chair in front of her dressing table. She put her face in her hands and stared at her reflection. Where did it all go wrong? she asked herself. Didn't she raise Elspeth with a good moral compass? She knew which way pointed north: how hard was it to follow? But she now insisted on marrying an Anglo-Irishman with no money to his name. Acclaim for being one of the best huntsmen in the land was not going to pay for their lifestyle. What would become of Elspeth in a country that was unraveling around their ears? Didn't she realize that her future was in England, where it was safe? Victoria had chosen well, she was a countess of a great country, not a Mrs. of nowhere. Maud rubbed her temples. One day Hubert would die and *she* would become Lady Deverill, but of what? A castle that was once one of the greatest in Ireland, but was now nothing more than a pile of stones with precious little land to call its own, surrounded by rebels intent on hounding them all out. What good was a castle in Ireland? She cursed herself for her own foolish choice of husband. As for happiness, how long had it been since she was happy? She bit her lip. She couldn't tell; it had been too many years. If one was going to be unhappily married the least one could do was marry an aristocrat with a stately home, pots of money and a grand title pertaining to the greatest empire on earth. Didn't Elspeth understand that there was consolation in *that?*

AT THE BEGINNING of the following year the British sent a special task force to Ireland to reinforce the police. Due to a shortage of traditional bottle-green uniforms they were given khaki trousers and black berets, a combination of colors that inspired their subsequent nickname: "Black and Tans." Shortly after they arrived, Hubert invited their colonel to dinner at the castle. A tall, oily man with glossy brown hair and a thick thatch of a mustache neatly trimmed above pink fleshy lips, Colonel Manley had returned from the war with a reputation for heroism and an equally high regard for himself. Hubert greeted him warmly, patting him on the back and offering him a glass of whiskey. "It's a good thing you've arrived, Colonel Manley," said the old man, showing him into the drawing room. "We're in a state of emergency. This sort of uncivilized behavior simply can't go on."

"You can rest assured, Lord Deverill, that we will see that it doesn't," Colonel Manley replied confidently. "We'll put Paddy in his place!"

"I'm glad to hear it," said Hubert. "The ladies will feel safer with you lot about."

When the Shrubs came down for dinner with Adeline, Colonel Manley bowed, most certainly *not* a nod, Laurel reported later, and brought their hands up to be tickled by his mustache, which they found thrilling. He sat on Adeline's right with Hazel on his right and Laurel opposite, gazing eagerly into his clear blue eyes that shone with equal brilliance on all three sisters.

"Charming man," said Hazel, when the ladies retired to the drawing room after dinner, leaving the men to their cigars and port.

"One has confidence in a man like that, wouldn't you say?" said Laurel.

"I don't know," Adeline deliberated. "I think he has a cruel glint in his eye."

"You think he was mocking us?" Hazel asked.

"Well, he knows how to compliment a lady," said Laurel. "He's a gentleman—only a *true* gentleman knows how to get the right balance between flirtation and good manners."

"If his eyes have a cruel glint, Adeline, it might be just what these people need to put them back in line. I must inform the colonel that only yesterday the shop girls in Flanagan's were sneering at me . . ." and Hazel sank into the sofa to tell her sisters all about it.

As WINTER THAWED into spring Bertie saw less and less of Grace even though he was trying to consume a reduced amount of alcohol and conduct their affair with the utmost discretion, as he had before the war. She claimed she had business to attend to in Dublin and disappeared for weeks at a time, which left him as heartbroken as a lovesick schoolboy. He saw Sir Ronald out hunting and at the races, but Grace, usually such a keen horsewoman, was often absent, and he missed her dreadfully. It had been *her* letters and *her* words of encouragement that had supported him through the war, like the wind beneath the wings of an eagle, he thought unhappily. Without her he didn't have the will to fly but remained earthbound and in despair like a miserable chicken.

Maud was no longer speaking to him. Bertie welcomed her silence but he didn't welcome the unpleasant atmosphere she created in the house. She was rude to the servants and ruder still to her daughters; only Harry was untouched by her desire to inflict gloom on everyone around her. While her daughters kept a safe distance from their mother, Harry remained close out of guilt and loyalty. Maud was adept at manipulating her son with a mixture of emotional blackmail and favoritism and she was determined not to lose him, as she had clearly lost Elspeth. If Kitty was the influence behind Elspeth's surprising rebellion she was damned if she was going to let Harry slip into her power as well.

One morning Bridie was leaving Kitty's bedroom with the dirty linen when she saw Mr. Deverill sitting in a heap at the other end of the corridor. At first she thought she should pretend she hadn't seen him and disappear behind the green baize door. But compassion overcame her caution and she put down the linen and approached him. "Mr. Deverill, are you all right, sir?" she asked. Bertie looked up at her, his eyes cloudy and alien. "Can I get someone to help you? Mr. O'Lynch, Mrs. Deverill?"

At the mention of his wife's name he seemed to come alive. "No no . . ." he stammered, trying to get up. Watching him there, floundering on the floor, impelled her to assist him. She held his arm and let him use her as a lever to push himself up. When he reeled, she held him tighter.

"Are you all right?" she repeated lamely, for it was clear that he wasn't.

"Take me to my room," he said, leaning on her. They walked slowly down the corridor. Once in his bedroom she made to leave. He sat on the side of the bed and shook his head. "I'm sorry you had to see that, Bridget."

"It's Bridie, sir," she corrected him. "I'm Miss Kitty's lady's maid."

"Bridie," he repeated.

Suddenly she noticed a trickle of blood running down the side of his face from his head. "You're bleeding, sir."

"Am I?" he asked, putting trembling fingers to the wound.

She hurried to the bathroom and returned with a towel. "May I, sir?" she asked. He nodded and frowned as if he wasn't quite sure why he was bleeding. As she dabbed his injury she could smell the alcohol seeping from his pores. "I think I'd better call for Mr. O'Lynch, sir," she said, referring to his valet.

"I must have fallen and hit my head," he muttered. "That's what happened. I hit my head. How silly of me."

"I think I should call for Mr. O'Lynch, sir," she said again.

"If you must."

She rang the bell beside the bed. "Can I get you a glass of water?" She went to the dresser where there was a jug of water and a glass.

"Thank you, Bridget," he said, taking it.

"It's Bridie, sir."

"Bridget to me, Bridget." He took the towel and looked at the bloodstains in bewilderment. Then he put it to his head again. Bridie noticed his hand was shaking. "You're a good girl, Bridget, and a pretty girl too. Let's keep this just between us, all right?"

Bridie smiled. "Of course, sir. Thank you, sir." She bobbed a curtsy and left the room. She retrieved the linen she had discarded on the floor and made her way back up the corridor, passing Mr. O'Lynch hurrying the other way.

"What are you up to, Bridie?" he asked.

"Fetching Miss Kitty's linen, Mr. O'Lynch."

"Then be quick about it," he said, marching on.

Bridie hummed a tune as she washed the linen. That was the first time anyone had ever said she was pretty.

THE SHRUBS REPORTED insults daily, taking unnecessary trips into Ballinakelly just so that they could return loaded with more ammunition for Colonel Manley. Every morning over breakfast, Hubert reported "atrocious acts of violence" committed by the "bloody Shinners." He would thrust his nose into the *Irish Times* and grunt and groan like an old walrus at the tales of murder and arson against the British Army and their property. "It's time Colonel Manley and his men showed their mettle," he said before describing the outrages to the women as they drank their tea and buttered their soda bread.

The Black and Tans were quick and decisive in their response to the atrocities. Rumors spread of reprisals carried out all over Ireland with the murder and abuse of innocent people. Shops and hay barns, homes and businesses were destroyed. Men were stopped and searched at random, shot at, assaulted, arrested, tortured, threatened and deported. It seemed that the Black and Tans could do just about anything they liked, without censure. "They're above the law," Jack told Kitty when they were able to meet at the Fairy Ring. "Colonel Manley's the most hated man in Ballinakelly. He doesn't think twice about killing innocent men if he thinks it'll terrorize people into line."

"Be careful, Jack," said Kitty anxiously. "Keep your head down. You have to be above suspicion."

"I don't like to say this, Kitty, but your grandfather must be careful. If I were him I wouldn't socialize with the likes of Manley."

"He only came to dinner."

"I know, but word gets round and he'll get into trouble."

"Grandpa's old."

"And we don't want him to see his grave before it's time."

Kitty blanched. "Ballinakelly people are loyal . . ."

"No they're not, Kitty," Jack growled. He took her arms as if he wanted to shake her. "It's war. It's not about soup kitchens and feeding the poor—they resent you all the same. Shooting those men after the Easter Rising did the British no favors. Oppressing the people with violence will only deepen their hatred and unite them in their determination to be free." He released her and wrapped his arms around her instead, pulling her against him with a ferocity that shocked her. "I wish to God you'd leave."

"Don't, Jack."

"I fear for your safety."

"You'll keep me safe."

He squeezed her hard. "I can't. The only way to be safe is to go to London—"

"I love you, Jack."

"Right now I wish you didn't." He buried his face in her neck. "And I wish to God I didn't love *you*. It's a blessing and a curse."

Chapter 17

Due to the violence Digby and Beatrice decided to break years of tradition and spend the summer months at Deverill Rising, their country estate in Wiltshire. The British press was full of the atrocities being committed in Ireland in the name of nationalism and they feared for the safety of their Anglo-Irish cousins. But Hubert and Adeline had faith in the British government and were certain that with the swift and efficient response of Colonel Manley, and other men like him, peace would be restored.

"He needs our support, Kitty," Hubert explained when his granddaughter tried to discourage him from entertaining Colonel Manley at the castle.

"Surely you have to be seen to be *above* the conflict, Grandpa?" she argued.

"If I was younger I'd take my gun and patrol the streets myself," Hubert responded. "Manley is our ticket to peace in this county and we must show our allegiance. It wasn't with a weak heart that Barton Deverill, the first Lord Deverill, won his title and land but by showing his loyalty to the King. We must do the same and uphold the family name."

Kitty sighed heavily. There was no point arguing with her grandfather. He was born in a different century when the Great British Empire was at the height of its power. So, to Kitty's despair, Colonel Manley became a frequent guest at the dining table at Castle Deverill and she had to endure his disingenuous charm and condescension, for in his eyes all women were as butterflies, to be admired, played with or crushed, depending on his whim. One of his favorites was Grace Rowan-Hampton, who was a regular visitor with her husband, Sir Ronald, when she wasn't in Dublin. Kitty had to suffer her, too, and endure the sight of her father watching his mistress from across the table while her mother's mouth grew thinner and thinner with resentment until it disappeared altogether.

WHILE THE CASTLE remained entrenched in the past, fearful of change, Ballinakelly was moving toward a different future. The town was seething with anti-British feeling and fertile with plotters who were sprouting in every dark corner like mushrooms: the fight for freedom went on. Bridie had the evenings off, while Kitty ate dinner downstairs in the dining room or up at the castle with her grandparents. Those five-course dinners would go on for hours so Bridie would run home, taking the shortcut through the woods, to find her brothers sitting huddled around the table with friends, talking in low voices over tumblers of stout. As she lifted the latch the room would fall silent and the men would stare at the door in fear of the Black and Tans until they saw that it was only Bridie. Then they'd put their heads together again and resume their plotting like a gang of thieves, a deck of cards at the ready to disguise their business in case of a raid.

Jack was often there. He'd smile at her as she entered and she'd smile back, encouraged by the affection in his eyes. She'd make herself a basin of hot milk, bread and sugar, sit in her mother's rocking chair and crush the bread into a mush while the men talked of stealing guns, ambushing the Auxiliaries and murdering colonel Manley. It was during those twilight hours that Bridie would hear stories of the colonel's brutality. The innocent men arrested, tortured and even killed as he went about the county in search of information like a dragon breathing fire indiscriminately. No one was more hated in Ballinakelly than Colonel Manley.

In response to the increasing bloodshed the British government declared martial law in much of southern Ireland. The Irish Republican Army was at last recognized as an army in the field instead of a band of murderous rebels. On Sunday, November 21, fourteen British soldiers were assassinated in Dublin and the Royal Irish Constabulary punished the people by opening fire on innocent spectators watching a football match, killing fourteen and wounding many others. That December the violence came to Cork with the burning of the city by British forces. Hubert read the *Irish Times* but failed to make any comment. He had run out of puff like an old steam engine that has at last reached the end of the line. It was all too horrific to contemplate and too close for comfort, for Cork City was a mere fifty miles from Ballinakelly. After that he retreated into his own world, where snipe and rabbits were plentiful, foxes fit for the chase and the weather fine for the hounds. He discussed horses, the races and the good old days when he was a boy, when the local people had had respect for the family and loyalty to the Crown, but the War of Independence had finally worn him down.

Adeline indulged him while the Shrubs grew anxious. If Hubert was scared, then what was the hope for *them*? They sipped Adeline's cannabis tea, played whist and prayed, for only God could get them out of *this* mess.

In January 1921 news reached the castle that Colonel Manley had been killed just outside Ballinakelly. "Good God!" Hubert exclaimed, hanging up the telephone receiver in the hall and walking into the dining room where Adeline and the Shrubs were having breakfast. "That was Lieutenant Driscoll. Colonel Manley has been murdered." The women gasped. Laurel dropped her teacup with a splash. "In an old farmhouse along the Dunashee road, yesterday evening. They only found his body this morning. Bloody idiot went without an escort. Why would he do that, do you think? Eh?" He sat down, suddenly looking every one of his seventy-four years. "Why, only two days ago he was sitting here at our dining-room table."

Adeline shook her head. "There will be terrible consequences for Ballinakelly," she said anxiously, thinking of the innocent civilians who would suffer the reprisals.

"This is an unfortunate setback." Hubert shook his head. "Manley was a good man."

"What happened?" Laurel asked, as pale as egg white.

"Yes, do tell us the details, Hubert," Hazel implored.

"Driscoll didn't have much information. He said Manley had set out along the Dunashee road yesterday evening with only one of his men . . ." Hubert looked at Adeline and frowned. "Surely he of all people knew how dangerous it is on those remote roads!"

"What happened to the man who was with him?"

"Shot."

"Dreadful!" Hazel gasped.

"So what happened to the colonel?" Laurel pressed.

"He was knifed in the ribs."

"Dreadful!" Hazel gasped again.

"Who was he meeting in that farmhouse?" Adeline pondered.

"The day is for the living, the night is for the dead," said Laurel.

"What was he up to, do you think?" Adeline narrowed her eyes. "I'd put money on a woman being involved."

"A woman he wants to hide," added Hazel excitedly. "A *Catholic* woman."

"On the Dunashee road? I very much doubt it," said Hubert. "Driscoll says he wants to come and talk to me this morning."

"Did he say why?" Adeline asked.

"No."

"I can't think how you can be of help."

"Neither can I," said Hubert.

"Oh dear," said Hazel. "He was such a charming man."

"And handsome," Laurel added.

"He was a gentleman. What a shame. We shall miss his company," said Hazel. She grinned behind her teacup. "I might be mistaken, but I could have sworn he took a shine to us."

KITTY WAS LYING on Elspeth's bed, discussing her sister's impending wedding, when Bridie knocked on the door. "I have a note for you, Miss Kitty," she said, reminding herself that she had to treat Kitty with due respect when they weren't alone. "Colonel Manley has been killed," she announced, watching the two girls sit up in astonishment.

"Killed? When?" Kitty asked.

"Last night. An ambush, they're saying."

"Goodness, how dreadful!" Elspeth gasped. "Does Papa know?"

"I think the whole of Ballinakelly knows by now, Miss Elspeth," said Bridie.

"To think it could have happened on the road to dinner with Grandpa," said Elspeth.

"I don't think the Ballinakelly road would be suitable for an ambush," said Kitty. She looked at the writing on the envelope and recognized it at once. It was from Jack.

"Who's the note from?" Elspeth asked.

"I don't know. I'll read it later," Kitty said dismissively, slipping it into her pocket. "I think lace, Elspeth. After all, it'll be spring and lace is so pretty."

Bridie left the room. She wondered who the note was from. The delivery boy who had brought it had asked especially for *her* and given her instructions to get it to Kitty without delay. Bridie had a horrible feeling that Michael and Sean were involved in the murder. She'd heard them discussing it often enough. If they were caught they'd be shot, for certain. If they were even suspected they'd be arrested and tortured. The only hope was that everyone in Co. Cork wanted Manley dead and they couldn't arrest everyone.

Later, when Kitty was alone, she opened Jack's note. *You were with Lady Rowan-Hampton last night at her house. A dinner just for the two of you. Beef and potatoes. You arrived at eight and left at eleven.*

J. Kitty was so shocked that Jack had something to do with Colonel Manley's murder that she read the note again. Why did she have to pretend that she had dined at Grace's house? Was *she* under suspicion? Surely, she could just as easily tell the truth, that she had had dinner alone with Elspeth and Harry while her parents dined at the castle with the Reverend and Mrs. Daunt. Anyway, why would they suspect *her*? As for Jack, her heart began to pound as she thought of the danger he was in. Killing Colonel Manley was akin to treason. The people involved would undoubtedly be shot, if they could find them. Kitty knew enough to know how hard it was to find the rebels when the entire Irish population rallied around them. But how would the Black and Tans avenge their colonel's killing?

Later that morning Lieutenant Driscoll's car drew up with two Army vehicles full of Auxiliaries and Tans. They were taking no chances now. While his men stood guard at the front door and patrolled the gardens, Driscoll was shown into the library, where Hubert was waiting for him. "Good morning, Lord Deverill," said Driscoll.

"Good morning, Lieutenant Driscoll. What a business. Please, take a seat."

O'Flynn closed the door and the two men were left alone. Driscoll sat down opposite Hubert, who popped a cigar between his teeth and proceeded to light it. "Yes indeed, it is a sickening example of what these people are capable of. Colonel Manley was an honest man, dedicated to his job. We've lost a fine man, Lord Deverill."

"You certainly have. As you know he was a regular guest at my dining table. So, how can I help you?"

"I trust that we are quite alone," said Driscoll, looking around warily.

"We are."

"Then let me speak frankly." He leaned forward and put his elbows on his knees, knitting his fingers. "We have reason to suspect Colonel Manley went to meet a woman yesterday evening."

Hubert raised his eyebrows; Adeline had been right. "Go on."

"This woman has been under suspicion for a while. We've been watching her closely. Suffice to say she has been seen to have Fenian friends in Dublin. Colonel Manley wanted to keep her close. We believe he was on his way to meet her, just the two of them, for an . . ." He hesitated, searching for the right word. "*Amorous* rendezvous. That's why he went without a full escort. We have reason to believe she was the bait, but *she* claims she was at home yesterday evening."

"So how can I help you?"

"You are a friend of hers, Lord Deverill, and while her husband was in London, she claims she was in the company of your granddaughter last night, Miss Kitty."

"Well, who is she, this scarlet woman?" Hubert chuckled on his cigar.

"Lady Rowan-Hampton."

The smoke caught in Hubert's throat and he coughed. "Good God, man, she's no Fenian. What an idea! Blarney, that's what it is. But if you want to speak to my granddaughter, I'll gladly send for her."

"If you will. I'd like to clear this up as a matter of urgency."

When Kitty received the summons she walked through the

gardens to the castle with a thumping heart. She had burned Jack's note, but she had read it so many times the words were impressed on her memory. Why did she need an alibi when she had one already? She was guilty of nothing. And why did she have to say she was with Grace? The mere mention of Grace's name made her stomach curdle.

She was shocked by the number of Auxiliaries surrounding the castle. Alert and jumpy, with their fingers on their triggers, they looked as if they had laid siege. They let her pass and she strode through the hall to the library, where her grandfather and Lieutenant Driscoll were waiting.

She shook Driscoll's plump hand and sat down on the sofa. "Lieutenant Driscoll wants to ask you a few questions," said Hubert. "You are aware that Colonel Manley was killed last night, are you not?"

"Yes, Grandpa," she replied, keeping her voice steady.

"I apologize for the intrusion, Miss Deverill. I'm just following orders. All I need to know is where you were yesterday evening."

"You don't think I had anything to do with Colonel Manley's death, do you?" she asked, shocked.

She looked at Driscoll. His round face was smooth and pink, like a schoolboy's, his fair hair greased back off his forehead. As she stared at him she sensed, to her horror, that it wasn't *she* who was under suspicion but Grace. *She* didn't need the alibi, Grace did. In that brief moment time stood still. She saw her father through the crack in the bedroom door, his hips thrusting back and forth like an animal as he took the woman she had always admired. She felt the hatred rise from her stomach to burn her throat, followed by a surge of power. She knew then that she had the chance to get rid of Grace Rowan-Hampton once and for all. If she was involved in Colonel Manley's murder Grace would go to prison at the very least. But Kitty looked into Lieutenant Driscoll's eyes and replied, "I was with Lady Rowan-Hampton." It felt like a dream, as if she were disconnected from her body and floating above it, detached, impassive.

"At her house?"

"Yes, at her house. Why, am I in trouble?" She looked at her grandfather, eyes wide and innocent.

"Not at all, my dear." Hubert turned to Lieutenant Driscoll. "Will that be all?"

Lieutenant Driscoll nodded. He sighed as if disappointed that *that* particular line of inquiry had led him nowhere. "Yes, that will be all. Thank you for your time, Miss Deverill." He replaced his cap.

"I'm dreadfully sorry about Colonel Manley. He was a charming man," said Kitty.

"Yes he was," said Lieutenant Driscoll, standing up. He walked to the door, but as he turned the handle he seemed to remember something. "Miss Deverill, one more thing. What did you have for supper?"

Kitty returned his stare with her own steady gaze. "Beef. I hate beef. It was overcooked and chewy." This satisfied and disheartened Lieutenant Driscoll in equal measure.

When he had gone Kitty rounded on her grandfather. "What was that all about?"

"I know, preposterous. I told him Grace had nothing to do with it."

"What's she accused of?"

"Being the bait. They've seen her mixing with the enemy in Dublin, so they say. Apparently they've been watching her for some time. They believe she arranged to meet Manley for a romantic liaison at the old farmhouse along the Dunashee road last night, then, when he turned up, she or her accomplices knifed him. I've never heard anything more ridiculous in my life. Grace is a lady, an *English* lady, not a Shinner. Wait till Ronald hears of this."

An image floated into Kitty's mind of Colonel Manley thrusting into Grace instead of her father and she promptly sat down again, feeling suddenly light-headed. Then another image replaced it, that of Grace in the farmhouse on the Dunashee road with a knife hidden in her skirt.

Kitty returned to the Hunting Lodge and hastily changed into her riding habit. "Where are you going?" Elspeth asked, entering her bedroom.

"I need to get some air."

Elspeth looked disappointed. She wanted to continue discussing her wedding. "What did Grandpa want you for?"

"He's worried about the Shrubs," Kitty improvised.

"Why?"

"They never go out anymore because they're frightened of the Shinners. They think they're going to get murdered like Colonel Manley."

"I don't think anyone's going to murder two defenseless old ladies."

"Just what I said," Kitty lied, pinning her hat onto her head.

"I suppose we could take them into Ballinakelly one afternoon. They won't be so frightened if they're with *us*."

"Quite." Kitty was brisk. She had already grown bored of her lie. "I'll see you later."

"You're not going into Ballinakelly on your own, are you?" Elspeth looked worried.

"No. I'm going over the hills."

"Are you sure you're safe on your own? Shouldn't you take Harry with you?"

"Perfectly safe. God help the Shinner who takes *me* on." She laughed and left the room.

KITTY GALLOPED OVER the hills to Grace's house. Sheep and cows grazed peacefully on thick, lush grass, unmoved by the cold. As she rode she felt her anger release on the wind, as if it had fingers to snatch her resentment and take it away. As she galloped she felt her love for Ireland swell in her heart like an expanding balloon. The more she looked around her, at the wild and rocky countryside, the bigger the balloon grew until she laughed out loud with unrestrained joy. Spurring her horse on, she jumped a stone wall, delighting in the risk.

When she reached Grace's large, gray-stone manor, she dismounted at the stable and handed her horse to the groom. Taking off her gloves as she went, she marched into the house through the front door. "I've come to see Lady Rowan-Hampton," she announced to the butler, who looked surprised and a little uncomfortable as Kitty strode past him without waiting in the hall as was customary.

"I will just go and inform her ladyship," said the butler, hurrying after her.

"Grace!" Kitty shouted. Before the butler could reach the sitting room, Grace appeared in the doorway. She looked pale and tired around the eyes, but her crimson dress and green cardigan revealed her usual penchant for color. Kitty couldn't imagine she'd have the nerve to thrust a knife into a man.

"It's all right, Brennan. Would you bring us some tea?"

"Yes, my lady," he replied, pursing his lips and shooting Kitty a disapproving look.

"Come in, Kitty." She smiled as Kitty followed her into the room. "So, I'm Grace at last," she said with satisfaction.

"It wouldn't be right to call you Lady Rowan-Hampton, seeing as we're such close friends. I gather I had dinner with you last night."

Grace turned and held Kitty with solemn eyes. "For that I thank you, Kitty," she said in a quiet voice.

Kitty walked past her and perched on the club fender in front of the fire. "So, are you going to tell me what this is all about?"

Grace went and sat beside her. She lowered her voice but her eyes were blazing with zeal. "I was there last night," she said. "With Michael and the boys . . ."

Kitty's jaw fell open. "*You* killed him?"

"No." Grace looked at Kitty steadily. "Jack did."

"Jack . . . ?"

"*Your* Jack."

Kitty was caught off guard. She didn't think anyone knew about her and Jack, least of all Grace. "I don't understand. How do you know?"

"I know lots of things, Kitty. I know you're one of us, though, which is why I chose to make *you* my alibi."

"You had no choice. Mama wouldn't have lied for you. I doubt any of your other English friends would have lied for you, either."

"But I knew *you* would."

"Even though you know I dislike you?"

"I knew you'd do it, not for me, but for Jack." Grace lowered her eyes unhappily. "I know why you dislike me but I make no apology."

"You have some nerve, Grace."

"I trust my instincts."

"So it was a test?"

"In a way."

"Weren't you perhaps a little reckless? One word from me and I could have had you hanged."

Grace's lips curled into a small smile. "But you didn't, did you? My gamble paid off."

"I gave you an alibi and saved your life, which means you owe me."

"No, it means you're one of us now."

Kitty raised an eyebrow. That *did* please her. "I'm involved, whether Jack likes it or not?"

"You are indeed, which is what you've always wanted. Am I right?"

"So what do I do now?" Kitty asked.

Grace turned her eyes to the door where Brennan was coming in with the tea, followed by a young maid with a porter cake on a plate. "Ah, the tea. I think this is going to be the beginning of a very interesting friendship."

WHEN KITTY RETURNED to the Hunting Lodge she summoned Harry and Elspeth to her bedroom. When they arrived she closed the door behind them and leaned against it as if fearful they might be overheard or spied on. Too many occasions when she'd peered through keyholes had taught her to be suspicious of others. "I need your help," she said gravely.

Elspeth glanced at Harry. "What's going on?" she asked.

"Are you in trouble?" Harry inquired.

"No, but I might be if you both decide not to help me."

"We'll help you, won't we, Harry?"

"Of course," Harry agreed. "What's the problem?"

Kitty took a deep breath. "I can't explain why, but I need you to pretend that I wasn't with you last night. That we didn't have dinner together. I went to have dinner with Lady Rowan-Hampton."

Harry frowned. "Why?"

"I told you. I can't explain. You just have to do this for me. It's complicated."

"Does it have anything to do with Grandpa summoning you this morning?" Elspeth asked.

"Yes," Kitty conceded. "It does."

Elspeth smiled. "You did seem a little upset."

"Well, will you do this for me? If anyone asks, anyone at all, I was *not* with you."

Harry nodded. Considering the secret she was keeping for *him*, this was the least he could do. Elspeth nodded too, although she longed to know why. "You have my word," she said.

"Thank you." Kitty smiled. "There was a time when I thought we'd never be friends," she said.

Harry grinned. "There's nothing that bonds people more surely than a secret."

Elspeth agreed, although she could never imagine the secret Kitty kept for their brother. "And there's nothing that bonds siblings more than a selfish mother."

Chapter 18

Bridie was wrong about the Black and Tans not being able to arrest everybody. They came in their Army vehicles, with their guns and their thirst for revenge, and rounded up all the young men of Ballinakelly while their women wailed and clung on, fearing they'd never see them again. Michael and Sean were among them, as was Jack. All taken away. God knew where. Bridie sobbed on Kitty's bed as Kitty held her tightly, trying not to give her heart away with her own burning tears. Mrs. Doyle ruined the lunch and curdled the cream, which was a very bad sign. She requested the day off, which Adeline readily agreed to, and spent the afternoon in church with her mother and the other Ballinakelly women, lighting candles, saying rosaries and novenas and making deals with God.

Bertie had heard from his father that Grace was under suspicion and drove over to see her at once. He parked the Daimler outside the house and knocked on the door. The butler led him through the hall to the sitting room, where his mistress was at her desk, writing letters. "Bertie," she exclaimed happily, noticing that he was sober and concerned. She put down her pen and stood up. "What's the matter?" The butler discreetly closed the door, as was his custom, leaving them alone.

"I heard that they are trying to implicate you in Manley's murder. Of all the—"

"Oh that," said Grace dismissively, cutting him off mid-sentence. "Well, they're only doing their jobs. I'm not sure why my name came up. But it did."

Bertie tried to embrace her, but she sidled away and settled into the armchair by the fire. "Why? Why you?" he asked, pacing the room in agitation.

Grace sighed. "I imagine it's got something to do with me teaching the children English. Their elder brothers and fathers come too, and we talk. They're suspicious of groups of people, aren't they? It's only natural. Apparently, they think I'm meeting Sinn Féiners in Dublin." She laughed lightly, as if the mere idea was ludicrous. "I'm not Countess Markievicz!" she added, referring to the infamous rebel imprisoned after the Easter Rising.

"But why you and Manley?" Bertie persisted, the fire in his cheeks exposing his jealousy.

"Because Manley took a shine to me."

"Manley?"

She laughed again. "He was a terrible flirt. Surely you know that? He was all over me like a rash. Really, he was very tiresome."

"But you're a married woman!"

She arched an eyebrow. "That never stopped *you*."

"I'm different. We're Ascendancy. He's just a professional soldier!"

"Whatever he was, he isn't anymore," she corrected.

"Why on earth would they think you had planned a liaison with *him*?"

"Because they're clutching at straws, my darling Bertie." She narrowed her eyes and smiled indulgently, as if at a petulant boy. "You don't think I was there, do you?"

"Of course not! It's just preposterous that your name ever came up in a conversation about Manley. Preposterous and I've told them so."

"I was with Kitty," she said, watching him carefully for his reaction.

"So Father told me." He looked uncomfortable.

"We've become friends," she said quietly.

His eyes darkened with dread as he read the tone of her voice. "Which has implications for us," he ventured, speaking her mind for her.

"Yes. I'm afraid our affair has to end."

Bertie blanched. "End? Why? I've sobered up for you, haven't I?"

Grace rose from her chair and took his hands in hers. "She knows about us. I don't know how, but she does and it's driven a wedge between us for all these years. I'm a fool for not working it out sooner." She gazed into his stricken face. "I'm sorry, Bertie, but it's run its course."

"Grace, please! Our affair has nothing to do with Kitty. I love you!"

"I love you, too, darling Bertie."

"You never minded about Maud."

"Maud is the reason you came running into *my* arms. She's the creator of her own fate. Kitty, on the other hand, is only an innocent child."

"She's not a child. She's a young woman of twenty, for God's sake."

"She's my friend. She's loyal to me, therefore I want to be loyal to her," she said deliberately.

Bertie frowned. "Loyalty? What's that got to do with it?"

Grace sighed. "I can't explain. It's a woman's business. She's done something for me and I can't repay her by carrying on as her father's mistress. It's not honorable."

"Since when are you so worried about honor? It's never bothered you before!"

"It was never called into question."

Bertie's face flushed with anger. "I don't understand you, Grace. I thought you loved me."

"I did and I still do, but we can't have everything in life. Sometimes one simply has to do the right thing, even if it breaks our hearts."

Bertie strode over to the window and gazed out onto the gardens in silence. He remained there for some time, lost in thought. Finally he turned on his heel. "I'm not giving up on you, Grace. I'll give you time to think this through." He made for the door. "I don't believe you can just dismiss me, after all we've meant to each other. I will not accept it." With that he opened the door and strode out, slamming it behind him with a loud bang that shook the room. Grace leaned on the back of the armchair to steady herself and heaved a regretful sigh.

When it came to Ireland she'd sacrifice everything and anyone she loved for freedom.

"THEY SHOULD HANG the bally lot of them," said Hubert that evening, refilling his glass with whiskey from the drinks tray.

Adeline and the Shrubs sat on the sofa while Maud perched stiffly on the club fender as her husband paced the floor distractedly. "They've taken Mrs. Doyle's sons, Hubert," said Adeline. "I don't believe they're part of the plot."

"I'm sure they're loyal to you," said Laurel.

"Oh yes, very loyal," Hazel agreed.

"They're not loyal to anyone but each other," Maud cut in. "I agree with Hubert. They should all be hanged, every one of them."

"The trouble is they're a slippery lot. Hard to catch," said Hubert.

"Well, they've arrested a whole lot of men from Ballinakelly, haven't they?" said Maud.

"And elsewhere besides," Adeline added. "They can't all be guilty."

"But they'll treat them all as if they're guilty," Maud added. "It's a case of throwing the baby out with the bathwater, but if they put away a few guilty ones in the process I'd say it'd be a job well done. They're frightfully surly. I can see them looking at me with their eyes full of hatred every time I go into Ballinakelly, which I try not to do, unless we're going to church. I don't trust a single one. Not even the ones who work for us."

"Oh really, Maud. You're taking it too far," said Adeline with a smile. Maud bristled; Adeline treated her as a source of amusement, as if she found her opinions self-indulgent and trite.

"Hazel and Laurel feel the same, don't you?" Maud appealed to the Shrubs.

"Well, I do feel a little timid," Laurel agreed.

"It's since the stone incident," Hazel added. "I feel safe here, though. The staff are very loyal, I have no doubt."

"They're loyal," said Hubert. "Indisputably so."

"Until they're pressured by their own kind to betray us," Maud said darkly, watching her silent husband walking the carpet, back and forth, with his hands in his pockets and his face grim. "Are you going to join in the conversation, Bertie, or are you just going to make us all dizzy with your pacing? Really, you're giving me a headache."

Bertie looked up in surprise. "I was just thinking that if they imprison all the lads they've taken there'll be no one left in Ballinakelly to do the work," he lied, dragging his thoughts away from Grace.

"Same as in England during the war," said Maud. "The women will have to roll up their sleeves."

"Which is what they do already," said Adeline. "Where are Harry and the girls? Don't they want any dinner?"

When Elspeth, Kitty and Harry arrived, flushed from hunting, the subject was swiftly changed to Elspeth's impending wedding. Maud had turned the whole event around to herself as usual, giving her opinions on the guest list, the bridesmaids' and pages' attire and the order of service. "It's going to be lavish and gay, just what people expect of a Deverill wedding, even though the groom might be a little disappointing to some.

It's exactly what we all need to cheer us up. Something positive to talk about for a change."

"Oh yes!" Hazel exclaimed excitedly. "It will be nice to read something positive about Ireland in the British newspapers."

"Victoria's wedding was all over *The Tatler*," added Laurel proudly.

"Because that took place in London," said Elspeth. "I don't think anyone's going to be particularly interested in *my* wedding." She grinned broadly. "I'd happily get married in a cowshed."

"A cowshed was good enough for Mary and Joseph, after all," said Harry laconically.

Adeline laughed. "Really, Harry, you do say the funniest things!"

"When are *you* going to get married?" Hazel asked.

"Oh yes, now *that* will be a splendid occasion," Laurel gushed.

"Harry has yet to find a bride," said Maud pointedly.

"No hurry for that," Hubert interjected. "Take your time, Harry. Play the field. Plenty of nice girls to choose from."

"Not in Ireland," Maud added hastily. "You should go to London. You'll have the pick of the crop." She glanced at Bertie, who was not listening.

"I'm happy here," said Harry and the way he was lying back against the cushions in the armchair suggested that he had no intention of *ever* leaving.

"Quite right, Harry," Hubert agreed. "Nothing like home, eh?"

"Nothing," Harry agreed. He caught Kitty's eye. She smiled at him knowingly. "You want me to leave, Mama, you'll have to prize me off Irish soil like a limpet off a rock."

Two AGONIZING DAYS later the men were released. Kitty at last found a note in the wall with a time and place to meet. She slipped it into the pocket of her skirt and hurried back to the Hunting Lodge to change into her riding habit. She rang the bell for Bridie. "They're out!" she exclaimed as her friend appeared in the doorway.

"I know, Mam told me. But what state are they in? Michael's got a shiner the size of a hurley ball. They've been beaten to pulp."

"But no one's been charged?"

"No."

Kitty slipped out of her skirt, leaving it to drop to the floor at her feet. "They all got off?"

"Every one." Bridie grinned. "Father Quinn came to the rescue. He said they were at Mass."

"All night?"

"Father Quinn said he kept them there because they needed sense talked into them."

"But that's obviously not true."

"No one argues with Father Quinn."

"Hand me my riding habit. I'm going out."

"Alone?"

"Aren't I always alone and don't I always come back in one piece?"

"Don't tempt the fates, Kitty," said Bridie anxiously. "It's not safe out there for an English girl like you."

Kitty rounded on her angrily. "I'm as Irish as you are, Bridie, and sick of saying it! What's in the heart is all that matters."

"Try telling that to Michael."

"You tell him for me then," Kitty snapped. Kitty knew that Michael and the others would know how Irish she was soon enough.

Once dressed she left the room without a backward glance. All she could think about was seeing Jack and healing his wounds with tender kisses. Bridie picked up her clothes and put them on the bed. She hung her blouse on a hanger and replaced it in the wardrobe. Then she picked up the skirt and shook it out. As she did so she heard the rustle of paper in the pocket. She slipped in her hand and pulled out the note. Normally it would not have occurred to her to read a private letter, but there was something compelling about this one. It was small and creased as if it had been folded into the tiniest square. Unable to resist the mysterious force of the note and instinctively knowing it had something to do with Kitty rushing off, she opened it.

As Bridie read the words her face blazed crimson right to the tips of her ears. She didn't need to read the *J* at the end because she knew it was from Jack. She could hear his voice as if he were speaking the words himself. She collapsed onto the bed and began to cry like a child. Then she pressed the note to her heart and stifled a sob. He had ended it *My love, as always, un-dimmed, J.*

All this time Kitty had been sneaking behind her back seeing Jack. The times she had gazed out of the window absent-mind-edly, the wistful smiles that warmed her face, the sudden haste to saddle her horse and ride out over the hills had all been for Jack. And Bridie had believed she was in love with Mr. Trench. How stupid could she be? All the while Kitty had loved Jack—and more vitally, Jack had loved *her*. With a trembling hand

Bridie replaced the note in the skirt pocket. Kitty must never know she had read it. She must never know that she had just broken Bridie's heart. Broken it so that it would never mend.

KITTY REACHED THE Fairy Ring. Jack was waiting for her. When he was sure that she was alone he stepped out from behind one of the tall stones. Her joy at seeing him was snatched away by the sight of his bloodied face and his left arm, which was bandaged and wrapped in a sling. "What did they do to you?" she wailed, slipping off her horse and running to him.

"Easy now, I'm all right."

"They hurt you!" Kitty's eyes glittered and then the tears spilled onto her cheeks. She ran gentle fingers down his bruised face. One eye was closed altogether. "I'll murder the man who did this to you, Jack," she whispered.

"Not if I get there first." He smiled, then winced. "They got a rib or two into the bargain."

"Oh Jack!" She kissed him softly on the mouth. "You foolish man."

"But you love your old fool, right?"

She laughed. "I love my old fool. I never thought Father Quinn would stand up for you."

"Father Quinn? He's one of us, Kitty."

She frowned. "One of you?"

"He hides guns for us in the sacristy."

"Lord preserve us!" she gasped.

"He will. We have God on our side, that's for sure." Jack slipped his good hand around her neck, beneath her hair. "Thank you for giving Grace an alibi."

"I did it for you. Not for her."

"I know."

She was suddenly overcome by a wave of emotion. "She seduced my father, Jack. She's been his mistress for years." She took a staggered breath. "I've hated her ever since I saw them . . . on the bed . . . at the Summer Ball . . ." She rested her forehead against his shoulder.

"It's all right, Kitty. He's still your da whatever he does. It's just a shame that you had to see it, that's all."

"It's haunted me for years."

"Enough now then. Enough hating. She's a good woman."

Kitty lifted her face and stared at him steadily. "I gave her an alibi. I'm involved now."

Jack shook his head. "No, you're not."

"I am," she said more forcefully. "You got me involved. There's no turning back now. I'm going to join the fight, Jack. We're in this together."

"I don't want you hurt."

"Then you should have thought about that before you used me. I'll be useful again, Jack, you'll see. You won't regret it. One day we'll celebrate a free and independent Ireland together."

"I'd drink to that," said Jack, running his thumb across her chin.

"Let's kiss to it instead." And she lifted her face and closed her eyes, holding the thought with every fiber of her spirit.

BRIDIE NEEDED AIR. She dried her eyes with her sleeve and made for the door. But just as she began to walk down the corridor the tears welled in her eyes and spilled down her cheeks again. There seemed no end to them. She bowed her head and walked on, her vision blurred. Suddenly she met with a thump, walking straight into none other than Mr. Deverill. She recognized the shoes at once and gasped in horror at her carelessness. Stepping back she bowed her head and mumbled an apology. "Are you crying, Bridget?"

She didn't have the will to correct him. "No, Mr. Deverill. Just something in my eye. I'm sorry to have trodden in your way."

"You're not in my way." He was slurring his words a little and she could smell the whiskey on his breath. It was not unpleasant.

"Yes, you are crying. I can see tears. Lots of them. This won't do, Bridget. A pretty girl like you crying. Not over a man, I hope. They're not worth it, you know. A bunch of rotten scoundrels, most of them."

Bridie began to cry. "I'm sorry . . ." she mumbled, hiding her face.

"Come, let's not stand in the corridor." He led her farther down the passage to his private quarters. "Sit on the bed and let's dry your tears."

She did as she was told. "You're very kind, sir."

"It's what any gentleman would do." He opened the top right-hand drawer of his dresser and pulled out a clean handkerchief. Kneeling before her he gently dabbed her eyes. "There, that's better. Can't have a pretty girl like you marred by tears." The way he said the word "pretty" made her aching heart lurch with longing.

"I don't think I'm pretty," she said sadly, hiccupping.

"You *are* pretty. You're very pretty." He swayed a little. "And you're young. Too young to have had time to break a man's heart. But you will, you know. They all do."

She lifted her eyes and gazed at him in confusion. He was staring at her with an unfamiliar look on his face. She hadn't seen that look before but she knew it instinctively. It was desire. She felt a sudden yearning to please him and reached out her hand to touch his face. Her fingers were trembling and for a horrible moment she thought he might grab her hand and shout at her. But he didn't. He wound his hand around her neck and brought her face close so that he could kiss her. Bridie had never been kissed before but the wet sensation of his tongue entering her lips and circling around hers, and the taste of whiskey on it, was deeply arousing and she let her eyelids close as she surrendered to the feeling.

A moment later she was lying on the bed and Mr. Deverill was kissing her neck. Her breath grew short and the sweat began to gather in beads on her nose. He undid the buttons on her blouse and slipped his hand inside, feeling the soft rise of her breast and the sharply erect nub of her nipple. Bridie ceased to think. Aware only of the strange new sensations that now took over, she gave in to the powerful awakening of every nerve. His mouth was on her breast, teasing her with his tongue, sending her into a confusing state of excitement such as she had never before experienced. Then his hand was rising up her skirt and tracing her thigh and she was barely able to stay still for the excruciating pleasure of it. She heard his breathing, deep, shallow, urgent, as his fingers found their way to the top of her thigh where they could go no farther, and the pleasure of his caresses increased still more, leaving Bridie dizzy in the head and now oblivious of the pain in her heart.

When she felt something hard slip inside her, it momentarily woke her from her stupor. A sudden pain, but then it was gone. She wrapped her arms around him and closed her eyes again and let him do what he wanted. Mr. Deverill believed she was pretty. He was kissing her and loving her as if she was the only woman in the world he cared about. Kitty surfaced for a second in her mind but Bridie's vengeful smile was fleeting, for once again she was sinking into the firm embrace of a man who thought she was pretty.

Chapter 19

Kitty was indeed useful to Jack. Being a Deverill meant that none of the Royal Irish Constabulary ever stopped and searched her when she went into town. No one asked her where she was going and on what business. She could walk through Ballinakelly with guns in her basket without raising an eyebrow. She delighted in the thrill of doing something illegal and she relished the fact that she was helping, in a small way, to free Ireland from British rule.

After the men were released, thanks to the intervention of Father Quinn, they had to be more cautious; the priest wouldn't be able to save them a second time. Already under suspicion, they were constantly stopped and searched, while walking to Mass, meeting at the end of the day for a pint of stout in O'Donovan's, buying and selling livestock at the monthly fair. They were never free from harassment. Therefore Kitty and Grace became more valuable to them than ever. Even Michael had to concede that they needed them, English though he believed them still.

Kitty was wary of Michael Doyle. She had known him from a distance as Bridie's brother but he'd always been much older than her and so dark and serious that she had been a little afraid of him. He was strong and robust like all Doyle men, but he lacked the gentleness of his late father and the sensitivity of his brother Sean. However, he was taller and more handsome than both and possessed a menacing charisma that women seemed to find compelling—indeed Bridie had told her that the girls in Ballinakelly would do anything for her brother, such were his powers of attraction. But Kitty found him alarming. He had a mop of black curls that fell over his forehead, giving him the sly, furtive look of a poacher, and his black eyes were as hard as coal, his jaw as rigid as wood, his gaze as steady as the barrel of a gun. No one messed with Michael Doyle. Only Grace seemed to command his respect and admiration, even though she stood for everything he opposed.

While Kitty became indispensable to the cause Michael seethed with resentment. He seemed to begrudge everything about her, from her fine clothes to her pampered lifestyle and her cleverness. He made snide remarks at every opportunity and hid his dislike badly beneath a thin veneer of prickly humor. As far as he was concerned she was part of the ruling power they were fighting against. "She might have a romantic vision of a free Ireland but what she doesn't see is that she has no place in it," he would say over a glass of stout. "Fight or no fight, she's still one of them." Jack would argue passionately in her defense, which only made Michael despise Jack as well, for having won Kitty's heart and her esteem. He would watch the two of them, and his eyes had the Devil in them. But Kitty could stand up for herself and took pleasure in letting loose her temper.

"I might not have suffered as you have, Michael, and my family roots might be in England, but my heart is Irish to its core just like yours. I'm risking my life running back and forth with notes, ammunition, even standing here in your house—and I'm not doing it for fun or for romance but for Ireland, and you know it. Get past your prejudice because it doesn't serve you well. We're in this together and we need to support each other or we'll get nowhere." Michael would glare at her with his smoldering black eyes and she'd feel his loathing as if it were able to penetrate her skin. He'd search for words to pull her down but she was more articulate than him, having had the advantage of a fine education, and that seemed to infuriate him all the more. No one made him feel less of a man than Kitty Deverill.

IN THE SPRING of 1921 Elspeth married Peter MacCartain in the church of St. Patrick in Ballinakelly. Family and a few brave friends came from London for four days of celebrations in spite of the negative publicity splashed across their newspapers. They were reassured by the heavy police presence on the estate and the sturdiness of the castle walls. Maud was determined to show her London friends the grand and glittering side of Ireland. No expense was spared. She was also determined to conceal the groom's shortcomings in the extravaganza and hoped that no one would notice that he had no title and no fortune worthy of note.

The castle was filled with English guests. Cousin Stoke and

Augusta had their usual rooms above the hall but complained after the first night of the noise rising up from the drawing room below so that they were duly moved to the remotest part of the castle for the second. However, Augusta grumbled loudly about the damp sheets and the queer sound of footsteps in the middle of the night, so they were promptly moved back into the rooms above the hall again. Augusta wasted the servants' time trying to find a suitable pair of earplugs, complaining that, if the rebels didn't kill her, this wedding *would*. Adeline's patience was sorely tried.

Maud had arranged for Hubert to have new clothes for the occasion—it wouldn't do to have him letting her down with his shabby wardrobe. She had had his measurements sent over to Bertie's tailor in Savile Row in London and presented him with a beautifully cut white tie for the ball, a green-velvet smoking jacket for dinner and traditional morning coat for the church service. Hubert sniffed his displeasure and complained to his wife. "She's trying to change me, the silly woman. Doesn't she know that this dog's too old for new tricks?" He ignored the pristine new attire and slipped into his old, tattered favorites with a mutinous grunt. Maud was outraged. Not only had the new clothes cost a small fortune but he would lower the tone of the wedding. It simply wasn't right that Lord Deverill of Castle Deverill should appear with holes in the elbows of his sweaters and patches sewn into the fabric of his jackets where the moths had dined most lavishly. By contrast Sir Digby Deverill of Deverill Rising in Wiltshire was as neat and shiny as one of his diamond shirt studs.

Victoria resided at the Hunting Lodge with her slack-jawed husband the Earl of Elmrod. It was Bridie's duty to look after her, as well as Kitty and the bride-to-be, and she barely had time to gather her thoughts for the demands of the countess. Victoria rang her bell for the smallest whim. She demanded that her sheets be aired during the day and warmed before bedtime. She sent clothes to be washed when they'd barely been worn and pressed when they had scarcely a crease. She turned her nose up at the limited plumbing, complaining that Ireland was still in the Dark Ages compared with England, where electricity and hot and cold running water were a given.

Bridie had never warmed to Victoria but now she liked her even less. Elspeth, on the other hand, had grown sweeter with age. She was polite and grateful and as undemanding as her elder sister was demanding. Maud barely paid her any attention, even though it was *her* wedding, running around after Victoria as if she were Queen Mary. It gave her enormous pleasure to have a daughter married to an earl and she used Victoria's title wherever possible. "Lady Elmrod would like her milk heated for her tea," or, "Countess Elmrod will be taking a walk at eleven, if any of Lord Deverill's guests would like to accompany her."

KITTY ENJOYED THE wedding celebrations all the more because of her double life. Her new role as rebel gave her a certain swagger and she reveled in the knowing smiles that she and Grace gave one another when no one else was looking. Her loathing for Lady Rowan-Hampton had been replaced by a healthy respect for a woman of surprising courage and mystery. They worked together now. They had a common goal and a common interest and they both knew too much about the other to be disloyal. Having spent the last twelve years despising her, Kitty discovered that the borders between love and hate were as fragile and easily broken as eggshell. Her affection for the woman she had always admired as a little girl flourished in the glow of their shared secret.

Beatrice had climbed out of her grief after losing her beloved George in the trenches by making a stairway of diamonds upon which, step by laborious step, she had ascended into the light. Turning her focus away from her battered heart into London's social whirl of parties and lunches and balls, she could adorn herself in Digby's diamonds and bask in the attention such riches afforded her, the more superficial the better, for anything remotely deep drove her dangerously close to that dark and painful place she was trying so hard to circumvent. She threw herself into the wedding celebrations with gusto. She danced until her feet ached, she drank until her head swam, she flirted until her husband discreetly took her outside for some air, and she laughed so loudly she surprised even herself. In her brief moments of reflection she found that she was drawn to Harry. He appealed to her maternal nature, so desperately underemployed. There was something of the lost soul about him. He had a furtive look around the eyes that made her want to gather him up and show him a good time in London. She watched him talking to the other young men, smoking and laughing in a particularly jaunty manner, and thought how terribly dashing he was. He'd certainly be an asset at her Tuesday evening salons.

Beatrice's daughters, Vivien and Leona, had made excellent matches, which exacerbated all the more acutely Maud's fury at Elspeth's disappointing choice. She watched Kitty dancing with her brother, Harry, and wondered whether with a little more persuasion she could find a suitable match for her in London; after all, she conceded grudgingly, Kitty was by far the most beautiful and intelligent of her daughters. As for Harry, so handsome and witty, it was about time he stepped onto the London stage. A man with the promise of a title and a magnificent Irish castle was sure to attract a woman with a fortune. An American would do, she mused: they would be the only people foolish enough to consider Ireland romantic.

The Shrubs delighted in all the wedding celebrations like children at Christmastime. Never had the castle looked so grand. Flares lit it up at night, flowers adorned it during the day as if the building itself were a bride. In fact, they had only ever seen so many flowers when their father had taken them to London's Covent Garden as little girls. They fluttered excitedly from arrangement to elaborate arrangement like a pair of canaries, twittering loudly on Maud's exquisite taste and extravagance. "No expense spared!" they cried for everyone to hear. Maud wished they wouldn't behave like a pair of provincials. She wanted her English friends to think the castle looked like this all the time.

The Anglo-Irish women had come out in their splendor like crocuses after a hard winter. Keen not to be outdone by the English guests, they paraded their finest jewels and silks, led by Co. Cork's two most beautiful women, Maud Deverill and Grace Rowan-Hampton. Not easily defeated in the beauty stakes, they had more competition in the fashion stakes, the Englishwomen having the advantage of the latest designs from the Paris couturiers. Where the Anglo-Irish women outdid their English counterparts, however, was in their skin, which had benefited from years of soft rain and moist air. Neither

Maud nor Grace had a line on her face; even Adeline and the Shrubs looked much younger than their years. The English-women could only gaze on them with envy, for no amount of expensive creams and foundation could disguise the corrosive effects of the smoggy London air.

Bertie found the celebrations excruciating, for Grace had never looked more beautiful. Every change of clothes brought a more radiant Lady Rowan-Hampton onto the scene. She sparkled in sapphires, dazzled in rich silks and glowed in the candlelight as if she herself were lit from within like a Chinese lantern. His heart ached for her and the distance that had opened between them only worsened his pain. Grace remained close to her husband throughout the four days, clearly avoiding any sort of uncomfortable discourse with her ex-lover.

On the last night, in a fever of frustration and high on al-cohol, Bertie left the ball and returned to the Hunting Lodge in search of Bridie. He found her tidying Victoria's bedroom. Without a word he took her to his own quarters where he laid her on the bed and unbuttoned her shirt. He lifted her skirts and pulled off her drawers. Sinking his face into her breasts he closed his eyes and imagined she was Grace. Bridie, on the other hand, flushed with pleasure that Mr. Deverill had left the celebrations to be with *her*. She basked in his attention and allowed his caresses to lift her out of her pain.

ELSPETH AND PETER left at the end of the four days to honey-moon in Rome. They sped away to the station in the Daimler, which Kitty had decorated with ribbons and flowers, and Harry with cans tied with string that clattered on the ground as they went. The guests left with the impression that, while

Ireland crashed about the castle's borders, the castle itself remained the final bastion of civilization, glamour and wealth, exactly what Maud wanted them to think.

Not long after the wedding Harry surprised his mother by announcing that he wanted to go to London. "Cousin Beatrice has invited me to spend the Season with her and I think I should go."

Maud's pretty lips parted in astonishment. "Why, Harry, this is wonderful news. I shall accompany you, of course. With you in London there'll be little reason for me to stay here. Besides, it's becoming so dangerous. We're prisoners in our own homes." Maud immediately perked up at the thought of parties, lunches at the Ritz, the Chelsea Flower Show, Henley Regatta and Royal Ascot. She would give her expensive frocks a good airing and be admired by men of sophistication and women of class. There was no admiration here in Ballinakelly and Bertie was moping about the place, lovesick for Grace, who had obviously cut him loose. Maud lifted her chin, damned if she was going to show him an ounce of sympathy. "We shall leave at once," she said, getting up from her chair and smoothing her dress. "With Elspeth gone to Italy and Victoria back in Kent I need something to lift my spirits. Cousin Beatrice's beautiful home in Kensington is just the ticket."

Kitty was sorry to see her brother leave. She had enjoyed having him at home. Not only was he good company, but he was a vital buffer between her and her mother. While Harry was around Maud was blind to everyone else. Kitty embraced him fiercely and in that very physical moment when brother and sister held each other close, Kitty felt the intensity of their secrets bond them even tighter. Reluctantly, she let him go.

"Write to me, won't you, Harry?" she asked and he nodded, his eyes straying a moment behind her as if he was unwilling to leave the house. She waved as he sped off down the drive to take the boat across the water to Wales. She caught sight of her mother's hard profile as she looked ahead, her face impassive; there was nothing to keep her in Ireland anymore. Then they were gone.

When Kitty turned to walk into the house she saw Joseph's sad face gazing out of one of the upstairs windows. He was quite still, his skin translucent behind the glass, like the ghosts of Deverill heirs staring out onto their loss. She wondered whether in the vastness of London Harry would find his secret easier to bear. Whether he'd unearth others like him. Perhaps there were many lost men seeking solace and acceptance out there in the metropolis. She pitied the woman who would give him her hand, because he would never give her his heart.

BERTIE KNEW THAT Grace was avoiding him. She declined invitations to dine at the Hunting Lodge and spent increasingly more time in Dublin. Ronald took regular trips to London, which frustrated Bertie because, had he and Grace still been lovers, those weeks could have been spent together. He missed her dreadfully. He missed the smell of her, the soft timbre of her voice, the bubbling warmth of her laugh. With his wife gone the heavy atmosphere had lifted in the Hunting Lodge. It was as if the building had been holding its breath and could at last breathe easily again. Summer flowered into long sunny days and balmy nights. Bertie slept with the windows wide open and the sweet smells from the garden rose on the air to torment him, for everything beautiful reminded him of Grace.

Kitty was a comfort to him, accompanying him out riding, playing tennis and joining him and his parents for games of whist and bridge up at the castle. His daughter did much to take his mind off his aching heart. Occasionally, when the desire took him, Bridie did much to take his mind off his aching loins.

Then, in mid-summer, Bridie appeared white-faced and white-lipped at the library door. She knocked so quietly he didn't hear her at first. On her second attempt he turned to see her standing small and trembling, eyes on the floor as if too frightened to look at him.

"What is it, Bridget?" he asked impatiently. He didn't appreciate her turning up like this.

"May I speak with you, sir?"

He sighed. It wasn't her place to interrupt his work. "Come in," he said. He didn't notice her flinch at his uncaring tone.

"It's a private matter, sir."

"Then close the door behind you." He was irritated. It was all very well taking her every now and again, but for her to come and demand his attention when he was busy at his desk was not part of the arrangement. "What is it?" He noticed her cheeks flush weakly like the remaining embers of a fire, before dying away.

She picked at the skin around her thumbnail. "I'm . . ."

"You're what?" he asked.

"I'm . . ." She hesitated and he knew. Of course he knew. He should have known the moment she stepped into the doorway. He stood up and went to the cold fireplace. Placing his hands on the mantelpiece he stared into the void.

"You're with child." His voice was a whisper but she heard the words as if they were the sound of church bells.

She swallowed her fear. "I am, sir," she replied.

Bertie felt the room spin and gripped the mantelpiece to steady himself. He gritted his teeth and closed his eyes. Why hadn't he been more careful? At last he turned to face her, eyes dropping to her belly concealed behind her white apron. "Are you showing yet?"

She shook her head. "No."

"Are you sure you're with child?"

"I'm sure."

"How do you know it's mine?"

Her lips parted and her cheeks burned with the light of a rekindled fire. "Because you are the only one, sir," she replied, astonished that he might think otherwise.

Bertie sniffed, unconvinced. "One can't be too sure, you know."

Bridie's eyes filled with tears. "There will never be another but you, Mr. Deverill."

"Yes, yes, well, that's all very well." Bertie didn't know what to say.

"What shall I do?" She began to cry.

Bertie was now uncomfortable. Under normal circumstances he wasn't good with women's tears, especially women of Bridie's class. Servants were not his department. "Does anyone else know about this?"

She shook her head vigorously, horrified by the suggestion. "No!"

Bertie was relieved. "Good. This must be our secret, Bridget. Do you understand?"

"Yes, sir."

He wished the problem would just go away. Then he was

struck by an idea. "I will send you to Dublin," he suggested, feeling a little better. "Yes, I'll find you somewhere to go in Dublin. You can have the baby there. No one here will know anything about it. You can tell your family that I have found you a good position in the city, working for a cousin who is in need of a lady's maid. You can say it's a promotion. I'll arrange for the child to be given to a convent. Isn't that what one does with illegitimate children? Then you can come back. It will be as if nothing has happened."

Bridie's legs began to shake. She wasn't sure she could stand much longer. She stared at him in horror and disbelief. He was going to give her baby . . . *their* baby, away? The words echoed around her head but sounded distant and hard, like an echo from a stone thrown into a deep well.

Bertie watched her staring at him with her dark eyes as big as black holes and wondered what he had said to offend her. "Is that all?" he asked, returning to his desk.

Bridie's heart was crushed by his coldness. She tried to speak but nothing escaped her throat besides her hot, shallow breathing. He sat down and picked up his pen. Afraid to remain a moment longer in his presence, she fled.

Bertie looked up to find she had gone. He took a fresh piece of paper. There was only one person to whom he could turn in such sensitive circumstances. One person he could trust above all others. He began to write in his neat, looped hand. *My dearest Grace . . .*

Chapter 20

Kitty walked down the main street in Ballinakelly. Her chin up, her gaze idle and wandering. She held a box in her hands containing a pair of shoes, a gun and a small amount of ammunition. She nodded occasionally as she passed an acquaintance, but mostly she allowed her eyes to browse the shops to give the impression that she had nowhere in particular to go—that she was carefree, aimless and most important above suspicion.

It was a blustery summer's day. It was lucky that she had pinned her hat firmly to her head to stop it flying away. Kitty held on to the shoebox, pressing the lid down with her hand, aware of the consequences should the contents be revealed. She had ridden into town in the pony and trap, taking pleasure from the deep red fuchsia growing wild in the hedges along with the habitual sight of crimson petticoats and white breeches hanging up to dry among them. She had hummed to herself as her excitement mounted. Every covert mission fired her up like a steam train, propelling her forward, leading her into adventure and intrigue and closer to Jack—always closer to Jack. Kitty believed she had been born for *this*.

As she walked toward the Catholic church of All Saints she began to get nervous. It was perfectly normal for her to be seen wandering around town, but why would a Protestant woman be making her way toward the Catholic church? She hummed to herself again to hide the sound of her heart, which beat against her ribs like a drum of war. She thought of Jack's sweet, earnest face, and the fear in his eyes at the thought of losing her gave her courage and she strode on, a small smile curling the corners of her mouth. She could taste the salt from the sea, or was it fear drying on her tongue? She had done this many times before, but never to the Catholic church. It had been Michael's idea. She wondered suddenly whether he had deliberately sent her on a fatal mission because he wanted her to get caught. As she strode on she wondered whether arrogance had made her inconsiderate of the dangers.

She noted the pair of Black and Tans standing in front of the church, their hands on their guns, eyes as narrow as stoats' as they watched the locals suspiciously. No one looked at them; everyone hurried on as if afraid to be noticed, stopped and searched. The Tans had the power of God and they weren't afraid of using it. Kitty felt their incisive gaze fall upon her shoulders like an executioner's axe. She caught her breath but continued, trying to sustain the hum that was dying in her throat. She could see them talking to each other out of the side of her vision. Then the fat one called out to her. "Where are you going, Miss Deverill?"

She stopped and smiled. "I'm going to see Father Quinn," she replied sweetly. "Is there a problem?"

"Father Quinn isn't here," said the other one.

"What have you got there?" asked the fat one.

"Shoes," she replied. "A gift from my grandmother, Lady Deverill."

"On what business are you going to see Father Quinn?"

"It's a delicate matter," she replied, stepping closer to the men and lowering her voice. "It's one of my lady's maids." She pulled a sorry face. "She's . . . I think it would be indelicate to give you the details. I need Father Quinn's advice."

The fat one dropped his eyes onto the shoebox and Kitty felt the weight of it in her hands. "My wife likes shoes," he said. "Let's see what you've got there, then."

Kitty's head flooded with blood. It crashed against her temples like waves against rock. "I don't think you'll find these very exciting," she said, making to lift the lid.

At that moment there came a loud hollering. The three turned to see Father Quinn striding furiously toward them, his gray hair wild about his head, his black robes billowing around him like an avenging angel's. In his hand was a white petticoat. He held it up as if it were the embodiment of carnal sin. "I found *this* on the beach," he raged. "God save us!" The Tans looked at him in bewilderment. "When I find the culprit I will voice God's displeasure at such an unholy show of disrespect and vulgarity. On the beach it was, in full view of the children playing there. What is the world coming to when people indulge their desires out in the open?" He settled his fiery gaze on Kitty. "And what might I ask are *you* doing at my door, Miss Kitty? I believe you have mistaken *my* church for *yours*."

Kitty paled. "Father Quinn, I have something I need to talk to you about. It's a delicate matter regarding a member of your church. May we talk in private or shall I come back when you have . . ." She hesitated and looked at the petticoat. "When you've found the owner of that petticoat?"

He scrunched the petticoat into a ball and tucked it under his arm. "I have time now. Come with me. Good day to you." He nodded at the Black and Tans who watched them disappear into the church, not knowing what to make of the scene.

"Only in Ireland," said the fat one, shaking his head.

"They're all as mad as bloody snakes," said the other one, popping a cigarette between his lips.

Kitty followed Father Quinn down the aisle to the sacristy. He closed the door behind him and took the shoebox out of her hands. "You're a bold girl, Miss Kitty."

"I thought they'd caught me," she said, suddenly feeling weak in the legs. She sank into a chair.

"So did I. I thought you were done for." He looked at the petticoat. "I'll have to return this to Mrs O'Dwyer or she'll think a seagull stole it. Though, I'll need another word of inspiration in order to explain how I came by it!" He dropped it onto the table.

Kitty looked at him in astonishment. "You invented that whole scene just to distract them?"

"Of course I did. I saw you were in trouble and it was the first thing that came into my head. Divine inspiration," he said, crossing himself. "Thanks be to God." He took out the gun and ammunition and gave her back the box. "You'd better take the shoebox home, just in case."

"Thank you, Father Quinn."

"Say no more, Miss Kitty. We are all fighting this war together and it appears that God is on our side, does it not?"

"It does indeed," Kitty agreed.

"You're a brave young woman. But I would say it was near suicidal for you to bring a gun into my church. That Michael is a reckless man. He's so busy gazing at the goal he's often unaware of the perils of the game. I will have to have a quiet word with him." He smiled at Kitty warmly. "You're not to do this again, do you understand? You're too valuable to us to get caught being reckless."

"I won't," she replied.

"Grand. Now, you'd better leave by the side door. At least if they stop you this time you'll only have a pair of shoes to show them."

"Thank you, Father Quinn."

"May God go with you, Miss Kitty."

Kitty returned to her patient pony. She stroked his muzzle affectionately, then mounted the trap. As she was leaving Ballinakelly, Michael was walking into town with his brother, Sean, hands in his pockets, cap hiding his mop of unruly curls. Kitty kept her eyes on the track ahead and ignored them both, which cost her dearly because she liked Sean very much. She shook the reins and the pony broke into a trot. As she passed Michael she felt a rising sense of triumph. She had pulled off the impossible. Out of the corner of her eye she saw him lift his chin and drop his heavy gaze upon her with a jolt. But she didn't waver and continued on up the track without so much as a twitch. Only the small smile that curled her lips betrayed her jubilation.

Once back in her bedroom she rang for Bridie. Her secret missions and liaisons with Jack had kept her so busy she hadn't noticed Bridie's increasingly white face and quiet demeanor as she discreetly went about her work. But now, when she came to the door, her raw eyes and swollen cheeks were too evident to overlook. "Bridie, what's the matter?" Kitty ran to her friend and led her to the bed where she sank into the mattress like a rag doll.

"I'm leaving, Kitty," she said, buckling beneath her sorrow.

"What do you mean you're leaving? Why would you want to leave?"

"Mr. Deverill says it's a good opportunity. A promotion. I'm going up in the world, Kitty." She began to sob.

"Papa is sending you away?" Kitty was aghast. Bridie nodded, withdrew a handkerchief out of her sleeve and patted her eyes. Kitty noticed her father's initials on the handkerchief and clicked her tongue. "He's sending you away even though you don't want to go!" She took the handkerchief out of Bridie's hand and held it up. "How callous of him! When did he tell you?"

"This morning." Bridie reached for the handkerchief and pressed it to her heart. Kitty would never know how much it meant to her.

"At least he gave you something to wipe your eyes with!" She stood up. "I shall go and talk to him. He can't send you away because I need you."

"I *want* to go," Bridie said quietly. "It's a good position for a girl like me. I've never been to Dublin."

Kitty swung round. "Dublin? Papa is sending you to Dublin?"

"Yes, Dublin." Bridie twisted the handkerchief into a knot. "Didn't I say?"

"You're not going to leave me, Bridie! We're like sisters, you and I. I *need* you!"

Bridie thought of Jack and his love for Kitty and her resolve hardened. She looked down at the handkerchief that Mr. Deverill had used to dry her eyes the first time he had kissed her, and folded it into her hands. "I have to go, Kitty. There's nothing for me here but you. If I stay I'll end up like my mother."

"That's not so terrible, surely," Kitty argued.

"I want more from my life than this."

"So, what's Papa arranged for you in Dublin?"

Bridie couldn't look at her and lie so brazenly. She stared into her lap. "I'll be working as a lady's maid for a grand lady in a beautiful house. That's all I know."

"What's the difference to working here? Aren't I grand enough for you?" Kitty grinned but Bridie could tell she was angry. "I'll always treat you well, Bridie. You know that. If it's money, I'm sure Papa can pay you more . . ."

"It's not money." Bridie looked at her steadily. "I had a fella, but now—"

"Well, why didn't you say?"

"It's over. He doesn't want me anymore." Bridie's shoulders began to shake. "I need to get away. Far away."

Kitty sat beside her and put her arms around her. "Oh Bridie, you should have told me. Did he break your heart?" Bridie nodded. "The toad!"

"It doesn't matter. He was too good for me anyway."

Kitty wondered whether she was speaking of Jack, but didn't dare ask; that subject was much too sensitive. "Nonsense," she soothed. "You're too good for *him*, Bridie. You have a heart of gold. Any man would be lucky to win it."

Bridie leaned her head against her friend and felt a warm feeling wrap her up like a blanket. "Whatever happens, we'll always be friends. Isn't that so?" she said.

Kitty held her fiercely. "You're my best friend in the whole world, Bridie. I love you like a sister. You promise to write to me every week?"

"I promise."

"If she's mean to you, or you're unhappy, or you simply miss home, your place here will always be open for you." She felt her own eyes prickling with tears. She squeezed Bridie harder. "Or if you simply miss me, I'll come up to Dublin. Yes, that's what I'll do. I'll come and visit you. You only have to say the word."

BRIDIE ARRIVED IN Dublin sick with nerves about leaving home and frightened about her uncertain future. The only consolation was the child growing inside her, whom she already loved with the passion of someone who has lost everything. When she pressed her hand to her belly she felt a wave of tenderness wash over her, drowning her fears and filling her with optimism. Surely she could persuade the nuns at the convent to let her keep her baby? But Bridie was naïve to believe that *her* wishes would ever be considered.

Grace had answered Bertie's cry for help and agreed to take Bridie in as a maid in her Dublin home for the duration of her pregnancy. When Bertie had told her of the girl's plight, Grace had understood the situation immediately and made the arrangements with the efficiency of a colonel in the British Army. The girl had to be removed discreetly and Bertie's child put up for adoption at once. Grace rose to the challenge; after all, she prided herself on her ability to get things done. "Once you have been delivered of your child I shall arrange for your passage to America," she told Bridie. "Sir Ronald and I have many friends in New York and I have already started looking for a position for you. It will be exciting starting a new life in a new city. I'm sure you'll make your family very proud." Grace faltered when she saw the girl's stricken face. It was clear from the light slowly extinguishing in her eyes that Bridie had hoped to keep her baby. But this wasn't just *any* baby: this was Bertie's baby, and there was nothing in the world that would have convinced Grace to let her keep it. "I'm afraid a girl in your position, Bridie, simply can't bring up a child on her own. This way is better for both of you." Grace averted her gaze. She couldn't bear the sight of Bridie's despair. She was only a child herself, the same age as Kitty. "One day you will thank me," she said, before leaving Bridie to the care of her housekeeper. But Bridie felt as if she had just been delivered her death sentence.

AFTER BRIDIE LEFT, the summer disintegrated into wet days and the leaves fell dejectedly onto the soggy ground. Autumn blew inland in gales that sent the waves crashing against the cliffs. The wind thrashed against the castle walls. Kitty met Jack whenever she could, but it was dangerous to be seen together. Kitty could not be observed associating with local men already under suspicion of being involved with the IRA for fear of breaking her cover. So they met in secret at the Fairy Ring, in the caves on Smuggler's Bay, in Adeline's greenhouses. Their kisses were stolen and therefore more precious than ever. They had become a small island surrounded by a hostile ocean, with enemy ships on every side. They clung to each other, living intensely and in the moment, because neither dared look beyond for the future was as dark as night.

In July both sides had agreed to a truce to end the fighting but the violence had continued nonetheless, especially in the North. When Hubert read that thirty people had been killed in Belfast he threw the paper onto the breakfast table in disgust and walked out with his gun, shouting through the hall that he was taking the dogs for a walk and woe betide any Shinner who dared step into his path. In December Kitty and Jack celebrated the Anglo-Irish Treaty, which was signed in London between the British government and the Irish delegation, declaring Southern Ireland a free state, but allowing the North to opt out and stay British if it so desired; and it did desire. This meant that Ireland would be partitioned into two parts: the independent south and the British North. But it was a compromise and compromises never please everyone. Many Irish nationalists regarded it as a betrayal and Michael Doyle was one of them. He challenged Jack to agree but Jack was growing tired of the violence. The fire in his spirit was now tempered by his deepening love for Kitty. The vision of settling down with her and starting a family was a pinprick of light at the end of a black tunnel, impossibly small but tantalizingly visible. The more he set his sights on it, the more real it became. He began to dream of peace so that he and Kitty could walk over the hills hand in hand for all the world to see. But Michael wasn't going to let him give in so easily.

THE NIGHT BEFORE Christmas Adeline sat up in bed. It was as dark as slate. Her heart beat frantically. She climbed out of bed and made her way across the cold room to the window. Pulling back the curtains revealed nothing but her own white face and nightdress reflected in the glass, staring uneasily back at her. She sighed heavily and wondered whether to wake Hubert. She could hear him snoring loudly in his bedroom next door. She was suddenly overcome by a desire to curl up beside him, like they had done in the old days when they were young and in love. She wanted to take comfort from his big, warm body. But she wasn't sure she'd be able to sleep with the noise. Finally she crept back into her own bed and curled into a ball beneath the blankets. She closed her eyes but her heart would not quieten for all the gentle thoughts she poured into it.

Kitty lay in bed blinking into the darkness. A pheasant screeched somewhere deep in the wood. Kitty shuddered. Her stomach churned with anxiety. She lay staring up at the ceiling, trying to learn the reason for her disquiet. Slowly she became aware of the presence of someone in her bedroom. She strained her eyes in the darkness, but as they adjusted she realized it wasn't a person but a spirit who had taken it upon himself to visit. She sat up and stared at the ghostly figure now standing before her. As he grew clearer she realized it was Tomas Doyle, Bridie's father. His light was dim, as if he was struggling to remain there, and his face full of worry. He held his cap in his hands and his kind eyes gazed at her with intensity but she understood nothing of what he was tying to communicate. At last he began to fade, but before he disappeared he pointed at the window, waving his finger in frustration.

Kitty pulled on her dressing gown and went to the window.

She tore back the heavy curtains and stared into the darkness. To her surprise it had a glow to it, as if dawn had begun to break in the wrong part of the sky. She gazed out in confusion. She was sure it was the middle of the night. Then she smelled smoke. It came thick and fast, carried on the wind like a sea fog, dense enough to swallow entire ships. Gripped by a terrible panic she ran out of her room and down the corridor, the smell of smoke growing stronger with every step. She ran to the top of the Hunting Lodge and looked out of the attic window. There, above the tree line, was a bright yellow light. It was so vivid it was setting the sky aflame. Sick with fright she realized the castle was on fire.

Adeline smelled the smoke before she sensed the spirits crowding her bedroom. She opened her eyes to find her room alight with ghosts. They had all squeezed into her room at once, to rouse her from sleep. "The castle is burning!" they exclaimed and Adeline sprang out of bed. She hurried into Hubert's room. Her heart was beating so loudly she could barely hear his snoring above the thumping it made. She shook him. "Hubert! Wake up! Wake up! The castle's on fire. We must get out!"

Hubert grunted and opened his eyes. He stared at her in horror. "What's the matter, woman?"

"The castle! It's on fire!" Adeline shouted. Hubert jumped out of bed and flung on his dressing gown. Smoke was sliding beneath the door like a malevolent gray snake. He grabbed a towel and plunged it into the water jug on the dresser. "Press this against your nose, my girl," he said, thrusting it into his wife's hands. He found another one for himself, then opened the door and stepped out into the smoke. They ran down the stairs as the cracking sound of burning wood and the deafening noise of flames grew ever louder.

When Hubert had delivered Adeline safely into the hall he told her he had to return to save the Shrubs. Adeline watched him disappear back up the stairs, his big body suddenly small and frighteningly vulnerable as it vanished into the smoke.

Now the whole household was spilling out onto the gravel in front of the castle with Hubert's wolfhounds, who looked around anxiously for their master. O'Flynn, Skiddy and the maids stood staring up at the building, their faces golden in the glow of the fire, their mouths agape, their eyes glittering with tears as they watched the flames blazing behind the glass windows as if Adeline were throwing the most lavish party ever. Adeline stood trembling and helpless. There was nothing anyone could do. No amount of water would put out such a fire. The castle, being so old, was going up like a tinder box and all she could do was pray for Hubert and her sisters.

She was so focused on the front door that she didn't notice Bertie and Kitty and the servants from the Hunting Lodge running toward them with reinforcements. Bertie dashed into the castle, deaf to Kitty's cries. Suddenly there were buckets of water and loyal men and women throwing them at the walls. They formed a chain, a useless, ineffectual chain that did nothing to arrest even the smallest flames. They must have known it was hopeless but they continued all the same. No one could stand and watch, except Adeline, who knew that only God could help them now.

For an agonizing length of time the door remained engulfed in smoke. The flames grew higher, the smell so intense that the water bearers had to stop and move away, coughing into their wet hands. The heat was so strong they began to sweat in the icy December night. And then Bertie emerged out of the smoke with a Shrub on each arm, choking, trembling, terrified but alive. Adeline felt a surge of relief. But when she saw that it was Bertie and not Hubert her legs buckled beneath her and she collapsed onto the ground. She hadn't noticed her son go in.

Kitty was beside her at once. "Grandma!" She wrapped her arms around her but there was nothing she could say to comfort her.

"Where's Hubert?" Adeline whispered. "My Hubert? Where is he?" But she knew. She could sense it. He had gone.

Chapter 21

As sunrise bled into the eastern sky the reds and golds of Heaven were nothing compared to the bleak brilliance of Castle Deverill. By now most of Ballinakelly had come to help put out the fire, Protestants and Catholics alike. The constabulary and all the members of the British forces available were on the scene. The grounds were swarming with people, but still no one could enter the skeleton castle to find Hubert. Adeline had been taken to the Hunting Lodge. Bertie remained at the castle. Kitty looked around. Sean was there with Mrs. Doyle, but there was no sign of Jack and there was no sign of Michael.

Kitty stayed with her grandmother until she fell asleep in Kitty's bed. The doctor had come to give her laudanum to dull her senses and she had closed her eyes like a child and sunk into the relief of slumber. Kitty dressed quickly and hurried around to the stables to saddle her horse. Without a word to anyone she galloped over the hills to Ballinakelly. There was a storm coming. She could see the purple clouds gathering on the horizon, like a fleet of black ships sailing in on an evil wind. Every instinct told her to turn back, but her anger was so great she ignored the internal warnings that had always served her so well and galloped on.

When she reached the Doyles' farm she tied her horse to a post and strode into the house. "Michael Doyle!" she shouted, marching through the rooms. "Michael Doyle! Don't be a coward and show yourself!" But only the fire smoldered in the grate from the night before. Old Mrs. Nagle's chair was empty. Suddenly the door opened and Michael stepped into the room, his bulk overwhelming the dwarfish door frame. His face was dark and damp with sweat. She could smell the oil on him, and the menace. He rubbed his bristly chin and his fingers were soiled with soot. "Top of the morning to you, Kitty. This is a pleasant surprise." But there was no joy in his voice.

"You murderer!" she hissed hysterically. "You set my home on fire! You've killed my grandfathe . . . my dear, sweet gran—" She swallowed her grief and willed herself to be strong. "You'll pay for this!"

Michael took off his cap, tossing it onto the table. His black curls fell about his head and he pushed them back with a dirty hand. "It wasn't my intention to kill anybody, but you can't bake a cake without breaking an egg or two."

Kitty stared at him in disgust. "Have you no conscience? You've murdered an innocent man."

"It was my intention to burn your father's inheritance," he

said and his face darkened with loathing. "If I've dealt him a blow to the heart, then all the better. Your grandfather? That's just the price of the struggle."

"I risked my life for the struggle and this is how you repay me? What do you have against my father? Hasn't he always been kind to you and your kin?"

Michael walked up to her and put his face so close to hers she could smell the alcohol on his lips and feel his pugnacious rage sucking the air out of the room and stealing her breath. "What do I have against your father, you ask?"

"I do indeed," she retaliated, rising to her full height.

"You mean you don't know?" His eyes glared at her, but she held her ground and stared right back at him.

"No, I don't know, Michael, so you had better tell me."

"He raped my sister."

The words hit Kitty so hard she reeled. "He raped Bridie?" she gasped, incredulous.

"Yes, indeed."

"You're lying. My father's no rapist."

"Is he not?" Michael laughed meanly. "Then why is Bridie in Dublin pregnant as a sow?"

"Bridie's pregnant!" Kitty held her stomach as if Michael had punched her beneath the ribs.

"Why do you think your father sent her to Dublin?"

"She said he had found her a job." But Bridie had broken her promise and never written. Kitty had been too distracted by Jack and her clandestine gun-running that she hadn't taken the trouble to ask herself why.

"He sent her to Dublin to get her out of the way because he violated her and when he laid his hands on her he insulted my family and our people. That's why I burned the castle. I took revenge on behalf of my kin, so help me God."

"I don't believe you!" But Kitty was unsure.

"Then ask him." He stepped away and casually took off his jacket. He began unbuttoning his shirt. "I don't think we have anything else to say to each other, do you? You'd better go and throw some water on that old fortress of yours, for all the good it will do."

"You bastard!" she shouted. "You won't get away with this. I'll tell the constabulary and they'll hang you!"

"Then they'll hang Jack too."

Kitty blanched. "Jack? What's he got to do with this?"

"Oh, he's part of the plot, all right. While the RIC are all up at the castle putting out the fire, he's stealing guns and taking them to a safe house, that is, if he doesn't get caught on the way. I have a very strong feeling that he *will* get caught on the way." He gave her a broad smile.

"How could you!" Kitty felt as if the wind had been knocked out of her. "This has nothing to do with my father, or Bridie, does it? This is about me!"

"Don't flatter yourself, Kitty Deverill. You're not my type." He took off his shirt, revealing a body honed by a life of manual labor. "Now, if you please, I have to clean myself up before my nanna comes back from Mass."

"You've set Jack up because you can't stand it that I love him and not you!" She began to laugh manically, overcome by a madness that derived from the wildness of love, war and fire. "You're a pathetic excuse for a man, Michael Doyle. Jack is worth ten of you!" Michael's face hardened. She realized then that he wanted her. In his own twisted way he probably even loved her.

"Killing and burning houses doesn't make you a man, Michael, and it never will. You'll never be the man your father was and you'll never be half the man Jack is."

She knew in that moment that she'd gone too far. The air in the room stilled. The light darkened as the purple clouds now closed in above the house. Michael grabbed her by the throat with his giant hands. "I'll show you how much of a man I am," he rasped, a diabolical look in his eyes. He threw her onto the table, pressing her nose into the wood, bruising her cheekbone. She struggled to free herself, but he had pinned her down so that she couldn't move her head. With the other hand he lifted her skirt to her waist. Panic seized her. She wriggled and writhed and banged her fists on the table but she was helpless. He roughly spread her legs with his knee and tore off her drawers, ripping them as if they were made of paper. She tried to scream but nothing came out. Her mind flooded with fear. Thick, suffocating fear that tightened and dried around her, leaving her immobile. She realized, to her horror, that *he* was going to do to *her* what *her father* had apparently done to *Bridie* and there was nothing she could do to stop him. She froze in terror as something hard prodded and probed between her legs, then forced its way inside her with unstoppable brutality. It jabbed her deep in her core, tearing her, and the pain was intense. Now suddenly she shrieked but he didn't seem to hear. His breath stentorian, his bulging black eyes fixed in the middle distance, he stabbed her again and again, faster and faster, deeper and deeper, thrusting into her with the full power of his weight as if in some perverse way he believed this act of violence would make her his. She closed her eyes and tried to think of the greenhouse in spring but all she could see was, through the gap in the door, her father thrusting into Grace. Then Grace became Bridie and Kitty opened her eyes in revulsion and began to cry.

When he was done he withdrew and buttoned up his trousers. Kitty pushed herself off the table. As she stood a trickle of warm fluid ran down her legs and her knees almost buckled beneath a wave of anguish and exhaustion. But years of suppressing her pain had taught her to dissemble. With deliberation she smoothed down her skirt and searched past her humiliation for her dignity. At last she lifted her eyes to see that Michael was as horrified as she was. He stared at her in silence, rooted to the spot, shocked by his own actions. "I hope you're satisfied, Michael Doyle," she said and her voice was surprisingly steady. He gazed at her in fear, as if he saw something truly frightening in her eyes. "As God is my witness, you will live to regret this for the rest of your life. You should have killed me. Instead you have created a Fury that will pursue you to the gates of Hell and beyond. You've no idea what a wounded woman can do. Yes, you'll wish you had killed me." She picked up her torn drawers, pulled back her shoulders, lifted her chin and left the house.

As soon as the door had slammed behind her Kitty was overcome by a swell of nausea. It began in her belly and rose up into her throat where it was duly exorcised. She held her stomach as she bent over and retched onto the grass. Fearful that Michael would witness her weakness she clamped her mouth shut and strained every muscle in her neck to suppress her distress, and staggered to her horse. It took her three attempts before her trembling knees found the strength to lift her into the saddle. Shaking the reins she galloped over the fields as fast as her mare could carry her, wincing with pain every time the motion of the horse jolted her.

Only when she was far away from the Doyle farm did she release her suffering into the wind. She howled so loudly and with such anger as to challenge even the Banshee herself. As tears rolled she wished she had plunged a dagger into his heart.

She rode to the Fairy Ring and dismounted. Standing in the center of the circle of stones where she had so often met Jack, she let the rain soothe her tormented spirit. Quite apart from the humiliation she had just suffered, the loss of her family home, her grandfather and the suggestion that her father had raped Bridie and sown a child into her belly, she feared for Jack. Had this ruined the one thing that was precious to her? Was she spoiled for him now? Would she be good enough for him? She knew that as soon as she could she would wash her body clean and then at least she'd be herself again.

For an hour she paced the soggy ground until the grass had turned to mud beneath her feet and she was sodden through and shivering with cold. When she could sob no more she found her breath and something else, deep in her core, that was always there like the still, calm ocean bed leagues below the waves. Slowly she was healed by the allure of her surroundings. Ireland—beautiful, wild, constant Ireland. The gentle rain, the desolate cry of a gull, the relentless wind that battered the coastline and the mysterious megaliths that had withstood it for hundreds of years, these things she treasured because they would never change and no one could ever take them from her.

Kitty gazed out into the mist and listening to the sounds she had known and loved all her life. She surrendered to it, and as she did so her mind cleared and her heart opened and from somewhere beyond her senses came a source of strength.

At last she mounted her horse and headed for home, whatever was left of it. But she knew now that she would cope. Michael had defiled her body but he hadn't touched her soul, and her mind was hers to command; she would lock away the memory and throw out the key. If her father had raped Bridie, why would she have held on to his handkerchief as if it was something to be treasured? Bridie had given herself to him willingly, for certain, but Kitty would never forgive him for taking her. As for her grandfather, he was dead, imprisoned now with Barton and Egerton and all the other restless heirs of Castle Deverill. Michael had burned the castle and killed its lord. But what about "A Deverill's castle is his kingdom"? The family constantly repeated that motto but now she doubted it. What did that mean anymore? Everything was ashes. The Deverills diminished. And then she understood, that in his disgusting way, Michael Doyle had recognized that spirit in her, and in his attempt to possess her and destroy her, he had in fact made her stronger. Now she was worthy of her name.

KITTY RETURNED HOME to find the castle still burning. When the rain put out the last of the embers all that remained was the western tower and the outer stone walls. It was as if that part of the building had been protected by a supernatural force, for the room where Barton Deverill resided remained unscathed. Adeline insisted she remain there, for not even Hubert's "bloody Shinners" could keep her from his spirit, which now haunted that tower with all his unfortunate ancestors. The Shrubs feared she had lost her mind. Bertie feared the tower was unstable and begged her to come back to the Hunting Lodge where it was safe. But Kitty understood her grandmother better than all of them. She took comfort, as she always had, from Adeline's presence up there in the tower where she lit a fire and lounged in Barton's chair, drinking cannabis tea and talking to her husband as if he were still made of flesh and blood and complaining about the state of the country, only now he was complaining about the other spirits who had the audacity to enter the tower he had claimed for himself.

Kitty soon heard from Grace that Jack and Michael had gone into hiding. Jack had been caught taking stolen guns to a safe house outside Ballinakelly but he had overpowered the two Auxiliaries who had arrested him and escaped into the hills. As for Michael, a warrant was out for his arrest for arson. Grace assumed they were together and that they would hear word as soon as they were able to contact them. "We have friends all over the country, Kitty. Jack and Michael will be safe, I promise you."

"Michael Doyle can rot in hell for all I care," Kitty replied and the venom in her voice gave Grace a jolt.

"My dear, you don't think he's responsible for setting fire to the castle? Surely . . . ?"

"He's a monster, Grace," Kitty interjected passionately. "He set Jack up and destroyed my home."

Grace stiffened. She put her hand on Kitty's arm and gripped her harder than she intended. "Michael is guilty of some terrible things," she said softly and Kitty was astonished that Grace didn't see Michael for the brute that he was. "But you are way off the mark here."

"He did it, Grace. I *know* he did it!" Kitty insisted. "He betrayed Jack . . ."

Grace's eyes filled with fear. "You're wrong," she interrupted firmly. "I can only assume that your judgment has been clouded by your emotions. Michael is . . . wild, strong, a bull in a china shop perhaps, but nothing if not loyal, Kitty. I assure you, when he finds out who destroyed Castle Deverill, the culprit shall be suitably punished. No one will be keener to see that happen than Michael Doyle. As for Jack, that was just unfortunate. However, he got away and he will be somewhere safe by now. You have to trust me." But Kitty's intuition screamed distrust. She was too ashamed of her father and of what had taken place in the Doyle farmhouse to ever tell Grace the truth and, even if she did, she somehow doubted Grace would believe her, because Grace didn't *want* to believe her. As the older woman stubbornly defended Michael there was something about her defense that led Kitty to suspect that she cared about him more than she should.

* * *

Hubert's funeral was almost a requiem for Anglo-Irish society itself. "*The Irish Ascendancy has been rocked by the untimely death of my dear old friend Lord Deverill of Ballinakelly, known to all as Hubert,*" wrote Viscount Castlerosse in his *Express* column. "*Even in London no one can talk of anything else, from the tea rooms of the Ritz to the drawing rooms of Mayfair. I attended the funeral myself . . .*" Maud cried for Hubert and for her husband's ruined inheritance. How would she hold her head up in London society now that her castle was reduced to cinders? Everyone expected Bertie, the new Lord Deverill, to flee his estate and settle in England as so many had. Maud, now Lady Deverill, returned to Ballinakelly for Hubert's funeral, but it was unsafe for Harry, who remained in London. He wasn't certain he'd be able to face the rubble or Joseph, who had been his first and enduring love. Victoria, now finally pregnant with her first child, sent her grandmother a letter of condolence on a gold-embossed letterhead with her initials *V.E.* but didn't want to jeopardize her pregnancy by sailing across the Irish Sea. A heavily pregnant Elspeth, however, attended with her new husband, Peter. They might not have much money, but at least their castle was still standing.

Stoke and Augusta braved the journey with Digby, Beatrice and their daughter Celia. They held their chins up in defiance of the outrages waged against their family. "We're Deverills, my dear Celia," said Digby as the Irish coastline loomed out of the fog. "We must give our family our support and show those Shinners that we Deverills aren't to be broken or cowed by their violence. A Deverill's castle is his kingdom."

Beatrice gazed out over the green hills and recalled those balmy summers at Castle Deverill, now gone forever, and her heart ached with nostalgia and a sudden, searing pain for her darling George, who had adored them as much as she had.

The funeral was a gray, solemn affair, the day drizzly and cold. The people of Ballinakelly gathered outside the church of St. Patrick to pay their respects, for even the most ardent supporters of Sinn Féin did not condone the murder of Lord Deverill, though some of them believed it right that the castle, a bastion of British supremacy, should be razed to the ground. Mrs. Doyle, Old Mrs. Nagle and Sean remained at the back, for they knew Michael had had a hand in the fire and their shame weighed heavily upon them—as did the uncertainty of their own future now that Mrs. Doyle's livelihood had been devastated along with the castle.

Celia found her cousin Kitty much changed. The mischief had gone out of her eyes and in its place a distance that made Celia long for the past when they had been as close as sisters. It seemed as if they had both grown up and apart. Their childhood belonged to another life, and to other people entirely. Celia couldn't understand why she didn't come back to London with her. "We'd have so much fun together, you and I," she explained excitedly. "Parties galore and handsome men calling day and night. It's a whirlwind of entertainment and I shall introduce you to everyone. You'll be the toast of London, Kitty. Please say you will."

But to Kitty the idea of leaving Ireland was akin to ripping out her heart. "I belong here," she replied and the solemn expression on her cousin's face told Celia that no amount of persuasion would change her mind.

"Will you at least consider it? What's left for you here, Kitty? The castle is all but demolished." She took her cousin's hand when she noticed Kitty's jaw tense and her cheeks blanch and a glimpse of the old Kitty shone through the cracks in her newly constructed armor. "Just because you come over to London doesn't mean you're not Irish. But you have to consider your future. Find a rich man and you can rebuild your castle." She smiled encouragingly.

"I don't care if I never marry, Celia. I will happily remain here for the rest of my days. Right now Grandma needs me. She's alone in that tower and I'm the only one who dares visit her. Everyone else thinks it's on the brink of falling down but Grandma will hear none of it. I'm all she has left." Kitty sighed and Celia felt its heaviness as if it were a solid thing. "The Shrubs have returned to their home but they barely ever leave it for fear of coming to harm. If anyone should leave for England, they should. But they won't, either. You see, we're Irish, Celia. We're all Irish. England is not our home, nor will it ever be. I'd rather die here on Irish soil than live my life in London, pining for my home."

"Your mother—"

"My mother never liked Ireland," Kitty snapped, interrupting her. "She's never liked me either. She's only ever liked herself, which is fortunate because she's the only person who does. I don't care if I never see her again."

Celia gasped. "Kitty, surely you don't mean that . . ."

"You know I do, Celia. I hope she leaves for England and never comes back."

Celia's heart swelled with compassion as Kitty suddenly looked forlorn in spite of her efforts to appear strong. "Oh Kitty, you seem so angry." Celia sighed. "And so alone."

"I'm not alone, Celia. Far from it. I have Ireland and Ireland is more constant than people." Celia knew then that grief had placed her cousin out of her reach. There was nothing more she could do to help.

WHEN EVERYONE LEFT, the only people who remained at Castle Deverill were Bertie, Adeline and Kitty and a small retinue of servants. Bertie wanted very much to leave for London but he had his mother to consider, mad though he thought she was, languishing up there in the castle tower talking to herself and drinking that intoxicating weed she called medicine. Busy with the business of his father's will and the salvaging of precious items from the castle ruins, he didn't notice his daughter's frostiness toward him. When his mind wasn't on his devastated home it was on Grace. She had been a tremendous support to him taking care of the maid's pregnancy and the birth of her son, keeping it quiet and dealing with it both discreetly and efficiently. He had seen a great deal of her since the fire. With Ronald away now so much of the time, she came to dine with him most evenings. Although they weren't lovers anymore at least they were friends. He was grateful for that.

Kitty waited anxiously for news from Jack. She visited the hole in the wall five times a day to check for messages but her own damp letter was all she ever found. She never gave in to crying and she never gave up hope. She imagined him hiding out in the hills and prayed that people were being kind and giving him food to eat and a warm bed to sleep in. When at last her monthly arrived she was overwhelmed with relief; she could now try and put the horror of her ordeal behind her. But in the back of her mind she worried that Jack might sense a difference in her and be repelled. And then, one late January morning, she discovered not a note, but Jack himself, hiding behind the wall. She stared at him in disbelief. Then her eyes filled with tears and her strength gave way to sobs, so long stifled by the force of her will. Without a word he jumped over the wall and gathered her into his arms, holding her tightly and pressing his lips to her temple. In that moment she cried for her lost virtue and for the fact that Jack would not be the first to take her as a woman. She cried too because she knew she would never tell him.

Jack believed her tears were for her burned home and her dead grandfather and he hugged her close and waited for her grief to pass through her. Finally, he held her steady and looked deeply into her eyes. "I've come back for you, Kitty. I want you to come away with me. We can start a new life together far, far away where no one will find us. I want to marry you. I want you to have my children. I want to grow old with you." Kitty was lost for words. "I love you, Kitty Deverill. I love the bones of you. But we can't be happy here. We have to go where the law won't find *me* and your family won't find *you*. We have to go where we can be free."

"Where?" Kitty asked. Her heart was thumping so loudly in her chest she could barely hear herself speak.

"America."

Kitty was astounded. "You want to leave Ireland?"

"Until things quieten down. I want to make a life for us, Kitty. I can't do that here."

"But what about Ireland? What about the fight?"

"It's over, Kitty. I accept the Treaty. I don't want to be part of the violence anymore. I want to live in peace, with you."

"I can't leave my grandmother . . . I can't leave my home . . ." Her gaze wandered over the gardens forlornly.

"Look at me, Kitty." She did as she was told. "There's nothing left here. The castle's gone. We have to leave. I have to leave before they bloody shoot me."

The thought of Jack facing the firing squad concentrated Kitty's mind. "All right. I'll leave with you as long as it's only temporary. As long as we come back. If I know we'll come back I'll be able to leave." She began to cry again. "Please reassure me that we'll come back."

"I promise you, we'll come back."

"Then I'll go with you," she conceded quietly.

"Good. There's a boat leaving from Queenstown the day after tomorrow. We have to leave at dawn on the early train. It's all arranged."

"How?"

"Trust me. I have friends in high places. I have two passages and someone to vouch for us when we get there."

"I have nothing, Jack. No money . . ."

"You have *me*." He hugged her again. "You have me, Kitty, and that's all you'll ever need." He grinned at her and her anxiety was dispelled by his confidence. "I'll meet you here at six in the morning. Don't be late."

As she hurried back to the Hunting Lodge she found that she was trembling all over. Jack had returned but her heart was pounding with dread. She hadn't anticipated leaving Ireland. She gazed upon the ruins of the castle and knew that Celia was right. There was nothing left for her here. But still, she didn't know whether she had the strength to tear herself away, for a tear it would be. How she would bleed. Without Ireland she would not be herself.

She slowed her pace and in her chest there grew a pressure so great that it caused her breathing to become labored. She put her hand to her heart and suddenly all the horror of the last month seemed to crash down on top of her. "I don't know if I can do this," she whispered to herself, pacing small circles on the grass. "I don't know if I can leave. I love you, Jack, but I love Ireland. I don't know if I have the courage." Her face crumpled with despair and indecision. She put her fist in her mouth and bit down onto her flesh to stifle another sob. "God help me. Am I going mad?" Then she managed to control herself again. "No, I can do it," she rallied. "I love Jack. There's nothing for me here. I love Jack. I love Jack, I love Jack with all my heart." She strode off toward the Hunting Lodge.

As she reached the front door she saw a basket in the porch. At first she thought it was a basket of food, but as she approached she realized that it was a baby. She bent down and gazed into the tiny pink face. A red curl was already falling over his pale forehead. She flinched as the baby opened his eyes and seemed to stare at her. His boldness took her breath away. Tucked into the blanket was a note. With a shaking hand she opened it. *Please take good care of me, Kitty. I am a Deverill and I belong to you.* She turned it over, hoping for more, but there was nothing. Tentatively she allowed the baby to grip her finger. He was so compelling she was unable to wrench her eyes away. She guessed at once. This must be Bridie's child; her half brother.

"Hello, my little friend," she said softly and her vision blurred. "I'm going to take good care of you. For Bridie. And for me, because I'm going to need someone to love."

Chapter 22

"This is an outrage!" Bertie thundered, averting his eyes from the baby Kitty had just brought into the library in a basket.

"He is your child, Papa, and I intend to keep him." Kitty gazed at her father steadily.

He knocked back a swig of whiskey and stared into the fire. "So you know," he said quietly.

"I know." There was a long pause. Kitty didn't want to hear the details. She feared suddenly that he might have raped Bridie, after all. Perhaps she was just being naïve because she wanted to believe her father incapable of brutality. She dispelled the image of him taking Grace and dared not imagine how he had taken Bridie. She wanted to admire him. For all the world she wanted him to be honorable. She dropped her eyes onto the child who was sleeping again. "Where is Bridie now?"

"America," he replied.

"You sent her to America?" Kitty was astounded.

"She's starting a new life, Kitty. It's what she wanted."

Kitty's eyes began to water. "You sent her away without her baby? How could you?"

"It's what she wanted," he repeated.

"I don't believe that. Bridie has a heart. I know she does." She gazed into the basket. "He's my half brother," she added.

"He's a bastard," Bertie retorted.

"Then he's *my* bastard." Kitty felt a swell of affection for the helpless creature and a keen sense of loyalty to her friend.

"I will not have him in this house." Her father's face reddened. When he turned to look at her she was surprised to see his countenance so void of compassion. "He will return to the convent as arranged. You're in no position to raise a child on your own. How do you imagine you're going to find a husband if you have a baby to tarnish your reputation?"

"You sound like Mama," she stated sharply.

"Perhaps she spoke sense, after all."

"I'll get by."

"And what of my reputation? How will you explain to people that you suddenly have a child?"

"He's a foundling I took in. Left on our doorstep. That's the truth, isn't it? I can't imagine how, but Bridie found a way of getting her baby to us. I admire her for her bravery. I'm not going to let her down. The child belongs here, at Castle Deverill."

Bertie drained his glass and went to the drinks tray to pour another. His hand was trembling as he lifted the crystal decanter. "She came to me willingly," he said quietly, pouring the golden liquid into the glass. Kitty didn't reply. The image of Michael's dark face loomed large in her mind, his voice insistent: *He raped my sister.* "I was careless," Bertie added. He put the glass to his lips and shook his head. "That is the result of my carelessness."

"But I will love him and bring him up as a Deverill. He's our flesh and blood. See, he's even got my red hair. I don't care what you say or what anyone else says. I owe it to Bridie."

"You won't get a penny from me," said her father, and Kitty felt the cold slap of rejection.

She delved deep and found her courage. "I won't ever ask." She walked out of the room and closed the door behind her. There was one person she knew she could call on to help her. After all, didn't Grace Rowan-Hampton owe her her life?

BERTIE SWALLOWED HIS second whiskey and closed his eyes to shut out the room, which was suddenly spinning and making him dizzy. He felt sick to his stomach. He had thought he could cover up his blunder by sending Bridie to America and giving her baby to the nuns. Grace had assured him that the whole unfortunate business would simply disappear. But no, the boy, by the inevitable march of fate, had found his way right to his doorstep. He rubbed his eyes. He couldn't face thinking about it. Guilt had stalked him like a hunter and finally caught him. He surrendered to it like a cornered animal with nowhere to run.

The fact that the bastard was his would not remain a secret for very long. The shame would be immense. Suddenly he worried what Maud would say. Maud, whom he despised for all her bourgeois pettiness and ambition. If she were an aristocrat like Grace she'd probably accept the child and raise it as her own, but Maud had no breeding and no taste for eccentricity.

He had married her for her beauty and her iciness, which had once posed so great a challenge for a man who could have anybody. Who would want him now? Even Grace had turned away from him.

He walked to his desk and sat down. Beads of sweat collected on his skin. He opened the bottom drawer and found his gun hidden beneath a pile of papers. Carefully he lifted it out. The last time he had held it was the day Grace had rejected him. The day he had put it to his temple. The day he had failed to end it all and fallen like a drunken coward, hitting his head on the side of the desk, only to be found later, bleeding and defeated in the corridor, by Bridie. That was where it had all started. Before that moment he hadn't ever noticed her. But every action has a consequence. That moment had changed his fate. Grace hadn't wanted him anymore but Bridie did.

Again he pressed the barrel to his temple. Again he closed his eyes. Again his finger trembled on the trigger. And again he lacked the courage to take his own life.

KITTY AND THE baby arrived at Grace's manor in the Daimler. The stables and garages had not been affected by the fire and the chauffeur was grateful he still had a job. Brennan the butler glanced at the baby curiously before showing her into the hall and telling her firmly to wait while he announced her to his mistress. Kitty did as she was told, shifting her weight from one foot to the other with impatience. He seemed to be gone a long time before Grace appeared at last, her shoes tapping lightly across the marble floor. Her eyes dropped to the basket and a look of concern blackened her face. "What is this?" she asked, and for a moment Kitty wondered whether it was asking too much of her friend to help with her father's illegitimate child.

"Oh Grace, it's a long story . . ." Kitty began, suddenly feeling weak beneath the burden of responsibility. "I'm sorry I brought him here. I had nowhere else to go."

"This is Bridie's child," Grace said.

"You know?"

"Don't look so surprised, my dear. Your father had no one to turn to either. It appears I'm the only available port in a storm."

"Do you know who put him on my doorstep?" Kitty asked.

"He was left on your doorstep?"

"With a note."

"May I see it?"

Kitty pulled it out of her pocket. Grace read it and her irritation appeared to deepen. "I don't know who wrote this," she said quickly, handing it back. "But it's clear to me that either Bridie herself managed to spirit her son out of the convent and send him down here, or someone who very much wants *you* to raise her child. I can imagine your father was none too pleased to see him."

"He wanted me to send him back. He was furious. I don't think I've ever seen him so angry."

"Give him time. He'll regret his outburst, I have no doubt. In the meantime, you can stay here as long as you like."

"Oh, thank you, Grace." Kitty sank onto the sofa and put her head in her hands. Her eyes filled with tears and she began to tremble. Grace's irritation evaporated and she sat down beside her and drew her against her breast as a mother with her child. "It's going to be all right, Kitty," she soothed. "This is a tremendous responsibility for a young girl like you, especially after everything you have been through." But Kitty was now thinking of Jack. She closed her eyes and let out her anguish into Grace's arms.

"Jack wants me to go to America with him," she told her. "He's going to be waiting for me at dawn, by the wall in the vegetable garden. But I can't . . ." Her voice broke. "I can't—"

"You can't go now." Grace spoke for her. "Of course you can't go. You have a duty to Bridie's child and the practicalities of taking a small baby to America are simply too complicated. How would you feed yourself, let alone a baby? Jack will understand. If you love each other, you'll both wait."

Kitty was reassured. "He'll come back when there's peace, won't he?"

Grace swept away a stray tear with her thumb. "Of course he will, my dear."

"You're very kind, Grace." Kitty looked deeply into her friend's gentle brown eyes and felt a swell of gratitude. "I regret ever having doubted you."

THE FOLLOWING MORNING Kitty went to the wall to wait for Jack. Dawn was riding the night's sky, illuminating the darkness with stripes of indigo and gold. She had been too nervous to sleep. She knew she was asking a lot of Jack to wait for her, but there was nothing else she could do. She owed it to her friend to take care of her son. She owed it to the Deverills.

At last Jack appeared at the wall in his jacket and cap, a shabby bag slung over his shoulder. He smiled at Kitty but his smile soon faded when he saw her inappropriate attire and the fact that she had not brought a bag. He paled. "You're not coming, are you?" he said, and his obvious disappointment made Kitty's heart buckle.

"I can't." Kitty thrust her hands into her coat pockets. She couldn't tell him about her father and Bridie and the baby; it was too complicated and still too raw. He'd ask her to leave the baby. He'd persuade her to elope with him. She might weaken and then what? "I can't leave Grandma, and Papa needs me," she said.

"Oh Kitty . . ." he groaned. He put his hand on his hip and turned away. His profile was as hard as if it were carved out of granite. He stared into the distance, lost in thought. His mouth, drawn into a bitter line, reminded her of the boy he had once been when the tinker had hit him on the jaw. For a moment she thought he was going to tell her it was all over. That good–bye was forever. But he took off his cap, settled his intense blue eyes on hers once again and gathered her into his arms, where he held her so tightly she could scarcely breathe. "Then as God is my witness, I'll come back for you," he said, and the passion in his voice left her in no doubt that he would. "When peace returns to Ireland I'll come back and marry you."

"And we'll remain here in Ballinakelly," she replied through her tears. "They'll all just have to get used to it." She pulled an envelope out of her pocket and gave it to him. "For you to take to America so you don't forget me."

"I'll never forget you, Kitty. For as long as I live your face will be engraved on my heart." He kissed her one last time and Kitty closed her eyes to commit it to memory.

Jack put the envelope in the inside pocket of his jacket and disappeared into the wood, leaving Kitty alone in the garden with only the sound of squabbling crows that picked at the castle ruins like thieves in a graveyard.

She let her gaze wander down the familiar paths of her childhood. The greenhouses with their domed roofs, the rows of growing vegetables, the walls where jasmine and clematis grew in abundance in the summertime, the immaculately manicured lawns where they had played croquet and tennis, which were neglected now and overgrown with weeds. Her heart pined for her lost youth and the girl she once was, rebellious, carefree and wild. She hadn't realized how happy she had been. In spite of Miss Grieve's cruelty and her mother's rejection, her cares had been few. She remembered watching the nature spirits that had danced in little balls of light around the flower beds, the ghosts who had been her most regular companions, the secret conversations about fairies she had enjoyed with her grandmother in her little sitting room that smelled of turf fire and lilac. It was all gone; all of it. Who was she now and where did she belong? She was nothing more than a ghost herself, haunting the castle.

Suddenly, she was seized by a dreadful sense of regret and the realization that she had just made an awful mistake. She put her hands to her head and let out a loud wail. "What have I done!" she shouted into the empty garden. With her heart thumping and the blood pulsating in her temples she ran toward the wall where she had left Jack. How could she give him up when she knew that living without him would be impossible? How could she sacrifice her love for a child who didn't even belong to her? What had she been thinking? Why was she so ready to forfeit her own happiness when no one demanded it of her, only her own misplaced sense of duty?

Her throat constricted with panic as she ran through the woods, taking the shortcut to Ballinakelly where Jack would be waiting for the train, reflecting perhaps on his loss. She could barely see the way for the tears that blurred her vision. It didn't matter that she had no belongings save the clothes she was wearing. If she was with Jack she'd have everything she needed. If they were together, they'd require only the air they breathed: love would do the rest. She sprinted on, falling over a tree stump as she hurried down the hill, not caring that her dress tore on the brambles and her skin ripped on the thorns. She was desperate not to miss him. Once gone, she feared, he might be gone forever.

She stumbled into town. Her face was smeared with tears and dirt, her hair a tangled mess. She envisaged herself running into his arms and the sense of relief was almost within her grasp. Everything was going be all right. Soon they'd be together and nothing would ever part them again.

She hastened through a small copse, reaching the station from behind. There, in the dull light, she saw the platform and the red-bricked station house with its white awning and the rickety bridge that straddled the tracks. Then she saw Jack. He cut a forlorn figure as he stood there alone, his heavy gaze lost in the no-man's-land between reality and the brighter realm of if-only. She was so overcome with relief her legs went weak and nearly gave way altogether. She lifted a hand to wave but, when she cried out, her voice was a breathy squeak, overwhelmed by the sudden eruption of thumping boots that echoed off the station walls as Black and Tans swarmed onto the platform with their guns pointing at Jack. Her heart stalled. She collapsed to her knees. The large number of men seemed excessive for the arrest of one rebel, but they clearly weren't taking any chances: he had outsmarted them before.

She watched, helpless, as Jack dropped his bag and put his hands in the air, his expression resigned. They handled him roughly, beating him about the head, thumping him in the stomach with the butts of their guns so that he bent double, then fell to the ground. Kitty hugged her own stomach and let out a wild and desperate shriek that was lost in the whistle of the train as it steamed into the station like a breathless dragon. She tried to see through the windows to the other side but her eyes were blinded by tears. When the train eventually moved away the platform was empty. Jack had gone. There was no evidence that he had ever been there, except the deep crack in Kitty's heart that would never mend.

With an ache of longing for all that was lost she ran to the castle and up the charred back staircase to the western tower where her grandmother sat reading and talking to her husband as if the fire had never happened. She burst in, which startled Adeline, for she was unused to living people coming into her room—Bertie insisted on meeting her downstairs in the re-mains of the boot room where he had set up a table so they could at least eat together, the food being brought up daily from the Hunting Lodge because Adeline refused to leave Hubert. Bertie hoped that the cold would change her mind.

"Grandma!" Kitty exclaimed, falling at Adeline's feet. "I'm so unhappy!" She dropped her head onto her grandmother's lap and sobbed.

Adeline put down her book and stroked her granddaugh-ter's hair, giving her grief time to pass. "My darling child, you must be strong," she said at length. "We must all be strong. Life is full of changes but we mustn't fear them. We must adapt."

"But *everything* has changed. Everything. I don't know who I am anymore."

"Come come now, Kitty. Just because things change around you doesn't mean *you* are any different."

"But you don't understand. I need to tell you everything. You're the only person I can truly trust." Kitty told her about Jack, her involvement with the rebels, her father's indiscretion with Bridie and the baby left on their doorstep. When she had finished she sat up and looked at her grandmother with large, glassy eyes. Adeline's face was serene, as if nothing Kitty told her had been in the least surprising. "He's been arrested now," she choked. "What if they execute him? What if I never see him again? I don't think I can go on without him, Grandma. I don't think I can do it."

"You can and you must," said Adeline fiercely. "Do you think Jack would want you to lie in a heap and give up on life? Of course he wouldn't."

"But he doesn't know I was there. He thought I wasn't coming. I shouted but he didn't hear me."

Adeline patted her head. "Then you must write to him and tell him, Kitty. When they release him you will be reunited."

"But will they release him? Do you *see* that, Grandma? Do you see us together? Tell me what you see because I see nothing but a void."

Adeline looked at her granddaughter steadily. "Didn't I tell you that you are a brave child of Mars? Life was never going to be an easy path but full of potholes that are of your choosing. It's in your nature to elect the roughest road." She sighed and ran a hand down Kitty's red hair. "You're my favorite grand-child. You always have been. We're so alike, you and I, and yet you're far more reckless than I ever was. I don't know who you get that from." She laughed. "Hubert says you get it from him, but I don't agree." Kitty raised her eyes to see her grandfather sitting in the armchair opposite. He looked so real for a moment she believed he hadn't perished in the flames and her heart gave a little jump. "No, my dear, I'm afraid he's a spirit, just like all the others. Were you to marry this Jack of yours, you could come and live here and set them all free."

"That would be a dream," said Kitty sadly.

"The child is your destiny, Kitty. Your father wants nothing to do with him, which is very predictable. He's a terrible coward, I'm afraid. So, *you* have to look after him."

"How? Papa won't give me a penny. He's my half brother. He's Bridie's boy . . ."

"And he's a Deverill. He's one of us." Adeline lifted her chin. "I will support you. Hubert has provided for me in his will and I have more than enough. This little boy is my grandson. You can count on me to give you everything you need." Kitty stood up and wiped her eyes. "Brace yourself, little child of Mars, for the road is a long one and it is full of peril. I suggest you leave now. I feel an urgency suddenly. You need to leave Ireland at once. May God go with you."

KITTY RETURNED TO the Hunting Lodge, where the chauffeur waited to drive her back to the manor. With a heavy heart she climbed into the car and was driven away.

When she reached the manor, Grace was waiting for her on the doorstep, wringing her hands. From the expression on her face Kitty knew something terrible had happened. "Thank God you're back," Grace exclaimed, running down the steps to meet her. "You must come inside quickly. Jack has been arrested at the station."

"How do *you* know about that?" Kitty asked in astonishment.

"Little goes on around here that I don't know about," she replied cagily, leading Kitty into the hall.

Kitty gripped Grace's arm. "I was there, Grace," she hissed. "I changed my mind. I was there and I saw it all."

"But they didn't see *you*?" Grace asked anxiously.

"No, they didn't. What will they do to him?" Her breaths came out in gasps. "They won't hurt him, will they?" Kitty panicked suddenly, remembering the envelope she had given him. "Dear God," she cried, squeezing Grace's arm harder. "I gave him a photograph of me . . . and a letter."

Grace was quick to act. "Then you must leave immediately. There's no time to waste."

"Where to?"

"London, of course. Where else?" Grace took her by the hand and led her briskly upstairs. "You must take the baby with you. You can stay in my house in Mayfair for as long as you like. Ireland is no longer a safe place for you, my dear. Now pack your bag and hurry."

Just before they disappeared onto the landing Grace glanced over her shoulder into the hall below, where a man stepped out of the shadows. He ran a rough hand through his thick, curly hair, then began to button up his shirt. Their eyes met and a silent understanding passed between them. Grace hurried Kitty on down the corridor. Michael Doyle replaced his cap, slipped into his jacket, then vanished.

BRIDIE WAS IN her narrow bunk in the steerage cabin she shared with three other Irish girls when she was woken by a loud commotion coming from the deck. She blinked a moment, then with a sinking feeling remembered where she was. The emerald hills of home had been no more than a dream. She sat up, stiff from the hard mattress, feeble after nearly two weeks of tiny portions of tasteless food, and listened. The disturbance grew into a roar. Her heart was seized with terror. Was the boat sinking? She called for Eileen, the girl from Co. Wicklow she had befriended on the voyage, but when she got up and looked onto the top bunk, Eileen's bed was empty. Urgently she dressed and gathering her small case of belongings she hurried out into the corridor and upstairs to the deck as fast as her trembling legs could carry her.

It seemed as if every single passenger was out on deck. Dawn had broken misty and cold but out of the gloom she could see the magnificent figure of a monumental statue rising out of the sea. Suddenly, a reverential silence fell upon the crowd. They stared at this symbol of liberty as if it were some kind of benevolent god, bestowing upon them a new and positive future. Christians fell to their knees and crossed themselves. Jews began to pray in their talliths. Old men and women cried with happiness. Children sobbed because their parents did. Bridie began to cry too, not for the sight of this promised land, but for the one she had left behind and the baby she had abandoned there. She stood, engulfed by this crowd of strangers all seeking a new life as she was, and cried for everything she had lost.

PART THREE

Chapter 23

London, England, 1922

Celia sat at her dressing table as Marcie, her maid, arranged her hair in preparation for her mother's regular Tuesday evening salon. She glanced absent-mindedly at that morning's *Express* newspaper where Viscount Castlerosse, the gossip columnist, had written in his London Log: *I can never bear to miss one of my dear friend Lady Deverill's weekly Salons at her gorgeous residence on Kensington Palace Gardens where American film actors mix with aristocrats and politicians, and drink the new American cocktails to jazz music. This week I saw Mr. Douglas Fairbanks and his new wife Mary Pickford, talking about his new film* Robin Hood *while Ivor Novello, the upcoming songwriter from Wales, was singing one of his hit tunes at the piano, accompanied by The Sax, the black musician from New Orleans who has won many intimate fans among our lady hostesses. In another corner the Russian émigré, Prince*

Yusopov, was telling the Foreign Secretary, Lord Curzon, about how he killed Rasputin (for the tenth time). Also there was . . .

Harry lounged on the chaise longue in his silk dressing gown, smoking one of Beatrice's Turkish cigarettes he had stolen from the pearl box in the drawing room. Since moving to London he had developed a close friendship with Celia and was rarely out of her company. With their angel-blond hair, alabaster skin and blue eyes they might easily have passed for siblings were it not for George's memory which remained clear and strong in the minds of all who had known him. While Maud trawled the scene for a suitable bride for her son, a bigger challenge than ever considering there was no castle to use as bait, Harry partied incessantly with his tireless cousin and George's childhood friend, the beautiful and laconic Boysie Bancroft.

"What did you think of Charlotte Stalbridge?" Celia asked. "Your mama was pushing her in your direction all evening."

Harry took a long drag of his cigarette and blew out a ring of smoke. "Frightfully dull," he replied.

"But she's pretty enough, isn't she?"

"What's the good of an attractive shop window if there's nothing worth buying in the shop?"

Celia giggled. "She might have lots of money but she doesn't have a clue how to dress herself."

"That pale pink was awfully unbecoming," Harry agreed. "A girl with her coloring should avoid pale colors. You, on the other hand, look exquisite in every shade."

"Will you write a poem about me one day? I'd like to be immortalized in verse. A long and musical poem like *The Lady of Shalott*."

"She came to a nasty end. *To look down to Camelot she knows not what the curse may be, and so she weaveth steadily, and little other care hath she, The Lady of Shalott."*

"Oh, how romantic it is and how clever of you to know it by heart." Her hair done, she waved away her maid, who left the room, closing the door behind her. "I saw you'd written a poem for Boysie." Harry sat up and took his ashtray to the window, where he stared onto the garden below at a pair of portly pigeons pecking the grass. "I didn't mean to pry. I saw it on your bedside table. Of course I didn't read it," she added hastily. "Only, I'd like you to write one about me. You're aw-fully talented. One day you'll be famous, like Oscar Wilde."

The comparison was not lost on Harry. He took a final drag of the cigarette and stubbed it out. "Oscar Wilde is remembered for more than his writing, poor, tragic man," he said quietly.

"He was wonderfully scandalous. There's nothing wrong with a man loving another man, is there? It's a brotherly love of sorts, wouldn't you say?"

"I don't love Boysie, if that's what you're insinuating. I admire him. He's a very intelligent man. I write poems about everybody."

"I know that. But if you did love him, there'd be no harm in it. That's all I'm saying."

"You do speak nonsense sometimes, old girl." He left the ashtray on the windowsill. "I suppose I'd better change. People will be arriving soon."

As he was about to leave the room Beatrice flung open the door and marched in, holding a telegram in her pudgy, bejew-eled hand. "Celia, Harry, sit down. I have some extraordinary news." Harry glanced at Celia and returned to the chaise longue. "Your sister Kitty is on her way to London."

"But that's wonderful news, Mama!" Celia exclaimed.

Beatrice's eyes widened. "She's bringing a baby!"

"A baby!" Harry repeated. "Whose baby?"

"A foundling."

"Really, her social conscience is a riot!" Celia laughed. "Do you remember that summer we had to pick and pod for the poor?"

"Who's the telegram from?" Harry asked. Beatrice handed it to him. "Ah, Lady Rowan-Hampton," he said. "I suppose Papa is having nothing to do with it, otherwise she'd be staying in Ireland. I didn't think anything would induce her to leave Castle Deverill."

"She was adamant she wasn't going to leave when I suggested it at Cousin Hubert's funeral. I tried every sort of persuasion but she wouldn't have it." Celia narrowed her eyes. "I wonder whose baby it is."

"Well, it's not hers," said Beatrice.

"Is she coming here?" Celia asked hopefully.

"No, she's staying at Grace's in Mayfair."

"Does Mama know?" Harry asked.

"Not yet. The duty has fallen to me to tell her," said Beatrice glumly.

"Ah," said Harry. "The best of luck, then."

"Why would she care?" Celia asked. "Your mother's never given a stuff about Kitty."

"Her unmarried daughter arriving in London with a baby will be scandalous. Everyone will assume it's hers," he told her.

"And so what?" said Celia, who enjoyed being avant-garde. "It's 1922, not 1822!"

"All the same, Mama's very conscious of her reputation," said Harry.

"Because it's all she has left," Celia added spitefully.

WHEN MAUD HEARD the news she sat down and put her delicate white hand to her lips. "Why on earth would Kitty bring a baby to London? Does she want to ruin me?"

Beatrice had anticipated Maud's reaction and was ready to console her. "She's taken in a foundling. I think it's admirable."

"It's not admirable, Beatrice. It's downright foolish! How's she going to find a husband with a baby in tow? How could Bertie allow her to leave like this? Couldn't she have stayed in Ireland?"

"The telegram came from Grace, Maud. I don't imagine Bertie wants anything to do with it."

"Of course he doesn't. Whose baby is it anyway?"

"I don't know. The telegram only says—"

Maud stood up. "How could she! Everything was going well for me at last. Victoria is expecting a baby. I think I might have found a bride for Harry. What will Lady Stalbridge think when Harry's sister appears with an illegitimate child? Will she want her only daughter to marry him then? I think not! After all I have suffered, how could she arrive to stain our family name?"

"I'm sure there's an explanation. Let's wait until she gets here before we pass judgment."

"She's always been a thorn in my side," said Maud bitterly. "I don't know what I've done to deserve it. But she hates me. My own daughter hates me. There's no other explanation. It would have been better if it were her child, then at least we could all pretend her husband had died! There's honor in that."

"It must be someone very dear to her," Beatrice suggested.

"When she arrives I will demand an explanation."

"She's not staying here, Maud. She's staying at Grace's."

"In Mayfair? Why on earth isn't she coming here?" Maud shook her head with self-pity. "Of course, how silly of me. Well, that's just another insult. I don't think I can bear to talk to anyone tonight. I'm going to retire to my room. Please tell Lady Stalbridge that I am unwell." And she disappeared to her bedroom just as the first guests were arriving for Beatrice's salon.

Harry enjoyed Beatrice's salons. People would appear, one never knew who or how many. They would eat, drink, play cards and charades, debate and discuss. It was where he had first met Boysie, and fallen hopelessly in love, for Boysie seemed unaware when Harry followed him with his eyes.

Boysie Bancroft was the most beautiful man Harry had ever seen. He was tall and slim like a willow, with long tapering fingers that caressed the keys when he played the piano and danced on the air when he recited poetry. He was an aesthete who had the singing tone of a fallen angel whose voice has grown husky on late nights, cognac and cigarettes. His eyes were deep and wistful, the color of green tourmaline and flecked with specks of gold, and although his lips were full and pink, like a cherub's, they were capable of delivering the put-downs of a demon. He was twenty-four but his skin was so smooth he hadn't yet begun to shave and his hair, a shiny mop of sugar brown, fell over his forehead like the mane of a lovely young horse. Everyone adored him on account of his charm, acerbic wit and self-deprecating humor, but Beatrice loved him especially because he had been George's dear friend and having him around somehow made her feel connected to her son.

Boysie and Harry had liked each other on sight. Both were handsome and clever, fanatical about art galleries and museums, theater and ballet, and equally fond of Celia. They were perfect companions, laughing at the same jokes (usually each other's) and finding the same tedious people intolerable. However, when it came to love, Harry couldn't be sure that Boysie admired him in the same way that *he* admired *him*. Just when he was beginning to believe that his feelings might be reciprocated, Boysie had turned up to a party with a pretty girl on his arm and declared that *she,* this rather plump, mousy Deirdre Mortimer, was the girl he intended to marry.

Now Harry loitered in the hall, greeting guests and waiting for Boysie, trying not to let his agitation show. He was so busy thinking about the man he loved that he had quite forgotten about his sister and the baby. When at last Boysie appeared, a simpering Deirdre Mortimer by his side in an unflattering green dress, he feigned surprise, pretending that he had only at that moment been passing through the hall. "What a coincidence!" he exclaimed, patting his friend on the back. "Miss Mortimer, how lovely to see you again."

"You've bought a new jacket, you devil," said Boysie, taking in Harry's immaculate attire. "Have you been to Savile Row again?"

"I'm afraid I have," Harry replied. His heart swelled with happiness now that Boysie was here.

"I feel very shoddy by comparison. I shall have to make up for it by playing the piano with gusto! Are you ready for a song?"

Just then, as Harry was about to lead Boysie upstairs to the drawing room, who should appear in the doorway but Lady Stalbridge and her daughter Charlotte. "Look, darling, here's Harry. So sweet of you to wait for Charlotte. You know how nervous she is walking into a room full of people."

Harry was bewildered, and secretly furious. "It's my pleasure," he replied as Charlotte handed her coat to a butler. "Why don't we all go upstairs together? I believe Boysie is going to play the piano. How is your singing voice, Charlotte?"

Charlotte blushed. "I can't sing at all," she said.

"Me neither," Deirdre agreed.

"Then Harry and I will sing for you, and you can both clap and make us believe we're brilliant and talented!" said Boysie, leading the way, and Harry marveled at how Boysie had the ability to make everybody feel good about themselves.

It wasn't long before the socializing descended into outright revelry. The singing grew louder, the laughter more raucous, the behavior less decorous. Harry was more confused than ever. Boysie gazed at him lovingly over the piano yet lavished his attentions on Deirdre. At midnight Celia started the dancing. The floor cleared and other young people joined in while the older guests moved into quieter rooms or left altogether. The gramophone replaced the piano and jazz music drove the dancers into a fever of energetic foxtrotting. Boysie was not a good dancer. He preferred to watch with a cocktail in one hand and a cigarette in the other, scrutinizing the revelers to gossip about later. Harry loved to dance and took Celia by the waist, much to the disappointment of Charlotte, who wanted nothing else than to be swung around the floor in Harry's arms.

In the downstairs study Beatrice played bridge with her inner circle of friends, boldly smoking Turkish cigarettes and lamenting the tragic state of Ireland. "Why don't *you* buy the castle?" one of her friends suggested. "After all, Digby has the wealth to buy it ten times over."

Beatrice sighed heavily and hesitated over her cards. "Digby loves Ireland but Castle Deverill does not belong to him. It's Bertie's and he's very proud. If Digby bought the castle, that is, assuming Bertie wanted to sell, or even paid for its renovation, it would ruin everything between them. I'm sorry to say that Bertie will have to rebuild the castle himself, or abandon it altogether. I fear that it's all over for the Anglo-Irish." She smiled wistfully. "Oh but we had some very good times."

"Better to come back to England than be murdered in his bed," her friend added. "I hear the Irish are an uncivilized lot."

"Quite so," Beatrice agreed. "But there's no country more beautiful. If Bertie loses Castle Deverill it will be a very great tragedy indeed."

As Harry danced around the room he felt the heavy weight of Boysie's stare following him like a shadow. When he managed to look at him he saw that his face was serious and desperately sad. Harry stopped dancing, only for Celia to tug his arm and insist he continue. "You're not tired, are you, Harry?"

"Certainly not!" Harry exclaimed, but he was watching Boysie leaving the room. "Give me a moment, old girl. I'll be back in a tick." He set off after his friend. Once out on the landing he saw a glimpse of Boysie's black shoe on the stairs as he disappeared onto the floor above. Harry called but there came no reply. He sprang up the steps two at a time. Once he was there, Boysie was nowhere to be seen. He called again. No response. He put his hands in his pockets and slowly wandered down the corridor, his heartbeat accelerating with every stride. At last he reached his own bedroom. He hesitated a moment before turning the knob. A hand grabbed him and pulled him inside. "Boysie?" he hissed. Before he could say anything else Boysie's mouth had found his and he was kissing him passionately. Harry's heart flooded with joy. He cupped Boysie's beautiful face and kissed him back. He tasted the soap on his skin and inhaled the spicy scent that was Boysie's alone and they were so familiar it was as if he had known them all his life. "But what about Deirdre?" he asked when they came up for air.

"I can't fool myself any longer, Harry. It's killing me. I love you, old boy. That's all there is to it. I know you love me."

"I do love you, Boysie," Harry replied. The word "love" had never sounded so sweet.

Boysie pressed his forehead to Harry's. "Then there's nothing more that needs saying."

AT LAST KITTY arrived at Grace's red-brick mansion on Mount Street. The train journey from Fishguard to Paddington had been long and tiring but Grace had sent a maid with her to help with the baby. Kitty had never been to England before and the countryside, which she had imagined so ugly, had surprised her with its beauty. Even in February there was a charm to the soft pastures of grazing sheep. Wales reminded her very much of Ireland and soothed her homesickness. She stared out of the window of the train and wondered where Jack was. She re-called the urgency in his voice when he had said, *I have to leave before they bloody shoot me.* And the tears fell again for the man she loved above all others, and for herself and her broken dreams. Where had her courage got her? She had thought she was indomitable. She had believed she could do anything. But in the end she was nothing but a weak and useless woman, no different from her sisters. Jack had been arrested. She had abandoned her home. Her father had all but disowned her. Only Grace and her grandmother were there for her now. But she couldn't live off them forever. When, oh when, would she be able to return to Ireland? And when she returned, would Jack be there?

It was dark by the time Kitty arrived at Paddington. A chauffeur had been sent to pick them up from the station and the drive to Mayfair had been short. Kitty had gazed around at this new city in wonder. The streets near the station had been busy with people, cars and omnibuses and in the middle of it all the odd horse and cart slowly plodding home, but as they had entered Mayfair the bustle had been left behind and the streets were suddenly empty, but for the odd Daimler and Bentley driving beneath the streetlamps as couples left to go out for dinner.

Grace's home was palatial, five-stories high with a tall gray portico and imposing black door. Rows of large windows with elegant stone pediments glowed golden in the darkness and Kitty felt an immediate sense of relief, knowing that once inside she would feel safe.

She was shown to her room by a gentle-faced, rotund lady called Mrs. Blythe. "As soon as you've freshened up there will be supper downstairs in the little sitting room. Lady Rowan-Hampton often eats in there when she is on her own. It's less formal and nice and warm. We'll take care of the baby so you can get some rest. Lady Rowan-Hampton has given us strict instructions to make sure you are as comfortable as possible." She opened the door to a large bedroom with a big brass bed and a cheery fire. On the bedside table was a small arrangement of heather. "Lady Rowan-Hampton specifically asked for that," Mrs. Blythe told her importantly. "She said it would remind you of home."

Kitty picked it up and brought it to her nose. "It does remind me of home," she said, but she was now too weary to feel homesick.

"Can I draw you a bath?"

"That would be lovely, thank you," said Kitty, expecting Mrs. Blythe to ring for a man to bring up the water in containers. To her surprise she walked into the bathroom and Kitty heard the gush of water. She remembered Victoria complaining of the lack of efficient plumbing and electricity and now knew what she had meant. She wandered into the bathroom to watch the tub fill up. Mrs. Blythe poured a green liquid into the water and Kitty's battered spirit was immediately calmed by the soothing scent of pine. She realized how dirty she must be from her journey and her limbs felt suddenly unbearably heavy with fatigue. "You have a bath now while Becky and I unpack for you. You only brought the one bag?" Mrs. Blythe was surprised. "It won't take us long, then, will it."

Kitty lay luxuriating in the bath for such a long time that Mrs. Blythe must have worried because she knocked on the door to check that she hadn't drowned. After her bath she dressed for supper and went downstairs. The house was large, but Grace's raffish charm and flirtatious personality ensured that it was cozy in spite of its grandeur. Kitty ate alone in the little sitting room with its bookcases, soft sofa and armchairs. The fire had been lit and her place laid at the round table, in the middle of which was a bright arrangement of red flowers. The food tasted scrumptious. As she forked the chicken and mashed potato into her mouth she realized how hungry she was. The meat was tender and succulent, the gravy full of flavor, not like the meals she'd had to endure in Ireland. Regretfully, she scraped the last remains of it off her plate and rose to go to bed. When her head hit the pillow she was too tired to miss home. Too emotionally exhausted to even think of Jack. Kitty closed her eyes and allowed the sweetness of sleep to release her from her troubles and the uncertainty of her future.

In the morning she was awoken by Mrs. Blythe knocking on her door. "Good morning, Miss Deverill. I'm sorry to wake you but Lady Deverill is in the hall. She asked me to tell you right away."

"What time is it, Mrs. Blythe?" Kitty asked sleepily.

"Eleven o'clock, Miss Deverill."

"Good Lord, I've slept the morning away."

"You have indeed. It's a lovely sunny day," she said, opening the curtains. "Perhaps you might enjoy a walk around the park later?"

"That would be very nice," said Kitty. "But first I think I'd better go and see my mother."

"I've laid up breakfast in the morning room. It's a lovely room, overlooking the gardens. Lady Rowan-Hampton likes to watch the birds. I'll ask Lady Deverill to wait for you in there."

"Thank you, Mrs. Blythe," said Kitty, her stomach already cramping with nerves at the thought of seeing her mother.

She dressed in the clothes Mrs. Blythe had put out for her. She noticed her traveling clothes had been taken away to be washed. She'd have to ask for the rest of her wardrobe to be sent over from Ireland as soon as possible. When she had made herself presentable she left her room and walked downstairs, wondering what she was going to tell her mother about the baby—she certainly couldn't tell her the truth.

Maud stood in the morning room in an ivory-colored dress with a fashionably low waist and tidy black hat. Her blond hair had been cut to her jawline, which made her face look much more severe, but most notable were her scarlet lips now drawn into a tight, thin line. "Hello, Mama," said Kitty, taking a seat at the table where her place had been set with a pretty blue mat and matching china. She poured herself a cup of tea. "Would you like one?"

"I won't be staying long," said Maud.

"Forgive me, but I'm ravenous." Kitty helped herself to a piece of toast and began to butter it.

"So you've fled Ireland with a baby." Maud was too agitated for pleasantries. "Whose baby is it and why did you have to bring it? Couldn't you have stayed in Ireland? Can you imagine what people are going to say? They'll think it's yours. There'll be a terrible scandal. How on earth do you hope to marry with a child? No man wants to raise another man's child. For goodness' sake, Kitty, have you no thought for anyone else but yourself?" Kitty calmly bit into her toast. "Well? What have you got to say for yourself?"

"Have you quite finished?"

Maud looked startled and sat down. "I need answers, Kitty, and you're going to give them to me."

At that moment a butler appeared. "Good morning, Miss Deverill. Would you like eggs this morning?"

"I'd love two boiled eggs, please," Kitty replied, feeling more confident.

"Is there anything I can get you, Lady Deverill?" he asked Maud.

"Nothing, no, I'm not staying," she answered. When he had left the room she looked at Kitty expectantly. "Well?"

Kitty sighed. "I've left Ireland, Mama, because Papa won't have the baby in the house." It wasn't the whole truth, but Kitty couldn't tell her mother the real reason she had abandoned her home.

"Quite right, too. You should have sent it to an orphanage or something. But instead you bring it here, where it's going to tarnish our good reputation. You know, your brother might have found a bride but this . . ." She struggled a moment with her emotions. "This might just ruin it. Have you considered your family?"

"I've considered the child," Kitty replied flatly.

"Whose child is it? It can't be yours."

"No, he's not mine biologically, but he belongs to me."

"What rot! It doesn't belong to you. You can't just take someone else's child and pass it off as your own."

"He's not just anybody's child, Mama."

Maud wasn't listening, she was so busy calculating how she could get rid of the problem as fast and discreetly as possible. "I will arrange for it to go somewhere. There are plenty of institutions in England where it will be very well looked after."

"He's not going anywhere."

Maud turned on her fiercely. "Why? What's this child to you?"

Just as the butler appeared with the eggs, the maid who had traveled with Kitty from Ireland entered with the baby, wrapped in a cotton blanket. Maud stood up and peered into the face of the child. His red hair and pale gray eyes made her recoil in horror. She turned to Kitty. "But this child is yours?"

"No, he's not mine."

"But he has your hair and your eyes."

"He has Grandma's hair and Grandma's eyes. As do I."

Maud turned back to the child, a white hand clutching her chest as if she was finding it hard to breathe. "Then . . . then . . . it's . . ."

"Yes, it's Papa's baby," Kitty told her coolly, feeling a sense of gleeful satisfaction at the shocked expression on her mother's face.

Maud swallowed hard. "Take it away," she hissed.

"Thank you, Hetty. I'll come and see him when Lady Deverill's gone."

"Excuse me, Miss Deverill, but what's he called?" Hetty asked.

Kitty considered her question a moment. Maud sank into a chair. "Jack," Kitty replied firmly. "He's called Jack. Master Jack Deverill."

Chapter 24

New York, America, 1922

B ridie had to wait on the ship for two days before a small ferryboat drew up to take her and the other third-class passengers to Ellis Island for immigration processing. The first- and second-class passengers had long gone and Bridie had to endure lengthy queues and hours of medical and legal inspections before she was at last claimed by Mrs. Bessie McGuire, the housekeeper of a friend of Lady Rowan-Hampton, and passed off as her niece. On the manifest, the official paperwork given to the immigration officers by the steamship's crew, Bridie's name had been misspelled as "Bridget." That was the name Mr. Deverill had called her. To Bridie it seemed like fate, so she didn't bother to correct it. From now on she'd start a new life with a new identity. She'd make something of herself. "Will I see you again, Bridie?" Eileen from Co. Wicklow asked.

Bridie shook her head. "This is good-bye, Eileen," she replied and left Ellis Island and her past behind her.

Bessie McGuire had emigrated with her husband twenty years before and settled in New York with so many others, like them, who had fled Ireland in search of a better life. Her late husband, Paddy, had been a construction worker, building roads, train tracks and skyscrapers in the city until one day the scaffolding had given way beneath him and he had perished in the fall. Bessie's children were grown-up now and working— her eldest son had gone as far as Texas to labor on a ranch. Bridie liked Mrs. McGuire immediately. She was warm, exuberant and efficient, and she didn't ask too many questions. All she wanted to know was whether Ireland still looked the same.

Bridie had never seen anything like New York. Not in her wildest dreams had she envisaged buildings as magnificent as the skyscrapers that soared so high the tops disappeared into cloud like mountain peaks. So many of the buildings in Dublin had been spoiled by years of violence; here they were grand and foreign to Bridie's unworldly eye. Having never been in a car before, she sat rigidly in the back seat beside Mrs. McGuire, gripping the leather for fear of falling out, while the chauffeur, sent by Mrs. McGuire's employer, drove into the heart of Manhattan. She gazed through the glass and felt the stirring of hope rising out of the ashes of her desolation.

"You're a lucky girl, Bridget. My boss, Mrs. Hamer, has found you a position," Mrs. McGuire told her as they entered the tall brownstone house by the servants' door below the sidewalk.

"Already?"

"Yes, indeed. You'll be starting tomorrow."

Bridie should have been happy with the news, but her body ached with fatigue. She longed to put her head on a pillow and sleep for a week. "Who will I be working for?"

Mrs. McGuire stopped in the corridor and her face was full of sympathy. "An elderly widow called Mrs. Grimsby, Mrs. Eliot Grimsby. She's a very wealthy woman but I won't pretend she's agreeable." Bridie must have looked anxious for Mrs. McGuire was quick to reassure her. "She gets through maids like my Paddy used to get through socks, but you're a strong girl, I don't doubt it. We Irish are as tough as old leather, so we are. With a bit of feeding you'll feel as good as new. Come now, let's give you something to eat, then a bath and you'll be as right as rain, so you will."

Later Bridie lay in bed almost too exhausted to sleep. She could hear loud snoring from the bedroom next door. One of the male servants, whom she hadn't met, grunted like a pig. For a moment it reminded her of home and she suffered a sharp pang of longing. She hadn't seen her mother since the previous summer when she had said good-bye before leaving for Dublin. She had lied about the job there when all she had wanted was to tell her the truth about her pregnancy. She had wanted her mother's sympathy and love, not Lady Rowan-Hampton's cold, efficient making of arrangements as if she was an inconvenience Mr. Deverill wanted to be rid of as quickly as possible. Bridie had seen Michael. He had waited for her around the corner of Lady Rowan-Hampton's house in Dublin and discovered her extended belly and her lie. "You little whore! I knew there was more to it!" he had exclaimed, dragging her down a side street by her hair and pressing her against the wall with such violence she had panicked and told him that Mr.

Deverill had raped her. She hadn't considered the consequences. She knew what Michael was capable of but she prayed he'd let the matter go—after all, he had far more important things to concern himself with like freeing Ireland from British rule. Michael said he would tell the family that she'd gone to America. "You can write to Mam from there," he had said. "But one word about your pregnancy and you'll be sorry, do you understand? I won't have you hurting her with tales of rape." Just before she had hurried back to the house he had called after her, "And don't tell anyone you saw me. I was never here."

She wondered where he was now. Whether they were all in the farmhouse together, believing her safe and well and making a new life for herself in America. Perhaps her mother was in her rocking chair, darning, her grandmother putting twigs under the bastible and smoking herring up the chimney for their supper. Perhaps Sean and Michael were huddled around the table with their friends, drinking stout and plotting. Maybe Jack was there too. She closed her eyes and let her mind settle on his gentle face that smiled at her with encouragement. From there she took herself off into the depths of her memories to the time they had hunted for a frog in the river with Kitty and Celia. To the games they had played on the wall. To the tender looks Jack had given her during Mass when Father Quinn had wagged his long finger at his transgressing congregation and threatened them all with the fires of Hell. Those days had been happy. She knew that now because unhappiness had given her perspective. Those days had been *truly* happy.

She thought of Kitty, her dearest friend, the woman Jack *really* loved, and her vision distorted like a pool of water disturbed by the tossing of a pebble. Did Kitty miss her? Did she

ever think of her? Or had she forgotten her secret friend belowstairs? Bridie rolled over in bed and banished all thoughts
of Ireland. She didn't think of her baby, either, or dare to
wonder how he was faring in the Convent of Our Lady Queen
of Heaven. The shock of giving birth to *two* babies, one who
had lived and its twin who had died, was too much to with-
stand. The nuns had spirited the dead one away before she had
even laid eyes on it. All they would tell her was that she had
been a girl—a poor little girl who was now in God's keeping.
Just as the aching for her lost babies became unbearable Bridie
shut that door. She shut it forever and vowed to herself that she
would never look back. She listened to her breathing instead
until sleep overcame her at last and she sank into the blissful
relief of oblivion.

The following morning she was awoken early by Mrs. Mc-
Guire. She dressed in the uniform she had worn at Castle Deverill and later in Dublin, until her belly had swollen so big she
hadn't been able to wear it. It was creased from being at the
bottom of the suitcase Lady Rowan-Hampton had given her,
but at least it was clean. After a hasty breakfast of porridge and
tea she walked with Bessie to Mrs. Eliot Grimsby's house on
Fifth Avenue, which was a pleasant stroll through a large and
beautiful park where uniformed nannies pushed babies in prams
and stylishly dressed ladies walked their dogs. When Bridie saw
the house she was seized with panic. It was a Gothic, fanciful
mansion built out of dark-brown stone with an ominous-looking
tower rising out of the roof, with a cap like a witch's hat. "Don't
be put off by the house," Mrs. McGuire said as she climbed the
steps to the large double doors. "It's quite informal inside, I
assure you." Bridie stood beside her and trembled. This was her

destiny. This was going to be her home now. She was Bridget Doyle and Bridget Doyle was not afraid.

An aged butler opened the door and asked them to wait in the hall. "If you don't mind, I'll be getting back to my work," said Mrs. McGuire. She turned to Bridie. "You'll be all right, now, Bridget. Come and see me when you've settled in and tell me how you're getting on. May God go with you and keep you safe."

"Thank you for taking care of me, Mrs. McGuire," said Bridie, suddenly afraid of being left alone in this eerie house.

"You have a friend in me now, so don't be frightened. Just work hard. Don't forget that poverty waits at the door of idleness." With that she was out of the door and down the steps before Bridie could grab her by the sleeve and beg her not to leave.

Bridie waited in the vast hall, sitting on a hard sofa, staring at the shiny black-and-white checkerboard floor and the elaborate stone fireplace opposite, above which a portrait of a porcine man in a top hat and winged collar looked imperiously down from a great height. The house smelled of rotten flowers and stale air. There were windows on the wall that backed onto the grand wooden staircase to her right but none of them was open. She heard the regular ticking of a grandfather clock and the distant noise of the city outside, but the house itself was shrouded in a heavy silence like a church where one was afraid to speak for fear of waking the dead.

The butler returned. "Mrs. Grimsby will see you now," he said and began to walk slowly upstairs, his stiff knees creaking on the steps. Bridie followed, anxious about the lady who went through maids as fast as Mrs. McGuire's late husband went through socks. She presumed it was a lot.

Down a corridor, at the back of the building, Bridie was shown into a sun parlor with a barreled glass roof and enormous green plants in brightly colored pots. In the midst of the jungle a voluminous lady sat on a wide chair, stroking a fat cat with fingers that resembled pink sausages glittering with gems. She wore a frilly white cap and a long black dress that reached the ground. Her bosom was so big it was as if her chins grew out of it, and dangling like a helpless climber over a precipice was a large gold locket on a chain. "Let me see you," she said as the butler quietly retreated. Bridie stepped before her and bobbed a curtsy. Mrs. Grimsby inhaled through her nose and slowly ran her hooded eyes over Bridie as if inspecting a horse. "Turn around." She waved a bejeweled hand. Bridie did as she was told. "Well, we'll have to change that uniform and we will cut your hair, you won't have time to put it up, and you're much too thin. I could eat you alive and no one would be any the wiser."

"Yes, my lady."

"I'm not a lady so you will call me madam. *You're* not a madam so I will call you Bridget." She moved her fingers to a silver button on the arm of her chair and pressed it. "Miss Ferrel will show you to your room and explain how I like things done. I hope you're stronger than the last one, and less sensitive. I cannot abide tears. You're not a crier, I hope."

"No, madam."

"Good. I trust you can read and write?"

"Yes, madam."

"Reading and writing are imperative. As you can see my

house is full of books. I love books above everything else in the world. They are my treasures and you are not to touch them unless I ask you to. Is that understood?"

"Yes, madam."

"And you mend and sew and clean and everything else?"

"Yes, madam."

"Mrs. Hamer told me you were a lady's maid for Lady Deverill of Castle Deverill in Cork, is that correct?"

Bridie didn't bother to correct her. "Yes, madam."

"Why did you leave Ireland?" Mrs. Grimsby narrowed her eyes and glanced momentarily at Bridie's belly as if she knew of her shame.

"To make something of my life, madam," Bridie replied without hesitation.

The old lady sniffed, but she accepted Bridie's answer. "I'm glad to see you have a wider vocabulary than 'Yes, madam'!"

"I do, madam."

"'Yes, madam, I do, madam.'" Mrs. Grimsby sighed so that her bosom swallowed a fold of chin. "I hope you're not going to be feeble. I can't bear itty-bitty frightened sparrows and neither can Precious here. She's my cat. She eats frightened little birds. Ah, Miss Ferrel." Bridie turned to see a severe-looking woman with brown hair pulled into a tight bun at the nape of her thin neck standing in the doorway, dressed in an unappealing starched brown uniform.

"Does she please you, madam?" Miss Ferrel asked.

"We'll see. She's perfectly plain. It wouldn't do to have a beauty distracting my guests, now would it? Cut her hair and give her Alice's uniform and explain how I like things done.

My nephew is arriving at eleven so she can bring us tea. Did you send round those invitations?"

Miss Ferrel nodded. "I did, madam. They were all hand-delivered at dawn."

"Good. You can leave me now."

Miss Ferrel showed Bridie to the servants' quarters down-stairs. Once out of earshot Miss Ferrel heaved a sigh. "I'm afraid you won't be here very long," she said, not unkindly. "She's a horrible bully to new maids. No one wants to work for her. She's simply lonely." She smiled sympathetically. "I hear you've just arrived off the boat from Ireland."

"Yes, I have," Bridie replied.

"Well, you might last a little longer seeing as you have no-where else to go."

"I will work hard."

"Of course you will. They all do, but in the end they find her intolerable."

"How long have you worked here?" Bridie asked.

"Twelve years."

"She can't be so bad then?"

"I have earned her trust, Miss Doyle. She trusts no one as much as she trusts me. And I don't have to undress her." Bridie paled. "Oh, didn't they tell you? You have to nurse her as well. Mrs. Grimsby is an old lady who needs a lot of care. I hope you have the stomach for it."

Miss Ferrel gave her an ugly brown uniform with a white apron and sat her down to cut her hair. "Shame we have to get rid of it. You have beautiful hair," she said, lifting it off her back and rubbing it between her thumb and fingers.

Bridie wanted to cry. She bit her lip to stop it wobbling. "It's only hair," she replied bravely.

"Did you leave a man back in Ireland?"

"No," Bridie replied as her hair began to fall around her shoulders like rook's feathers.

"That's good. You don't want to be pining on top of everything else. So, let me take you through your duties. Your bedroom is next to Mrs. Grimsby's so that she can call upon you in the night if she needs you. As mark my words, she *will* need you. You will rise at six A.M. and light her fire without waking her. You will run her a bath and put out her clothes for the day . . ." As Miss Ferrel listed her chores Bridie kept telling herself that nothing was beyond her capability. Hadn't she impressed Miss Lindsay with her sewing and mending? She was going to be better than all the other maids. She wouldn't let hard work scare her, or Mrs. Grimsby's bullying. She had suffered worse at the hands of the nuns. "You have one day off a month and leave to attend church on a Sunday. Are you Catholic?"

"Yes, I am," Bridie replied.

"There's a Catholic church around the corner. Trust me, you'll need God's help working here so I advise you to go as often as possible but hurry back. The old crow will time you so you mustn't hang around chatting or she'll have your hide!" She handed Bridie a mirror. If she was plain before, she was downright ugly now, she thought bleakly. Her hair was down to her chin. She gave the mirror back as the doorbell chimed through the house. "That will be her nephew, Mr. Heskin. He's very dutiful. He visits three times a week. Come, you'd better meet Mrs. Gottersman, the cook, and take up the tea.

She'll expect you to know what you're doing right away, so try not to drop the tray!"

Bridie covered her shocking new hairstyle with a white maid's cap and took up the tea as she was told. The tray was heavy with the silver teapot and china cups and a succulent fruitcake that made Bridie's mouth water, but she was careful not to trip on the stairs. Mrs. Grimsby didn't acknowledge her as she put down the tray and poured the tea. Bridie had seen tea being served enough at the castle to know how it was done, serving Mrs. Grimsby first and offering her a slice of cake, which she accepted greedily, picking it up in her pudgy fingers and stuffing it into her mouth, then serving her nephew. Neither thanked her, but she was used to being ignored by the Deverills and their guests so that didn't bother her.

Paul Heskin was thin and wiry with a weak chin and calculating eyes. He sat close to his aunt and seemed to be making a grand effort to entertain her. Bridie was sure he was even flirting with the old lady, flattering her and charming her as if she were a beautiful woman of twenty. Mrs. Grimsby listened to his stories, her hooded eyes impassive so that Bridie couldn't tell whether she was enjoying his company or loathing it. All the while, Precious lay on her knee, watching Bridie suspiciously, purring loudly as her mistress's fingers caressed her behind the ears.

When Bridie returned later to clear up the tea Mrs. Grimsby was alone, her nephew having left. She sat with her eyes shut, her hand resting on the cat's back. Bridie quietly put the cups on the tray and carried it downstairs. She then asked Miss Ferrel to show her to Mrs. Grimsby's room so she could collect her dirty linen and make her bed. When she entered her mistress's bedroom she was shocked to see the state of it. The vast bed was unmade, the heavy curtains still closed, clothes lying all over the floor and bottles of perfume and lotions sitting without lids on her dressing table. "Alice left this morning," Miss Ferrel told her, referring to the previous maid. "I'm afraid she didn't bother to make up Mrs. Grimsby's room before she left. She had simply had enough."

Bridie set about flinging open the windows and tidying the room. She gathered the dirty linen to be washed and hurried downstairs to the scullery. She derived a certain satisfaction from doing her job well. It was a way of living in the moment and not allowing her past to draw her back into a place of suffering. Guests arrived for lunch and Bridie helped the butler serve and clear away. She brought in the tea at five and cleared it away at six-thirty. She lit the fire in the drawing room and plumped up the cushions when everyone had left. At seven she was summoned to help Mrs. Grimsby undress and bathe. Mrs. McGuire had shown her how to turn the faucets to draw a bath the night before, but now she poured a little oil into the water from the crystal bottle on the marble surround, infusing the room with the scent of roses.

Mrs. Grimsby shouted commands and Bridie ran to attend to her without the slightest annoyance. She found relief in being busy. She also found a surprising respite in Mrs. Grimsby's bullying—had she been kind Bridie might have broken down and wept. This way Bridie remained protected behind the steely armor of her new persona, Bridget. Bridget took all the abuse but Bridie remained cocooned in the depths of her being, detached from the world that had hurt her so.

Bridie didn't balk at her mistress's grotesque obesity, or at having to scrub the folds of her back in the bath. She was awoken every couple of hours during the night and commanded to turn her mistress, which was no easy feat, considering how very heavy Mrs. Grimsby was. Sometimes the old lady would call for her chamber pot or shout at Bridie to cover her feet with the blanket because they had somehow found their way out and were getting cold. But her mistress's summons were an unexpected blessing for they rescued her from her nightmares where the nuns bore down on her like a coven of witches, scolding her for her sins and making off with her babies. As the days went on and she was required to cut Mrs. Grimsby's fingernails and toenails, wash her hair and rub lotion into the creases where her skin chafed, she grew accustomed to the old lady's pungent smell and her incessant demands. It was as if Mrs. Grimsby wanted to see how far she could push her— and Precious seemed to be watching and waiting, but Bridie didn't know what for.

On the first Sunday Bridie left the house to attend Mass. The church was a couple of blocks away. It was the first time Bridie had left the building since she had arrived and she relished the early spring sunlight that bathed her face in its glorious radiance, and the warm breeze that brushed her skin. She longed to walk in the park and listen to the birdsong. She had taken the countryside at home for granted. Now she remembered the sound of corncrakes and rooks and the twittering of sparrows in the hedgerows. She breathed in the smells of the city and her heart yearned for the scent of damp soil and sea.

The church was large and cool and the smell of incense reminded her of home. Beside the pulpit, in a large vase, was a grand display of white lilies. The sight of them uplifted Bridie and she found a chair near the front and waited for Mass to begin. This church was very different from the one in Ballinakelly. The priest was kind-looking and softly spoken, there was a choir who sang like angels and people in the congregation smiled at her and made her feel welcome. It was a far cry from the fear engendered in Father Quinn's church. At the end of Mass she lit candles and sent up prayers for her family back home. Once again she suffered a pang of homesickness at the thought of her mother and grandmother beside the fire and her brothers plotting at the table, and the memory of her father loomed large and bright out of the darkness of her longing. Then the pang turned to pain as her taper trembled over the candle she lit for her two babies, abandoned at the convent, and she clutched her chest in a hopeless bid to nurse her battered heart beneath. Remembering what Miss Ferrel had told her about Mrs. Grimsby timing her absence, she didn't wait to speak to anyone but hurried back to the house. She was relieved she hadn't dawdled for no sooner had she reached the kitchen than the bell rang and she was summoned to the sun parlor.

Mrs. Grimsby had many visitors. Sometimes she saw her attorney, Mr. Williams, a round tub of a man with slick black hair combed off his forehead and spectacles, which gave him an air of authority and intelligence. He came in his three-piece suit with a gold pocket watch on a chain emphasizing the ballooning of his belly, and a black hat, which he took off in Mrs. Grimsby's presence. He sat with Mrs. Grimsby for a long while, drinking tea and pulling out official-looking sheets of paper from his briefcase. Sometimes, after he had gone, Mrs. Grimsby would call for her trusty butler, Mr. Gordon, who had worked for her for over forty years. He was as tall as a broom, with a shiny bald head and a long square chin. She would gently pat his hand and whisper confidentially to him as if sharing a secret. Other times she would send for Miss Ferrel and pat *her* hand. "What would I do without you, Ferrel? Lord, the world is a hard place but you, Ferrel, reassure me that there is goodness in it." Her nephew came often and paid court to his queen. There was something distasteful in the smug expression on his face as he left the house, but Bridie wasn't sure what it was about.

THE MONTHS PASSED. The days lengthened and summer arrived, stifling and hot in the city. Bridie worked without complaint. Her sewing was neat, her mending almost invisible, her washing and pressing immaculate. She told herself that God would forgive her sins if she worked hard. Hadn't Father Quinn preached that suffering purified the soul? As well as the possibility of saving her from damnation her labor also served to distract her from thinking of home, which only scorched her heart with longing and plagued her with regret. Therefore she sought solace in her duties. She learned to be one step ahead of Mrs. Grimsby. When she asked her to do something Mrs. Grimsby found, to her surprise, that Bridie had already done it. She was patient, tireless and dutiful. Miss Ferrel was astonished, for Mrs. Grimsby's maids had never lasted more than a month.

In July the heat was too intense to bear. Mrs. Grimsby announced that the whole household would move to her "Cottage" in the Hamptons until September. Bridie didn't want to leave New York, in spite of the rising temperature, because she had made a home for herself there, between the Gothic mansion on Fifth Avenue and the church. She had found comfort in the familiarity of her routine. Now she would have to get to know another house and rely once again on the severe Miss Ferrel to tell her how Mrs. Grimsby liked things done.

Unlike the mansion in Manhattan, Mrs. Grimsby's Cottage resembled a magnificent pink château with green shutters and a wide veranda, overlooking the sea. The rooms were large and airy with tall windows, wooden floors and pale fabrics on the sofas and chairs. It had a completely different feel to the oppressive, unhappy mansion in the city. Here, Mrs. Grimsby held court as she did in New York. People came to visit her in droves and invitations were delivered daily by boys in uniform. She left the Cottage often to visit neighbors and friends and returned late and sometimes even a little tipsy, but she seemed to derive no pleasure from her outings. Her face was set in a permanent scowl and she was as bullying and unpleasant as she had been in Manhattan. Bridie was overcome by the serenity of the long white beaches and the bright, azure sea, but Mrs. Grimsby seemed not to be moved by it. Bridie wondered what, if anything, made her mistress happy. Surely, the old woman had a heart. And, if she did, what would it take to open it?

Chapter 25

"Bridget, you have shrunk my dress," Mrs. Grimsby accused as Bridie struggled to attach the little hooks into the eyes at her mistress's back. "How do you expect me go out in *this*?" Bridie wanted to tell her that it wasn't the dress that had got smaller but her huge body that had got bigger, but she knew better and remained silent. "Really, I can't imagine how Lady Deverill put up with you. A slovenly maid isn't worth having. There's no future for you if you can't even wash a dress without shrinking it to the size of a child's. I suppose you're thinking *I've* expanded? Yes, I know what goes on in your unpleasant little mind!"

Bridie let her rant on. Experience had taught her that it was better to say nothing for Mrs. Grimsby liked answering back least of all. At last the hooks grabbed the eyes and the dress was firmly put together, though straining badly at the seams. "I can barely breathe, Bridget. Do you want to kill me? Is that it? You want to see me to my grave like everyone else." Mrs. Grimsby turned around, her face pink and sweating. "They all think I don't see through them, but I do. They take me for a fool but *they* are the fools, because I know them for what they are: greedy, avaricious, two-faced scavengers. Money is a great curse, Bridget. You may think me wrong for saying so, but when one is rich one doesn't know if people like one for oneself or for what they can get out of one. Sometimes I'd rather be poor like you, with one friend who loves me for who I am. Do you have a friend, Bridget?"

"No," Bridie replied quietly.

"That's because you don't make yourself very appealing. Smiling would help." The old lady chuckled with difficulty in her straitjacket of a dress. "I suppose you're going to whine and tell me I make your life difficult. Well, *my* life is difficult, Bridget. After Eliot died everything changed. I was on my own like you are now. I had to fend for myself. Like me, you'll grow to be strong and resilient. Perhaps you'll even learn to smile. Smiling might win you a husband and then you can shrink his clothes as well. Now help me out of this dress. I can't possibly wear it. You've ruined it. Find me another, the blue one, or have you shrunk that, too?"

Mrs. Grimsby left the Cottage in her blue dress, her great bosom almost bursting the seams at the front, and already fanning herself vigorously and breathing with effort. Bridie watched her go and heaved a sigh of relief. She was used to her abuse now but not impervious to it. Her mind wandered to the first time Mr. Deverill had held her and her heart burned with longing to be loved. She leaned against the wall in the hall as Mrs. Grimsby was driven away by the chauffeur and felt her mind spin as the memories somehow slipped through her defenses to remind her of a time when she had had not only a friend in Kitty but a lover in Mr. Deverill. A man with strong arms and a handsome smile and eyes that looked deeply into her soul and made her feel cherished. Her mother's face floated before her and her grandmother, Old Mrs. Nagle, smoking her clay pipe in her chair by the fire. But before she surrendered to the images Mr. Gordon stepped into the hall and coughed deliberately, rousing her from her reverie. "And what are *you* doing?" he asked imperiously, for it was not her place to stand there by the front door.

"I was seeing Mrs. Grimsby to the car," Bridie replied, shaking away the pictures of Ireland and the sense of melancholy they induced.

"You should have called me. I've worked for Mrs. Grimsby for forty years. She would prefer *me* to see her to the car and settle her in. Did you make sure she had a bottle of water?"

"No . . . I . . ."

"Oh dear," he said, clearly taking pleasure from her oversight. "Well, it is very hot and she will get thirsty. She always likes a bottle of water in the car."

"I presumed the chauffeur—" Bridie began.

"Don't ever presume, Miss Doyle. It's not by presuming that I am her most devoted and trusted servant. You have to use your head so that she doesn't have to use hers. She is old and fragile, although you may not think so. I see the softer side, of course, which very few have the privilege to see. She will be hot and uncomfortable when she comes home. You had better be ready with a cool bath and some cold water. Did she tell you where she was going?"

"No," Bridie replied.

Mr. Gordon gave a superior little smile. "Oh, well, for fear of being indiscreet I will simply say that she is having luncheon with relations whom she despises. She will be in very bad humor when she returns. You had better brace yourself. It is a miracle that you've survived this long. Miss Ferrel says it's because you have nowhere else to go." He shook his head. "This must be quite an endurance test. Or do you think you'll find her soft center?"

"No, Mr. Gordon, I don't."

"That is one thing you *may* presume, Miss Doyle. It took me thirty years to win her trust. I doubt she'll be here in thirty years. As for you, I'll be surprised if you last another thirty days."

Bridie left the hall and retreated upstairs. She wiped away tears as she busied herself tidying Mrs. Grimsby's bedroom and hanging up the discarded dresses that lay draped over the bed, too small for the old woman's inflating body. She wondered why Mrs. Gottersman kept making her cakes; surely the cook could see that her mistress was getting bigger and bigger. Bridie sat for a moment and put her head in her hands. She was tired. She hadn't had a full night's sleep in months. Mrs. Grimsby thought nothing of waking her up for the smallest thing, like checking behind the curtains for a ghost or simply because she wanted the reassurance that she wasn't alone—and the chamber pot. How could any living creature fill it so often and with such relish?

Bridie would have loved to have asked Mrs. McGuire who had claimed her at Ellis Island to help her find another position. But she had been kind enough already. If she had had the time Bridie would have knocked on Mrs. McGuire's door, just to see a friendly face, but she was rarely allowed out of the house and her days off were few. Besides, she didn't want to admit defeat, not to Mrs. McGuire or even to herself. She had transgressed in the eyes of God by bearing children out of wedlock; she had to put it right now through hard work and sacrifice. She had to ask for God's forgiveness. She had to be good.

When Mrs. Grimsby returned in the late afternoon, Mr. Gordon welcomed her home at the door. Bridie watched them from behind the wall on the landing above the hall. They spoke together in low voices, the butler inclining like a drooping reed so that their heads were almost touching. Mrs. Grimsby patted his hand and shook her wobbly chins, showing her gratitude for something he said. Mr. Gordon put his head on one side, listened attentively and sympathetically when she talked. The old woman smiled feebly, fanning her perspiring face, which was flushed from the heat and a little wine, Bridie thought, judging by the way she was swaying slightly. Mrs. Grimsby gave Mr. Gordon's hand another pat, looked up at him from beneath her painted eyelashes and pulled a face, a face that Bridie thought was almost flirtatious; the face of a girl giving a smidgen of hope to a boy who fancied her.

As Mrs. Grimsby began to climb the stairs, Bridie walked out to meet her. "Good afternoon, madam," she said.

Mrs. Grimsby's face hardened. Gone was the smiling girl she had been with Mr. Gordon; back was the grouchy old woman struggling to move in a dress that was much too tight. "Get me out of this thing at once!" she snapped, striding across the landing toward her bedroom. "You should never have let me wear this dress. I've been feeling faint all day." She staggered into the room and leaned on the chest of drawers, thrusting her back at Bridie so that she could unhook the dress. As soon as Mrs. Grimsby was relieved of it she went to her bed and lay down in her petticoat. Her mountainous body lay inert on the covers, spread out like a waxy corpse, eyes shut, mouth agape, her breath rattling in her chest. "Fan me!" she demanded. Bridie found her fan on the top of the chest and opened it. As she waved it in front of Mrs. Grimsby's face, little wisps of gray hair quivered at her hairline. The sweat slowly dried around her nose and on her upper lip where it glistened among the fine down that grew there. Bridie said nothing. She listened to her mistress's breathing and fanned her until it was obvious that she was asleep. Every now and then she gave a snort and her body twitched. Once, she opened her eyes in surprise to see that her maid was still standing over her and the cool breeze from the fan was still blowing. Bridie was too afraid to leave. She knew that, if Mrs. Grimsby were to wake up and find her gone, she would be in terrible trouble. So, she remained, fanning until her arms ached.

THE SUMMER DAYS grew shorter. Mrs. Grimsby took tea on the veranda and wrapped her shoulders in a shawl as the sun dipped behind the Cottage and the air grew cooler. She seemed to grow tired of people and went out less, receiving fewer guests. She preferred to sit alone, gazing out over the ocean, or deep in a book, her reading glasses propped on her nose. Then one Sunday at the end of August Bridie was called to the garden. Mrs. Grimsby was sitting on the swing chair, listening to the birdsong in a long dove-gray dress. She was lost in thought, her face surprisingly soft in repose.

"Read to me," she demanded, handing Bridie a book. "And

read with expression. Alice had such a dead voice. She even looked like a dead fish hanging in a frame on the wall. Well, off you go. No need to sit on ceremony." She stroked her cat and closed her eyes expectantly.

"*A Collection of Poems, by William Butler Yeats*," Bridie read.

"It's my favorite book. He's an Irish writer. I thought you'd like that. I want to hear it read with an Irish accent. It's appropriate that it should be read with authenticity." Mrs. Grimsby did not open her eyes. Bridie was astonished by the kindness of her words, or perhaps she had chosen an Irish writer to torment her. "Do you know Yeats?" Mrs. Grimsby asked.

"Yes," Bridie replied.

"Good. There's nothing more tedious than a stupid woman, that's what my father used to say. He taught my mother everything he knew. She wasn't born to privilege but she had a lively mind. You're no beauty, Bridget, but if you're stupid as well as plain no man will *ever* marry you." She opened her eyes and looked at Bridie like a hawk considering its prey. "You do want to marry, don't you?"

"I won't ever marry," Bridie replied firmly, returning Mrs. Grimsby's stare with a boldness that even took *her* by surprise.

"How very unusual," said Mrs. Grimsby. Bridie lowered her eyes, for Mrs. Grimsby's inquiring stare was much too intense to endure."Of course you *will* marry," Mrs. Grimsby continued stridently. "All girls marry in the end because we live in a man's world, Bridget, and a woman on her own is a helpless creature, unless she has money. Money doesn't guarantee happiness; I am a fine example of *that*. But it gives one power, Bridget." Her fat fingers stroked her cat. "The trick is in finding the *right* man. Now that's a gamble."

"I am in service to you, madam. I think no further than that."

Mrs. Grimsby frowned. "Children?"

Bridie answered without flinching. "No, I don't long for children." She squeezed her heart shut and suffered the agony in silence.

"I was not blessed with children but with great wealth. Eliot was a talented industrialist. I have no one, you see, only parasites who leech on to me for my fortune. Take Paul, my hyena nephew. Do you think he enjoys coming to see me?"

"Does he not?"

"Of course he doesn't. He's waiting for me to die. They all want a piece of my wealth." She sniffed disdainfully. "Well, you might as well begin. Read 'The Stolen Child.'"

Bridie found the right page. She took a deep breath. "*Where dips the rocky highland Of Seuth Wood in the lake . . .*" She glanced at Mrs. Grimsby, who sat with her eyes closed and her chins tucked into her bosom. Her fingers were still, buried in the fur of her cat, who slept peacefully in her lap. "*Come away, O human child! To the waters and the wild With a faery, hand in hand, For the world's more full of weeping than you can understand . . .*"

Without opening her eyes Mrs. Grimsby began to recite it with her. "*Where the wave of moonlight glosses, The dim gray sands with light, Far off by the furthest Rosses We foot it all the night . . .*" The old lady's voice trailed off and she sighed with rare pleasure. "Beautiful, Bridget. Beautiful," she sighed.

Bridie read on, her face flushing at the extraordinary compliment and the tone in her mistress's voice that suggested she meant it. When she reached the final verse, Bridie's eyes filled with tears. She struggled to stop her voice from quivering with emotion for every line brought her closer to her home. *"Away with us he's going, The solemn-eyed: He'll hear no more the lowing Of the calves on the warm hillside Or the kettle on the hob Sing peace into his breast, Or see the brown mice bob Round and round the oatmeal chest . . ."* In that moment she saw her mother and father dancing round the kitchen table, their eyes sparkling with pleasure, their unguarded smiles only for each other, and she was sure she could hear the sound of fiddles carried on the breeze from across the ocean of time and space.

"You read that superbly," said Mrs. Grimsby quietly when Bridie had finished. Bridie looked up from the book to see that her mistress's cheeks were pink and shiny, like the cheeks of a child. "Tell me about Ireland," she asked, and her gentle tone caught Bridie off guard. "Is it really as beautiful as Yeats describes it?"

"It's more beautiful," Bridie replied, her heart lurching painfully at the thought of the lowing calves on the warm hillside.

"Are there really fairies?"

"My friend Kitty sees fairies all the time," said Bridie softly, suddenly afraid that she had said too much and that Mrs. Grimsby would chastise her for being outspoken.

But she didn't. She pondered on Bridie's words, then said, "Miss Kitty Deverill?"

"Yes."

"She was your *friend*?"

"She was . . ." Bridie's voice died. Kitty was her friend no longer.

"How very unusual." Mrs. Grimsby opened her eyes. "I

don't imagine Kitty's mother was very happy about your friendship."

"She never knew."

Mrs. Grimsby arched her eyebrows. "Of course she didn't. How very sly of you!" Bridie felt ashamed, but Mrs. Grimsby only laughed. "Tell me about Kitty."

"She's very bold."

"And . . . ?" Mrs. Grimsby wanted more. "What does she look like? What is her nature?"

Bridie put the book on her lap. "She has Titian-red hair and a wild character. She sees ghosts too. That's a gift she inherited from her grandmother."

"Ghosts? What sort of ghosts?" Mrs. Grimsby leaned forward on her chair.

Bridie closed the book. "There are many ghosts at Castle Deverill."

"How so?"

"It's a long story."

"We've got all afternoon." The old lady sat back in her chair and seemed to settle into it like a nesting hen. "Start at the beginning."

Bridie took a breath, still mistrustful of Mrs. Grimsby's enthusiasm. "Then let me tell you about the Cursing of Barton Deverill."

Chapter 26

London, England, 1922

Kitty waited for news of Jack. It was agony not knowing what had become of him. She took solace in the baby, named after him, and in the social events that Celia dragged her to, but Jack was never far from her thoughts. Then, at last, in March she received a letter, passed on by Grace.

March 15, 1922

My darling Kitty

    I write to you from Cork where I languish in prison for my sins. You probably heard, but I never made it to America. At least this way I am closer to you. I can gaze at the sky and know that you are seeing the same blue. That is the only consolation. I don't think I'll face the firing squad. Perhaps the Brits learned from their mistakes in 1916! But, I don't think they're going to let me go. So, my darling, heed my words, for rotting in here will not grieve me too much if I can think of you getting on with your life and not pining for me. Don't waste time in waiting for you'll grow old and sour before I'm out! Beautiful Kitty, find a man to love you, and love him back. I release you from your promise as you must release me from mine. We are not destined to be together. I know that now. But my life has been sweeter for having been loved by you.

There's truth in the expression, if you love something, let it go. I love you more than I love myself, Kitty.

Jack

Kitty's tears splashed onto the paper, smudging the ink. Hastily she put the letter down and hung her head in her hands. She'd wait for Jack. For as long as it took. The idea of falling in love with someone else was an anathema. Her heart belonged to him and always would.

Since she had arrived in London with baby Jack she had been pleasantly surprised by people's reactions. Celia thought it "a riot" for an unmarried woman to have a baby. Beatrice admired her "charity," Digby thought he looked just like her, to which Maud replied tartly that half of Ireland had red hair. Victoria wasn't in the least interested. Harry, on the other hand, took Kitty to one side and, in their tradition of keeping each other's secrets, demanded to know the truth. When she told him, he criticized their father for being a fool, but supported Kitty's decision to raise the baby. "I might be grateful for him one day, considering my chances of fathering a child," he whispered with a smirk.

"Mama will be very disappointed if you don't further the family line," said Kitty.

"Poor Mama, so many disappointments. I'm beginning to feel rather sorry for her."

"Don't be fooled, Harry. Mama's like a weed, very resilient and spreading her influence in all the places one doesn't want it."

Kitty wrote to her sister Elspeth explaining that she had taken in a foundling child left on the doorstep of the Hunting Lodge in an act of charity. She told her that she had gone to London because their father refused to have her in the house with a child that didn't belong to her. It was as close to the truth as she dared go and she didn't want her hearing rumors from other sources. She knew Elspeth would support her. If she ever needed a refuge in Ireland she could count on her sister.

If London society gossiped about her, Kitty never knew—nor did she care. With Ireland behind her she threw herself onto London's party scene with such abandon, trying to lose herself. She attended Beatrice's Tuesday night salons and charmed and bewildered the other guests for she was outspoken and intelligent and debated the issues of the day with the boldness of a man. If anyone was imprudent enough to challenge her on Irish politics they soon wished they hadn't, for she was unafraid to show her support for the IRA and was better informed than most. Beatrice welcomed her outrageous niece for she added pepper to her salons. Kitty lunched with Celia and her large circle of friends in London's most fashionable restaurants and danced the nights away in the clubs where live bands played jazz, recently imported from America. She learned to dance the Charleston, adopted the latest attire of dropped waists and shorter hemlines and took up smoking. She visited museums and the theater with Harry and Boysie and pretended she didn't see their secret looks and furtive caresses. She was like sunshine to the social butterflies who clamored to have her at their parties, even though the old dowagers condemned her for being both "fast" and Irish, which was, to them, a dangerous combination.

Kitty embraced her new life, but she never forgot Jack. Every few days she wrote him another letter, posting it to the prison in Cork. She waited anxiously for his replies, but they never came.

If Maud had feared Kitty would never find a husband, her fears were unfounded. The war might have depleted London's supply of young men, but the ones there quickly lost their hearts to Kitty. It didn't seem to matter that she was caring for a child; it wasn't hers and, besides, the way she loved the little foundling only made them admire her more. But Kitty teased them and encouraged them and like the wind was one moment warm, the next moment cold, but always fanning their interest because they couldn't quite pin her down.

SUMMER CAME AND with it Victoria's baby girl, pompously named Lady Alexandra Mary Victoria Casselwright. "Could she not have thought of a name that wasn't a queen's," Kitty complained to Celia.

"Next she'll have a boy—George William Edward *Eric*,"

Celia replied with a snigger. "Eric will have to go in there somewhere, poor child!"

"At least Mama won't be spending the summer with us, now Victoria's got a baby for her to coo over," said Kitty. "Elspeth's son doesn't count, because he's plain John MacCartain, and Mama doesn't care for Elspeth or Ireland. How she must relish having a legitimate, aristocratic child in the family she can boast about."

The summer was spent at Deverill Rising, Digby's large estate nestled in the Wiltshire hills. When Kitty was driven up the impressive drive that swept through undulating meadows of wild flowers and long grasses and over a pretty stone bridge that straddled the Deverill stream, she realized how much she had missed the countryside. Sheep dotted the hills like fluffy dandelions, birds flew in and out of hedges of blackthorn and beech, towering chestnut trees gave shelter to horses as the summer sunshine grew intense and fat flies braved their nodding heads to gather at their eyes and on their mouths. Kitty's heart swelled at the prospect of riding once again and she gazed over the chalk hills with longing.

The house itself was an imposing stately home of natural stone with a giant pediment crowning the facade and a bold balustrade circling the roof with vast ornamental urns punctuating it at intervals. Tall windows looked out over gardens that had been expensively planted and lovingly nurtured. Celia jumped out of the car as soon as it pulled up on the gravel and took Kitty by the hand to show her around, leaving Hetty to look after the baby and see to the luggage. They ran through the house to the back where French windows opened onto a paved garden where wild thyme grew in abundance with *Al-*

chemilla mollis and forget-me-nots, and vast urns sprouted great heaps of rosemary. Beyond, on the horizon, a circular white dovecote with a thatched roof was positioned serenely in front of a thick wood.

They ran through all the gardens, under wire arches of climbing roses, down meandering paths that led them between wide borders of campanula and peony, into the walled vegetable gardens, where sweet peas grew among rows of carrots and spinach. Celia pulled Kitty on, keen to show her the tennis court and croquet lawn and the elaborate treehouse that her father had commissioned for her tenth birthday. At last they sat down on a wooden bench that circled a pear tree. They were both out of breath and laughing excitedly. "Isn't it lovely?" Celia exclaimed.

"I didn't think anywhere could be as beautiful as home, but Deverill Rising has taken my breath away," Kitty replied, panting heavily.

"We're going to have such fun. Just like we did in Ireland. Vivien and Leona are coming with their boring husbands and squeaking babies. Harry and Boysie arrive tonight with Archie Mayberry, who I think is going to propose to me at any minute."

"What'll you say?" Kitty asked.

Celia shrugged. "Yes, I suppose. After all, I have to marry somebody and Archie's no worse than anyone else. He has heaps of money. Heap and heaps and heaps."

"And he's handsome at least," said Kitty helpfully.

"Yes, he's not unpleasant to look at, is he? I don't love him, but I think he loves me. One has to be practical in choosing a husband. He's rich, comes from a good family and is intelligent, which is important because I can't bear to be bored. God forbid I'm bored. I can behave very badly if I'm not entertained. So, I'll have a couple of babies and then fall in love with someone else." Celia gave a contented sigh. "Isn't that how it all works?"

"I've never really considered it. I know Papa has strayed from his marital bed."

"Of course he has. So has mine. If Mama has had lovers she's been more discreet. I say, when the boys arrive, let's go riding? I bet you miss it."

"I do," said Kitty. "I miss it terribly."

"No hunting at this time of year, but we can gallop over the hills and I can show you the Man. He's a giant carving on the hillside, for there's chalk beneath the grass. It's not as impressive as your Fairy Ring because the Man doesn't come alive at sunset." Celia took Kitty's hand and squeezed it. "I do wish we could turn the clock back and spend just one more summer at Castle Deverill, don't you?" Kitty's eyes dimmed so Celia changed the subject. "Come on, let me show you the inside."

It wasn't long before the house was filled with guests. They seemed to come unexpectedly and stay for days on end. Beatrice didn't mind. She sat on the terrace in a wide sunhat holding court, while Digby, in a brand-new yellow-checked jacket and breeches, took the men off around the estate to show them the farm. Sir Digby Deverill might have come from an old family but he lived like a complete nouveau riche. Beatrice enjoyed the young people best. They motored down in their shiny new cars, the girls with their fashionably short haircuts, long red nails and lipstick to match, the men in pale suits, cricket sweaters and boater hats, fun-loving and cheerful. She watched them play croquet and tennis, charades and kick the can, picnic on the hill, tease each other, flirt, smoke, dance and banter. *Oh to be young again*, she thought wistfully. *These young people have it all.*

Archie took Celia by the hand one starry night in August and asked her to marry him. Celia accepted and they ran into the house, breaking up a game of Cocky Ollie, which the Deverills had invented and which had, over time, become legendary, and announced it to the entire house party. Champagne was popped, congratulations given and Celia hurried off with her girlfriends to discuss the dress and choose her bridesmaids. "You, Kitty, will catch my bouquet, because you're going to be next." But Kitty knew that the only man she'd ever marry would be Jack. When, oh when, would he be released?

ON AUGUST 22, Michael Collins, the Irish leader who had negotiated the partition of Ireland, was ambushed by diehard nationalists in Co. Cork and murdered. Kitty was devastated when she read about it in the newspaper. "How could they murder Michael Collins!" she wailed, throwing *The Times* onto the breakfast table, thinking of Jack rotting away in prison. "When will the violence end?"

"Wasn't he just another Irish terrorist?" Celia asked, wondering what the fuss was about.

Kitty shook her head in astonishment. "I despair of you, Celia," she cried out. "Michael Collins was a hero. He was a rebel, a freedom fighter, a brave and selfless man. I hope they find the people who did this and string them up by their necks!" The house party glanced at each other uncomfortably.

None of them, besides Harry, cared what happened in Ireland. Harry took the paper and read it in silence. Boysie's face darkened with concern. The room was plunged into an awkward stillness.

"Oh dear, well, it's all very sad, isn't it? I tell you what, let's have a picnic today. That'll cheer you up, Kitty. We can play rounders on the hill," Celia suggested.

"Capital idea, darling," Archie agreed, gazing at her with soppy eyes. "We'll take your mind off your Michael Collins."

THE WEDDING DATE was set for the following spring. Autumn was filled with endless engagement parties and the usual revelry. Kitty kept in close contact with her grandmother, whose letters were long and poetic and increasingly mad. She wrote of the leprechauns in the hedges and the fairies in the flower beds and said that Bertie had made her move into the Hunting Lodge on account of the cold weather. She said she only went there to eat and sleep, because Hubert was very demanding and insisted on her company during the day. The Shrubs were too afraid to visit and had become virtual recluses in their home in Ballinakelly. She sent them cannabis to calm their nerves but who would know if they died in their beds? She asked whether the allowance she had set up for Kitty was enough. *I don't want you to live like a pauper, my darling Kitty, you deserve to live well. As for me, I need very little now, my life is confined to the tower. I feel like Rapunzel, except there is no witch, and Hubert, my prince, is in no position to rescue me. Be safe and pray for an end to the violence so that you can come back with the baby and bring him up here at Castle Deverill, where he belongs.*

Kitty continued to write to Jack. Even though he had told

her not to wait for him she was bewildered and hurt by his refusal to write back. Didn't he know that she loved him enough to wait a lifetime for him? Then, on December 17, 1922, following the creation of the Irish Free State, the last of the British forces handed over the Royal Barracks in Dublin and left. The South was independent at last. Surely Jack would be released now.

Liberation was a tremendous moment and one which Kitty had fantasized about for so long. She was proud that she had played a small part in winning this freedom. She and Grace celebrated with champagne and a sumptuous dinner at the Ritz. The two women reminisced about their rebel days, the gruesome murder of Colonel Manley, the moment Kitty had realized that Grace was an ally and not an enemy and the time Kitty had nearly been caught carrying a gun in a shoebox by the Auxiliaries. "Had it not been for the fast-thinking priest you might have been thrown into jail like Countess Markievicz," said Grace, who clearly missed those exciting times. Kitty expected Jack's immediate release but, as the weeks went by, she heard nothing and her sense of triumph dissolved into bitterness and disappointment.

Little Jack Deverill was growing big and strong. No longer the frail little baby who had been left on the doorstep, he was now fat and bonny. As Kitty didn't know his date of birth, she decided that January 1 would be his birthday. She made him a little cake and invited Celia and Harry to celebrate with her. As she blew out the candle she wondered where Bridie was and whether she had returned to Ballinakelly. She wanted to write to her and reassure her that her child was safe and that she loved him with all her heart because Bridie couldn't. Sometimes,

when he was sleeping, she'd sit and gaze at him without noticing the time. Who'd have thought such a little person could
bring her such joy? It pained her to think what Bridie was
missing out on.

Grace came to London from time to time but she brought
no news of Jack. As for Kitty's father, he was more adamant
than ever that Kitty would never return to Castle Deverill.
"He does not recognize his child," Grace told her gently. "In
his eyes Jack is not a Deverill."

"Then I cannot go back," Kitty declared, lifting her chin to
restrain her sorrow. "But one day Jack Deverill will know his
home. He's more Irish than I am and I intend to reunite him
with his roots."

"You are always welcome to stay with me," Grace told her.

"And gaze upon my home from afar? That would finish me
off completely. No, Papa will have to relent, for Grandma's
sake. You have to talk some sense into him, Grace." She put a
hand on Grace's arm. "You're the only person who can."

Grace didn't tell her that Bertie was drowning himself in
drink and that she barely saw him these days. He hunted only
occasionally, was never seen at the races and rarely accepted
visitors. He was a husk of the charismatic man he used to be.
Once dashing and insouciant, he had grown paranoid and
twitchy. Only whiskey in large quantities soothed his troubled
soul—soon she feared he'd be seeing Adeline's leprechauns and
fairies.

"Is there any news of Bridie?" Kitty asked.

"The last I heard was that she had started working as a maid
for a woman in Manhattan. She's well and happy, Kitty. You
don't need to worry about her," Grace said, turning her eyes to

the window. "She wanted to start a new life. Your father has been more than generous. I don't know another man who would have looked after her so well."

"Will she ever come back?"

Grace looked at Kitty solemnly. "Do you want her to come back and claim her child?"

Kitty hadn't thought of that. "No. No, I don't. If I'm honest, I want little Jack for myself. Am I a brute?"

"You'd be a very heartless girl if you didn't want him."

"I love him like my own, Grace." Kitty beamed a smile. "When I look into his face everything is right with the world and all my cares are washed away."

"Then think nothing more of Bridie. She chose to abandon her child. Whoever left him on your doorstep knew you'd take care of him and bring him up as a Deverill, which is what he is. I'm sure Bridie arranged it herself. She knew she could trust you, her friend, to look after him."

"Yes, I'm sure she did," said Kitty, feeling better. "If our roles were reversed I know she'd do the same for me."

As HER WEDDING approached Celia grew increasingly nervous about the wedding night. "I wonder what *it's* like," she said to Kitty. "Do you think *it* hurts?"

Michael Doyle flashed in front of Kitty's eyes and she winced. "I'm sure it doesn't hurt if the man is kind," she replied.

"I'd rather make love with Lachlan," Celia said, referring to Archie's best man.

"Celia!" Her cousin's confession distracted her for a blessed moment.

"Oh, I know, I shouldn't think of these things. But when he

looks at me all the hairs stand up on my body like little soldiers standing to attention, just waiting for a command. That doesn't happen when Archie looks at me, handsome though he is."

"What are you saying, Celia?"

"I'm not saying anything. I'm getting married in a fortnight and that's all there is to it. Perhaps when I've given Archie an heir and a spare I'll fall in love with Lachlan Kirkpatrick."

Celia Deverill's wedding might have been one of the most exciting events of the Season had it not been for the marriage of Prince George, Duke of York, to Lady Elizabeth Bowes-Lyon that April. The royal wedding was held at Westminster Abbey rather than the more traditional Royal Chapel, which made it a grand public affair, presumably to lift the spirits of the nation after the misery of the war. Beatrice was put out that Celia's wedding in May should be overshadowed by a wedding with which she was unable to compete, even with Digby's millions and her unique cocktail of guests. Still, the marriage was held in St. Peter's in Belgravia with the reception at the Ritz. Celia was resplendent in an ivory silk dress with an impressive diamond tiara Digby had commissioned for Leona's wedding, and which her sister Vivien had worn later at her wedding. Both marriages had been written up in the newspapers with a photograph in *The Tatler.* Beatrice expected no less for her youngest daughter's wedding.

Kitty was a bridesmaid with jasmine threaded through her hair and a long white dress to complement Celia's. Her bouquet was fragrant with lilies and cherry blossoms, which she kept pressing against her nose and remembering with a touch of sadness springtime at Castle Deverill. Celia vowed to love and obey Archie Mayberry and the choir sang hymns that had the power to melt the iciest heart. Or so Kitty thought, but one look at her mother's taut profile reminded her that the only thing capable of melting her mother's heart would be her own marriage to an aristocrat who met Maud's impossibly high expectations. What a shame Prince George had just been snapped up, she thought wickedly, masking a smile.

After the marriage the guests went to the Ritz for tea. This Kitty found rather dull, considering that the guest list was comprised mostly of Digby and Beatrice's friends and not Celia's or Archie's, which was customary. She mingled with her cup of tea and humored old Augusta, who was as disagreeable as ever, giving her, with ill-concealed relish, a long list of friends who had recently died. "Bunny Spencer died in the flower border last week," she told her eagerly. "One minute she was smelling the roses, the next she was compost! Arthur Sillars is terribly ill. They say it's only a matter of time. Look at Stoke over there." She pointed at her husband, who had never looked more spritely with his sweeping mustache and ruddy face. "One can't imagine him dying, can one? But it could come at any moment."

Kitty managed to extricate herself with the excuse of attending the bride and hurried out onto the terrace. She took a deep breath and leaned on the balustrade to look into Green Park at the people wandering aimlessly beneath the plane trees. "Well, if it isn't Miss Deverill," came a voice beside her.

She turned to find Mr. Trench standing next to her. She was surprised at how happy she was to see him. "Mr. Trench, how unexpected . . ."

He took her hand and bowed. "It's a great pleasure to see you after all this time. Might I say how lovely you look."

"Thank you." She smiled: something about him had changed.

He was less stiff, more sure of himself, perhaps, less solemn. "This is the last place I would expect to see you," she said.

"Why, was it not through your cousin Beatrice that your mother employed me to be your tutor? Digby and Beatrice are very dear friends of my family."

"Then why have we not met before? I've been in London over a year."

"I've just returned from Italy."

"Italy, how marvelous. What were you doing in Italy?"

"I'm writing a book."

"An academic book?"

He shook his head and grinned bashfully. "A novel."

"Why, Mr. Trench, how very exciting. What's it about?"

"Love."

"Love?"

"Don't look so startled. What else in the world is more important than that?"

Kitty didn't know what to say. "Goodness, Mr. Trench, I don't know. I don't think anything in the world is more important than that."

"Please, you must stop calling me Mr. Trench. I'm not your tutor now. My name is Robert."

"Robert then. You must call me Kitty."

His face became suddenly serious. "I heard about the castle and your poor grandfather. I'm so sorry."

She lowered her eyes. "Yes, it was dreadful."

"Is that why you left?"

"No." Kitty hesitated and felt a weariness descend upon her. "It's a long story. A sad story. I don't think I'm quite ready to share it."

"I understand. Forgive me. May I . . ."

At that moment someone stepped onto the terrace, looking about frantically. "Has anyone seen the bride? We've looked everywhere!"

"Dear God!" Kitty exclaimed.

"Miss Deverill, you're a bridesmaid. When did you last see her? She's meant to be cutting the cake."

"Are you sure she's not powdering her nose?" Kitty suggested.

The man looked desperate. "We've searched everywhere."

"You don't think she's done a runner, do you?" said Robert under his breath, watching the panic ripple through the room as heads turned and people whispered behind their hands.

"I don't know what to think," said Kitty anxiously. "But I suggest we start by looking for Lachlan Kirkpatrick, the best man."

Chapter 27

New York, America, 1922

Bridie discovered that, beneath Mrs. Grimsby's hard outer coating, there was a soft and sentimental woman. She knew nothing of the old lady's past to understand why she had become embittered and unhappy, but she discovered that poetry and stories in the present were the nutcracker that occasionally exposed this vulnerable center. Mrs. Grimsby loved beautiful words. She'd repeat them, rolling them on her tongue like boiled sweets, savoring their taste. She made Bridie read every afternoon on the veranda overlooking the ocean and demanded more stories of Ireland. Mrs. Grimsby loved stories of Castle Deverill best of all. She was fascinated by the ghosts imprisoned by a curse within the castle walls and gripped by Lady Deverill and Kitty's extraordinary gift of sight. Thus Bridie was forced into the past. The door she had shut with such determination opened a crack and her memories were at once exposed like the secret corners of a darkened room suddenly thrown into light. At night she dreamed of her father, the smell of smoked herring, the sound of the fiddle and the old Irish songs that had accompanied her growing up. Sometimes she dreamed of the Banshee, the tinkers and the awesome black figure of Father Quinn, his eyes burning into her soul in search of sin, and she'd awake with tears rolling down her cheeks and soaking into her pillow.

The smells of the sea in America were nothing like the smells in Ireland and Bridie was grateful for the difference. She didn't allow herself to pine. America was her home now and her past existed only in her mind. Ireland was so far away—the other side of a world that was too enormous for Bridie to fully comprehend. She didn't read the newspapers, she didn't listen to gossip in church and when she did hear snippets of conversation in the drawing room about the civil war she suppressed her curiosity and smothered her sense of dismay. The only contact she had with her country of birth were the regular letters she wrote to her mother and the money she sent home; the only sign of surrender her pillow wet with tears.

Miss Ferrel, Mrs. Gottersman and Mr. Gordon were Bridie's only companions, although none of them was her friend. Bridie remembered helping her mother in the kitchen of the castle as a child. There had been a strong sense of unity among Lord Deverill's servants and a genuine affection for the Deverill family. She remembered her mother laughing with the kitchen maids, chiding them as they gossiped but secretly enjoying their spirited banter. She remembered Skiddy, Lord Deverill's aged valet, and O'Flynn the butler, who had been older than Mr.

Gordon. Skiddy had allowed her to help him polish the gold buttons on Lord Deverill's hunting coat and O'Flynn had once chased her around the kitchen table with a dishcloth, until she had collapsed onto the flagstone floor in a fit of giggles. Those two men had been full of affection and mirth. Mrs. Grimsby's houses were silent and cold, like tombs, and laughter was never heard anywhere, only the occasional cynical chuckle from Mrs. Grimsby as she considered her greedy family. Bridie thought Mrs. Gottersman was as sour as a lemon, Mr. Gordon as stiff as a stick of celery and Miss Ferrel, though friendly enough, was as formal as a dinner service. They attended to Mrs. Grimsby's every need and, one after the other, were summoned to her presence for "confidential little chats." They eyed each other with suspicion. They trusted no one. They lived for that pat on the hand and that "confidential little chat." Mrs. Grimsby sat on her grand chair like a fat spider contemplating the flies caught in her web. And Bridie observed them all, kept her head down and got on with her job.

In the autumn when they returned to New York Bridie made her first real friend. A plucky girl called Rosetta from Italy. They met at Mass and after a few Sundays smiling tentatively at each other they finally spoke. Rosetta had traveled from Italy on a steamship. Her parents had settled in Brooklyn, where her father had gone into business with other Italians and her mother looked after her siblings and worked from home as a seamstress. Rosetta was a maid in one of the big houses around the corner from the church where the lady of the house was an actress married to a theater producer. She was temperamental, highly strung and spoiled and had lots of lovers, according to Rosetta, who was adept at listening at doors and peeping through keyholes. She reminded Bridie a little of Kitty. As they grew closer Rosetta and Bridie spent their days off together, sitting huddled on benches in Central Park or drinking cups of tea in cafés until, in midwinter, they took the train into Brooklyn and spent the day at Rosetta's house, eating the best food Bridie had ever tasted. Rosetta made her realize how thirsty she was for friendship and how lonely she had been.

It wasn't long after Christmas that strange things began to happen in Mrs. Grimsby's mansion. The first incident was Bridie's discovery of a thick roll of dollar bills tied up with string beneath her employer's bed. It was more money than Bridie had ever seen in her life, more money than she thought she'd ever be able to spend, were it to belong to her. She held it in trembling hands and stared at it in wonder. She recalled reading Jack's note to Kitty and the same guilty feeling arose in her conscience as if the eye of God was upon her and waiting to see what she would do. Without another thought she put the money on Mrs. Grimsby's bedside table, where she presumed it had initially been before it fell off, and continued tidying the room. The next incident was Bridie's discovery of a pair of diamond earrings that had somehow found their way into the pocket of one of Mrs. Grimsby's dresses. Bridie admired the glittering beauty of the valuable gems and again she did what was right and put them on Mrs. Grimsby's dressing table. The third incident concerned a china figurine on the mantelpiece above the fireplace in the dining room. When she picked it up to clean, the torso came apart from the skirt. Mortified that she might be reprimanded for carelessness, she was going to put it back together again, for the break was very clean and the top would rest nicely on the bottom and no one would be the wiser, but her honesty prevailed and she went to inform her mistress.

"Madam," she said, bobbing a curtsy. Mrs. Grimsby was in the sun parlor in her usual chair, reading a letter with some difficulty for her eyesight was fading.

"What is it, Bridget?" Bridie held out the two halves of the figurine. Mrs. Grimsby's face clouded. "Are you coming to confess that you broke it?"

"It was broken when I picked it up, madam," Bridie told her.

"Was it indeed." The old lady looked skeptical. "Do you know how valuable that is?"

Bridie felt her cheeks burning with shame. "No, madam, I do not."

"It's worth hundreds of dollars. Hundreds. You couldn't afford to repay the money if you saved your salary for a lifetime. What do you have to say for yourself?"

Bridie knew there was no point proclaiming her innocence. Mrs. Grimsby wouldn't believe her. "I'm very sorry, madam." She hung her head.

This seemed to satisfy the old lady. She held out the letter she had been reading. "Do you know what this says?"

"No, madam."

"My two nieces are coming down from Boston and they've asked to stay here. Do you think you can look after all of us?"

Bridie remembered when Lady Elmrod had come to stay at the Hunting Lodge for Miss Elspeth's wedding and she had had to look after all three sisters at once. "I think I can, madam," she replied, knowing she was in no position to refuse, having supposedly broken the figurine.

"They're incredibly tiresome. You see, they think I'm about to die and they want to make sure they are accounted for in my will." Mrs. Grimsby smiled smugly and sighed. "Let's see how hard they work." She chuckled into her chins, which wobbled like aspic.

When Bridie left the room Mr. Gordon was standing there in the shadows, listening. He looked down his imperious nose and shook his head as she passed. Bridie went hot with indignation. No one was more diligent in her duties than her. She watched him enter Mrs. Grimsby's room and close the door behind him.

When Bridie told Rosetta about the strange incidents, Rosetta was quick to see foul play. "Is there somebody who might be jealous of you in the house?" she asked.

Bridie immediately thought of Miss Ferrel. "Well, there's a woman who has worked for Mrs. Grimsby for over twelve years. We're not friends but she's kind to me."

"Snake in the grass," said Rosetta. "I'd be careful if I were you. It sounds to me like she wants to trap you. She was probably hoping you'd steal the money and the earrings. She probably broke the figurine herself."

Bridie was shocked. "Do you really think so?"

"Be careful, Bridget. It's not easy finding work in this city."

"Now that I think of it, she was expecting me to leave within the month. She said no maid had ever lasted longer. But Mrs. Grimsby is good to me. She likes me to read to her and to tell her stories of Ireland."

"Does she like this other woman to read to her?"

"No."

"*Ecco!*" Rosetta exclaimed happily. "She's a jealous snake in the grass! Be careful, Bridget."

It had never occurred to Bridie that Miss Ferrel might be jealous of her. But it did seem a little odd that suddenly Bridie was finding money and jewelry around the mansion, as if someone was trying to prove her dishonesty. It most certainly wasn't Mr. Gordon, the butler, for he had no access to Mrs. Grimsby's bedroom, although he clearly didn't like her. Miss Ferrel, on the other hand, had access to every room in the mansion, even to Mrs. Grimsby's most personal drawers, for she had seen her pulling out papers from her desk and putting red-velvet jewelry boxes in the safe the morning after Mrs. Grimsby had attended a grand ball or the opera. She was Mrs. Grimsby's most trusted companion. It was entirely possible that she didn't like the intimacy of those afternoons reading in the sun parlor. Bridie wanted to reassure her that Mrs. Grimsby had no affection for her whatsoever. She was simply available to read to a bored and lonely old woman.

From that moment on Bridie became suspicious of Miss Ferrel. She checked her bedroom every evening before bed in case Miss Ferrel had slipped something valuable into her drawer or beneath her pillow to frame her. She dusted with extra care in case something had been placed dangerously near the edge of a table or a mantelpiece and she was alert to any valuable items lying around, putting them back where they belonged, each time with a sense of satisfaction that she had outwitted Miss Ferrel. Miss Ferrel seemed to notice Bridie's sudden coolness and tried to be extra friendly, but Bridie didn't fall for that. She kept her distance and watched the woman with distrust, knowing that her affability was just a front and that in reality she was the enemy.

IN THE SPRING Mrs. Grimsby's two nieces arrived from Boston. Mrs. Halloway and Mrs. Kesler. They were sisters, both in their early thirties, married with young children they had left behind and barely mentioned. They embraced their aunt with great exclamations of affection. "It's been too long!" they gushed, complimenting her jewelry and giving her gifts wrapped in exquisite paper and brightly colored silk ribbons. Mrs. Grimsby received them with apparent pleasure, putting the gifts aside to open later—Mrs. Grimsby did not care very much for presents.

She hosted dinner parties for their entertainment and accompanied them to the ballet and the opera. The nieces were both pretty and fashionably dressed and seemingly without a care, like a pair of colorful hummingbirds fluttering about the mansion in their fine feathers. "Oh, everything's perfectly dandy in Boston," they told their aunt, recounting their husbands' business successes and the glamour of their relentlessly sociable lives. They spoke of their illustrious circle of friends, dropping famous names into the conversation and describing the extravagance of the parties they went to.

Bridie thought them gilded and privileged and blessed by God with beauty. Yet as she crept silently around the mansion, unnoticed in the shadows, she heard them discussing the terrible debts they had incurred trying to keep up with their friends and the anxiety their endless struggle gave them. "The old bat is sitting on millions," said Mrs. Halloway as Bridie passed their room unnoticed.

"She's as mean as a wolf, Evie," added her sister. "Mama says she'll give her money to Paul. Apparently he comes to see her at least three times a week and she adores him."

"Nonsense," Mrs. Halloway snapped. "Paul is Uncle Joe's son and apparently Aunt can't abide her brother on account of his gambling. I doubt very much she'll give Paul or his siblings a penny."

"What makes you think she'll give *us* anything?"

"Because she has no children and Mama is her sister. She has to leave it to somebody. We're her only family and she has two houses full of treasures, not to mention the money. Mama says she's as rich as Croesus, whoever he is."

"She's looking much too well, wouldn't you say?"

"Fat people don't live long," said Mrs. Halloway meanly.

"I hope you're right, because I can't ask Papa for any more money."

"You're not the only one." Mrs. Halloway sighed heavily. "We only have to humor her for a few more days, then we can go home and wait. It might even be a matter of months."

"Isn't it lucky she didn't have any children?"

"Very," Mrs. Halloway agreed. "She's come a long way, considering her mother grew up in the bogs of Ireland."

"Don't breathe a word about that. She likes to keep it secret that our grandmother was a bogtrotter." They both giggled.

"I tell everyone our ancestors arrived on the *Mayflower*!" said Mrs. Halloway. "You should, too, Tally. Irish immigrants are the lowest!"

Bridie hurried down the corridor and into Mrs. Grimsby's room to draw the curtains and turn down the bed. Did she hear right? Mrs. Grimsby's own mother was Irish? Bridie was astonished. Mrs. Grimsby had never mentioned it, but now

Bridie knew, she wondered whether her mistress's curiosity about Bridie's past had something to do with her desire to learn more about her mother's roots. She felt sorry for Mrs. Grimsby: all these relations pretending to like her when they really only liked her money. At least Bridie knew that Rosetta liked her for herself.

Shortly, the nieces returned to Boston and Mrs. Grimsby was left with her nephew, Paul Heskin, who continued to visit her regularly, drinking tea in the sun parlor and asking after her health with a little too much interest, Bridie thought.

Since Bridie had become aware of Miss Ferrel's tactics to diminish her in the eyes of their mistress, no more strange incidents had occurred in the mansion. But Bridie did not allow herself to be lulled into a false sense of security. She needed this job, although the pay was small, and she was determined that Miss Ferrel wouldn't ruin it for her.

THAT SUMMER THE heat in New York was intense. Mrs. Grimsby closed the mansion earlier than usual and the entire household departed for the Hamptons. However, the journey was tiring and she seemed to labor getting in and out of the car and moving from one place to the other. Bridie and Miss Ferrel helped her together, each taking an arm, but even they struggled with her weight and had to ask the chauffeur to help them. When at last they reached the Hamptons, Mrs. Grimsby took to her bed with Precious and remained there for the entire month of July. Mr. Gordon and Miss Ferrel attempted to see her, but she wasn't up to her secretive chats, asking only for Bridie to turn her, cover her feet when they peeped out of the sheet and mop her brow when she overheated. Finally in

August she ventured onto the veranda to gaze at the sea, and only then did she find peace.

"Read to me," she said to Bridie one evening as the sun sank behind the Cottage.

"What would you like me to read you?" Bridie asked.

"Yeats. I want you to read me Yeats."

Bridie went into her bedroom and found the book on her bedside table, where she liked to keep it nowadays. She sat down on the wicker chair and opened the book. "Which poem shall I read, madam?"

"'The Lake Isle of Innisfree,'" said Mrs. Grimsby. "You know my mother was from Ireland."

Bridie feigned ignorance. "No, madam, I didn't."

"She spoke like you. She had an Irish accent from the South. Soft, lyrical, like a song, it was. Her father taught her to recite poetry. *By the rising of the moon, by the rising of the moon. For the pikes must be together by the rising of the moon.*" Her clumsy hand grabbed the locket that always hung over her bosom. "She later gave me this. It's not worth anything, but it's precious to me." She heaved a labored sigh. "Read to me, Bridget." She closed her eyes expectantly.

Precious sat in Bridie's lap, as she so often did now, and Bridie began to read. "*I will arise and go now, and go to Innisfree, And a small cabin build there, of clay and wattles made; Nine bean-rows will I have there, a hive for the honeybee, And live alone in the bee-loud glade . . .*" Halfway through the poem she glanced at Mrs. Grimsby. Her heavy lids were shut and she was breathing gently. A tear glittered like glass in the corner of her eye. Bridie read on. When she had finished she didn't bother Mrs. Grimsby but chose another poem and continued seamlessly. "*When you are old and gray and full of sleep, And nodding by the fire, take down this book, And slowly read, and dream of the soft look Your eyes had once, and of their shadows deep . . .*" Something made Bridie look up from the page. It might have been the cry of a seabird or the slackening of Mrs. Grimsby's face and the dropping of her hand to her side or the intuitive sense that something had shifted, like the unseen plates below the earth's surface. A spirit leaving for a better place. She looked at Mrs. Grimsby and knew at once that she had gone.

Slowly Bridie stood up and crossed herself. Her heart flooded with sorrow. It was both unexpected and deep. Suddenly she felt very alone, like a raft cut adrift to float on the sea, rudderless and vulnerable to storms and high waves. Mrs. Grimsby was all she had and now she had no one.

She called for Miss Ferrel, who came running. The older woman felt her mistress's pulse and shook her head. "She's dead," she said in a quiet voice. "She's finally let go. May she rest in peace. May God forgive her sins." Precious had curled up in the old lady's lap. Mr. Gordon appeared in the doorway like a specter and bowed his head, but Bridie saw no trace of sorrow in his features. Bridie left them alone and went to the beach to walk up the sand. It was the first free moment she had enjoyed since they had arrived the month before, but there was no pleasure in it now. What was to become of her? Would the inheritor of Mrs. Grimsby's homes continue her employment or would she be released from her duties and left to find another job?

When she returned to the Cottage Mrs. Grimsby's body had been taken away. Her chair was vacant. The Cottage seemed big and cold and very empty. Miss Ferrel told Bridie that she had informed the family. "They'll come like vultures now and take everything she had," said Miss Ferrel bitterly. She sat on the steps of the veranda and hugged her knees.

"What will become of us?" Bridie asked.

"I don't know," said Miss Ferrel. "I should think they'll want to keep you on. As for me, I'm not so sure. Everyone needs a maid. I'm harder to place." Miss Ferrel smiled at Bridie. "She was very fond of you, you know. All that reading she asked you to do."

"I think she liked my accent."

"It touched her, for sure. Her mother was Irish."

"I know. She told me only today."

"She was ashamed of being of Irish descent. She never talked about it. I don't think she had ever opened that book of Yeats's poetry before you arrived. Alice used to read her other writers, but not Yeats. You stirred something in her, Bridget, if I may call you that." She smiled. "I'd like to think we're friends."

Bridie was confused. "I thought you didn't like me."

Miss Ferrel frowned. "Whatever gave you that idea?"

Bridie stiffened. "I thought you resented me. You had worked for her for twelve years and I arrived and she asked me to read—"

"You think I was jealous of you?"

Bridie shrugged. "You left money under the bed to trap me, did you not?"

Miss Ferrel was baffled. "What money?"

"And the earrings . . ."

"Earrings? What are you saying, Bridget?"

"You were trying to show her that I was dishonest."

"I don't know what you're talking about."

Bridie began to feel uncomfortable. "The thousands of dollars I found under her bed and a pair of diamond earrings I discovered in the pocket of one of her dresses? Who else but you left those things there?"

"I swear it wasn't me, Bridget."

"Then who was it?"

"Mr. Gordon?" said Miss Ferrel slowly. "Could it have been Mr. Gordon?"

"Why would he do that?"

"Because *he* was jealous. He was closer to her than anyone, even me."

"Well, it doesn't matter now, does it," said Bridie. "She's gone."

"No, it doesn't matter," Miss Ferrel agreed, looking pensive. She said nothing about the money *she* had found on Mrs. Grimsby's floor—and kept.

ONCE BACK IN New York it wasn't long before Mrs. Grimsby's nieces arrived with their mother, just as Miss Ferrel had predicted, and walked around the mansion arguing over which paintings, ornaments and pieces of furniture should go to whom. "That table will look charming in my dining room," said Mrs. Halloway. "I must have the chairs too."

"But I'd like the chairs," said Mrs. Kesler, sticking out her bottom lip and appealing to their mother.

"The chairs must go with the table, Tally. I'm afraid you'll have to choose something else. Why don't you have her bed? It's a mighty fine bed."

Mrs. Kesler screwed up her nose. "I don't want her bed.

She's lain in it. That great big whale of a woman. It probably sags in the middle."

"You can buy a new mattress," her sister suggested with a smirk.

"With the money I'm going to inherit, Evie, I can buy twenty new mattresses!" Mrs. Kesler exclaimed, cheering up. "All right, you can have the chairs, Evie, and I'll have the bed, without the mattress. I want the Persian rugs. All of them."

"Isn't that a little greedy?" their mother asked.

"Evie doesn't need them. She already has beautiful rugs. She got the chairs. I'm choosing the rugs. I'll *have* those rugs, do you hear!"

Bridie left the room. She couldn't bear to listen to the women fighting over Mrs. Grimsby's possessions when they hadn't even buried her yet. When the women had previously come to New York they had been united in their plot to endear themselves to their aunt; now they were squabbling like crows over carrion. If Mrs. Grimsby had known how disrespectful and avaricious they were going to be she might have considered burning down her houses so they got nothing.

"Of course they can't take anything until the will is read," Miss Ferrel told Bridie later when the three women had gone. They had departed in silence, furious with each other. "You know, it wouldn't surprise me if she has left everything to charity."

"Indeed and that would serve them right," Bridie agreed. "They don't deserve a dollar of her money."

"They don't even deserve Precious," Miss Ferrel added. "Those women will kick her out onto the street."

"A job's a job, but I don't think I'd like to work for them," said Bridie. "I never thought I'd miss Mrs. Grimsby."

Miss Ferrel raised her eyebrows and shook her head. "You're an odd girl, Bridget," she said.

Bridie and Miss Ferrel remained at the mansion for a week. They heard nothing from the family so they continued to do their jobs as normal, even though Mrs. Grimsby was no longer there. Bridie kept the place dusted and Miss Ferrel went through her desk and tidied her papers. When she had done that she took all the books down from the shelves and rearranged them in alphabetical order just to keep busy.

Then, at the end of the week, Mr. Williams drew up outside the mansion in a shiny car. He stepped out in a pristine suit and hat and rang the bell. Miss Ferrel answered and showed him into the hall. He asked to see Miss Doyle. He had something important to say to her.

He put his briefcase down on Mrs. Grimsby's desk in the study and smiled at Bridie. "Good morning, Miss Doyle. As you know, I'm Mrs. Grimsby's attorney, Beaumont Williams. I'm sorry for your loss." Once the pleasantries were out of the way, he sat down and put on his spectacles in a businesslike fashion. "Now, you might be aware that the reading of the will took place yesterday in the presence of Mrs. Grimsby's family." She dropped her gaze into her lap where her fingers fidgeted nervously. "It came as quite a surprise to the family when they were told that Mrs. Grimsby has left her entire estate to you, Miss Doyle."

"Excuse me, sir?" Bridie had gone white with shock.

Mr. Williams's eyes twinkled in amusement. He was clearly enjoying this. "Let me speak plainly, Miss Doyle. Mrs. Grimsby changed her will only a few months ago. She said this would be one hell of a surprise for her family, who had never given her an ounce of affection until the very end. If I recall correctly, she said, 'Miss Doyle has been more loyal to me than anyone I have ever known, in truth she is the only member of my staff to prove her honesty, therefore it gives me enormous pleasure to reward her with everything I own. But it gives me even more pleasure to deny my family an inheritance they don't deserve.'" He opened his briefcase with short, nimble fingers. "Now, let me show you the paperwork. It is a considerable fortune by anyone's standards." He grinned at her with satisfaction. "She was very specific about two things, however. She requested that you cherish her book of Yeats's poetry, and *this*." He pulled out the gold locket on the chain that the old lady had always worn and handed it to Bridie. She held it a moment in her trembling hand. "Don't be frightened to open it, Miss Doyle," said Mr. Williams encouragingly. As her eyes blurred with tears she clicked it open. Inside was a green shamrock set behind glass.

Chapter 28

London, England, spring 1923

Celia Deverill and Lachlan Kirkpatrick's scandalous flight to his father's estate in Scotland sent waves of astonishment and disbelief through the grand drawing rooms of London society. Digby and Beatrice were devastated by their daughter's incomprehensible decision to abandon her new husband; Vivien and Leona furious that their sister should bring dishonor to their family name; Kitty bewildered that her cousin had decided to run off after she had taken her marriage vows and not before, which would have been more sensible. The grandees who smoked cigars and drank port in the exclusive London clubs rallied around Digby, patting him on the back and reassuring him that his daughter would soon come to her senses and hoof it back to London like a runaway horse when she realized that her lover was not as exceptional as she had previously thought. If he was anything like his dishonest and puffed-up father, Porky Kirkpatrick, she'd regret her choice and beg Archie Mayberry to have her back. Those women who envied Beatrice's eclectic wealth and collection of friends relished her daughter's sudden fall from grace and gossiped maliciously in the tea rooms of Fortnum & Mason and the Ritz Hotel, where the ill-fated wedding reception had taken place. No one, however, enjoyed the scandal more than Maud Deverill.

"Poor Beatrice," she sighed disingenuously, bringing the delicate china teacup to her lips. "People are fickle. I doubt her salons will be so well attended in future."

"I can't say I'm surprised," said Victoria, sitting opposite her mother in the pretty green sitting room of her London home that looked out onto pink camellias and white viburnum blossoming brightly in her lavish garden. "Celia always had a wild streak. Don't you remember those summers when she and Kitty would run off like feral dogs and get up to all sorts of mischief?"

"They were as bad as each other but Beatrice was much too indulgent. Anything Celia did was amusing in her eyes. Frankly, I wanted to give her a good smack."

"I wouldn't be so sure that Beatrice's salons will be diminished by the scandal. There's nothing people love more than a drama and everyone will be longing to be in the know. I predict they'll be flocking there in droves just to be at the center of it all."

"Do you really think so?" Maud was disappointed.

"At least it's distracted everyone from Kitty's baby. You should be grateful to Celia for that."

Maud sighed. "Kitty's baby. I don't want to speak of it. She's irresponsible and selfish. She hasn't considered me for a minute. Or you, for that matter. What does Eric think?"

"Oh, Eric couldn't give a monkey. He doesn't relish gossip and like most men he finds Kitty compelling."

"She needs to marry," said Maud firmly. "A strong man will put her in her place."

Victoria wasn't convinced. "Then she needs to find a *very* strong man indeed."

As SOON AS Harry discovered where Celia was, he and Boysie took the Flying Scotsman to Edinburgh. "Who wants to live in Scotland?" said Boysie, settling into the seat of the first-class dining carriage. "It's full of Scottish people."

Harry laughed at Boysie's irreverence. "I doubt Celia thought of that before she ran off with him."

"It's all very well going north to fish and stalk but a week of wet feet and cold toes is enough to send anyone in their right mind shooting back down south. I really can't abide those dreadful kilts. Most of the men who wear them have bulging calves and knobbly knees. I find the knee the least attractive part of the human body. It shouldn't ever be on show."

"I hate to think what part of the body you *do* want on show. I suppose Lachlan wears a kilt, does he?"

"Most certainly. He's without doubt a kilt wearer and offensive with it. No one but the King should wear a kilt. Kings are meant to dress up, it's what they do, and tourists love the pageantry. But aristocrats harping on about their clans and their tartans and their silly Scottish reels are really very tiresome."

He pulled a face at Harry. "Remind me, old boy, why we're going to Scotland!"

The stationmaster blew his whistle and a puff of steam billowed up the platform in a quickly evaporating cloud. Slowly the wheels screeched and the train began to move out of the station. "We have to make Celia see the error of her ways," said Harry. "She might have to beg but I'm sure Archie will take her back. They're married, after all. For better or for worse and all that."

"Lachlan might be devilishly handsome and unconventional, but really, one doesn't want *that* every day of one's life. He's a terrible egoist. Poor Celia!"

"If he had given *her* a thought he wouldn't have encouraged her to run off with him. Her reputation is in tatters."

"On the contrary, old boy, she's become much more interesting because of it. If she returns to Archie they'll be the toast of the town. You wait, there won't be a hostess in London who won't want them at her table—excluding a few stuffy old dowagers, of course. There are always those." Boysie extracted his silver cigarette case from the inside pocket of his jacket and opened it. "Fancy a smoke?" Harry took one and popped it between his lips. Boysie flicked his lighter and Harry puffed on the flame. "I hope she sees sense," Boysie added, lighting a cigarette for himself. "I'm not going all the way to Scotland for nothing."

"Then you'd better hone your powers of persuasion," said Harry.

"I'm hoping that pea-size brain of hers will have worked it out already. Darling Celia, I do love her most ardently, but it seems to me that the brains in the Deverill family went directly to Kitty. No offense, old boy, but it's not for your brains that I love you."

"No offense taken, Boysie," Harry replied with a grin. "But to make up for your slight you must now list all the reasons why, brains apart, you love me so dearly."

THE FOLLOWING DAY Celia was waiting for Harry and Boysie in one of the cold drawing rooms, huddling by the fire, drinking a mug of hot cocoa. They arrived mid-morning, having spent the night in a small hotel in Edinburgh. The butler showed them through an austere hall where antlers of all sizes hung on the walls and a giant bearskin was spread on the flagstone floor, the bear baring his teeth in a silent growl. He announced them at the drawing-room door while two young footmen went outside to attend to their luggage. "Darling boys, you're *too* good to come to my rescue!" Celia gushed, running to greet them with hugs and kisses.

"Do you *need* rescuing, darling?" Boysie asked.

"But of course I do." She beamed a smile. "You're my knights in shining armor."

"It's a rather splendid house this, or could be if one heated it up a little and redecorated," said Boysie, rubbing his hands to warm them. "Where is he, the wife stealer?"

"Hush, Boysie! There are spies everywhere!" Celia hissed, loving the drama. "You must be tired. It's a ghastly journey, don't you think?"

"I think Scotland is ghastly, if you ask me," said Boysie, running his eyes over the tired furniture and faded upholstery.

"What were you thinking?" Harry asked.

Celia looked sheepish. "Whatever it was, I'm not thinking it now," she said. "Do you believe Archie will have me back *even though I'm no longer intact*?" she whispered.

"You might have to grovel," said Harry.

"Oh, I can grovel. Can't we just pretend that Lachlan abducted me and had his wicked way?" she suggested.

"Is that really fair?" said Harry.

"Nothing's fair in love or war," Boysie added, falling into the sofa.

"Have some tea," suggested Celia. "Patterson, a pot of tea for my friends. Now sit down and warm up. It's frightfully cold in here. Makes Castle Deverill seem as hot as a greenhouse by comparison."

She perched on the club fender so that the fire could warm her back. "What are we going to do? Lachlan thinks it's all perfectly wonderful. He loves the fact that everyone in London is talking about it. He wants to marry me."

"Then he should have run off with you *before* you made your marriage vows," said Harry.

"I don't think he's very clever, do you?" said Celia, crinkling her pretty nose. "I think I've made a terrible mistake."

Boysie lit a cigarette. "You have two choices. One: you annul the marriage and marry Lachlan instead. But frankly, living up here will drive you mad."

"What's two?" Celia asked anxiously.

"You come back to London with us. Explain to Archie that you had a terrible attack of wedding nerves and beg him to forgive you."

"Of course you'll have to explain your decision to Lachlan," Harry reminded her.

Celia was shocked. "Lord no. I'll run off into the night and leave him a note. I couldn't possibly tell him to his face."

Patterson soon brought them tea. He placed the tray on the coffee table then disappeared discreetly back into the hall, closing the door behind him. "Why did you run off at your wedding, Celia? Why not later?" Boysie asked. "Did you really have to humiliate poor Archie, not to mention your poor mother?"

"It was the thought of the wedding night. I didn't think I could go through with it. Archie leaves me cold, you see. Lachlan is another matter entirely. He's so devilishly attractive."

"I thought you girls just lay back and thought of England. Then after an heir and a spare, found a man who really satisfied you in the bedroom. Sounds very sensible to me. Marriage isn't about love, it's about alliance." Boysie glanced at Harry. "I'll marry 'the pudding' because it's my duty as the only son to further the family line. But I won't love her. If she loves me she'll be desperately unhappy."

"Poor Deirdre," said Celia without really meaning it. "Dreary Deirdre. It rolls off the tongue, doesn't it?" She sighed heavily as if the travails of womankind rested on her shoulders alone. "I suppose I must return to Archie."

"Where's Lachlan?" Boysie asked.

"Fishing. He'll be out all day." She looked suddenly forlorn. "He spends a lot of time doing that."

"And what are you meant to be doing while he entertains himself?" Harry said.

Celia smiled pathetically. "I don't know. What *do* women in Scotland do?" she asked.

"Brush their husbands' sporrans," said Boysie with a chuckle.

"Really, Boysie, you're too much!" Celia laughed. "How do you bear him, Harry?"

The three friends had lunch together in the dining room while Lachlan, blissfully unaware of Celia's plans, sat beside the river with his gillie, watching his fishing line and eating the picnic the cook had prepared for him. When he returned home that evening he would find a note on the table in the hall and Celia gone.

BEATRICE WAS ETERNALLY grateful to Harry and Boysie for bringing Celia home. She threw her arms around her daughter and wept profusely as if Celia were the liberator of her unhappiness, not the cause of it. Digby was much less forgiving. "You've made us a laughingstock!" he declared furiously. "After all we have done for you! Do you have any idea how much your wedding cost us, in both money and effort? I hope Archie takes you back, but I wouldn't blame him if he got rid of you and chose someone else. You'd better beg, my girl. Without Archie I don't think you have much of a future."

Celia was stunned. Her father had always been indulgent, quick to laugh, slow to chastise. She thought he might see the amusing side, smile at her courage, perhaps shake his head at her foolishness in a "Really, so typical of you, Celia, my dear" sort of way, but certainly not be furious. She disintegrated into passionate sobs. "Is it really so hopeless, Papa?"

Digby lifted his hands and shrugged, the light catching the gold on his large signet ring. "There might be a way," he said.

Digby met Archie in the library at Deverill House on Kensington Palace Gardens. He gave the young man a stiff drink, then made him an offer he couldn't refuse. "I can only apologize for my daughter's deplorable behavior. Wedding nerves might explain her foolishness, but not justify it. However, she is married to you and in the eyes of God marriage is a bond that no man can put asunder. Therefore I have decided to increase her dowry by £100,000 as a small recompense for the ordeal she has put you through. I hope you see it in your heart to forgive, or at least to take her back to save us all from further scandal. She has seen the error of her ways and is keen to make it up to you." Digby knew that the offer was, in truth, a humiliating one that no man would accept unless it happened that his family was on the verge of complete bankruptcy. Through his contacts in the city he had discovered that the Mayberrys were being overwhelmed by colossal debts. That house of cards was on the point of collapse. He knitted his fingers and watched the color rise to his son-in-law's cheeks.

Archie inhaled through his nostrils as he considered Digby's words. "You are asking a great deal of me, Sir Digby," he said finally, but Digby knew it was a good offer. "Had she fled with a girlfriend, I might have understood her wedding nerves. But to run off to Scotland with Lachlan Kirkpatrick and live with him is a clear case of adultery. However, we are married, as you say, and in God's eyes must remain so. I will take her back, but this is a blight on our happiness. I'm not sure I'll ever be able to trust her, much less love her, but I will strive to forgive." The two men shook hands. Money had, as it so often did, eased the pain of the recent events and cast Digby's daughter in a more favorable light. Certainly it softened the atmosphere in the library so that, when the door was opened and Celia summoned, the two men were on excellent terms, discussing the roaring start to the London Season.

Celia appeared, sufficiently contrite. Archie glanced at her, but he couldn't meet her eye. He shook Digby's hand again and walked out into the square where his chauffeur waited for him on the curb beside his shiny Ford Model T, a wedding present from his father, bought with borrowed money. Celia followed, uncertain what to do, wanting to cling on to her childhood and the security of her home, but knowing she had willingly left her girlhood behind in Lachlan Kirkpatrick's bed from where she could never get it back. Her father didn't want her at home, Archie probably didn't want her either, and Lachlan had wanted her very badly but seemed to want her less when the excitement of their grand escape had worn off. The drama had been thrilling, but the aftershock now left her cold. She climbed into the back seat beside Archie.

"Are you going to forgive me?" she asked, trying to find the old Archie beneath his hard and pitiless mask.

"I thought I understood you, Celia." He shook his head and gazed out of the window as the car drove around the square and off toward Mayfair. "But I don't know you anymore."

"I'm sorry," she said in a quiet voice. "I didn't mean to hurt you. I was thinking only of myself. I was a fool and I will live with that for the rest of my life."

"Yes, you will." His profile remained unmoved. "And you will accept everything I demand of you."

THEY SETTLED INTO their new home in Mayfair and Celia tried very hard to be a good wife. She ran the house, arranged dinner parties and accepted the sudden deluge of invitations that arrived from the grandest hostesses in London. As Boysie had predicted, the drama had only made them more interesting as a couple and when in public they put on a convincing display of unity. However, Celia's bed remained empty at night, their marriage unconsummated. Archie didn't speak to her at all, unless in company, so Celia made sure the house was full of guests whenever possible. Her front door was forever open and callers most welcome. They came in their droves, simply so they could report what they'd seen of the "runaway bride" and her poor cuckolded husband, and both Celia and Archie did their best to keep up appearances.

"It's a sham," Celia confessed to Kitty when they were alone together in the garden one afternoon, sitting side by side on an iron bench, a gift from one of the wedding guests. "We look like the happiest couple in the world, yet we're the most miserable and it's all my fault."

"It will settle down," Kitty reassured her, taking her hand.

"He won't forgive me, Kitty. I hurt him and he won't ever forgive me for it."

"You'll have children soon and they'll bring you together."

Celia laughed huskily, throwing her head back so her throat flashed white and vulnerable in the sunshine. "He doesn't come to my bed," she said. "He hasn't visited me once. Not once. I'm a pariah."

"He will."

Celia stared at Kitty, her eyes wide and desperate. "The irony is I so want him to."

"Oh Celia."

"I ache for him, Kitty. I long for him to hold me. I long for things to be the way they were before we got married. Back then I dreaded him touching me. But now I wish he would."

Her voice lowered as she struggled with her emotions. "But I'm a tainted woman. I've been with another man. I'm spoiled goods. No one wants me anymore. I hear Lachlan is courting that dreadful Annabel Whitely. He didn't waste time pining for me, did he?"

"Forget about Lachlan. Concentrate on your marriage. You have to be patient. You can't expect wounds to heal overnight. Archie will soften, I'm sure."

"He'd better or I'll wither away. The virgin bride, they'll call me." She smiled at Kitty sadly. "And what about you?"

"Me?"

"Yes, Jack will have to have a father, you know. You can't bring him up without a man to look up to."

Kitty frowned at Celia. She hadn't thought about that. But Celia was right. It wouldn't be fair to deny Jack a father's love. "I always believed I'd marry the man I loved," she said. "I was starry-eyed and dreamy. But it isn't like that, is it?" She was lost now in the half distance, her mind dragging her back to Ireland and the memories she had left there.

"One has to be lucky." Celia sighed. "I didn't realize how lucky I was."

"I loved a man," Kitty confessed suddenly, her eyes filling with tears. "I loved a man with all my heart, Celia. I loved him enough to die for him. But I couldn't have him."

Celia stared at her cousin in astonishment. "Was he Irish?" Kitty nodded. "What happened to him?"

"He was imprisoned." Kitty turned her eyes away. She didn't want anyone to see the pain behind them, not even Celia.

"For what?"

"For being a rebel."

"Oh," Celia gasped, not really understanding what that meant, but knowing it had something to do with the reason they had stopped spending summers at Castle Deverill.

"I told him I'd wait for him," Kitty continued. "I would have waited forever. But he let me go. I wrote letters. So many letters. But he never replied." She dropped her shoulders. "He knows, you see. There are too many obstacles in our way. There always were. But I believed we could jump them." She laughed unhappily. "I could jump anything on a horse, couldn't I?"

Celia wrapped her arms around her cousin. "Aren't we a sorry pair?" she said, squeezing her. "The Deverill cousins and their complicated love lives. Do you think it's in our blood?"

"I don't know. Our sisters have all married, haven't they?"

"To the most dreary men in England! I wouldn't want their boring husbands. I'd still rather be married to Archie, even though he's not talking to me."

"I'll have to marry a man I don't love because I'll never love anyone as much as I love Jack."

Celia pulled away. "Jack? You mean Jack O'Leary, the boy who loved frogs?"

Kitty nodded. "I named little Jack Deverill after him. He is brave, handsome, funny, intelligent and kind. I couldn't think of a better man to name him after."

"Don't expect to love like that again, Kitty, or you'll never be happy," said Celia with rare wisdom. "You have to find someone you respect and who respects you. A partner for life. He's out there somewhere, Kitty. You can't live off your grandmother forever. You need to give Jack Deverill security." *It's truly over then*, Kitty thought to herself, and the last ember of hope died.

ONE NIGHT AT the end of the summer Archie came to Celia's bedroom. He didn't say a word. He took off his dressing gown and hung it on the back of her chair. He slid out of his slippers and unbuttoned his pyjama top, untying the drawstring of his trousers and stepping out of them. Celia watched him from the bed, too nervous to speak. His naked body shone golden in the glow of the streetlamp that poured a fountain of light through the gap in the curtains, but his expression was cast in shadow and Celia longed to see whether he was coming in love, to take her in his arms as she had so often dreamed, or in loathing to do his duty as a husband but nothing more.

Quietly he pulled back the covers and climbed in. Celia bit her lip and a tremor of anticipation rippled across her skin. She felt his hand glide over her belly. Tentatively she placed hers on top of it, holding it still against her nightdress. At once she felt something silky in his grasp. She searched for his eyes through the darkness. At last he looked at her. "I want you to put these on," he said.

She frowned. "What are they?"

"White gloves," he replied. She made to object. "Celia, darling, the deal was you'd do anything I demand of you."

She felt the heat rise to her cheeks. "If it's only a pair of white gloves . . ."

"That's all it is, *and nothing else.*"

For a moment she looked horrified . . . but then her face broke into a smile and she started to laugh. "If that's your only peccadillo, then we're going to be very happy together." And he bent his head to kiss her.

Chapter 29

London, England, autumn 1923

Kitty opened her eyes. The dark face of Michael Doyle was staring down at her, smirking triumphantly as he buttoned up his trousers. Her virtue was a prize to celebrate, like the murder of Colonel Manley and the many Auxiliaries he had no doubt killed in the name of a free Ireland. "I own you now," he was saying. "I filled you with my seed and, even though it never took root, it embedded itself deep inside you like a thorn that you can never remove, however hard you try to forget." She blinked into the darkness, her pulse racing, her breath scratching her throat. Had he come in death to haunt her? She blinked again, then fumbled for the light. The room was empty. She realized it had only been a dream, but she could smell the blend of alcohol and smoke as if he had really been there and shuddered. She took a sip of water. She had sworn that she would never let him go, but in truth it was *he* who had never let *her* go. The ripping of her flesh had healed but the memory of his attack remained forever branded on her soul like the mark of the Devil. If she hadn't ridden over to confront him . . . if she hadn't been so arrogant . . . if only . . .

Little Jack Deverill was now one and a half and more adorable than any child Kitty had ever seen. Without restraint she poured all the love she had saved for Jack O'Leary onto the half brother who bore his name. Harry and Boysie visited often and spent time with the child, cooing over him like a pair of pigeons, but their regular calls only emphasized the lack of interest from the rest of her family. In Maud's case it was on account of her hurt; in Victoria's her disapproval; in her father's his shame. Kitty accepted that Jack would never be recognized by that branch of the Deverill family. The Wiltshire branch, however, embraced him with their habitual aplomb.

Harry had got engaged to Charlotte Stalbridge at the same time that Boysie had asked Dreary Deirdre to marry him. Maud was ecstatic. The Stalbridges were a wealthy, well-established landed family with a large estate in Norfolk, near the royal Sandringham estate. Indeed, Sir Charles Stalbridge was a friend of the King. Although Harry no longer had a grand castle to inherit, the Stalbridges were delighted owing to Harry's charm. There was a certain romance in the black ruins of a fortress burned by Fenian rebels during the Troubles. Harry was a Deverill, destined to be Lord Deverill, castle or no castle, and they were perfectly satisfied with that. Besides, Charlotte was madly in love, which to Lady Stalbridge was more important than ancient stone walls and worthless lands.

Beatrice offered to throw the happy couple a joint engagement party at Deverill Rising with Boysie and Deirdre, and set about organizing it for New Year's Eve. Maud spent Christmas with Victoria. Elspeth, pregnant with her second child, invited her father and grandmother for the festivities, for he and Maud seemed to lead totally separate lives now. Bertie remained at the Hunting Lodge with his increasingly eccentric mother while Maud stayed in England with Victoria, or during the Season with Beatrice. She had begged Bertie to buy her a house of her own, explaining that it was hard to depend on the hospitality of Digby and Beatrice "like a poor relation." But Bertie told her there was no money left for that sort of extravagance. If she didn't like it she could always return to Co. Cork. The thought of returning *there* appalled Maud. Without the castle she could no longer hold her head up in Ireland—and besides, she had severed all ties with the country she had never really warmed to. Betrayed by her best friend, rejected by her husband, insulted by his illegitimate child Kitty had insisted on raising and chatelaine of a heap of stones and ashes were reasons enough to never set foot in that godforsaken country again.

Kitty longed to return to Ireland with every fiber of her body and it took a great force of will to remain in England. She spent Christmas at Deverill Rising with Digby and Beatrice. The house filled once again with their family and friends and for a brief moment Kitty lost her craving for home in the excitement of endless parties. As long as she kept herself occupied she could bury Ireland beneath the buzz of activity. She could wander around their splendid gardens in Wiltshire and not yearn for the walled vegetable garden where she had looked for messages from Jack, or the greenhouses where she, Celia and

Bridie had held their secret meetings in the summertime, or the box garden where she had so often lost herself as a child, her footsteps in the frost doubling up until she no longer knew where she was. She stifled her sorrow by taking pleasure from the loveliness of Deverill Rising, and it was, quite simply, magnificent.

It was at the boys' engagement party on New Year's Eve that she found herself talking to Robert Trench. Seated next to him at dinner she inquired after his book. "I've finished it," he said happily. "It's going to be published this spring."

"How delightful," Kitty enthused. "I look forward to reading it."

"I will send you a copy," he volunteered. "You can be the first to receive one."

"I'm flattered. I'm sure I shall enjoy it very much."

He smiled and Kitty thought how handsome he was when he looked happy. He had been so terribly solemn in Ireland. He gazed at her with affection and Kitty wondered at people's ability to change. There was something reassuring about the familiarity of him; he reminded her of home. "You never smiled in Ireland," she ventured. "Why?"

"I was unhappy," he confessed.

"Didn't Ireland make you happy?"

"Those years made me more unhappy than I have ever been in my life. I should have been fighting in the war. I felt a failure. I felt less of a man."

She frowned. "I'm sorry, Robert. I never knew."

"You were very young. How could you have known?"

"I should have been more sensitive. I think I was beastly."

"You weren't beastly. You were distracted."

Kitty thought of Jack but hastily suppressed it. "I was very concerned about Ireland," she said.

"You were certainly idealistic."

"We got our Free State, though, didn't we?"

"But Ireland is still divided."

"Yes, but we won independence for the South."

"Yet, at what cost?"

She looked at him steadily and at once she felt the desire to share things that had remained hidden for so long. She knew that, out of all the people in her new life, Robert was the only man who would truly understand her. "The War of Independence robbed me of everything I have ever loved," she said quietly. "It was a war I believed in and in a small way I played a part. But I never thought I'd be personally affected."

"Might that be an understatement?"

She lowered her eyes sadly, overwhelmed by the compassion in his voice and the emotions it provoked. "Oh, Robert, you have no idea how true that is." She sighed. "But Ireland has her independence now."

"And you?"

"I have lost her." Kitty picked up her glass of wine, rallying her strength from the deep reserves she could always count on. "But I'll get her back one day. She's not going to go away. I might have lost my home and . . ." She hesitated. "But Ireland is still wild and green and beautiful." She stood up from the table and hurried out of the dining room, through the house to the French windows that opened onto the wintry terrace.

The fountain was frozen, the hedges glittered with freshly fallen snow, an icy moon shone through an aura of mist. Stars glimmered brighter than she had ever seen them and somewhere in the woods, beyond the dovecote, an owl hooted through the darkness. "You'll die of cold," said Robert, stepping out to join her. He took off his jacket and placed it over her shoulders. He stood beside her. "I'm sorry, perhaps I shouldn't have asked you about Ireland."

Kitty shivered and put the jacket on. It was warm where his body had been. "I try so hard to suppress it, Robert. I try all the time but every day it's a struggle. My heart bleeds for my home. I love it, you see. I love it more than anything in the world."

"I understand your love, Kitty. Castle Deverill was one of the most wonderful places I have ever been to in my life. I've traveled to Italy and Spain, Morocco and France and yet, those rugged green hills of Cork are among the most beautiful sights my eyes have witnessed. They seem to touch one deeply, in one's soul. I was so lucky to have spent those years there with you."

"But you were so unhappy?"

"Unhappy, yes, but surrounded by such beauty." Her eyes glittered in the moonlight and Robert gazed into them, his heart swelling with love. "I'd give you Ireland if I could," he said softly, looking at her earnestly through his round spectacles. "I'd take you back and watch you flower like the purple heather on the hills." He ran his fingers down her damp cheek. "Nothing would make me happier than to return to Castle Deverill and rebuild your home stone by stone. I'd sell my soul to do it."

"Oh Robert." She sighed, suddenly understanding everything. "You were unhappy because . . ."

"Yes, I loved you." He nodded. "Every day was a struggle, Kitty, just like you are struggling now with your yearning for

Ireland. But I survived and here I am, looking down upon the woman I love who has stars in her eyes." He laughed at his own foolishness. "One day you'll return to Ireland and your struggle will have been worth it. For your absence will only deepen your love and increase your appreciation. When you lay eyes on your beloved Ireland again you'll believe its splendor more intense than before, more vibrant, more uplifting, just like I believe you more beautiful than before."

"You're going to make me cry," she said. "If your book is as moving as your words are to me now, I don't think I'll be able to read it."

He brushed away a tear with his thumb. "It's inspired by you, Kitty."

"Does it have a happy ending?"

"No," he replied. "It doesn't."

She placed her hand on top of his, holding it against her cheek. "Do we?" she asked.

"That depends on you."

She lifted her chin and he bent his head to place his lips on hers in a long and tender kiss. She squeezed her eyes shut, releasing a final tear for Jack, for that chapter had to close now. The book that contained within its pages all the tragedy and pain of Ireland's Troubles and Kitty's suffering must be put away on the shelf and a new book begun. A positive book, one filled with joy and light.

She knew that, although she didn't love Robert, she needed him. She couldn't endure her exile alone. Robert understood her love of Ireland—he connected her to a time in her life when she had been truly happy. He knew the gardens at Castle Deverill as well as she did. He appreciated the rocky hills and their deep and enduring majesty. He knew her better than anyone else for he had taught her everything she knew. She respected his superior mind and yet, at the same time, knew he admired her for her inquiring one. There was no one more qualified than him to lay claim to her heart.

She wrapped her arms around him and let him shelter her from the cold, from the fears that rose up from her past like monsters, from the future that was still so uncertain. She kissed him gratefully, because, having doubted she would find someone to love her, she had found someone who always had. In Robert's arms she felt the warm comfort of the familiar and she silently thanked God for giving her a second chance.

GRACE WAS IN the garden when the butler approached her across the lawn. Spring had breathed her sugar-scented breath over the grass, turning it a bright, vibrant green, and through the branches of the ancient oak trees, opening their delicate little buds and awakening the flowers on the horse chestnuts and elders to scatter their petals on the wind like confetti. She loved this time of year the best and it pained her to leave for London just as Ireland was blossoming in all her glory. "I'm sorry to disturb you, m'lady, but there's a young man in the hall. He says he needs to speak to you."

Grace sighed irritably. She had been enjoying the peace of the garden and the sight of birds frolicking among the new leaves, building their nests and twittering merrily. There was nothing like the sound of birdsong to lift the spirits. "Did he say his name?" she inquired. Perhaps she could ask him to come back later.

"Yes, m'lady. Jack O'Leary."

She gave a start. "Thank you, Brennan. I'll see him at once."

Grace followed the butler across the grass and entered the house through the side door. When she reached the sitting room Jack was by the window, gazing out over the gardens. He heard her enter. "When I was in prison, I missed the sight of birds, the smell of soil, the budding of leaves." He turned around and took off his cap. "It's good to be free. How are you, Lady Rowan-Hampton?"

She stood in the doorway and took in the sight of the eager boy war had hardened into a rugged and world-weary man, older than his years. The passion she had witnessed in his eyes the night he had plunged the knife into Colonel Manley had gone and in its place a resignation and a sorrow that touched her deeply. "Why did they keep you so long?" she asked.

"They thought I had more information than I was giving them," he told her.

Grace was astonished. "Did they know about Kitty?"

"They found a letter she had given me in my pocket." He grinned and Grace noticed that one of his teeth was missing. "It's lucky she left when she did."

"I'm surprised they let you live."

"Only thanks to Father Quinn. I owe him my life."

"For the second time," Grace added drily, remembering the aftermath of Colonel Manley's murder.

"Indeed and God was always on our side."

Grace knew why he had come. "Let's walk around the garden," she suggested.

They stepped into the sunshine where the call of a corncrake resonated across the lawn with the hum of spring's first bees, buzzing about the dandelions that shone enticingly in the long grass. "How could they have bloody burned down the castle?" Jack asked. "That's a tragedy, that is. Considering what Kitty did for the cause." Her name hung like a weight between them. "She should have left when I told her to."

"You should have both left. You should have gone to America."

"It was too late."

"You should have asked for my help. The advantage of having a rich husband is that it enables me to help those who can't afford to help themselves."

"Where is she, Lady Rowan-Hampton?"

Grace heaved a sigh. "She's in London, Jack."

"I let her go, but she continued to write to me. Now I'm free, am I a fool to hope?"

"Yes, you are."

He nodded and dropped his gaze to the ground. She could almost hear it thud onto the grass with disappointment. "I should have let her wait."

"You did the right thing, Jack. She has a little boy." Grace put a hand on his arm as he stared at her in bewilderment. "Oh no, he doesn't belong to her. He was left on the doorstep of the Hunting Lodge. She made the decision to keep him. That's why she can't come back. Her father won't have her in the house with an illegitimate child. She's started a new life with him in London." Jack's eyes dimmed. Grace couldn't bear to look at him as she dealt the final blow. "She's engaged to be married."

"Jaysus." He shook his head as if trying to shake away the image of Kitty with another man.

"The boy needs a father and she needs security."

"I'd fight for her if I believed I'd win."

"I'd finance your fight if I believed it was the right thing to do. But it isn't. Leave her, Jack. She's found happiness. After all she's suffered, doesn't she deserve to be happy?"

They wandered through a wooden gate, into a field of yellow cowslips. As they walked through it they disturbed a flock of pigeons that took to the skies in fright. "We won our independence," said Jack with a wry grin. "The Irish Free State. Those words are sweet on the tongue. But now brother is set against brother. We're like a hideous creature feeding on itself."

"The IRA won't rest until Ireland is united and fully independent," said Grace solemnly. "But I'm content with what we have. My days as a rebel are over." She looked at him and smiled fondly. "So are yours."

"It's good to walk in Ballinakelly as a free man. Our children will thank us for our sacrifice when they learn of Ireland's history in their schools and at the family table."

"History never gives its gratitude in the right places. What are you going to do?" Grace asked.

He shrugged. "What I've always done. I'll go home."

"You'll look after animals?"

"Ballinakelly needs a good vet. My father's getting on now and the war affected him physically so he's not as fit as he once was. I'll pick up the pieces and carry on. What else is there for me to do?"

"You'll always find work around here. That hasn't changed."

He looked at her sadly. "Everything else has, though, hasn't it, Lady Rowan-Hampton? The War of Independence robbed us of everything we loved."

"Yet it gave us the thing we all love the most: Ireland. Don't forget that. Your sacrifice, Kitty's sacrifice, God knows I've made my own, were not for nothing." She gazed around at the soft velvet hills and sighed with pleasure both bitter and sweet. "We have all *this*, Jack. It belongs to *us* and we all played our part in its liberation."

GRACE RETURNED TO London for Kitty's wedding, which was a small and modest affair. Kitty didn't want a big society wedding like Harry was going to have. She had no father to give her away and no mother to help her choose her dress and the flowers for her bouquet. Instead, she and Robert married at Old Church in Chelsea at the end of the summer, for which Elspeth and Peter traveled all the way from Co. Cork. Beatrice insisted on paying for the reception at a venue on Pavilion Road, and took the liberty of filling it with an extravagance of white roses, hoping to shame Maud into feeling guilty for having pushed her youngest daughter and the little child she loved as her own out of her life. Had Kitty married a duke Maud might have been roused out of her sulk, but as Kitty's choice was the humble Mr. Trench, the man who had once been her tutor, Maud was less than satisfied. She hadn't been too happy about Peter MacCartain but at least *he* had had a castle.

Elspeth took one look at little Jack and gasped. "But he's yours!" she exclaimed, just like her mother had.

Kitty grinned. "He does look like me, doesn't he?"

"When did you have him?"

"He's not mine, Elspeth." Kitty laughed at the astonished look on her sister's face.

Elspeth sat down. "Then whose is he?"

Kitty was tired of keeping secrets. "He's Papa's," she stated coolly. She watched Elspeth's mouth open and draw in a horrified gasp. "Papa was a little indiscreet with one of the maids," she told her carefully. "Jack is our half brother."

"Oh Kitty! No wonder he won't let you come home!"

"Jack is his son. He has to let us come home eventually."

"God, Kitty. Why didn't you tell me sooner?"

"I didn't want to upset you."

"You've held this in all this time?"

"Harry knows. Robert too, of course. So does Mama . . ."

"No wonder she looked so miserable at your wedding."

"She can't look at Jack. She sees Papa's betrayal. I can't blame her for that."

"She's a deeply unhappy woman but I feel no compassion for her, Kitty. She deserves her unhappiness. You, on the other hand, deserve every happiness. I'm so pleased you've found a decent, kind man." She took her sister's hands. "Please come back to Ireland. I miss you, Kitty. You can stay with us for as long as you like." She lowered her voice. "There's always Uncle Rupert's old house. It's all boarded up and no one's been in there since he died, but I'm sure if Robert talks to Papa, he'll let you have it. Please try," she implored. "I know you miss Ireland. No one loved Castle Deverill more than you."

KITTY HAD DREADED the wedding night for some time. Robert had chosen a small hotel in Chelsea and Kitty had arranged for Jack to remain at home with his nanny. When at last they were alone, Robert had taken her by the hand and led her into the bedroom. But after a few kisses Kitty had put him off, complaining of tiredness, and changed into her nightdress behind a screen, slipping modestly into bed and pulling the covers around her chin. Robert had lain beside her, holding her in his arms, gently pressing his lips to her forehead, respecting her need for sleep. If he was disappointed he didn't show it. The following morning they had traveled to Italy by boat and train, arriving in Florence in a pony and trap two days later, and Kitty could put him off yet again, for the journey had been long and arduous.

The foreign smells of parched earth, eucalyptus trees, wild rosemary and thyme filled Kitty's nostrils and lifted her out of her pining for home. Gone were the rugged green hills and chuckling streams of Ballinakelly, the soft rain and tempestuous skies of Ireland. She allowed herself to be relieved of the past and committed to the present with a sense of reprieve. She took in the splendor of that ancient city of pale buildings, terra-cotta roofs, narrow cobbled streets, and colonnaded squares with the excitement of a person starved of culture and beauty. From her balcony she could see the magnificent basilica rising above the city like a glorious ship in an ocean of red tiles. The gigantic dome seemed to defy the laws of gravity and human limitation. Kitty gazed on it in wonder as the setting sun cloaked the city in a soft veil of dusty pink.

Robert wrapped his arms around her from behind and kissed her neck. "Isn't it beautiful?" Kitty sighed, attempting to delay the inevitable for as long as possible.

"I want you, Kitty," he murmured. "I want to make love to my wife."

Kitty was almost paralyzed with fear. Robert must have felt her stiffen for he lifted his head from her neck. "What is it, darling?" She gripped his arms. "Are you frightened? I won't hurt you, I promise." When she didn't reply he turned her around so he could read the expression on her face. He was astonished to see her eyes so full of real terror. "Kitty, what is it?"

Her natural pallor had turned to gray and her lips trembled with the secret that balanced upon them. But she didn't know how to articulate what Michael Doyle had done to her that day in the farmhouse. If she did, would the words unleash the memory to feed on her happiness? Would it rob her of everything that was now good in her life?

Robert was alarmed. He held her upper arms and gazed anxiously into her eyes. "Kitty, you have to tell me. I'm your husband and I love you. Whatever it is, I won't love you less."

Kitty swallowed. A calmness came over her. A surreal tranquillity as if she were floating somewhere over Brunelleschi's heavenly dome. "I was raped," she whispered. The words were a mere ribbon of sound but Robert heard them.

He too paled. "Who?" he gasped. "When . . . ?"

A hot tear slowly trickled down her cheek. "In Ireland. The day the castle burned. I knew who had done it, Robert. So I went to find him."

"Oh Kitty." He pulled her into his arms and held her more fiercely than he had ever done. "My darling, darling, sweet Kitty. No one will ever hurt you again. As God is my witness, no one will ever hurt you again." She closed her eyes and gave in to the suffering Michael Doyle had inflicted. With a giant, shuddering breath, she released it into Robert's chest.

Chapter 30

New York, America, 1923

Bridie sat in the garden of Mrs. Grimsby's mansion on Fifth Avenue and hugged the shoebox she had brought all the way from Ballinakelly. It was all she had to connect her to her past, and to herself. The vast inheritance should have made her the happiest girl in the world but she felt afraid; small, lost and very very far from home.

Bridie had never been in charge of her destiny. She had done what she was told. She had obeyed orders. She had allowed life's current to carry her down the stream and she had always known where it ended. But Mr. Deverill had changed its course and she had been carried off to a foreign country on the other side of the world. In spite of the uncertainty, she had taken comfort from the boundaries imposed upon her by Mrs. Grimsby's autocracy. Now, with the old lady's death and her sudden independence, Bridie was adrift; there was no one to tell her what to do.

Slowly she opened the box. Inside shone the pair of dancing shoes with their bright buckles and fine black patent leather that Lady Deverill had given her all those years ago. A sob escaped her throat and a fat tear dropped onto her hand as she lifted out one of the shoes and held it up to the light. She looked at the silver buckle that glinted in the sunshine and remembered her father. She'd give away all the money she had inherited just to have him back for a day. *He* would know what to do. She tried to rouse her drooping spirits, but her heart remained leaden, full of homesickness and the emptiness of her solitude that weighed heaviest of all.

Just as she was about to unravel she suddenly saw the faces of the girls at school reflected in the metal buckles, taunting her for wearing her fine shoes "like a tinker" and her misery swiftly turned to resentment. She lifted her chin in defiance and wiped her eyes with the back of her hand. She was no tinker. She was a wealthy woman now; a lady of means and property at the age of twenty-three. She could buy a hundred pairs of fine shoes if she so wanted. At that moment all the fear that made her soft inside hardened like clay. She'd show them all, she resolved, even Kitty who had stolen Jack's heart and broken hers. If it hadn't been for Kitty she would not have been vulnerable to Mr. Deverill's advances. None of this would have happened. She'd be by the hearth still, with her mother and her nanna and, who knows, perhaps Jack would be there too and perhaps he'd love her back.

She stood up and walked into the house. Miss Ferrel, Mr. Gordon and Mrs. Gottersman had all departed, their lips pursed with bitterness, their unspoken words burning with their sense of injustice. Bridie realized that they had all hoped for a slice of Mrs. Grimsby's fortune, depended on it even. Those little pats and "confidential chats" had led them each to believe they were special in her eyes. The old spider had enjoyed manipulating them, Bridie mused, and ultimately disappointing them. She realized, too, that it hadn't been Mr. Gordon or Miss Ferrel who had left the money under the bed but Mrs. Grimsby herself; a test, perhaps, to see if she was trustworthy; a trial to see if she was deserving of her fortune. Well, she was far less deserving than they were, of that she was certain. Now she was rich, she would share her money with them. It would give her pleasure to thwart the old lady's plan. After all, Mrs. Grimsby had inflicted misery on her servants during her lifetime; it seemed right that with her death they should be rewarded for their suffering.

Bridie recalled the times Kitty and Celia had dressed up for the Castle Deverill Summer Ball while *she* had had to help belowstairs and watch the glamour of the evening through cracks in doors and gaps in curtains. She remembered their beautiful dresses and carefully braided hair, their thick leather boots and silk stockings, their fine coats and gloves, and a hatred she had never felt before seeded itself inside her like bindweed, from where it would grow, winding around and around her heart to stifle her sweetness, which had never gotten her anywhere. She would buy pretty shoes and dresses, she thought sourly, just like Kitty, and Celia's, and marry the richest man she could find because that's how one acquired status and respect. Now that she was wealthy she was a prize worth having.

Determined to be someone, Bridie settled into the old house on Fifth Avenue with the witch's tower that no longer gave her the chills. She knew how to be a lady, having spent so long observing Kitty. She knew how to dress and how to stand and how to behave in company. She knew how to speak with less of an Irish accent, she knew how to walk with her chin in the air; she knew how to dissemble. Wasn't this what she had always wanted? To be somebody else; anybody but her.

First, she asked Rosetta to work as her maid. The role reversal gave her pleasure. Now *she* was the lady of the house and Rosetta her servant, just like *she* had been to Kitty. At first Rosetta declined her offer, explaining that it would be awkward working for her friend, but Bridie managed to persuade her by offering her a more generous wage than she would ever have earned anywhere else. "You can be my companion," Bridie told her. "I don't care what title you give yourself. I want you with me. It's as simple as that. You're my only real friend and I need you." Finally, Rosetta gave in. Bridie asked Mrs. McGuire for help in finding her a suitable cook and butler and paid her handsomely for her trouble. She threw open the windows and let the air blow away the stale smell of Mrs. Grimsby's aged body and the lingering remains of her sour presence. She filled the house with sunlight so that it would radiate with happiness like Castle Deverill had done in summertime, when the Irish sun had shone through the tall glass windows and turned the hall to gold.

The news that the wealthy widow had left her entire fortune to her maid hit the newspapers and she soon became a cause célèbre. Debate ensued. There were those who thought it disgraceful that the widow had denied her family her money and denounced Bridie as a gold digger who had manipulated an old lady, while there were others who believed the hard-working woman in Mrs. Grimsby's employ deserved every penny she had given her. After all, America was the land of prosperity through hard work and Miss Doyle had earned her riches while Mrs. Grimsby's family had done nothing to merit her fortune besides some tactical flattery in the final months of her life. The argument extended from the press to private houses, where New York society discussed it ad infinitum at their grand luncheons and dinner parties. No one could agree. The grand old families of Fifth Avenue turned up their noses at this upstart from Ireland who was now their neighbor and barred their doors against her, but the brash young people who wore feathers in their hair and danced to jazz in the speakeasies where bootlegged alcohol flowed in fountains were curious to meet the now infamous Miss Doyle.

It wasn't long before women came calling, out of inquisitiveness and the desire to generate funds for their charities, and unscrupulous gentlemen came looking for a wealthy wife. The first young man to pay Bridie a visit was none other than Mrs. Grimsby's hyena nephew, Paul Heskin. Bridie had never liked him with his receding chin and calculating eyes. He had never so much as tossed her a thank-you when she had worked as his aunt's maid, but now he was full of sycophancy and false charm. Bridie sat in Mrs. Grimsby's chair in the sun parlor and looked at him disdainfully, seeing him for what he was, an opportunist preying on her naïveté and inexperience. But she was no fool—Mrs. Grimsby had taught her to be cynical about people's motivations. She dismissed him brutally as she believed a lady in her position would and set her sights on finding a man who could equal her in wealth. Now that she had it, she wasn't going to lose it by marrying unwisely.

But Bridie was a young woman on her own and this made her vulnerable and exposed to all sorts of degenerates. It wasn't possible to head out into society alone, without a companion or chaperone to accompany her. She had no father or brother to escort her and no friend to take her under her wing. However, there was one man she could call upon to advise her in this most unusual and delicate of situations.

"Thank you for coming, Mr. Williams," she said from Mrs. Grimsby's chair in the sun parlor, where the soft light of early autumn streamed through the windows, bathing Bridie in a warm golden radiance.

The attorney looked Miss Doyle over with an amused and admiring eye. She was indeed an ugly duckling turned swan. "Might I say how well you look, Miss Doyle?"

"Yes indeed, Mr. Williams, money certainly enables a woman to look her best."

"Money solves nothing but it eases everything. Mrs. Grimsby would be proud to see the fine young lady you have become."

"I am grateful to her for her generosity. She had no affection for her family. In fact, she used to receive them in this very room and put up with their false flattery. She knew why they visited."

"You know, she began rather like you, Miss Doyle. Her mother came over from Ireland as a little girl with her parents and siblings. They had nothing but the clothes on their backs. What she had that set her apart from the rest of her family was a love of literature. She adored to read. As a child she read everything she could get her hands on. Mr. Grimsby was a well-educated, scholarly man. He was much older than she was, but he was struck by her intelligence, so they say. They met in the library of all the places!"

"How did he make his money?"

"Printing presses." Mr. Williams grinned. "He was an entrepreneur, one of those brilliant men whose touch turns everything to gold. Before he died Mrs. Grimsby was the queen of New York society. Sadly, after he passed she put her glad rags away and became increasingly morose and cynical about people. You can imagine the men who wanted to marry her for her fortune. She trusted no one. I flatter myself to think that she trusted me. I was not after her hand in marriage or eligible· for her fortune. As an adviser and confidant she depended on me. She was old when you met her, Miss Doyle, but she was a beautiful woman when young."

"I used to read to her in here," said Bridie wistfully. "When I read, she softened. It was as if the words somehow got through that hard shell she hid behind and reached the real person underneath. I liked to read to her."

"Now you have all her books to choose from."

"Indeed I do, Mr. Williams." She ran her eyes over the bookshelves. "They were probably more precious to her than anything else."

She sighed and brought her mind back to the present. "Mr. Williams, I need your help."

"Of course, Miss Doyle. How may I be of assistance?"

"I'm in a difficult position . . ." She hesitated, not wanting to be indelicate, and knitted her fingers. "I'm alone in New York without a friend in society . . ."

Mr. Williams smiled sympathetically. "Might I suggest I introduce you to Mrs. Williams? My wife is a lively, sociable young woman who would enjoy nothing more than to introduce you to people—colorful people, people who would find you interesting. What you need, Miss Doyle, is entertainment."

"Indeed I do."

"It's all very well having a fine house and fine clothes, but a woman in your position needs friends."

"A woman in my position needs a husband, Mr. Williams, if I may speak plainly. A woman without a husband has no standing in society and no protection. I need a man of equal wealth. I will not be taken advantage of."

Mr. Williams looked surprised by her candor. "I understand."

She stood up. "I know you do, Mr. Williams. I think you understand everything, which is why I called you."

Mr. Williams followed her onto the landing. "New York is the place for you, Miss Doyle." He shook her hand.

"I'd like to meet your wife as soon as it can be arranged."

"Dinner tomorrow night?" he suggested enthusiastically.

Bridie smiled. "I'd love to."

BRIDIE LIKED MRS. Williams immediately. She was a brassy, vivacious and energetic woman in her early thirties with the restlessness of a little bird. Never still, she chattered away without pause, her small white hands fluttering in the air as her laughter seemed to leave her throat in light chirrups. Her hair was short and blond with perky curls around the hairline, her eyes wide and blue and full of spirit, her ready smile warm and mischievous.

"Beaumont says the way to meet the right people," Elaine Williams told her, "is to donate money to charity. Fundraisers are where the rich mingle with other rich people. Money talks in this town, Bridget. Old money only talks to old money very quietly but new money is wonderfully noisy. There's no reason why yours won't talk any louder than anyone else's!"

Elaine wasted no time in taking Bridie to the salon to have her short hair trimmed into a fashionable bob with gentle waves curling at the temples. She helped her choose the most glamorous, loose-fitting dresses that reached as high as the knee, rayon stockings, cloche hats, feather boas, sequined headbands and heeled shoes, and taught her how to paint her face with makeup as they sat in Elaine's untidy bedroom listening to jazz on the wireless. Bridie was quick to learn. She applied the same dedication to her new role as she had done all those years ago at Castle Deverill when she had been promoted to lady's maid. While Mr. Williams advised her on financial matters, his wife saw to her personal life. Both reveled in associating with the girl the whole of New York City seemed to be talking about.

In Elaine's company Bridie was unafraid to shine. She relished the attention she received at the charity fundraisers. Photographers took her picture on arrival and everyone made a fuss of her inside. She was treated with respect, as if she was important. No one except the old New York families seemed to care that she had been a maid only a very short time ago. No one imagined the life she had lived in Ballinakelly and how very far she had come. She played the role like a seasoned actress and they all accepted it as truth. Bridie accepted it as truth too, because she had to. She threw herself into the part for it was the greatest performance of her life. Soon she began to forget who Bridie Doyle really was and where she had come from. *Bridget* Doyle was beautiful, fabulous and, most thrilling of all, in demand. She had no past, no pain, no cares at all for she had enough money to buy happiness. With such a vast fortune she was confident she would never be unhappy again.

In the new year Bridie was swept up into a thrilling new world of excess. She suddenly had more friends than she could count and suitors all vying for her hand. There were parties, lots of parties, where illegally bought alcohol was enjoyed in spite of Prohibition. Bridie discovered to her delight that alcohol made her feel more confident. With a gin cocktail she was able to impersonate Kitty Deverill to perfection. She liked who she was with a little liquor inside her to loosen her tongue and liberate her laughter. A dash of alcohol ensured she lost her inhibitions. She loved to dance. She loved to feel a man's hands on her waist, she loved to be admired; she thought of those mean girls in Ballinakelly and wished they could see who she had become. She wondered whether *this* had been inevitable right from the start. That it had truly been written in her stars. That it was all meant to be.

The young men who courted her were as diverse as chocolates in a box. There were the simply wrapped ones. They tended to be more romantic, though lacking in the only thing important to Bridie: money. There were the elaborately wrapped ones who had the money, but they were vulgar and pushy and much too pleased with themselves. Then there were the unusual ones who came wrapped in bright colors and tasted spicy and those frightened Bridie, who wasn't used to Europeans, although their grand foreign titles held a certain appeal. She was careful to share all her adventures with Rosetta, who patiently waited up for her at night, helped her into her nightdress when she had drunk too much and seemed to enjoy her stories of unsuitable suitors. When they laughed together in Bridie's bedroom, lying across the bed, they both forgot their new positions and they were simply friends again, as they had been before.

Once or twice Bridie was led astray by a poet or a writer whose sensitive face and gentle manners made her think of Jack, but she quickly reminded herself of her mission and coldly rebuffed them. She'd never fall in love again, she vowed. Not with anyone. Love had got her nowhere. It had only hurt her irrevocably. She would marry for security, partnership and because that was what society demanded of women. But she would never love again.

AT CHRISTMAS SHE went to Mass alone. Rosetta had gone to spend the day with her family. Bridie's thoughts turned to her mother and nanna, Sean and Michael and she stifled a sharp longing for home. It was quiet in the church. So quiet she could hear the small, distant voice of her conscience. Without the noise of music, dancing, talking and laughing to distract her, Bridie remembered Ballinakelly. She remembered the farmhouse, the warm hearth, the cowsheds, the cold, the mud, the damp, the poverty. Yes, she remembered the *poverty*. It wasn't so long ago that she hadn't a pair of shoes for her feet save the ones from Lady Deverill, which she still kept in their box. She stared at the marble sculpture of Christ on the cross that was placed above the altar and remembered how she had prayed twice a day at the sound of the Angelus, how they had all knelt in prayer after tea, how her mother had led it with the words: *Thou oh Lord will open my lips* . . . Did she miss her daughter? Did she pray for her? Bridie bent her head in shame and resolved to attend Mass more often. She might forget who *she* was but she must not forget who *God* was.

Then the thought of going home floated to the surface of her mind like a cork. For a fleeting moment her heart lurched with yearning for the farmhouse and her grandmother's stew, the smell of wet soil and cows, the sound of her brothers discussing the sorry state of Ireland over tumblers of stout. She longed for the taste of buttermilk and soda bread, the thud of dancing feet, the stirring crescendo of singing voices, the heart-wrenching strains of a lone fiddle. But the cork sank as quickly as it had risen. Going home now was impossible. She was no longer the girl she had been. She had no life left in Ireland. All that remained there was pain and loss, memories of Jack, Mr. Deverill and the baby she had been forced to give away and the one who had died. Here she had reinvented herself. She liked who she was. How could she go back in all her fine clothes and sleep in her old bed with the straw mattress? Her life was so different now and she was used to certain luxuries. As much as she tried to avoid it, her wealth would inevitably set her apart from Rosetta; what would it do to her family? She had moved on and the door had closed behind her, this time for good.

When the service was over she went to the front and lit four candles for her family, two for the children she had given birth to and a seventh for her father's soul, may he rest in peace. Despondently, she began to walk out of the church. Just as she neared the door she caught eyes with a silver-haired gentleman with a tidy gray beard, who smiled at her kindly. "You're not meant to look sad at Christmas, young lady," he said.

"I'm not sad," she replied, putting her head down and walking into the December sunshine.

"Like hell you're not sad," he persisted, walking alongside her. "I've been watching you. If that's your happy face what does your sad face look like?" He put out his hand. "Mr. Lockwood."

Bridie looked at his fine coat, expensive suit and hat, the umbrella with the silver collar engraved with initials and shook his hand. "Miss Doyle," she replied.

"Oh, I know who you are." He grinned. "Quite a famous lady, aren't you?" Bridie blushed. "I'm sorry, I didn't mean to embarrass you. You just look so alone. I don't like to see a woman on her own, looking sad. Especially such a pretty one." She smiled, won over by his charm and the shiny green car that waited for him on the curb with a watchful chauffeur standing to attention in his starched uniform and cap, even on Christmas Day. "There, that's better. Now, you only live a block away from here so allow me to walk you to your door." Mr. Lockwood waved at the chauffeur. "I'm going to walk, Maxwell, so you might as well go home," he said. The chauffeur climbed into the car and motored off through the slush.

Bridie cast her eyes around the street. It was empty now. Everyone had returned home for Christmas lunch. She put her hands in her coat pockets and walked on. "You look like you're on your own too, Mr. Lockwood," she said with a grin.

"My son has run on ahead. He's keen to put something in his stomach. I have four children but three are scattered all over. A son in Canada and two daughters, one on the West Coast, the other down south. Ashley is my youngest." He settled his twinkling gray eyes on Bridie's house. "We're almost neighbors, you and I. I knew Mrs. Grimsby. She was a strong-willed woman, that's for sure. No one pushed her around. I always found this house a little austere, though. Something about the tower. It looks like a witch's hat."

Bridie laughed. "That's just what I thought when I first saw it. But it doesn't frighten me now."

"I don't imagine much frightens you, Miss Doyle." He looked down at Bridie and smiled sympathetically. "You sure you're not lonely in there all on your own?"

"Oh, I'm not on my own, Mr. Lockwood. I have lots of friends and—"

"Of course you do," he said, cutting her off. "A pretty, wealthy young woman such as yourself must have hundreds of friends." He chuckled in a world-weary manner. "But who are you spending Christmas with? From what I understand your family is in Ireland."

"Yes, they . . ."

"I'm a Christian man, Miss Doyle. I would like to extend you an invitation to Christmas lunch. It's not right that a young woman like you should be alone on Christmas Day. My son Ashley will be delighted to have a pretty girl at the table and I'd be grateful for the company. Ashley and I are an uninspiring couple, just the two of us."

"Isn't there a Mrs. Lockwood?" Bridie asked.

"I'm afraid there is no Mrs. Lockwood. I'm a widower."

"I'm sorry," Bridie apologized.

"No need. Life ebbs and flows. We all come, we all go. You'll make an old man happy. What do you say, Miss Doyle? Will you come and share our Christmas feast?" There was something jaunty about him. An amused twinkle in his eye, a raffish crookedness to his smile, a complete lack of self-doubt; he knew who she was and he presumably wanted her for his son. Bridie was curious. She liked this Mr. Lockwood. She liked his manner. Perhaps she'd like his son. Maybe he'd be rich enough for her, but perhaps . . .

With a smile she linked her arm through his. "How very generous of you, Mr. Lockwood. I'd love to come and share your Christmas feast and meet your son. But you know what we say in Ireland: the older the fiddle the sweeter the tune."

Mr. Lockwood chuckled and led her down the wet street. "You've clearly brought the charm of the Irish with you, Miss Doyle." He patted her hand. "We can all benefit from a touch of that."

Chapter 31

London, England, 1925

London looked like a magical kingdom made out of sugar. The streets were covered in a thick layer of snow and the flakes twirled on the wind, illuminated like gilded feathers in the golden aura of the streetlamps. They settled onto the bare branches of the plane and horse chestnut trees in the communal gardens and insulated the spring bulbs that hibernated beneath the soil along with dormice and hedgehogs, sleeping through the cold winter in their warm holes.

Kitty gazed out of the window of her Notting Hill house on Ladbroke Square. It wasn't a stylish address but she didn't care. The development of the Ladbroke family farmland in the mid-nineteenth century had originally been intended as a fashionable suburb of London but it hadn't yet attracted the wealthy Londoners who preferred to live nearer the center in Mayfair and Belgravia. However, it appealed to the upper middle classes who could live in large Belgravia-style houses for a fraction of the price. Kitty was just happy to be far away from her mother, who now resided in Victoria's townhouse in Belgravia during the Season and in her country house in Kent for the rest of the year. Her father only appeared in London for occasions such as Harry's wedding and Royal Ascot. Otherwise he remained at Castle Deverill in the Hunting Lodge, in which his wife hadn't set so much as a toe since the fire. Kitty had received no correspondence from him. He hadn't even come to her wedding. His rejection hurt her deeply but she was used to burying her pain—and she had the love of little Jack and Robert to console her. Adeline had been too frail to travel, but from her beloved grandmother Kitty received regular letters; she treasured every one.

It had been five months since Florence. Five months since she had told Robert about Michael Doyle. Five months of patience, compassion and restraint that must have been a great trial for her new husband. But Kitty couldn't let him touch her. She reassured him that she would, but she couldn't say when that moment would come. Sometimes, as she lay in bed staring up at the ceiling, she wondered whether it might *never* come. Michael Doyle had stolen more than her virginity that morning; he had stolen her essence.

Kitty did not love Robert in the way that she loved Jack, and she didn't expect to. Her and Jack's love had been forged in the innocence of childhood and driven deeper with every test God had seen fit to send them. Robert could never compete with that. But he was a devoted father to little Jack and the boy loved him unreservedly. She hoped that, in time, she would grow to love him too.

As soon as it was light she walked out into the flurry, wrapped snugly in a thick coat. The gardens were quiet and unspoiled. A red-breasted robin hopped about in search of food, leaving barely a print in the snow, and a blackbird watched her from the top of a fir tree. Kitty inhaled the cold air and felt her spirits soar with the beauty of this secret white world in the heart of the busy city. She exhaled luxuriously. The tension in her shoulders melted away as she stood in the middle of the garden, allowing the eternal stillness of nature to resonate with the eternal stillness deep inside her. How her heart ached with longing for the countryside.

Suddenly, something bright caught her eye. She turned to see a small, vibrating orb dancing above the bushes. She stared at it in wonder, recognizing it at once as a nature spirit. She hadn't seen one of those since childhood. There had been plenty playing about the flowers at Castle Deverill. With rising excitement she walked softly through the snow and crouched down, smiling with the innocence of her girlhood long gone.

It was at that moment of finally rediscovering her gift that she realized with all clarity of mind and certainty of heart that her future was not here in this concrete metropolis, but at Castle Deverill. She felt her chest expand with a bubbling joy, like the chuckling stream that wound its way through Ballina-kelly to the sea, and she laughed out loud. The blackbird began to sing from the fir tree and the robin flew off into the snow-covered bushes. She knew now that it didn't matter what her father thought, or that the castle was no longer fit to live in, because she belonged there. She loved it unconditionally. She would never be happy anywhere else.

With her heart full of optimism she ran back into the house where Robert was sitting at the dining-room table, reading the papers. He looked up from *The Times* with surprise. He hadn't seen Kitty this animated since they married. "Robert!" she exclaimed, throwing her arms around him and making him put the paper down. "You remember you said you'd give me Ireland if you could?"

"Yes?" he replied, taking off his reading glasses.

"Well, you can."

"Can I?"

She pulled out the chair beside him. "I want to go home," she told him. "I know we can be happy there. You can write. You'll be inspired in Ireland much more than in this dreary city."

Robert smiled and touched her face. "If that's what you want, Kitty, we'll go," he said.

"I want Jack to know where he comes from. Castle Deverill is in his blood. But I need you to go and talk to Papa. I know you can persuade him. Uncle Rupert's house is vacant. No one's lived in it for ten years. Elspeth told me it's all boarded up. Grandma couldn't bear to go in there after Uncle Rupert was killed, so she left it just as it was. But it's part of the estate. It's in my father's power to gift it to me. I know he will if *you* ask."

Robert was so keen to please his new wife that he made the arrangements to travel immediately. They decided not to tell anyone of their plans. They would simply leave quietly and then, when everything was sorted out, inform Harry, Beatrice and Celia. Kitty packed with the help of her maid. When they were ready Kitty and Robert left London with little Jack and Hetty, Kitty's lady's maid and Robert's valet Bridgeman—a small retinue of servants made possible by the modest annuity Robert received from his father. Robert would send for the rest of the household when they had found a home. In the meantime they would stay with Elspeth and Peter.

WHEN KITTY STEPPED off the boat onto Irish soil she shed tears of joy and relief. She turned her face toward the soft rain. She was home at last.

Elspeth had sent their chauffeur to pick them up. Bridgeman would follow in a hackney cab with the luggage. Kitty sat in the back seat holding Robert's hand, gazing out of the window at the velvet green hills whose heather-coated summits were shrouded in mist. The trees were bare, their branches knobbly and glistening in the drizzle. Big black rooks hopped about the roof of an abandoned farmhouse. Cows grazed in fields of thick grass and woolly sheep were white dots on the hillsides, camouflaged among the rocks. Kitty was too emotional to speak. Occasionally she put her hand to her chest and sighed, as if every sight triggered memories she wanted to hold on to and savor. In spite of all the violence that had taken place there, Ireland still had the power to seize her heart with its constant beauty.

Peter and Elspeth MacCartain's neo-Palladian castle was a weathered old building of little charm. The gray walls were austere and bleak, the tall windows foggy like the failing eyes of an old man. It sat on the top of a hill without the luxury of trees to shelter it from the sharp winter winds and enhance its appeal. It looked isolated and abandoned, like a colonel deserted by his soldiers, alone with the years that had gradually robbed him of his gloss. Once it had rivaled Castle Deverill in its splendor, but now there were no gardens, no lovingly tended lawns, nothing that alluded to its former prestige, only fields of sheep. It made Kitty feel a tremendous sorrow, as if this castle was symbolic of all that the Anglo-Irish had lost in the War of Independence.

As soon as the car drew up outside the front door, Elspeth flew down the steps to greet them. She embraced her sister with excitement, barely pausing for breath. "I'm so happy you've come to stay, Kitty. It's lovely to see you and little Jack. We're going to have such fun. Peter has the perfect mare for you to ride. You'll love her, she goes like the wind. I'm sure you're going to want to hunt. There are plenty of snipe for you, Robert. Do you shoot? I can't recall. Do come inside. There's a lovely fire in the drawing room." She laughed nervously. "We tend to use only a small number of rooms because it's so cold! We run from one to the other like mice. But of course you don't mind the damp, do you, Kitty?"

They entered the hall. It was just as chilly as outside, in spite of the threadbare rugs that covered the flagstone floor. The vast fireplace was empty. Dusty portraits of ancestors in fine silks and suits of armor hung on the walls to remind the family of their illustrious heritage, now frayed and shabby. The place had a feeling of deprivation that would have horrified Maud. Kitty noticed there was no butler to greet them. Even if there had been she would have been reluctant to relinquish her coat. A scruffy maid stepped out of the shadows to take Hetty and little

Jack upstairs. Robert informed her that the luggage was about to arrive but she just blinked at him dumbly, like a sweet cow.

The drawing room was surprisingly charming. It seemed to Kitty that Elspeth and Peter must have lived only in that room, for it was warm, thanks to a lively turf fire, and full of family photographs, books, objects and other paraphernalia belonging to a married couple who never threw anything away. The sofa had a hole in the back, which Elspeth had tried to conceal behind a cushion, and the velvet on the chairs had worn away on the arms and was markedly stained. There clearly wasn't the money for repairs.

Peter appeared at once with two large dogs at his heels. His face was ruddy from outdoors, his boots leaving mud on the carpets. His tweed coat was as shabby as Hubert's had been. He embraced Kitty with affection and shook Robert's hand. "Welcome to Dunderry Castle," he said jovially. "You haven't got a drink?" He looked at Robert's empty hands with dismay. "Where's O'Malley?"

"Parking the car, darling," said Elspeth. She turned to Kitty sheepishly. "O'Malley is our butler, driver and odd-job man. Whatever we need him for, really. He's wonderful. He can do anything."

"Except be in two places at once," said Peter drily. "Right, what can I get you? Sherry? Whiskey and soda?"

"I'm sure Kitty will have sherry," Robert replied.

"I'll join you for a glass of whiskey then," Peter added happily. He trailed mud all the way to the drinks tray, which was placed at the other end of the room near a dilapidated grand piano. "How was your crossing? Rough as usual, no doubt!"

"Quite rough," said Kitty. "It's lovely to be here though."

"Ireland doesn't change, does it?" said Elspeth. "People come and go and do such awful things to each other, but Ireland is always the same. As it's been for thousands of years."

Kitty sat near the fire. A log of turf had fallen onto the front of the grate and was smoking into the room but neither Elspeth nor Peter seemed to notice. "Have you seen Papa?" Kitty asked, waving a hand in front of her nose to clear the smoke.

"Yes, I'm afraid he's much changed, Kitty," Elspeth told her, her forehead creasing into a frown. "He drinks too much. Has terrible mood swings and is altogether very disagreeable. Grandma spends all day in the castle talking to herself. It's all very sad. Not like it used to be. I go and see the Shrubs every day. You must come. They'll be so happy to see you. They barely leave their house, so I do the shopping for them and make sure they have everything they need. They seem to think everyone in Ballinakelly is the enemy, even though I've told them hundreds of times that the wars are over and any animosity now is between the Irish. We Anglo-Irish have never been safer. But they miss the security of the British Army's presence on the streets and they complain that there's a distinct feeling of unrest and suspicion."

"I'd like to go today and see Grandma," said Kitty. "I thought perhaps Robert could talk to Papa about Uncle Rupert's house. I don't want to be a burden to you and Peter."

"You're not a burden," Elspeth gushed. "We've been longing for you to come."

Peter handed them both a glass of sherry. "I'll drive Kitty over myself," he suggested.

"I'd prefer to meet you there," said Kitty, knowing that

when she returned to Castle Deverill she'd want to be alone. "Elspeth says you have a mare I'll like," she added hopefully.

"I do. She's called Tempest and she goes like the wind," Peter replied.

"So I heard. She sounds perfect. I can't think of anything nicer than riding out on my own. Just like the old days."

Elspeth smiled shyly. "I'd come with you, Kitty," she said, placing a hand on her belly. "But I'm expecting another baby."

"Oh Elspeth!" Kitty exclaimed. "Your third!"

"It's early days, but I want you to be the first to know."

Peter raised his glass. "To my clever wife," he said, beaming with pleasure. Robert and Kitty raised theirs too. "It'll be *you* next," Peter added to Kitty.

Kitty smiled tightly. "When shall we go?" she asked, swiftly changing the subject. At this rate the only chance of a child for her was by immaculate conception.

"We'll go to Castle Deverill after lunch. I'll take Robert in the car. Kitty will meet us there and you, my darling, will rest."

"Then I will show Kitty around before lunch and introduce her to her nephews!" She turned to her sister. "The castle is rather run down, I'm afraid. But I love it. Peter and I are so very happy here with the boys." She patted her stomach again. "I do so hope this one's a girl. I'll cherish her in the way a mother *should* cherish her daughter."

"So Mama doesn't know?"

Elspeth grinned. "I'll tell her when the baby's born. The only response I got after the boys' births was rather stilted telegrams of congratulations. She's never shown the slightest interest in meeting them."

"Come, *I* want to meet John and Jasper," said Kitty, getting up. "Let's not depress ourselves by talking about Mama. I want you to show me everything!"

Later, dressed in a pair of slacks, tweed jacket and riding boots, Kitty rode like a man over the hills toward Castle Deverill. The last time she had worn a long skirt to ride had been the day she had confronted Michael Doyle at the farmhouse. Afterward, she had shed it like a snake sheds its skin and cast it into the furnace of oblivion, along with everything else that had happened that morning. Never again would she be that woman. Now, the feeling of sitting astride a horse gave her a reassuring sense of control and disconnected her from the girl she had lost.

When the sight of the charred ruins of the castle came into view Kitty's throat constricted with emotion. She stopped her horse and remained for a long moment gazing down with glassy eyes on what had once been her home, rising forlornly out of the mist that edged in over the water. Nestled among the trees, its dull, lifeless eyes looked out over the gardens where its memories lay scattered among the rooks and crows that hopped about among the weeds. There was no sign of life in those blind windows. No sign of life behind those walls, only a thin ribbon of smoke that slipped out of the chimney in the western wing to be carried off by an unforgiving wind.

Kitty cantered as fast as she could down the hill and over the fields. She jumped the wall with ease, halting where once the croquet lawn had been and dismounting. She walked her horse around to a suitable tree and tied it there. Taking a deep breath to steady herself, she took in the ruins, fighting the memories that crept out of every corner of the building like ghosts. With a heart full of sorrow she walked around to the old kitchen entrance. Inside, there was much that was untouched by the fire. The flagstone corridor was as it had been when Kitty and Bridie had run up and down it. Their little cupboard beneath the stairs was unchanged. The kitchen itself, where Mrs. Doyle had cooked for the family, and the maids and footmen had dashed in and out with heavy trays, had only gathered a thick layer of dust. The long oak table was still there, the pots and pans hanging from a rack on the ceiling as they always had, the stove cold with a light sprinkling of ash, but the tall chests and dressers were unharmed. It was a small oasis of normality. Kitty almost expected Mrs. Doyle to bustle out of the larder and look at her with surprise. *What are you doing staring at me with eyes the size of saucers, Miss Kitty? Can't you see I'm busy!*

But as she climbed the stairs the smell of burned wood hung heavy in the air. She opened the old green baize door into her grandparents' side of the castle to find the rooms black with soot, piled high with rubble, open to the elements and crows who still found small treasures among the debris. In the midst of the rubble were patches of wall where the fire had not reached, glimpses of the castle's former life revealed like flashes of memory that Kitty seized upon with nostalgia. Dizzy with sadness, she retreated to the stairs and climbed up to the little room in the western tower where she had so often hidden with Celia and Bridie and talked to Barton Deverill, who used to sit in the silk chair with his feet up on the footstool.

She heard her grandmother's voice long before she entered the room. It rose and fell like a song as she merrily reminisced with Hubert by the turf fire as if they were still in the library. Kitty stifled a sob and pushed open the door. Adeline turned her attention to the visitor. Her eyes widened and her face broke into a smile. "I was just saying to Hubert, now we haven't seen Kitty for some time. Have you been hunting, my dear? It's fine weather for the hunt, so they tell me. Hubert shot some snipe this morning. He says there are plenty in the marshlands. Those dogs are frightfully good at putting them up."

Kitty blinked back tears and knelt beside her and allowed her grandmother to stroke her hair. "I've missed you," she said, gazing into the face that time had suddenly remembered and aged in a hurry to make up for the years it had overlooked.

"I had lovely red hair like yours when I was a girl. Of course in my day they made me put it up, but as soon as I was out of sight I'd pull out all the ribbons and let it fall about my shoulders." She scrunched Kitty's hair in her fingers. "Your mother never liked your hair. She thought it terribly ugly. She didn't know it was made of spun gold and sunbeams. I never liked Maud. When your father married her I was very sad. I saw what she really was, but men are blinded by beauty, aren't they? She was full of ambition and pretense. Then her head was turned by the Duke of Rothmeade. I'm not sure whether she loved *him* or what he represented, but she would have left Bertie, I think, and run off with him if it hadn't been for you."

Kitty sat up. She had a vague memory of the Shrubs discussing Eddie Rothmeade in the library. "What are you talking about, Grandma?"

"The Duke of Rothmeade. He was very handsome. He used to come and stay to shoot and hunt. He was a terrific horseman and a great friend of Bertie's. Maud went out with the hunt, sometimes three times a week, which is why she suffered those miscarriages after Harry. She was so keen to be with him she went flying over the hedges without a thought for the children she carried inside her. The Duke was very taken with her, you see. Then she became pregnant with you and no amount of hunting could dislodge *you* from her belly. You see, only rotten apples fall from the tree. You were the finest apple in the orchard. Because of you Eddie Rothmeade gave up on her. I heard the whole scene from the greenhouse. He was furious. I suppose she had said her marriage to Bertie was in name only and he had believed her. She was very manipulative." Adeline narrowed her eyes. "I even think, the stars in her eyes as bright as they were, that she would have turned her back on Harry had the Duke asked her to. But he gave her up without a backward glance. Between you and me, I think he was simply looking for an excuse and you were a very good one."

Kitty was astonished. She didn't know what to say. "Would you like some cake? It's terribly good," Adeline continued. "Mrs. Doyle makes wonderful porter cakes." Kitty looked around the room. There was no cake to be seen anywhere. "Hubert would love a rubber of bridge. The Shrubs will come down when they're ready. Laurel takes so long over her bath. Colonel Manley is coming for dinner. Do you think he likes to play bridge? What do you think, Hubert?" Adeline looked at the chair opposite, listening to Hubert's reply. It had been so long since Kitty had seen a ghost that she was almost surprised when Hubert came into focus, a faint, fuzzy light, but undeniably him.

"It won't be long now," he said and Kitty looked at her grandmother fearfully.

"I would love a rubber of bridge," she said, putting her head on Adeline's lap and closing her eyes to hold back the tears. "Do you have any cannabis, Grandma? I'd like to drink cannabis tea and laugh and gossip like we used to in the library. Those were happy times."

"I have lots of cannabis in the greenhouse. Why don't you go and pick some. The Shrubs will be down soon and they'd love a little tea. It does wonders to calm their nerves. Colonel Manley has a soft spot for Hazel, I'm sure of it."

Kitty hurried into the vegetable garden, choking back her sobs. Her grandmother was losing her mind. Up there in the tower all day she was slipping slowly toward death. Hadn't her grandfather said it wouldn't be long? Not only was she losing her mind but she was losing her sense of discretion as well. What about this Duke of Rothmeade? Was it true that her mother's pregnancy had ruined their affair? Was that the real reason Maud had so resented her? She stumbled over the weeds that had grown thick and tall and finally reached the greenhouses, whose glass windows were now covered with lichen and moss. She pushed open the door that had grown stiff due to the damp, and stepped inside. In spite of the neglect it was pleasantly warm and smelled as it always had. Kitty searched the overgrown plants and vegetation for cannabis. She remembered what it looked like. The leaves were very distinctively star-shaped.

At last she found them. Great heaps of vibrant green leaves that seemed to have seeded themselves and grown beyond all measure. Adeline wouldn't be able to drink this much cannabis tea even if she lived for a thousand years, Kitty thought in amusement, but *she* could make a start. After all, if it was good enough to calm her grandmother's nerves, it was good enough for *her*. Kitty picked a big handful, then headed back out into the drizzle. As she began to walk toward the castle she saw, out of the corner of her eye, the wall where she had exchanged notes with Jack. Her heart gave a little tug. She stopped and stared at it, remembering the last time she had seen him on the station platform, falling to the ground with a rifle butt in his stomach. If his plan had worked they'd have been in America now and who knows what their lives would have been like.

Slowly she found herself walking toward the wall. Jack's face materialized in her mind and she felt her legs go weak beneath her. She could almost *feel* him. The memory was so strong she could smell the scent of his skin and taste his kiss. Dizzy with the sudden assault from the past she bent down and traced her fingers over the stone that concealed the hole where they had kept their secret messages. Slowly she removed it. When she saw the little square paper inside, her heart gave a greater lurch. Confused, she pulled it out and unfolded it.

My darling Kitty

I'm free but you are not. I hear you are to marry and I only have myself to blame for letting you go. I got all your letters but I never replied because I really meant it when I told you to get on with your life. I thought I'd rot in there forever. But I'm free and I hoped, indeed I prayed, that you would still be there for me. You are not. My darling Kitty, I love you more than you'll ever know. I leave this letter here in the unlikely chance

you'll find it. Grace told me not to ruin your happiness
so I won't. But I can't leave this unsaid. I love you,
dear friend and compatriot. I love you with all my heart
and always will.

Jack

Kitty slumped onto the wet grass, put her head in her hands, and wept.

Chapter 32

Driven by an uncontrollable rage Kitty marched over the long grasses to the tree where she had tied her horse. She stuffed the cannabis into her jacket pocket with Jack's note and mounted. The sky had darkened above her as heavy clouds rolled in, carrying in their bellies the promise of rain. There was a sharp edge to the wind and it grazed her skin as she galloped over the hills to Ballinakelly.

She was furious with Grace for having told Jack not to contact her and she was furious with Jack for having listened to her. She put her head down and spurred the horse on. If Jack was in Ballinakelly she'd find him. Once she had found him she didn't know what she was going to do.

The town was just as she had left it. The houses looked gray in the dim light of mid-afternoon, the road glistened with rain and the sea reflected the dreary color of the leaden skies above it. Kitty trotted through the mud, digging her chin into her chest, not wanting to see anyone she knew. Her heart thumped with anticipation of bumping into Michael Doyle even though her head told her she had no reason to fear him now.

When she reached the O'Leary house, she dismounted and knocked heavily on the door. A moment later it opened a crack and the small, suspicious face of Jack's mother peered through. "What is it you want?" she asked when she saw Kitty.

"I'm after Jack. Is he here?"

"A problem with your horse, is there?" she said and Kitty chose to ignore the sarcasm in her voice.

"I need to see him urgently. Where might I find him?"

"He was called to John Whiting's farm outside Bandon."

Kitty's heart sank. There was no point riding all the way to Bandon. "Tell him I came by," she said.

"You might as well know that he doesn't live here anymore. Jack has his own place now, as he should."

"Oh, I didn't know."

"Well, good day to you, Miss Deverill."

"It's Mrs. Trench, actually," said Kitty haughtily. She mounted her horse and trotted off, leaving Mrs. O'Leary full of questions she was too proud to ask.

Kitty rode slowly up to the Fairy Ring. Leaning against one of the massive boulders she closed her eyes. She wished she could turn back the clock, open her eyes and find herself sixteen again, before she had gotten involved in the war, before she had gotten too close to Michael Doyle, before everything had gone so horribly wrong. She was transported back to those times she had met Jack here, in this mystical place where stones came alive at sunset and nature spirits played in summertime.

She longed to recapture that time of innocence and optimism, when she had believed love to be uncomplicated. When she had believed she and Jack had a future.

As she gazed upon the ocean she sensed she was no longer alone. She turned her head to see Jack. He had left his horse with hers and was standing outside the stone circle, watching her. Her breath caught in her throat and all the anger she had felt toward him welled up once again. He stepped toward her. But Kitty didn't notice the toll that prison had taken on his youth or the downward turn to his mouth, which had come from regret and bitterness. All she saw was the man she loved who had forsaken her.

"Why did you wait until *after* I was married to tell me that you're free?" she exclaimed, marching toward him. "Why didn't you write to me? Why didn't you come for me? I waited for you, Jack. I pined for you. I didn't give up even when you told me to, because I didn't want anyone else but you. I would have waited until old age for you."

"But you didn't," he said.

Kitty's anger boiled over. "You're accusing me of not waiting for you? Christ, Jack, what do you want from me!" She dropped her hands in defeat. "I have a child."

"I know," he said softly. "Grace told me."

"Then she should have told you that I had to give him a father. I had to put my own wishes aside for *him*. You had robbed me of all hope so I married Robert Trench who was always kind to me and he is a wonderful father to Jack." At the mention of the child's name they both stared at each other. Kitty gasped as if scalded.

"Jack?" he repeated.

Kitty nodded. "I named him after you."

"Oh Kitty." He came closer and Kitty flinched at the wounded expression in his eyes. "Do you love Robert Trench?" he asked, looking down at her, his face full of hope.

"No, I don't." She wanted to explain that she was fond of Robert. That she respected him and that she was grateful to him, but something stopped her.

"Don't be angry, Kitty. I thought I was doing the best thing for you but I did the worst thing for both of us. I'll regret it for the rest of my life."

"But you left this note!" She fumbled in her pocket because he was so close now that she had to avert her eyes. He took her hand and pulled it out of her jacket. The feeling of his warm skin weakened her resolve. She met his gaze and her fury dissipated.

"I left the note because I had to tell you I love you."

"You knew I'd come back and that I'd be married."

"I honestly thought you'd never read it. I thought the days of secret notes and meetings were over. I thought you'd left Ireland and everything in it." His voice cracked and his lips trembled and Kitty's heart buckled as she realized that everything she adored about Ireland was embodied in this man she had always loved.

"Oh Jack," she groaned. "What have we done?"

When he pulled her into his embrace she fell against him willingly. Their kiss peeled back the years and in that moment they were young again, undamaged by war, untainted by brutality, unwithered by time.

WHEN KITTY FINALLY returned to Dunderry Castle, Robert and Peter were celebrating their successful meeting with Lord Deverill at the Hunting Lodge. "He's allowed us to take it on as tenants," said Robert joyfully, not noticing the pallor in his wife's cheeks.

"The man's like a lion without his teeth," said Peter. "It was easier than I had anticipated."

"Kitty is his daughter, regardless of their differences, and Castle Deverill is her home. It's her right to live there," said Robert.

"Goodness, you're wet through," said Elspeth, walking into the room. "You must go and have a bath immediately or you'll catch your death of cold. I'll ask O'Malley to bring up hot water," she said, taking Kitty by the hand and leading her out into the freezing hall. "Are you all right?" she asked, as they made their way up the stairs.

"I saw Grandma," Kitty replied flatly. "She's lost her mind."

"I was afraid of this. Seeing her like that must be very distressing for you. I know how close you are. What's that you've got in your pocket?" she asked, looking down at the green leaves spilling out of it.

Kitty grinned wearily. "Cannabis."

"Oh Kitty, you didn't!"

"Yes, I did. Grandma asked for some, but I never got to give it to her as I had to come back. I thought perhaps it would calm *my* nerves."

"All you need is a hot bath and a good night's sleep and you'll feel as right as rain." Kitty followed her upstairs, knowing that her sister would never understand the turmoil in her heart. How could she?

THAT NIGHT, KITTY crept into Robert's bedroom. The light was off and he appeared to be sleeping. She slipped out of her dressing gown and let it fall to the carpet. He heard the creaking of the floorboards as she stepped toward the bed and rolled over. "Kitty? Is that you?" he asked.

"Yes," she whispered. "It's cold."

"Then you'd better come and snuggle up," he said, pulling back the blankets.

She slipped beneath them and edged into his arms. "I want to be your wife in body as well as in my soul," she said, tracing her hand up his chest.

Robert pulled her against him. "My darling Kitty!" He found her lips and kissed her tenderly. Kitty closed her eyes and wound her arms around his body. She needed him now more than ever. Jack was free and he still loved her. She couldn't trust herself with that knowledge, nor with the spark in the deepest corner of her heart that still smoldered for him. She had to give herself to Robert. She had to feel she belonged to him. She had to commit to her marriage with such force of will that there was no danger of her losing her head and consequently losing the security she had found for herself and little Jack. So she gave herself to her husband and hoped that, by this act, so distasteful to her now, she might conceive a child that would tie her irrevocably to Robert.

The following day Peter drove them all to Rupert's pretty white house that was built on the cliffs overlooking the sea. Robert had sent word to London for the rest of the servants to join them with what remained of their belongings and his car. With the help of O'Malley, Elspeth's maid and Robert's valet, Bridgeman, they set about lifting the dust sheets off the furniture and opening the windows to circulate the fresh air. No one had set foot in there since Rupert had been killed in the war so everything was just as he had left it. Kitty was grateful for the distraction. She threw herself into the activity with vigor in order to keep her mind from wandering into Ballinakelly or up to the Fairy Ring where she might find Jack. Robert, flushed with happiness after the final consummation of their marriage, looked upon his wife with extra tenderness, ignorant of the turbulence that raged beneath the mask of her smile.

While laborers from Ballinakelly worked on the various leaks in the roof and repainted some of the rooms, Robert and Kitty stayed at Dunderry Castle. The rest of their household arrived. The cook settled into the kitchen and began cleaning all the pots and pans and stocking the larder. Bridgeman unpacked the cases. Kitty's maid polished the cupboards inside and out and hung up all her clothes. The beds were aired and made up with fresh sheets. Turf was bought and fires lit to get rid of the damp. Rupert's papers were boxed up and stored in the attic. His clothes were shared between the two brothers-in-law because no one else wanted them.

Kitty knew it was unwise to see Jack. She had accepted that as a married woman meeting him in private again was not possible. However, she longed to see Grace. In spite of Grace telling Jack to let her go, she missed the one friend she was able to confide in. As the days passed her anger toward her ally and coconspirator was assuaged by the certainty that, whatever her reasons for putting Jack off, Grace had acted out of affection for her. There was no doubt that Robert Trench was a more suitable husband for her in every way even though she didn't love him like she loved Jack.

As soon as she heard that Grace was back in Co. Cork, Kitty drove over to see her. Robert's car was a menace to drive, but with determination she managed to navigate the roads and avoided crashing into a shepherd driving his flock of sheep from one field to the next. Grace was delighted that Kitty had returned to Ballinakelly. "I'm glad your father has allowed you to rent the White House. Your uncle Rupert was a man of great style and taste. I'm sure it's full of treasures," she said.

"My grandmother sits in the tower growing madder and madder. I couldn't bear it. It broke my heart to see her like that."

"She's in a very happy world," Grace reassured her. "It might not be our world, but it's not making her unhappy."

"I don't think she'll live much longer," Kitty said, thinking of her grandfather and what he had said.

"I'm afraid your father will not be displeased. Your grandmother has become quite a burden to him. He barely goes out because he's looking after her."

"He's not looking after her, Grace. She's in the tower all on her own."

"But he's there should she need him. He rarely hunts now and he doesn't have many friends. He used to be the most popular man in West Cork. He's half the man he used to be."

"I hear he's drinking."

Grace shook her head in frustration. "I've tried so many times to make him drink less, but it's a demon that won't let him go. Losing the castle was one thing, discovering he had fathered an illegitimate child was quite another. The fact that you insisted on keeping the child just drove him further into the bottle, I'm afraid."

"Do you still see him?"

"As often as I can. He needs some company or he'll go mad too and start talking to himself like his mother does."

Kitty drained her glass of sherry. "I saw Jack," she said. She met Grace's eyes and held them steadily. "I understand why you told him not to tell me he was free, but I wish you hadn't interfered. I still love him."

"Of course you understand," said Grace, returning Kitty's stare with equal boldness. "You're much too clever not to know what's good for you. In life we don't always get what we want. Often we have to put others before ourselves. You and I know all about self-sacrifice, Kitty."

"He still loves me."

"He'll have to get over it, and you, my dear Kitty, will have to learn to live with it. You have a little boy to think of now. You're a mother. Your child's a Deverill."

"But *you* were unfaithful to Sir Ronald."

"Only after I had given him sons to bear his name." Grace put down her glass and went over to sit next to Kitty on the sofa. "I loved your father very much. We enjoyed many happy times together. Ronald understood and didn't mind, so long as it was a private affair. Goodness, *he* had enough mistresses to keep him happy. But it's not an ideal way to live, Kitty."

"Did you stop loving my father?"

"No, I ended our affair because of you."

"Me?"

"Of course. You saved my life. I was not going to repay you by cheating with your father behind your back. Besides, it was our affair that set you against me in the first place, was it not?"

"It was," Kitty replied.

"How did you find out?"

"I saw you at the Summer Ball, in the bedroom."

Grace flushed with embarrassment. "You *saw* us?"

"Yes. I was playing with Celia. We came across a room with light glowing beneath the door and opened it a crack. I saw you and my father . . ."

"Oh Kitty," she groaned, putting a hand against her mouth. "How dreadful. I'm so sorry."

"It's a long time ago now."

"Long in time, less long in memory. I hope you have forgiven me."

"There's nothing to forgive. It was none of my business." Kitty smiled magnanimously. "After all you have done for me, Grace, you don't even need to ask."

"I will always love your father, even though the man I fell in love with has gone and in his place a man I sometimes fail to recognize. You will always love Jack and I'm sure he will always love you. But you have done the right thing in marrying Robert. He's a good, kind man who will look after you and little Jack. He will give you security and hopefully children of your own to love. Don't be rash and lose your head, because your heart is very strong, Kitty, and quite uncontrollable." Kitty knew Grace was right. Even *she,* with her determination to do what was right, was afraid of her heart.

ON THE FIRST Friday in March Kitty and Robert drove into Ballinakelly to buy a horse. She had taken what tack she needed from the stables at Castle Deverill but she couldn't very well take a horse without her father noticing.

It was a crisp day. The sun shone brightly. People had come from all around to buy and sell their animals and tinkers weaved among them, selling heather and cursing those who refused to purchase. Children were bribed to look after the cows as they had been when Kitty was a child, and the same children grew bored of their work and ran off to play with their friends, leaving the cows to wander, sometimes into people's parlors if they'd left their front doors open. The pubs were full; Kitty could smell the stout in the air along with the smell of horse sweat and manure. The noise of people's voices rose with the squawking of sea gulls perching on the rooftops, their beady black eyes searching the square for scraps to eat.

"Do you remember the last time we came here together?" said Robert, taking Kitty's hand.

"The time that man threw a potato at me," Kitty replied.

"Or at me, as you so wisely suggested," he added with a smile.

"I'm sorry. That was awfully mean of me."

"It was the truth."

"No, he threw a potato at *me*. I represented the British even though in my heart I've always considered myself Irish."

"It's your heart that matters."

Kitty felt a sudden swell of affection for this man who had given up his life in London so that she could be happy in Ireland. "Robert, if I haven't thanked you properly for bringing me here, it is only because I have been so distracted with all the arrangements. I really do want to thank you."

He took her hands in his. "I know you do, my darling. You don't need to thank me. To see you happy is thanks enough."

"Are you happy too?"

"You've made me the happiest man on earth," he replied. "How could I suffer a moment's unhappiness being married to you? I'm the envy of every man in London and, I'm sure, in Ballinakelly, too." He led her through the crowd. "Let's go and find you the best horse this town has to offer."

As Kitty's eyes floated over the faces of the men in caps, they suddenly rested on the familiar countenance of Michael Doyle. She gasped as if singed and dropped her gaze to the ground, but not before *he* had seen *her*. She gripped Robert's hand and hurried on, but the sweat gathered in her palms and her skin grew damp. Suddenly, her hand slipped out of Robert's. At once she found herself alone in the sea of people, frantically trying to keep her head up without catching the eye of the man who had haunted her nightmares since that fateful morning after the fire.

She jumped as she felt a hand grab her arm. She turned in fright. Michael Doyle was bearing down upon her just like he had done in the farmhouse, before he had thrown her onto the table and violated her. His malevolent face was so close to hers she could smell the alcohol on his breath. She stepped back in horror and cried out. The crowd parted as she fell into the mud. When she opened her eyes Michael had melted into the throng. Jack was gazing down at her in confusion, but it was Robert who was beside her, pulling her to her feet, putting his arm around her shoulders and leading her away.

Chapter 33

New York, America, 1924

Bridie was impressed with Mr. Lockwood's house. It was a five-story, white-stone palace with ornate pediments over the windows like eyebrows and a partially curved facade, which gave it a warm, inviting look as if it were smiling.

"It ain't much but it's home," joked Mr. Lockwood as he stepped up to the front door. It opened at once and a butler in a crisp white shirt and black tailcoat stepped aside with a courteous bow. Mr. Lockwood helped Bridie out of her coat and handed it to the butler, who took his master's camel-hair coat, felt hat and umbrella, hooking the polished wooden crook over his arm. Underneath, Mr. Lockwood's three-piece suit was expensively cut with a gold pocket watch on a chain hanging loosely across his somewhat rounded stomach. Bridie noticed the large gold signet ring he wore on his left hand and the diamond cuff links at his wrists. Even Mr. Deverill at his most debonair had never looked as refined as Mr. Lockwood. Bridie's heart began to race. "Now, let me introduce you to my son," he said as a young man stepped into the hall.

If Mr. Lockwood was an impressive figure, his son was a disappointment. It wasn't that he was plain or chinless like the hyena Paul Heskin, but he lacked his father's gravitas. He shook her hand and it was soft like dough and a little damp. His eyes were watery and wistful, his lips full and pink, his smile very handsome indeed, but Bridie thought him boyish and a little too fresh-faced for her tastes. He looked like he had no experience of life, as if everything had come to him much too easily. He looked weak. "I found Miss Doyle at Mass," Mr. Lockwood explained. "I thought she'd brighten up our Christmas. Who needs a tree when we have a pretty girl like Miss Doyle at our table?"

They climbed the grand staircase, which led up to a vast corridor with tall ceilings and heavy wooden doors with big brass knobs. Through one of those doors was a drawing room dominated by a glittering crystal chandelier and a merry fire. The walls were lined with wooden bookcases full of books bound in dark brown leather, embossed in gold, the floors covered in rich Persian rugs. The furniture was not unlike the furniture at Castle Deverill but everything here was shiny like new. The crimson silk chairs were spotless, the gilt on the mirror hanging above the marble fireplace was as bright as the sun and the walls themselves shimmered, setting off the paintings so that they shimmered too. What struck her most was the light that streamed in through the tall windows, infusing the room with happiness and a soft femininity. She was certain that this room had been decorated by Mr. Lockwood's late wife and she presumed she had been a woman of the finest taste.

Bridie was offered a glass of champagne, which she eagerly drank, allowing the bubbles to calm her self-doubt. "You have so many books, Mr. Lockwood," she said, walking up to run her hands over their spines. "I love books. I love to read more than anything in the world," she told him deliberately.

Mr. Lockwood looked surprised. "Do you?"

"Oh yes!" she exclaimed.

"What books do you like to read?" he asked, standing beside her.

She listed all the titles she had read to Mrs. Grimsby. "Yeats is my favorite poet. Of course he's Irish, which is probably why I love him. He reminds me of home." She looked up at Mr. Lockwood and smiled sweetly. *"He'll hear no more the lowing Of the calves on the warm hillside Or the kettle on the hob Sing peace into his breast, Or see the brown mice bob Round and round the oatmeal chest . . ."*

"Well, Miss Doyle, you surprise me. I know that Mrs. Grimsby collected books, but if you would like to borrow mine I'd be happy to lend them to you," he offered, his eyes now full of admiration.

"Oh, I'd love that, thank you. Mr. Lockwood, do you like to read too?" she asked his son.

Ashley looked bashful. "I'm afraid I'm not very interested in books. Father encouraged me as a boy, but I prefer more physical entertainment."

"Ashley plays tennis and golf," said Mr. Lockwood. "He put

his last book down about five years ago and hasn't picked one up since."

Bridie turned back to the elder Mr. Lockwood. "Will you recommend me something to read?" she asked, remembering that it was through books that Mrs. Grimsby had won Mr. Grimsby. "What is your favorite novel?"

Mr. Lockwood began to look through his library. "Well now, let me see. I'm not certain that you'd be partial to my tastes, Miss Doyle, being a woman of female sensibility. But my wife loved to read so let me offer you one of her favorites." He searched the spines for a moment, then pulled one out and handed it to Bridie. "*The Scarlet Letter.* I think you will enjoy it. It's an American classic and is very popular."

"Thank you so much," she gushed, holding it against her chest as if it were a treasure. "I can't think of anything nicer than curling up in front of the fire and reading a good novel while winter blows cold outside."

Mr. Lockwood looked pleased. "Let's eat," he said. "I don't know about you but I'm ravenous."

It was clear right from the start that Bridie had no interest in Ashley Lockwood. Ashley, it appeared, was not very interested in her either, but he dutifully courted her as his father commanded. Bridie read *The Scarlet Letter*, which was full of notes written in the margins by Mrs. Lockwood, which helped Bridie to make intelligent comments when she discussed the book with the elder Mr. Lockwood. She made sure that Ashley invited her to the house as much as possible, which enabled her to borrow more books from his father and to discuss them with him in front of the fire in that beautiful drawing room. When she talked to Mr. Lockwood Ashley would slip away, relieved to be left to his own devices, and Mr. Lockwood didn't seem to mind.

Bridie sensed that this silver fox was quite taken with her. Sometimes he had the same look in his eyes that Mr. Deverill had had the day he seduced her in his bedroom. Mr. Lockwood would gaze at her admiringly, a small smile curling the corners of his mouth, and she would return his gaze with as much sweetness as she could muster, before lowering it demurely and parting her lips a little to show that she was fighting her growing feelings for him, but only just managing to keep them under control.

It was on one of these occasions that Mr. Lockwood lost his composure. They were looking through the bookcase when he suddenly grabbed her by the shoulders and pressed his lips to hers. Bridie hadn't expected him to pounce so soon but she was not surprised; she had prepared for this moment. She closed her eyes, allowed her knees to buckle slightly and opened her mouth a little as if her desire was overpowering. He kissed her deeply and Bridie found she didn't have to pretend because she liked the feeling of his wet tongue curling around hers and his soft beard brushing against her face. It felt like years since she had been held by a man.

"Oh, Mr. Lockwood," she breathed, opening her eyes. "We shouldn't!"

"Why? Because of Ashley?" He chuckled and kissed her again. Bridie had not expected to feel so aroused. She thought of Mr. Deverill and longed for Mr. Lockwood to put his hand up her skirt and touch her like Mr. Deverill had done.

"Oh, Mr. Lockwood," she said again. "You're a devil, you

are, for making me feel things I've never felt before. I'm going dizzy in the head."

Mr. Lockwood smiled and buried his beard in her neck. She could feel the hardness of his own arousal pressing against her pelvis and she moved her hips, rubbing herself softly against him. This seemed to drive Mr. Lockwood into a hot fever of desire. "You smell so nice, Mr. Lockwood," she whispered and indeed the very male lemon and spice scent of his cologne did enhance her excitement. His hand found her breast as his tongue explored her mouth again with increasing ardor. His nostrils dilated and his breathing grew louder as he cupped her bosom. He pressed her against the bookcase and began to lift her skirt. "Oh, Mr. Lockwood," she protested, pushing him away. "We mustn't."

"Are you worried about my son?" he asked again. "Forget my son, Miss Doyle. I want you for myself." His hand began to wander to the tops of her stockings where they lingered a moment against her bare skin. She almost let him, so delicious were the feelings his fingers provoked. But she remembered her goal. She didn't want him to treat her like Mr. Deverill had treated her, but like he'd treat a lady of class.

"Then marry me, Mr. Lockwood," she said breathlessly. "Because I intend to go to my marital bed intact."

He considered her offer. It didn't take him long. "I'll marry you, Miss Doyle, and my final years will be full of pleasure."

"Then you'd better call me Bridget," she said with a smile.

"And you'd better call me Walter." He kissed her again but his hand returned to her waist where it remained. "We'll marry soon before you drive me insane with desire, and before my family have the time to object."

WALTER LOCKWOOD'S FAMILY did indeed object, but Bridie didn't care. They were married within the month just as the first buds of spring were beginning to peep out of the thawing winter earth. Ashley moved out of the house in disgust and Bridie sold Mrs. Grimsby's houses without a backward glance. She brought Rosetta with her to her new home and dismissed the cook and the butler who had worked for her for only six months. The newspapers were quick to write about this unlikely couple with nearly forty years between them, pointing out that their combined fortune was immense. Society gossiped about the new Mrs. Lockwood's extraordinary rise with both contempt and wonder. "She's not even beautiful," some of the women complained.

"It's not like he needs the money," said others.

"But she's young and old men can't resist the feel of young flesh," commented the more vulgar observers.

The old ladies clicked their tongues and shook their heads. "Poor Heather Lockwood must be turning in her grave," they said of his first wife. But none of this was noticed by the newlyweds, whose happiness was armor against disapproval and condemnation.

Mr. Williams continued to take care of Bridie's financial affairs, but Mr. Lockwood oversaw her investments with the same cunning and skill that had made *him* so rich. The stock market was a game the silver fox relished and he proudly boasted that he'd double her money by investing in gold. While their husbands took care of Bridie's business affairs Bridie and Elaine became closer than ever. Indeed, the two women were inseparable. When Bridie bought something for herself, she bought something for Elaine. When she was invited to lunch,

Elaine came as well. When her husband was too exhausted to go out in the evenings, Bridie partied with Elaine and the two of them returned to those old basement clubs, drank champagne in the speakeasies and danced until the sun rose in the sky to turn the Hudson gold.

Bridie had never felt more secure. Mr. Lockwood was a sensitive and gentle lover and Bridie managed to play the innocent without any difficulty. He spoiled her, indulged her and cherished her and Bridie relished having a distinguished, fearless husband to escort her through all the doors of Fifth Avenue that had previously barred her. She was Mrs. Lockwood, now infamous as the most determined social climber in New York.

Walter had gained a wife but he had lost his children. Furious that he had married a girl young enough to be his daughter they refused to speak to him. His daughters wept and raged and vented their wrath to anyone who would listen, while his sons insisted he arrange his will so that *his* fortune went directly to them and not to any children he might have with his new wife. While Bridie pressed her ear to his study door she heard the accusations his sons threw about the room. They told their father he had married an *Irish whore,* a *gold-digger,* a *tramp,* a *trollop,* a *ruthless opportunist who preyed on old people.* They told him she'd wear him out with her insatiable desire for entertainment and that he'd be dead before the year was over. They begged him to divorce her. They implored him to remember their mother, whom he had dearly loved. *It's her or us,* they told him. But Walter defended her with strong language, accusing them of selfishness and of denying him happiness in his autumn years. The boys left the house and Walter watched them go with a hardened heart. Any hurt he felt he buried deep so that even *he* couldn't find it. Bridie crept out of the shadows and wrapped her arms around him. "They'll accept me in the end," she said, kissing his beard. But she knew they never would.

Bridie made sure she distracted her new husband sufficiently so that he didn't have time to worry about his children. They were out most evenings and the invitations kept coming. When he complained he was tired, she laughed and kissed his white beard, pulling him back onto the dance floor, insisting she was too happy to remain still. When they stayed at home she crept into his arms like a needy black cat, demanding to be stroked.

Bridie had never been so happy. She had everything she believed she wanted. She didn't love her husband but she liked him very much. He allowed her to lead the life she had always craved. Those stars upon which she had gazed from her small bedroom window in Ballinakelly had made her wish come true. She was somebody now and no one could look down their nose at her. Not Kitty, not Celia, not Elspeth, not Victoria, Countess of Elmrod. No one would dare.

Then one night in late summer, as Bridie pressed her naked body against Walter's, his weary old heart gave up and stopped ticking. Just as quickly as Bridie had found happiness, it was lost to her. The last seven months of Walter's life had indeed been filled with pleasure. But Bridie's joy had come to an untimely end.

She stared in horror as her husband's face turned white. His lips became a dark shade of blue. His hand, which was resting on her waist, went limp and fell onto the mattress. His final breath was exhaled quietly, without any resistance, as if he gave up his ghost willingly. Bridie shook him. She shouted at him. She tried everything to rouse him from death, but to no avail. He had passed away, leaving her a widow at twenty-five years old.

Sobbing hysterically, she rang for the butler. She rang and she rang and she didn't stop ringing until he burst into the room in alarm. He found Bridie in her dressing gown clinging to the lifeless body of his master. Bridie was too distraught to see the accusation in the butler's eyes as he lifted Mr. Lockwood's hand to feel for a pulse. He shook his head dolefully and left the room to call an ambulance. Bridie watched them cover her husband in a sheet, lift him onto a stretcher and carry him away forever. With him went her security, her social standing and her happiness, which she had thought could never be taken away on account of her enormous wealth.

She remained in her bedroom, staring out of the window onto the empty street below, wondering where she could go from here. Without Walter she didn't belong in this house. His children would quickly reclaim it and she would have to move somewhere else. But where? Her heart flagged at the thought of summoning Mr. Williams again and searching for somewhere to live. Walter's children would make sure that every door that had opened for her on Fifth Avenue would close again and she would find herself an outcast. People would look on her with suspicion. No sooner had she arrived at Mrs. Grimsby's house than the old lady had died. No sooner had she married Mr. Lockwood than the old man had died. Rosetta had come to comfort her but she had sent her away. She didn't want to speak to anyone. Just as she had begun to feel she belonged God had seen fit to cast her adrift again.

The following day she telephoned Elaine to tell her the news. Elaine was horrified. "I'm coming over," she said, putting down the telephone. Shortly after, Elaine arrived at the house to comfort her friend while her husband came to discuss Bridie's future. Mr. Williams spoke plainly as Bridie had spoken to him when she had set out to find a husband. "I strongly advise you to leave New York," he said. "Mr. Lockwood's family will make it their business to make your life here very difficult. They know everyone in this town."

"Indeed and they'll want their revenge."

"I'm afraid they will," said Mr. Williams.

"Where am I to go?" Bridie asked, wringing her hands and throwing her gaze out of the window. "I have nowhere to go!"

"This is a very big country, Mrs. Lockwood. With your fortune you can settle anywhere you want."

"But I don't know anyone. You and Elaine are my only friends in the world."

"Beaumont is right, Bridget," Elaine replied, shaking her head. "You've done it before, you can do it again. What about Texas? It's sunny there."

"Texas? I don't even know where that is on a map!" Bridie swallowed a sob.

"You tell me where you want to go and I'll make the arrangements," said Mr. Williams, standing up.

"I'll help you decide. It'll be fun," enthused Elaine, glancing anxiously at her husband. "You can buy a big house and start afresh where no one knows you."

"But that's just it. I don't want to go where no one knows me. I don't want to start again. I ache for the familiar, Elaine."

When they had gone Rosetta appeared in the doorway holding a book. "What is it, Rosetta?" Bridie asked.

"I thought you might like this." She handed Bridie the old book of Yeats's poems.

Bridie took it and gazed down at it sadly. "Thank you, Rosetta," she said softly. "You're quite right. I *do* need it." She curled up on the sofa beside the fire in the most beautiful room of the house and opened the first page. Slowly she began to read:

> *"I am of Ireland,*
> *And the Holy Land of Ireland,*
> *And time runs on," cried she.*
> *"Come out of charity,*
> *Come dance with me in Ireland."*

Bridie stared at the words until they had all blurred into one dark stain. She knew where she had to go. She knew what she had to do. It was no use moving to another part of the country because her past would only go with her, for it was locked away in the secret chambers of her heart. Wherever she went it would follow, and in the quiet moments when she dared gaze into her soul she would see the child she had given away who was part of her and always would be. She had the money now to give him a finer home than she had ever had. She could give him a world-class education and a future in a country where he belonged; she could deny Ireland in loud protestations but that beautiful land was in her veins and, with every heartbeat, was calling her home.

Bridie attended her husband's funeral hidden behind a black veil. She did not meet the eyes of any of his children but she felt their loathing like little knives on her skin, viciously prodding.

The large congregation of his friends who had fawned over her when she had been married to him now turned their cold shoulders and ignored her. Bridie felt more isolated and alone than ever.

When it was over she left the house on Fifth Avenue forever. Her bags were already on their way to the Shelbourne Hotel in Dublin. She embraced Elaine fiercely and thanked Mr. Williams for his advice and friendship, then with Rosetta to accompany her, she boarded the boat for Ireland.

Bridie had arrived in America as a naïve and penniless child; now she was leaving as a shrewd and wealthy woman. The thought of seeing her homeland again gave her a thrilling sense of anticipation. She was returning for the child who belonged to her. Surely God could not deny her *him*.

Chapter 34

London, England, 1925

When Celia heard that Kitty and Robert had moved to Ireland she was devastated. Furious that her cousin hadn't told her, she complained bitterly to Harry and Boysie, who, in spite of each being married, were more together than ever. "Does she have so little respect for our friendship that she makes this decision without me?" she moaned into her wineglass. "Our lunches aren't the same without her." Indeed, their table for four at Claridge's was achingly incomplete.

"I imagine she told no one, so that there was minimal chance of the one person she really didn't want to know finding out," said Boysie.

"Mother!" Harry drew on his cigarette. "Mama despises Ireland now that my inheritance is gone."

"It's not gone," Celia reminded him. "It's a pile of rubble, but rubble can always be rebuilt."

"Who has the money to do that?" Harry asked.

"Your dreary wife," Boysie chuckled, winking at Celia.

"Yours is more dreary than mine," Harry laughed. "In fact, I think we've both married the most insipid girls in London."

"At least yours has money. I should think her father would happily rebuild your castle," said Boysie.

Harry pulled a face. "You know I don't want to live in Ireland. My inheritance was an unwelcome bind. I was never happy there," he said, forgetting Joseph. "My life is in England now."

"What will happen to the castle? I was at my *most* happy there," said Celia, sipping her wine and suddenly smelling the scent of tomatoes in the greenhouses at Castle Deverill.

"Mother says she's going to persuade Father to sell it."

Celia was appalled. "You can't sell your family home, however much you don't want to live in it! It's your inheritance. It's the *Deverill* family heritage. I've been boasting about our Irish castle since I was a little girl! What will I boast about if it's sold to a stranger?"

"Darling, it's over. Ireland is over. It belongs to the Irish now and we Anglo-Irish have no business to be there. It'll be bought by some Irishman with more money than sense."

"There aren't any with money, are there?" Celia said.

"There certainly aren't many with sense," Boysie added. "From what I understand they're still killing each other."

Celia threw her hands up in despair. "They can't sell it. Your grandmother will die!"

"She's going to die anyway. Mother says she's gone mad with

grief. As soon as she's gone, Mother will go to Ireland and persuade Papa that they need a proper house in England. She can't
go on living with Victoria."

Boysie arched an eyebrow. "That's an accident waiting to
happen. I don't know who will turn who mad first—Victoria
or your mother. They're both equally dreadful." Boysie flicked
his fingers at the waiter and ordered another bottle of wine.

"Before they sell it, let's go and spend one last summer
there!" Celia suggested excitedly. "Oh, do let's! It'll be such a
hoot. We can rummage around the rubble. Goodness knows
what we might find. We can stay with Kitty. Do you have to
bring your wives? Can't you say it's a family-only affair and
they must remain at home? Can't you hurry up and get them
pregnant? I simply couldn't stomach them all summer!"

Harry looked at Boysie through the veil of smoke. "What do
you say, old boy?"

Boysie shrugged. "It's certainly possible." The waiter came
and filled their glasses with wine. "Could *you* leave Archie
behind?"

"Of course I can," Celia answered without hesitation. "He
disappears to Scotland from the twelfth of August to shoot,
stalk and fish and goodness knows what else. You both know
how I feel about Scotland. I can leave him to his pleasure and I
can take mine. Oh, do let's. Harry, you can tell Charlotte that
you have to go home to discuss family matters that don't concern her. Boysie, you can tell Deirdre anything you like so long
as you come on your own. You're ingenious—you'll think of
something."

The three of them raised their glasses. "To our last summer,"
they said.

CELIA WAS FORCED to send Kitty a letter, for there was yet to be a telephone line installed in Dunderry Castle. After that moment at the fair Kitty had not left the house for fear of seeing Michael Doyle again. She had lied to Robert about her sudden "turn," explaining it away as an unexpected bout of claustrophobia. He had taken her home and returned later with Peter, who knew more about horses than he did, and chosen a fine gray mare, which had delighted Kitty, not least because it meant she didn't have to return to Ballinakelly.

When she received the letter from Celia her spirits lifted with excitement. She hurried into the nursery where Elspeth was playing with the children and announced that Celia, Harry and Boysie were coming to stay in August. "I can hardly wait!" she exclaimed happily. "To think, we can all be together again. Just like old times."

"Except there's no castle," said Elspeth sadly.

"It doesn't matter. We'll all be together." She thought of Bridie suddenly and her heart gave a little wince. "Well, *almost* all. It doesn't matter, we'll have Celia and Harry and Boysie's such fun. We can picnic on the beach, paddle in the water, ride out over the hills and do all the things we used to do." She sat down on the floor and drew little Jack into her arms. He was busy playing with a toy engine. "I must show Jack how to find nature spirits." She kissed his fat cheek. "I wonder whether he has the gift."

Elspeth rolled her eyes. "You and your fanciful imagination," she said. But Kitty raked her fingers through the little boy's red hair and wondered.

By the middle of March the White House was ready. Kitty moved in with Robert and little Jack and set about making it into a home. She left her dresses in the cupboard and spent most of the time in a pair of slacks with her sleeves rolled up, digging up the garden and planting seeds for vegetables and flowers. Her uncle Rupert had employed laborers, who had created and maintained beautiful gardens overlooking the sea, but Robert didn't have the money to waste on unnecessary pleasures, so Kitty was forced to do it all herself. But she enjoyed getting her hands dirty and watching little Jack scouring the overturned earth for worms and snails. The two of them spent many hours watching the birds that came to nest in the hawthorn bushes and the rabbits that nibbled at the little green shoots just as soon as they came up. Jack especially loved the flowers and Kitty wondered whether he could see the little dancing lights that hovered around them. She couldn't tell whether he sensed those happy spirits or whether it was the bees and butterflies that grabbed his attention.

Although Kitty was busy creating a home she could love, her thoughts were never far from Jack O'Leary. His face swam to the front of her mind in both memories and fantasies and instead of fighting them she let them come. It was impossible for her to be in Ireland without Jack being part of her world. Jack was Ireland and Ireland was Jack and the one was incomplete without the other. It was no use trying to restrain her feelings because she loved him in the same way she loved the soft rain, the craggy hills, the white sands and tempestuous sea: with her whole being.

Seeing Michael Doyle had opened a chamber in her memory that she had long ago sealed and now he too surfaced with his threatening face and ominous presence when she lost control of her thoughts. She had been struck by the murky aura that had surrounded him at the fair, as if he were an evil spirit trapped in a limbo like Egerton Deverill. But she sensed he was still very much alive and the thought of seeing him again struck her heart with fear. She wished she could overcome her terror. She'd overcome so much already. But Miss Grieve's unpleasantness was nothing compared with the violence of that morning at the farmhouse. He still lived in Ballinakelly and that marred the joy of her homecoming.

It wasn't long, however, before her fears began to materialize. At first she thought she was seeing things, shadows and plays of light in the distant shrubbery that made her feel Michael was there, watching her. She retreated inside the house, then peered like a spy from behind the curtain at her bedroom window. At night she lay in bed believing the wind rattling the glass was Michael climbing up the wall to steal in through the window and rape her all over again. She took to sleeping with Robert every night, curling up against him, which was the only place she really felt safe. When she gardened she asked Hetty to stay outside with her and, when the girl went inside to give little Jack his lunch, she dug with sweat on her brow and her heart thumping in her chest, keeping her eyes on the ground, telling herself she was just being silly: Michael wouldn't dare to come here.

But Michael *did* dare. He strode up to the door one morning and rang the bell. Kitty hid and told Bridgeman to send him away. If he had the audacity to come to her door, what might he do next? In a fever of panic she sent the stableboy into Ballinakelly with a note for Jack. He must come to the house at once on the pretense of attending a lame horse. She needed his help and she needed it *now*.

Kitty waited, pacing the garden impatiently, wringing her hands. At last Jack's small car trundled up the drive. She ran across the lawn to meet him. He climbed out and took off his cap. "Good day to you, Mrs. Trench," he said, sliding his eyes to the house to see if they were being watched.

"Thank you for coming, Mr. O'Leary. The mare is in the stables. Let me walk with you." Kitty shoved her hands into her pockets where they trembled out of sight. "Isn't it fine today," she said lamely.

"It's just grand," he replied.

They walked around to the stables where the boy who had cycled into Ballinakelly with the letter was now sweeping. "Seamus, would you do me the favor of emptying my wheelbarrow? It's in the garden, full of weeds. It can all go on the bonfire in the field. I'll show Mr. O'Leary my mare." The boy nodded, leaned his brush against the wall and hurried off.

Kitty opened the stable door and they stepped inside to where Kitty's gray mare stood on a bed of straw, in rude health. Jack patted her neck and looked down at Kitty. "So, what's the urgency?"

"It's Michael. He's after me," she hissed, putting her hand on her chest to quieten her heart. "I'm afraid, Jack."

"What have you got to be afraid of Michael for?" he asked, frowning.

"He burned the castle, Jack."

Jack nodded, not surprised. "I suspected as much."

"He burned the castle and he set a trap so the British would catch you red-handed."

At this, Jack stopped patting the horse. "What are you saying, Kitty?"

"I'm telling you the truth."

"How do you know?"

"He told me himself."

"When?"

"When I rode over to the farmhouse the morning after the fire. I knew it was him. I went to confront him."

"And he told you he'd betrayed me?"

"Yes. He told me he burned the castle and betrayed you."

"Why would he do that now? We were fighting on the same side."

"Because of *me*." Her eyes glittered in the dark stable. "He didn't want you to have me." The horse gave an impatient snort and nudged Jack for some attention. He put a hand on her muzzle absent-mindedly. "I would have told you, but you were arrested and then when we finally saw each other I didn't know where to start."

"Well, you can start now." His voice was hard. He looked at Kitty steadily. "From the beginning."

KITTY TOOK A deep breath. "Bridie is little Jack's mother."

Jack reeled. "Jaysus!"

"My father took her." She swallowed. "Michael claims he raped her." She shook her head vigorously. "But I can't believe that. I *won't* believe it. I don't believe my father is capable of that sort of . . . *violence*." She hit the word hard and rubbed her neck. "So Michael burned the castle in revenge."

"Jaysus!" he said again. "How did you come by the child?"

"Bridie must have sent him to me somehow before she left for America. That's why my father won't let me come home, because Jack is his and he's too ashamed to look at him." She took a deep breath, recalling the morning at the Doyles' farmhouse. "Michael told me that while the RIC were all distracted up at the castle, you were stealing guns and taking them to a safe house. But he made it very clear he didn't intend for you to get there."

Jack pulled Kitty into his arms and held her fiercely. "Michael didn't betray me because I was in love with a Prod, but because he wanted you for himself. The bloody bastard!"

"He's been watching me, Jack. I'm frightened he's going to hurt me."

"I won't let him hurt you, Kitty." She closed her eyes, squeezing out a tear. How she longed to tell him that he already had.

JACK WAITED IN a ditch for Michael Doyle. The sky was bright with stars but thick clouds gathered above the ocean, moving swiftly inland on an ill wind. He had fortified himself with whiskey and sufficiently blunted the edge of his anger so that he was no longer crazed and irrational. His heart was a stone in his chest. Because of Michael Doyle he had been locked away by the British. Because of Michael Doyle his dream of starting a new life in America with Kitty had been shattered. Because of Michael Doyle the girl he loved had been forced to leave her home and move to London where he couldn't find her. The rage now simmered quietly in his gut as he waited for Michael Doyle.

The eerie hooting of an owl was carried on the breeze from the distant woods where the shriek of the Banshee came loud and often these days. The sea was a constant hiss as it crashed against the rocks in great swells. Cows slept in spite of the wind and occasionally lowed. Jack heard the rustle of a small animal in the heather and then the sound of footsteps on the track as Michael slowly made his way home from the pub.

It was a lonely road, that road from Ballinakelly to the Doyle farmhouse. It wound through the rocky hills, meandering softly like a stream, benign in the moonlight. The footsteps grew louder, scrunching on the grit and stones. At last the black, burly figure of a man came into view, silhouetted against the charcoal sky. Jack got to his feet and walked into the middle of the road. Michael flinched. He had too much of a history of ambushes not to be alarmed.

"Jack O'Leary," he said and his voice betrayed his relief and the fact that he was drunk. "I thought you were a hoor of a garda! What are you doing here?"

"I've come to see *you*."

Michael swayed like a ship's mast. "To what do I owe the pleasure?" He slurred his words as if they were too big for his tongue. The two men faced each other—two men who had once fought side by side as brothers.

"Did you or did you not burn down Castle Deverill?" Jack's eyes glinted like steel as the wind tore a fleeting hole in the clouds, allowing the moon to shine down like a light.

"What if I did? That castle was a symbol of British supremacy. You know that. It had to go." He laughed wildly. "Is that why you've waited all night in the ditch to see me, Jack O'Leary?"

"You didn't do it because it was British. You did it to avenge your sister. Don't lie to me, Michael!" Michael grimaced but said nothing. "You set a trap for me, didn't you? You wanted me out of the way!"

"Who the devil have you been speaking to? Get your facts right, O'Leary! Why would I want to lose a good man?" He blinked hard, trying to remain focused.

"Because I had the woman you couldn't have!"

"You think I'd send you to your death over a woman! Jaysus, you had too much time to think inside!"

"I didn't think enough! I never thought you'd rat on one of your own!"

"You've been listening to women's gossip," he snarled.

As Michael's lip curled Jack realized just how naïve he'd been. "You told the Tans I'd be at the railway station, didn't you?" he said, the full truth exploding in a blast of clarity. "That's why you walked free when I was put away! A warrant was out for *both* our arrests, but *you* walked free. You bastard! I should have worked it out, but I never thought you'd stoop so low."

"You've lost your mind, Jack. Go home and get some rest!" Michael began to walk again, but Jack stood in his way.

"What are you doing sniffing around Kitty Deverill's place? What business do you have to be there?" he demanded.

"What business is it of yours to ask?"

"I'm asking now."

"She has my nephew or didn't you know?"

"You leave that boy alone."

Michael grinned, his teeth white against his inky face. "Has she sent you out like a hound to warn me off?"

"You'll not lay a finger on her or her boy. Do you hear?" Jack raised his voice against the wind. "You'll leave them both alone."

"When did you become so soft? The fight's not over. But you sold out, didn't you, Jack O'Leary! There was a time you burned for a free and independent Ireland, and yet now you want to settle down by the hearth with that whore—" Jack's fist hit him before he could finish his sentence. Michael recoiled, putting his fingers to his face and tasting the blood on his tongue. "Jaysus! What's got into you?"

Jack was trembling. He held up his fist. "You call her a whore again and I'll finish you off for good."

But Michael Doyle enjoyed taunting him and, propelled by drink, was unable to stop. "She asked for it, Jack. She came to my house. She came to me willingly. I didn't ask her but I gave her what she wanted." He narrowed his eyes and smirked. "I threw her onto the table and fucked her, Jack! I fucked her from behind like a whore. Did she tell you *that*?" Jack was stunned. He hesitated, arm in the air, trying to make sense of Michael's words. He was slow to react: Michael's fist dealt him a blow to the stomach before he had time to strike. Jack bent double and gasped for breath. "Were you not man enough to take her, Jack? Did you have to leave it to me to show her what a *real* man is capable of?" Michael kneed him in the ribs and Jack fell to the ground with a groan. "Don't you ever threaten me again, do you hear?" he shouted. "We're not on the same side anymore, Jack. You were too lily-livered to continue the fight. Michael Collins sold us down the river and you were right there behind him, happy to give it all away! But look what happened to him? Dead on the road in Béal na Bláth. The war is not over, Jack. And you're on the losing side."

Michael drew his foot back and kicked him in the kidneys, but Jack's fingers had found a large stone and were curling around it. His fury numbed the pain in his ribs. All he could think of was his beloved Kitty, thrown over the table, and Michael thrusting into her. He lifted the stone off the ground and threw it at Michael, hoping it would make contact somewhere. Hoping it would give him time. It did more than that. It struck him on the temple. Michael fell backward, hitting the grass like a vanquished giant in a fairy tale.

Jack staggered to his feet, holding his winded stomach. The clouds opened again and the silver eye gazed down at Michael Doyle, nursing his wounded head. "Jaysus, Jack!" he cried, writhing in agony. Jack was so full of rage he wanted to finish him off. He wanted to kick the life out of him. But Michael was drunk, and helpless now as he tended to his injury with a trembling hand and Jack didn't have the flint heart to kill him.

"Don't you ever go near Kitty again, do you understand?" he growled. "Or I'll finish what I started and the Devil will take your soul."

THE FOLLOWING MORNING Kitty was in the dining room having breakfast when there was a knock at the door. A moment later Bridgeman stood in the doorway. "Mr. O'Leary is here to see you, Mrs. Trench," he said.

Robert frowned at Kitty. "Isn't that the vet?"

"Yes," Kitty replied calmly.

"Did you call for him?"

"No."

"Oh." Robert raised his eyebrows. "Odd lot, the Irish."

Kitty smiled. "Darling, that's not kind. I'll go and see what he wants." Kitty hurried into the hall. When she saw Jack, one eye black, his lip cut and bruised, her heart went cold.

"Good day to you, Mrs. Trench." He took off his cap.

Kitty stared at him in horror. In her mind's eye she saw Miss

Grieve dead on the gravel. Hadn't they been here before? "What have you done?" she whispered.

"Michael Doyle won't be troubling you anymore," he replied flatly. "I'd have killed him if he hadn't been so blind drunk."

Kitty drew in a sharp gulp of air and put her hand on the doorframe to steady herself. "I think you should take a look at her, Mr. O'Leary," she said loudly, striding past him toward the stables. She didn't speak until they were alone. Only the mare was once more privy to their conversation.

"Oh Jack. What happened?" she asked, gazing up at his battered face.

"Why didn't you tell me, Kitty?" he groaned. The dreadful pain in his eyes told her that he knew what Michael had done. "Why didn't you . . . ?"

"I couldn't . . ." she whispered.

"That's not something you can carry on your own, Kitty. It's too big for one person." He put a hand on her arm. "I would have helped you bear it."

"I was ashamed."

"Of what? You have nothing to be ashamed of. You didn't ask for it."

Kitty's face burned. "But I went there, Jack. I went there of my own accord. I went to shout at him for burning the castle. What was I thinking?"

He took her stricken face in his hands and held her gaze. "You're a bold girl, Kitty Deverill. But boldness isn't a crime and he had no right to touch you. No right at all. May he burn in Hell." He wiped her tears with gentle thumbs and pressed his lips to her forehead. "Let me carry this for you, my darling. Let it all go."

Kitty howled against his jacket. "I can't live without you, Jack," she said, wondering how she had ever thought it possible. "And I don't want to."

Chapter 35

Kitty rode her mare over the hills at a gallop. The sea was a violet bed of satin, its foam like lace, as the wind swept over it. Jack's house was isolated, surrounded by woolly fields and a sandy inlet that went out to the ocean. He was waiting for her there, ready to take her horse to the stable where there was water and shelter. He pulled her into his arms and kissed her. This time his face was full of joy. The lines of trouble had eased, his eyes were no longer windows into pain and his mouth curled with delight as it always used to do before Michael Doyle had taken away everything he loved.

Holding her hand he led her into the cottage. The fire was lit in the parlor. The place smelled of turf smoke, dusty books and baking bread. He turned back and grinned and in that moment he was the boy she had known all those years ago, with his hawk and his dog and his love of every living creature, even the spiders and rats that Bridie had been so afraid of. He stepped onto the stair where the carpet was frayed with age and began to climb. Neither said a word as she followed him upstairs. There was something magical in the silence that neither wanted to break.

He took her to his bedroom. He didn't have much: a large bed, a simple wooden chest of drawers, a wardrobe, a standing mirror and a bookcase. The window was open, the curtains billowing on the breeze that carried on its breath the earthy smell of early spring. His eyes told her he had waited years for this. They told her that his love had no limits and no conditions. They reassured her that it would heal the wounds of the past and reduce to ash the residual memory of Michael Doyle.

He slipped his hands around her neck, beneath her hair where she was still hot from her ride, and caressed her cheeks with his thumbs. He gazed upon her face as if his desire was to commit every feature to memory. They needn't rush. They had time. Here in this remote cottage they were a world apart. Jack bent his head and all the longing, all the dreams and fantasies of youth, went into his kiss. Kitty ran her hands over his shirt, feeling the warmth of his body beneath, and closed her eyes. She wasn't afraid. In Jack's arms she was safe. In his familiar embrace she could erase everything that had come before.

She pulled his shirt out of his trousers and unbuttoned it. She traced his ribs with her fingertips, where the bruise had muted to a dirty brown, and over his chest. Unlike Robert's, Jack's was hairy and muscular, the chest of a man who hadn't the money to pay others to do his work for him. Kitty found it deeply arousing and pressed her ear to hear his heart beating beneath and to inhale the scent that she knew so well.

Jack tugged her blouse out of her slacks and lifted it over her head. She stood in her chemise and breeches, the skin of her shoulders pale against the red of her hair as it tumbled about them in thick waves. Unable to resist, he sank his face into her neck and kissed her there. The sensation of his rough bristles and lips was too much and Kitty pulled away and sat on the bed so that Jack could help her remove her boots and breeches. They both sensed an urgency now, an accelerating impulse to entwine so tightly that nothing could untangle them. Kitty's inhibitions had no place in this room, with Jack who had known and loved her for as long as they could both remember.

He stood at the foot of the bed and unbelted his trousers. As he bent his head his brown hair fell over his forehead and Kitty was reminded of the time he had helped her hunt for frogs in the river. He was still the same, just more weathered, time and experience having deepened the lines around his mouth and eyes, and darkened his skin. She felt her heart expand with gratitude that God had seen fit to preserve him, in spite of everything he had put himself through.

When at last Jack climbed over the bed to lie beside her, it was as if the intervening years had never been. He ran his hands over the soft undulations of her body as if he were the first and she took pleasure from his caresses as if her trust in a man's touch had never been broken. As Jack made love to her she discovered that this act that she had so abhorred was not a repulsive thing after all, but the manifestation of two people's deep and enduring devotion.

ROBERT'S NOVEL WAS published at the beginning of May. Kitty was the first to read it. She lay on a rug on the lawn, surrounded by flowers and shrubs that *she* had planted, inhaling the sweet spring air and devouring the love story that Robert had so clearly written for *her*. It was a beautiful tale and Kitty couldn't put it down. He wrote with a fluid, lyrical style that drew the reader into the plot, and on occasions she laughed out loud, which was unusual because Robert wasn't particularly witty in person. She was so proud of her husband. Although he had been paid very little for it, she hoped that it would sell well enough to justify writing another. They had sold the house in London, turning their backs on England forever. She had committed to a future in Ireland. It was where she belonged. It was where she was happy at last and it was where she could be close to Jack.

The spring flowered into summer and little Jack was growing boisterous. He loved exploring the beaches, playing with the dogs Robert had bought from Peter's bitch's litter and having fun with his cousins. Kitty didn't seek out her father. She visited her grandmother and the Shrubs, spent time with her sister and Grace and sneaked off to see Jack whenever she was able to disappear without raising suspicion. As long as her father didn't wish to see her, she would give him a wide berth. She was too busy thinking about Jack to care.

In August Celia, Harry and Boysie arrived with their high spirits and laughter and their demand for constant entertainment. Kitty arranged picnics, rides over the hills, excursions to Cork, lunch parties and dinners with their neighbors where Boysie entertained them all on the piano and Celia led everyone into a dance. Indeed, no one was happier to be back in Ballinakelly than Celia.

"Oh, I do so love this old place," she said, sitting in Adeline's tower, squashed onto a mouse-eaten sofa with Boysie and Harry, while Kitty took Hubert's chair.

"It's very crowded now," said Adeline, sipping the cannabis tea Kitty had prepared for her. "Hubert is jolly fierce but he can't keep Barton out. He says he was here first so it's his right. One can't argue with that."

Celia giggled. "I think you're drinking too much weed tea, Adeline!" But Kitty knew she wasn't making it up, for both Hubert and Barton were standing by the window looking extremely put out at having their room invaded in this way.

Adeline passed the teapot to Boysie. "At least I'm never alone," she said.

"And I have a lovely fire, even in the summertime. It gets very damp in here otherwise. But truly, I wouldn't want to be anywhere else. I can't leave Hubert to fend off all his relatives on his own, now can I?"

Boysie poured tea into his cup, then passed the pot to Harry. "We should drink more of this. I want to inhabit Lady Deverill's world."

"I'm afraid it's not the weed," said Harry. "Grandma and Kitty both see dead people. They say it's a gift. I say it's a design fault."

Kitty caught Adeline's eye and grinned. "In the olden days we'd have been burned at the stake," she said.

"I always thought you made it up," said Celia. "That story about the curse and Barton Deverill and his heirs being stuck in the castle until an O'Leary returned to live here." She took the pot from Harry and refilled her empty cup. Then she looked at Kitty steadily, remembering her confession in the garden about loving the man after whom she had named little Jack. "Whatever happened to Jack O'Leary?" she asked.

"He's the local vet," said Kitty smoothly, averting her eyes. "His father was wounded in the war so Jack took over."

"Yes, that's right," said Celia, narrowing her eyes. "He was always very good with animals. They were all unafraid of him. Even wild rabbits and deer. Do you remember how he used to tell us the names of all the birds? He knew every one."

"He sounds like St. Francis of Assisi," said Boysie drily.

"I don't think there was anything saintly about him. He was always devilishly handsome if I recall," said Celia. "Tell me, Kitty, has he married?"

"No, he's alone," Kitty replied.

Celia grinned. "Oh dear. That's frightfully dangerous." She passed the pot to Kitty who poured out the last few drops, thinking of Jack alone in the cottage by the sea. Would he crave a family one day? She took a gulp and banished the shadow of guilt that drifted into her heart like a black cloud across a clear sky.

"One day an O'Leary will return to claim the land," said Adeline portentously.

"Do you think?" said Celia. "Perhaps Harry and Charlotte's future son will marry Jack's future daughter. That would be enough to lift the curse, wouldn't it?"

"Oh, I think it would," said Adeline firmly. "Then all these poor spirits can return home, to where they belong." Harry nudged Boysie and smirked, because he didn't believe in things one couldn't see with the eye. "If it doesn't happen," Adeline continued, looking sternly at her grandson, "you will end your days here too, Harry. A wandering, angry soul unable to move into the light. It's a dark world in Limbo."

Harry stopped smirking. "I'm afraid I don't believe in ghosts, Grandma."

"You can't see the radio waves that wiggle their way through the ether, but it doesn't prevent you listening to the wireless. I'm afraid, my dear, your skepticism does not alter your destiny, nor does it protect you from it. Maggie O'Leary's curse holds firm and nothing but an O'Leary reclaiming the land will lift it."

Celia wriggled on the sofa. "Ooooh, I do love a ghost story. Tell us another one, Adeline."

"You're doomed, old boy," said Boysie. "You might end up here, after all."

Harry rolled his eyes. "Well, at least I won't be alone."

A FEW DAYS later Adeline's spirit left her weary old body and floated into the light as she always knew it would. Bertie returned to the Hunting Lodge after dark to find his mother wasn't there. Reluctantly, he climbed the stairs into the west wing of the castle to discover her cold corpse eerily lit by the dying embers of the fire. He carried her down as his father watched from the gloom of his existence between worlds. Hubert had seen her depart and she had left him with the promise that she would return just as soon as she could. "Love will connect us forever and always," she had told him. So he would wait; after all, there was nothing else to do.

Adeline was laid out on her bed in the Hunting Lodge. Bertie lit candles and placed a Bible in her hands. She looked serene, he thought, as if she had just taken an enormous gulp of that cannabis tea she liked to drink. Her eyes were shut, her skin translucent, a small smile playing about her lips—the smile of a person sure of Heaven and her place in it. He sat on the bed and put his head in his hands. Both parents were gone now, his brother Rupert also. All he had left was his sister who had long ago emigrated to America in disgrace, his estranged wife, his estranged daughter, Harry, Victoria and Elspeth . . . and his son, Jack. The boy he refused to acknowledge; the materialization of his greatest shame. What had become of his family, once so united, now so fragmented?

Adeline was buried in the church of St. Patrick in Ballina-kelly, alongside Hubert and other members of the Deverill family, right back to Barton himself, whose gravestone was barely legible due to the moss and lichen that had grown there. Stoke and Augusta, Digby and Beatrice, Victoria and Eric, Maud and the twins, Vivien and Leona, had traveled to Co. Cork for the funeral. The family came together again on this sad occasion and there was a sense of finality in the air. A feeling that it was indeed the end of an era. Adeline's presence had somehow held them all together, even though her hold had been tenuous. It was as if the string had broken and, like a flock of birds, the Deverills were about to take to the skies, each headed for a different destination.

The Shrubs wept into their hankies, Maud sat with a face of marble. Bertie had drunk enough of his mother's cannabis tea to smile on her with indulgence, as he used to do before her unhappiness had pierced his seemingly impenetrable *joie de vivre*. Kitty cried, remembering the refuge her little sitting room had been when as a child she had fled Miss Grieve's hostile companionship in search of her grandmother's warm and certain affection. Robert took her hand and squeezed it and she was grateful. Victoria sat beside her mother, dry-eyed, thinking of all the things she was missing in London, while Elspeth's tears were shed for the grandmother she had never really known. Harry and Boysie sat together, Boysie wondering how soon they could get away, Harry wondering whether his grandmother was right about the curse of Maggie O'Leary and whether his attempts at leaving Ireland for good would only be thwarted in death. Eternity locked up in the castle was a very long time. Celia dabbed her eyes and remembered the good old days and in her sorrow they inflated and grew out of all proportion. She wondered whether she would ever be as happy in the present as she had been in the past, at Castle Deverill.

The family gathered together in the Hunting Lodge for lunch. The Rector came and gave the occasion an air of formality, like the days when Hubert and Adeline had invited Reverend Daunt to dine with tedious regularity. Bertie sat at the head. He had a cloudy look in his eyes, as if he was in fact far away and only going through the motions with his lips loose, his once beautiful face red and puffy and glistening with sweat. He had greeted Kitty with affection, surprising them both, and inquired about her comfort in the White House. Then he had asked about little Jack. When Kitty had told him he was growing into a handsome Deverill, the corners of his flabby lips had twitched and he had nodded. "Good, good." But then his mind had drifted somewhere else again.

After lunch Bertie stood up to address the family. He was

unsteady on his feet. He swayed a little as if he were on a ship, listing on the waves. "Friends and family," he began, and Kitty caught eyes with Harry and pulled a nervous face. She wasn't sure he was going to make it to the end of his speech. Harry lowered his eyes guiltily. Kitty frowned at him, but he fixed his gaze on the table and refused to look up. "It saddens me that we gather here today on this most cheerless of days, to say a fond farewell to my dear mother, Adeline. Indeed it is the end of an era. But with every ending there is a new beginning and so it shall be for all of us. Thank you to those who came from England. My grandfather always used to say the English Deverills were the lucky Deverills, or 'lucky devils' as he called you." Bertie chuckled. "In many ways he was right. But we all fought in the war, united against a common enemy, and we all suffered for England together. You lost your beloved George and we lost Rupert. Both branches of Deverills suffered greatly. Once again we were united in our grief. While the war ended in Europe, we over here had to endure the Republicans' fight for freedom. Because of it we lost our home. Our once great castle; one of the finest in Ireland. In that respect we are not the fortunate ones. But I wouldn't have had it any other way. I wouldn't have lived anywhere else. There is no place on earth more beautiful to me than the west coast of Co. Cork."

He paused and inhaled through his nostrils. The room was silent. Only eyes slid from one to the other as the family began to sense a horrible purpose to this address. "So it is, with great regret, that I announce to you all that we are to do what no landowner in his right mind would do unless in dire circumstances. We are to sell." There was a collective gasp. Kitty felt as if the breath had been knocked out of her. She glanced at her mother. Maud's thin lips were drawn into a grim line, but Kitty knew that she had persuaded her father to let the castle go. It's what she had wanted since the fire. Before the fire it had been worth holding on to, but without a castle to her name there was no point in her continuing to live here; Maud had given up on Ireland long ago.

"I know this comes as a shock to most of you," Bertie continued. "I discussed my plans with Harry and he supports me. Maud and I will move permanently to London as soon as we find a buyer for Castle Deverill. I'm sure Barton Deverill, the first Lord Deverill, will turn in his grave but it can't be helped." He swept his eyes around the room, over the astonished faces of his relatives. Maud patted his hand as if it were a rather distasteful pet. Bertie grimaced. He stared down at her cold white fingers and curled his lip. "And just when you think things couldn't get any worse, I have something else to announce." Maud's hand flew up to her throat. "I would like to formally and publicly recognize my young son, Jack Deverill. Kitty is raising him here in Ireland where he belongs. A moment of weakness for which I am not proud, but I *am* proud of my son." He smiled at Kitty, his twitching face full of remorse. "Castles, property, land and trinkets come and go but family is forever."

Maud pushed out her chair with a loud scrape, threw down her napkin and marched out of the room. No one moved. Everyone stared at Bertie, trying to comprehend what he had just announced. The room was silent. Then a shaky voice spoke from the other end of the table. It was Augusta and as usual she was a little confused.

"Can somebody tell me what the devil he said?"

AFTER ADELINE'S FUNERAL Maud fled to London in a temper. Now everyone would know about Bertie's bastard son and the shame would throw a dirty stain over their family name. She'd have to hide out in the country at Victoria's until the scandal blew over. She cursed her husband, and herself for having married him. She should have run off with the Duke of Rothmeade when she'd had the chance! At least she had managed to persuade Bertie to sell the castle. Now she could start looking for a house in London.

Kitty was devastated. Her joy at her father's decision to recognize his son was completely eclipsed by the extraordinary announcement that he was selling their home. Of course, she knew who was behind it. If it wasn't for her father's penchant for whiskey she didn't think he'd have allowed his wife to manipulate him, but Bertie had grown weak and disenchanted with his life, and alcohol had numbed his heart. As for Harry, he didn't mind what happened to Castle Deverill; as long as he was close to Boysie he was happy. Kitty felt she was the only person who cared.

"I'd buy the castle if I had the money," she said to Jack as they lay together in the bed she now knew so well. "But I don't have it. Robert doesn't have it."

Jack grinned. "Perhaps he has a rich aunt who might suddenly die."

Kitty laughed. "Really, Jack, you're wicked."

"I'd buy it for you if I could." He kissed her forehead. "And I'd rebuild it brick by brick."

"I know you would." She traced her nails over his chest. "I'd like to live with you in the castle, Jack. A normal life. No sneaking around. You, me and little Jack."

506 · SANTA MONTEFIORE

"Then we'd release all those ghosts of yours."

"Yes. They'd all be free. It would be much less crowded."

"We'd restore the gardens. Buy lots of horses. Make lots of children."

Kitty sighed. "Oh Jack . . ."

He gently pushed her back onto the pillow and gazed into her eyes. "We'd have lots of children to fill up the castle."

"If only . . ." But he was running his hand over her belly.

"I want more than this, Kitty. I want more than stolen moments with you." He pressed his lips to the gentle rise of her stomach. "I want you body and soul."

"You already have my body and my soul."

He brought his head up and looked at her steadily. "Then I want your hand," he said. "I want to be your husband and I want to walk down the street in Ballinakelly with you on my arm, for all the world to see. This isn't enough anymore."

Chapter 36

When Bridie saw the Irish coastline from the first-class deck of the steamship she was overcome by a surge of emotion that rose in her chest like a great tide and broke onto her cheeks in waves of tears. A kindly gentleman in a felt hat put his hand into his inside coat pocket and pulled out a hand-kerchief. She took it with gratitude and blew her nose. "It's a grand sight, is it not?" he said, resting his eyes on those familiar cliffs like a gull settling into her nest.

"I've come home," said Bridie. "I can't believe I've finally come home."

"Indeed, and there's no place like it in all the world."

"Have you been away long?"

"Very long," he said, sighing with pleasure. "I've been away fifty years, no less."

Bridie stopped crying. "That *is* long," she said with feeling.

"The longest road out is the shortest road home," he said,

and with a smile he left her on the deck to contemplate her future.

Bridie arrived at the Shelbourne Hotel in Dublin. A grand Regency red-brick mansion overlooking St. Stephen's Green, the beautiful gardens where Bridie had often walked during the months she had worked for Lady Rowan-Hampton. She hadn't known then that she would leave Dublin a disgraced maid and return three years later a lady of great wealth with cases of fine clothes and a maid of her own.

She was greeted by a porter who escorted her into the foyer, where crimson carpets, elaborate moldings and a sweeping staircase gave the famous hotel an air of luxury and class. The hotel staff smiled at her warmly and welcomed her as if she were a duchess, while the porter clicked his fingers and summoned for help with all the expensive luggage she had brought with her. Bridie, dressed in a sumptuous coat and cloche hat, a long string of pearls hanging down to her waist, returned their hospitality with a gracious nod and a small curling of the lips, as she had seen Kitty's mother do, and in Bridie's opinion Maud Deverill was the most superior lady she had ever seen. She signed with her right hand, making sure that her left hand was placed conspicuously on the counter so that her diamond engagement ring and gold marriage band shone brightly to show everyone that not only was she wealthy but she was wealthy *and* respectable. She answered questions politely as the man behind the desk checked her in. "Yes, from New York . . . such a long way, but a most comfortable crossing . . . yes, I'm sure I'll be very comfortable here, thank you . . . no, I don't know how long I will be staying. More than a week, certainly."

As soon as Bridie reached the suite of rooms she flopped

onto the bed as Rosetta drew her a bath and waited for the luggage. She gazed at the exquisite furniture, the vase of bright flowers on the desk, the silk curtains and rich carpet and took a deep and satisfied breath. How she had imagined places like this from her small bed in Ballinakelly. How she had longed for a new life, perhaps in London as Kitty's lady's maid, if she was lucky. But how could she have possibly known that she would be here now, Mrs. Lockwood, heiress and widow, an independent, well-traveled woman, of only twenty-five? She closed her eyes and smiled. She'd find her child and then her world would be complete.

Bridie slept better than she had ever slept. She was home, in Ireland, on the same mass of land as her mother, her nanna and her brothers. She breathed a sigh of relief and allowed pleasant dreams to wrap their feathered wings around her.

In the morning she felt recharged after the long voyage across the Atlantic. Rosetta was up and dressed and had already laid out her mistress's clothes. Bridie left her companion to eat in the suite and went downstairs to breakfast in the dining room. She wanted to be part of Dublin life. She wanted to see people. The hotel was suitably busy. Stylish ladies and expensively dressed gentlemen sat at round tables conversing in low voices. The clinking of china teacups on saucers and silver cutlery onto plates gave the room a genteel dignity as waiters and waitresses brought in mouthwatering dishes and carried out the empty ones. As soon as Bridie appeared the head waiter bade her good morning and escorted her to a table at the window where the sunlight streamed in through the glass. Outside, the street was full of activity with cars, horses and carriages, and people going about their business, walking up and down the sidewalks and setting off into the gardens. No one broke off their conversation to stare at her; there was only the odd admiring glance from both women and men as they took in her fashionable attire, chic haircut and probably the fact that she was on her own. But she didn't think she looked out of place. She fitted in. She was one of them.

She smiled at the waiter and ordered a cup of tea and a hearty breakfast. He handed her the *Irish Times* and went off with her order. Bridie glanced at the paper. She didn't particularly want to read it but, as she was alone with no one to talk to, she flicked her eyes over the main stories. Then, further into the newspaper, one story caught her attention. *Lord Deverill of Ballinakelly to sell tragic Castle Deverill.* Bridie read the article in horror, burying her face so deeply in the paper that she didn't notice the waiter bring her tea and pour her a cup.

She read how the castle had been burned by the revolutionaries during the Troubles. She learned that Lord Deverill had been killed in the fire and that Lady Deverill had passed away only a couple of weeks ago. She learned that the present Lord Deverill had found the cost of living there too great and had decided to sell and move to London. There was a black-and-white photograph of the castle ruins and an old picture of Lord and Lady Deverill at the Dublin Horse Show. Bridie gazed into the face of the man she had loved and felt the prickle of tears behind her eyes. He had taken her innocence but she had let him. She had enjoyed every minute of their encounters. Then she remembered the brutality of his dismissal of her, as if she was an inconvenience, and her heart hardened. She had given birth to his children. A little girl who had died and a little boy who lived, and he had packed her off to America without even saying good-bye, leaving his son to languish in a convent, hiding his secret behind the discreet walls of the Church. But Bridie had come back, determined to right this wrong. She was no longer young and naïve. She had come to claim what was hers. Only God had the right to take him from her.

She folded the paper away and sipped her tea. If the castle had been destroyed, her mother would have lost her job. Had she been forced to find employment elsewhere? Or had the money Bridie sent been enough? What had become of Kitty? Did she still live in the Hunting Lodge? Bridie ate her breakfast in a fever of anxiety. What had become of them all?

After breakfast she and Rosetta set out in a taxi to visit the Convent of Our Lady Queen of Heaven, tucked away in a remote corner of Dublin. The sight of those walls made Bridie's palms sweat. She had come here to give birth and she had left without her babies. What had taken place behind those brown walls was unspeakable. She asked Rosetta to remain in the taxi while she went to inquire about her child. Rosetta watched her pull the knocker on the great door and wondered why she needed to visit a convent and why it had made her so nervous.

The door was opened by a nun in a dark blue habit. Bridie told her why she had come and that she wished to speak to the Mother Superior. The nun looked a little awkward but invited her inside nonetheless. She followed her down a corridor. The familiar smell of the place, a sort of dampness mixed with detergent and candlewax, made her head swim. She recalled being brought here after her waters had broken. For a moment she felt the same sense of confusion, the same feeling of alienation, the same *fear,* and she had to concentrate on breathing regularly to stem the rising nausea in her stomach. She was asked to sit in a waiting room. There was a measly bunch of yellow flowers in a glass on the coffee table and a meager fireplace, which was empty. Bridie sat on the hard sofa and knitted her fingers. She kept reminding herself that she was a wealthy woman now. If they wouldn't give her her baby she'd *buy* him back.

At last an older nun appeared. She smiled kindly in her blue habit. Bridie's spirits rose at the pleasant expression on the woman's face and sensed that she'd be only too happy to return her child. "Mrs. Lockwood," she said, sitting down on the edge of a chair. "My name is Sister Agatha. I understand that you have come back for your son."

"Yes, I have," said Bridie, trying to hear the woman speak over the thumping of her heart.

"You were Bridie Doyle, were you not?"

"Yes."

"I remember your son. A bonny baby he was."

"Yes."

"And I remember the little girl, God save her soul." Sister Agatha sighed. "I wish I could help you, but I cannot. You see, your child isn't here."

The world spun away from Bridie. She had never anticipated that her baby would have *gone*. "Where is he?"

"He's gone to a very happy home. We always take the utmost care to place our children with the very best families."

Bridie put her fingers to her mouth to stifle a moan. She stared at the nun, not knowing what to say. She shook her head. "No . . . no . . . he can't have gone!"

"Even if I knew where he was," Sister Agatha continued, "I wouldn't be able to tell you. That family adopted your baby in good faith. It wouldn't be right to give away their details. You have to let him go, Mrs. Lockwood."

"But I can't," Bridie croaked. "He's my son." In a flash she saw the little face in swaddling as if he were before her now. She could smell the vanilla scent of his skin. She could almost touch it. "Oh Lord Jaysus, what have I done?"

Sister Agatha stood up. "Please take your time, Mrs. Lockwood. I'm sorry for your distress." She had clearly witnessed this scene many times before and was unmoved by it. Bridie put her hand to her forehead and cried. Her whole body shook as she realized she would never see her baby again.

A moment later Sister Agatha returned with a glass of water. "There is no hurry to leave. If you would like to visit the chapel, you are most welcome. Sister Margaret will show you where to go and see you out."

"May I at least visit my daughter's grave?" Bridie asked.

Sister Agatha's lips thinned into a hard line. "There is no grave, Mrs. Lockwood. But you are welcome to pray for her soul in the chapel."

Bridie sat on the sofa until her breath grew ragged and her grief was reduced to the odd hiccup. She realized that Sister Margaret was waiting in the doorway.

"I'd like to visit the chapel," she said, standing up. At least she could pray for her daughter's soul.

"Please, follow me," said Sister Margaret. Bridie trailed her through the building to a courtyard where the nuns grew their own vegetables. It was a damp, miserable site and Bridie hurried on, not wishing to spend more time than necessary in this unforgiving place.

The chapel was warm, with a high, vaulted ceiling and two

graceful colonnades of arches on either side. Candles burned, giving the place an inviting glow, and the air smelled pleasantly of incense. Bridie walked down the aisle, crossing herself in front of the altar, before making her way to the table where she could light a candle of her own. Swallowing back her sorrow she lit two, closing her eyes and sending up a silent prayer to God. "Please help me, Lord. Please look after the little one who died and help me find the one who lived. As God is my witness, I will not rest until I find my baby. I will not give up. With the help of your angels I will bring my baby home."

She stood a moment staring at the richly colored paintings of Mary and the Saints depicted on the walls. Then her eyes settled on a surprisingly lavish gold cross, encrusted with precious gems that sparkled in the candlelight, hanging in glorious splendor behind the altar. It was magnificent, luxurious even, and quite out of place in that simple chapel. She wiped her wet face with the back of her hand and wondered how the nuns had come by it. Then she went to the front pew, knelt down on the cushion and said the Lord's Prayer. When she was finished she asked Sister Margaret to show her out. There was nothing left for her here but painful memories and disappointment.

Sister Margaret showed her to the door. As she opened it, she threw a furtive glance down the corridor, then put her hand on Bridie's arm. "I know what happened to your son," she whispered urgently.

Bridie grabbed her. "What? What happened to him?"

"A man came and took him."

"What man? Who?"

"His name was Michael, that much I heard."

Bridie felt her heart surge with gratitude and hope. "Michael? Michael Doyle?"

"I don't know. He was big, burly, black curls . . ."

"Yes, that's my brother." Bridie smiled through her tears. "Oh thank you, Sister Margaret. I won't forget your kindness. May the Good Lord shower you with a thousand blessings."

"No need, Mrs. Lockwood. I'm just happy that I was able to help you."

Bridie hurried out to the taxi, where Rosetta was waiting for her and beginning to grow anxious. "Is everything all right?" she asked as Bridie climbed in beside her.

"Everything is just grand," Bridie replied. "We will go back to the hotel. There are a few things I need to see to. When I'm done we will leave for Ballinakelly."

"Ballinakelly?"

"Yes, Rosetta. I'm going home."

Bridie returned to the hotel and tore out the article from the *Irish Times* about Lord Deverill selling the castle. She had enough money to buy that castle ten times over, she mused. She could rebuild it; restore it to its former glory. *That* would show them all, it would. Show them that she would never allow anyone to treat her the way Lord Deverill had treated her. Never allow anyone to call her a tinker again. She'd be mistress of a grand castle with a grand history and it would be *her* descendants who would live on in it and share the stories of the illustrious Deverill past. And one day, many years into the future, it would be *her* family name that people would talk about.

"I'd like to send a telegram to Mr. Beaumont Williams in New York," she told the receptionist.

Leaving her luggage in the suite, she took the train to Cork, remembering the journey to Dublin when she had sat in third class with a small bag, a growing belly and a heart full of anxiety. Now she was comfortable in first class. Everyone was polite to her. No one could do enough to please her. The difference money made to a person's life was immeasurable.

From Cork she took a hackney cab to Ballinakelly, under an hour's drive away. As she neared her home town her heart began to race. The terrain grew familiar. Those bumpy roads, those rocky hills, the heather and gorse, gray-stone walls, bushy hedges and fields full of woolly sheep all whispered to her, their voices calling her home.

At last she saw the white farmhouse, nestled in the crook of the hill beside the barns where Michael and Sean kept the horse and farming equipment. The field was full of cows, grazing on the long grass. Behind the hills the sky was a pale, watery blue embellished with cotton-wool clouds. It looked just the same. Bridie's heart stalled. "This is where I grew up," she told Rosetta.

"It's so pretty," said the maid. "And so green."

Bridie laughed. "That's because it rains all the time."

The car drove down the stony track and stopped outside the house. Bridie paid the driver and carried her bag to the door. She didn't bother to knock, but pushed it open. There, sitting in her usual chair by the hearth, was Old Mrs. Nagle. When the grandmother saw Bridie she looked at her blankly. "It's me, Nanna. Bridie." Rosetta stood behind her, wondering why she called herself Bridie and not Bridget.

Old Mrs. Nagle squinted. "Bridie?" she asked. Then her voice quivered. "Bridie? *Our* Bridie?"

"Oh, Nanna, I'm your Bridie all right. I've come home."

She knelt on the floor beside her grandmother and wrapped her arms around her. She felt as small and frail as a little mouse.

"Well, don't you look grand," said Old Mrs. Nagle. "You've done well in America, thank the Lord."

At that moment Mrs. Doyle hurried into the room. "That's not Bridie?" she exclaimed, her eyes welling with tears.

"Mam!" Bridie forgot that she was a woman of wealth. She forgot that she was Mrs. Lockwood with her fine clothes and expensive shoes. She was Bridie Doyle again, running into the arms of her mother.

"Well, would you look at you!" Mrs. Doyle's voice broke. She took her daughter's face in her hands and stared into her features, searching for her lost child.

"I'm rich, Mam. I can buy you anything you want. Anything at all!"

"God save us from wealth, Bridie Doyle. Money only brings misery. Only hard work and a love of God bring any kind of happiness." She looked at Bridie, but her daughter was too distracted to notice the pain in her mother's eyes. "Have you come home, Bridie?"

"Where's Michael?" Bridie asked, longing to see her son. Old Mrs. Nagle bowed her head. Mrs. Doyle put her hand to her mouth. Bridie looked from one to the other.

"Michael is at Mount Melleray in Waterford, Bridie," said her mother in a quiet voice.

"Where?" Bridie sank into a chair.

"Father Quinn sent him to the Abbey to cure him of the drink, God save us."

Old Mrs. Nagle crossed herself. "He's in the Lord's care, Bridie. The Devil can't touch him now."

Bridie wanted to ask about her child. If he had taken him from the convent, where would he have brought him if not here? "I read that they burned the castle," she said numbly.

"Oh, they did indeed. A dreadful thing it was, too. Now Lord Deverill is selling the estate."

"Tell her about the child, God save us!" said Old Mrs. Nagle.

"What child?" Bridie clung on to a small shard of hope.

"Lord Deverill has a bastard boy," said Mrs. Doyle, shaking her head disapprovingly. "No one can talk of anything else."

"Who's the mother?"

"He didn't say. But the boy is being raised by Kitty Deverill, now Mrs. Trench."

"God save us!" Old Mrs. Nagle exclaimed again, crossing herself more passionately.

Bridie's spirits revived. "Kitty married Mr. Trench?"

"She did indeed."

"Are they in Ireland?"

"In the White House. You know, where Mr. Rupert Deverill used to live."

"*Poor* Mr. Rupert Deverill," said Old Mrs. Nagle. "He often brought me a salmon and he always brought it gutted. A grand creature."

"Have you seen the boy?"

"No, but I hear he's a bonny lad with red hair like his sister and grandmother."

"Oh Michael," Bridie sighed, quietly thanking him for bringing her son home. "What's his name?"

"Jack," said Mrs. Doyle.

Bridie was stung. "Jack?"

"A grand name, is it not?" Now Bridie knew who had named him and she bristled with jealousy. "You must be hungry." Mrs. Doyle turned to Rosetta who still stood by the door. "Who's your friend?"

"This is Rosetta, my companion," Bridie replied.

"You have a companion? God save us!" said Mrs. Doyle in disapproval. "Well, you might as well make yourselves at home. Bridie, you can have your old room and Rosetta will have to share your bed or sleep on the floor. We don't have separate rooms for servants here. 'T'was far from maids and companions you were reared." She shook her head in displeasure. "I think America has spoiled you, Bridie. The world is gone red mad." Bridie caught Rosetta's eye. If her mother knew only *half* the truth, she'd send her off to Father Quinn to confess her sins and she'd spend the rest of her life in a heap of Hail Marys.

THAT EVENING SEAN returned for tea. He took one look at the pretty, amber-skinned Rosetta and his mood lifted. She was the first Italian to ever visit Ballinakelly. Rosetta instantly became more animated and her cheeks flushed a pretty pink. Bridie sat in the familiar room, with what was left of her family, and let the memories close in around her; but they felt distant, as if they belonged to another life long ago. She tasted the food she had loved as a child, but now it lacked flavor and she left half on her plate, much to her mother's annoyance. She knelt for prayer, but the floor was hard on her knees and she couldn't concentrate on the words. She visualized her father and Michael talking at the table with their heads together, their conflicting ideas creating sparks, and tried to feel part of that picture. But the little girl drinking buttermilk on the foot of the stair had nothing to do with her now. She might just as well have been a stranger.

Later, as she listened to the familiar sounds of the night, she didn't find comfort in them, but an unsettling sense of alienation. She wasn't Bridie Doyle anymore. She had grown out of that skin, like a hairy molly out of its chrysalis. She didn't belong here in this house either.

Chapter 37

The following day Bridie went alone to the White House in Sean's pony and trap, leaving Rosetta to help her mother in the house, while Sean found any excuse to keep coming back inside. It was another warm September day. The light was soft and autumnal, the wind smelling strongly of the sea. Bridie wanted to take pleasure from the echoes of the past that came to her from every corner of the land, but all she could think about now was her son.

The blood pumped feverishly through her veins. Her nerves churned her stomach with nausea. She didn't know what she was going to say to Kitty, now that Kitty knew the truth. She certainly didn't know what she was going to say to her son. She imagined him, as a three-and-a-half-year-old now, running into her arms, and she held on to that image to stop herself from losing heart and turning back. She tried to feel gratitude toward Kitty for looking after him; after all, he could have been sent away to strangers, lost without a trace. At least here, she knew where he was and that he was in a good home, but she couldn't help feeling resentful. He shouldn't have been taken away from her in the first place.

At last she saw the White House through the trees. It was positioned up a drive on a hill, with a clear view of the sea. She climbed down and tethered her pony to the gate post. As she walked up the drive she wondered what had become of Jack. Kitty had married her tutor, the man she had written off as dull and humorless. She wondered why she hadn't eloped with Jack. The fact that she hadn't gave Bridie a small sense of triumph, a malicious feeling of satisfaction. Neither of them had been able to have him. There was a certain justice in that.

Suddenly she heard the sound of voices. A woman's laughter and a child's squeals of delight. Bridie walked toward it. As the sounds grew louder she realized that she hadn't dared breathe. She was holding her breath in dread and fear and anticipation. Then she saw him and she let out a deep moan. A little boy in a pair of brown trousers and a white shirt, a cap on his head like the one Jack used to wear, trotted along beside a woman, holding her hand, but it wasn't Kitty. Bridie clutched her heart and stopped walking, taking in the sight of this small stranger who carried her blood in his veins. He was handsome and his smile broke her heart all over again. Then Kitty appeared in the doorway. She opened her arms and grinned. The little boy shouted "Kitty" and ran unsteadily toward her. With a whoop of delight Kitty swept him up and cuddled him against her bosom. She took off his cap and put it on her own head. The boy giggled and reached up to grab it. Before Bridie could digest the scene, Kitty had retreated inside, taking the boy with her.

Bridie stood rooted to the ground with a deep and searing

pain burning in her chest. The woman who had been holding Jack's hand turned and saw her. Bridie must have cut an unlikely figure there on the drive, alone, clearly distraught. The woman shielded her eyes from the sun with her hand and walked toward her. "Hello?" she said. "Can I help you?"

Bridie struggled to find her voice. "I'm sorry. I think I've come to the wrong address," she managed before turning and fleeing down the drive. The woman frowned as she watched her disappear in a hurry through the gate at the bottom.

Once out of the gate Bridie slumped onto the grass, put her face in her hands and sobbed. Her hope had turned to vapor. In her dreams she had imagined him a baby still. But he was a little boy and in his eyes Kitty was his mother, even though he hadn't called her by that name. Had she really believed that Kitty would rejoice at seeing her and hand the child back? Had she really been so foolish as to expect Kitty not to love the child as her own? Bridie might be the boy's natural mother but Kitty was his mother in every other way and with that thought her heart twisted with a fierce and desperate jealousy. She clutched her stomach and let her despair engulf her.

After a while she stood up shakily. As she untied the horse's reins she heard the sound of footsteps behind her. She turned. It was Kitty, pale and serious in the sunlight. "Bridie?" she said, stepping forward. "Is that you?"

Bridie stared back at the woman who had once been as dear to her as a sister and recognized the fear in her eyes. It was wild and undisguised, like the foxes people had always likened her to, and it opened a canyon between them. "Aye, it's me, Kitty."

"You've come back," Kitty croaked.

"I've come back for my son," Bridie replied with emphasis,

lifting her chin, and Kitty noticed how the years in America had hardened her face almost beyond all recognition.

"You've been gone a long time," Kitty reminded her. "He's a little boy now."

"He's *my* little boy."

"You gave him to *me*, Bridie. You left him on my doorstep and I vowed to raise him and love him as my own. I sacrificed everything for him, for *you*."

"I didn't give him to you," Bridie replied tightly. "Michael did."

"Michael?" The mention of her brother's name made Kitty shudder.

"The nuns took him away from me. They stole my child." Bridie's voice rose a tone in anguish. "Michael rescued him and put him into your safekeeping so that, one day, when I was able, I could come back and find him. Well, I'm here now. He's my child, Kitty. Where is your compassion?"

"It was compassion that propelled me to give up the man I loved and do my duty for your son. He was left on my doorstep because he's a Deverill. My father has recognized him. He is my brother and he belongs with me."

"But *I* am his mother," Bridie insisted.

"You gave birth to him but you abandoned him."

"I was left no choice."

"Jack believes he doesn't have a mother, Bridie."

Kitty's words, although delivered softly, dealt Bridie a mighty blow. Her hand flew to her throat and she stifled a cry. "You told him I was dead?" she gasped.

"What would you have had me do? I could not have told him that his mother abandoned him in a convent."

"There had to be another way?" Bridie groaned.

"He prays for you," Kitty said softly, suddenly suffering a pang of guilt at the sight of Bridie's distress. "He prays every night for his mother who looks down on him from the stars."

"God save us," Bridie wailed.

"I'm only thinking of Jack."

Bridie rounded on her friend with fury. "You're only thinking of yourself, Kitty. You stole Jack O'Leary and now you have stolen my son as well!" she cried.

"Don't bring Jack O'Leary into this," Kitty retorted, any sympathy for Bridie suddenly evaporating. "He never belonged to you in the first place."

"Well, now he belongs to neither of us," said Bridie with grim satisfaction. "I will not let this matter go, Kitty. Do you hear? This is not over." She climbed into the trap and shook the reins. "The years in America have given me not only great wealth but great strength. Jack Deverill is my son. He belongs to me. I had to leave him once, but I won't do it a second time."

When she had gone, and only when she had gone, did Kitty give in to her pain. She fell to her knees, wrapped her arms around her body and howled.

BERTIE PUT DOWN the telephone and stared into his glass of whiskey with an aching sense of hopelessness. So, the castle was sold. Just like that. It hadn't taken long. The buyer was very insistent that the whole business be done as quickly as possible, according to his solicitor, and in the utmost secrecy. He had paid the full price. He hadn't even tried to negotiate. Bertie wasn't sure why the buyer wanted the purchase to be secret, but he didn't inquire. He was so full of sorrow he just wanted the deal signed so that he didn't have to think about it anymore.

"The castle's sold? Already?" Maud exclaimed into the telephone. "Who's bought it, Bertie?" When she hung up she strode into the sitting room, where Victoria and Eric sat in evening dress, drinking sherry. "Can you believe it, somebody's already bought the castle!"

"Good Lord," said Eric. "That was swift."

"The buyer is very keen to have it as quickly as possible," Maud informed them. She sat down and picked up her half-drunk glass of sherry. "Well, so long as we get our money, I don't care."

"Do we know who's bought it?" Victoria asked.

"No, Bertie says it's a secret."

"How silly. Why would anyone want to keep the purchase of a castle secret?" Victoria sniffed.

"I don't know but we'll find out in the end," said Maud.

"Perhaps he thinks you won't sell it to him if you know who he is," said Eric, scratching his beard.

"That's a good point," Victoria agreed. "Who *wouldn't* we want to buy it?"

Maud shook her head. Her white-blond hair, cut into a stylish bob, didn't move. "I don't think I'd mind who bought it."

"Really?" said Victoria. "Oh, I think you'd be a bit peeved if a member of the family bought it. Like Digby, for example."

"Well, of course I wouldn't like Digby to buy it, because if a Deverill is going to live in there it's going to be Harry. But Digby doesn't want it. Beatrice certainly doesn't want it either.

They have Deverill Rising. Why on earth would they want a pile of old stones?"

"Kitty?" Victoria suggested.

"They don't have the money," said Maud meanly.

"Grace?"

Maud turned to Victoria and blanched. "Grace Rowan-Hampton? Is that a joke?"

Victoria shrugged. "She's rich enough to buy it."

"Why would *she* want it?"

"Because it's beautiful," said Victoria. "I wouldn't want it because I don't want to live in Ireland, but, if you love Ireland like she does, you'd prize Castle Deverill above everywhere else. Of course she'd want it."

Grace loved Bertie so it would make sense to rebuild his castle. Maud put her fingers to her lips and gasped. "Do you think . . . ?" The implications were too horrible to consider.

DIGBY RETURNED TO the dining room, where his wife was enjoying dinner with Stoke and Augusta. "Somebody's already bought the castle," he said, sitting down and flicking his napkin over his knee. "But Bertie says he doesn't know who."

"How wonderful for Maud," said Beatrice. "She must be delighted it's all happened so quickly. You know she was looking at a house in Chester Square only yesterday."

"What's poor Bertie going to do?" Stoke asked. "He can't abide the woman."

"I don't imagine they'll have the money to buy two houses," said Beatrice. "They're just going to have to learn to live with each other again."

"Maud is a very avaricious woman," said Augusta. "I could have told him that before he married her and saved him all the trouble."

"They were happy at the beginning," Digby argued.

"But then they weren't," Augusta added firmly. "It's no good being happy at the beginning. Life has a middle and an end. I'm near the end now and I can safely say, can I not, that in spite of all I have suffered Stoke and I are still happy."

"Blissfully happy," Stoke agreed *un*happily.

"One mustn't allow one's eye to stray," Augusta continued stridently. "You see, Maud was much too beautiful to remain devoted to one man. Wasn't it Eddie Rothmeade who caught her eye?"

"Eddie Rothmeade?" Digby repeated. "I've never heard such tripe."

"Oh yes, it was indeed. Adeline and I discussed it a great deal. There was a moment I thought they might run off into the sunset and never be seen again. Maud was that sort of woman. But Eddie tired of her. Now Bertie has tired of her too. Vain women like that eventually wear a man down. A woman must give as well as take in a marriage but Maud doesn't know much about giving."

"Good Lord, Augusta, you never told me about that," said Stoke, his winged mustache twitching like a walrus's snout.

"That's because Adeline would have killed me. Now she's dead, she can't."

Augusta dabbed her lips with her napkin. "I'm a deep well of information, Stoke dear. But I'll take all my other secrets to the grave, I suspect. Pity. I do hope I live long enough to find out who has bought the castle. I'm frightfully curious."

Chapter 38

Co. Cork, Ireland, 1925

The little boys looked at each other in bewilderment. The woman had clearly stated that she was going to rebuild the castle. That would mean an end to their games. They listened harder. "To think I used to play in those rooms. I used to watch the glamorous ladies arriving for the Summer Ball in their fine gowns and sparkling jewels and marvel at the beauty of it all. Because it really *was* beautiful then. I don't think there was anywhere else in the world more beautiful than Castle Deverill at that time of the year, on that night, when the sun was setting and turning it all to gold. You can't imagine how magnificent it was. But I remember. I've always remembered. That's why I wanted to preserve it. I couldn't bear to see it go to anyone else." She sighed and shook her head. "But now it's mine. I will rebuild it stone by stone, brick by brick and bring back those glory days. We'll bring them back together because this wouldn't have been possible if it hadn't been for you. Oh, Archie, you're just wonderful to me." Celia took his hand. "And our children will play with Kitty's just like *we* used to do. History will repeat itself. One big happy family." Archie put his arm around her and smiled. "One big happy family," she repeated with pleasure, conveniently forgetting the centuries of family curses, brutality, greed and self-indulgence. "Just the way it should be. A Deverill's castle is his kingdom, after all."

And so it was that Deverill money had gone full circle, because when Digby had rescued Archie Mayberry in return for taking back his disgraceful wife he had given him the means with which he would eventually show his gratitude for their unexpectedly happy marriage. In some ways, one could say that an empty-headed girl wearing nothing but a pair of white silk gloves had saved Castle Deverill.

Epilogue

Connecticut, America, 1925

The little girl with dark hair and freckles lay on her stomach on the lawn and stared at the yellow flower. Around it danced a tiny, quivering orb of light. She smiled. Every time she blinked the orb moved somewhere else, as if it enjoyed the game. The child reached out her hand and tried to catch it but the orb jumped away. She tried again: this time she thought she had it. But when she opened her fingers there was nothing there. The orb remained, hovering around the flower.

"She's been staring at that flower for ages," said the child's mother from the window of the house. "Is that normal?"

"She just loves nature, Pam darling, I wouldn't worry."

"I'm not worried, Mom. It's just, you know, when you adopt a child you never quite know what you're getting."

"She just loves flowers," said the older woman.

Pam frowned. "Perhaps. But it's as if she sees something else.

Something more than just the flower. Look how she's trying to grab it."

"It's probably a little bug."

Pam shook her head. "No, it's not. I've watched her before. She has an imaginary friend."

Pam's mother smiled. "All children have imaginary friends. Children are very inventive. It's very normal that an only child should invent a buddy to play with. After all, she is a twin, don't forget. Perhaps she senses the loss of her brother."

"I don't know . . . I have a funny feeling she sees things other people don't see."

"She's happy, right?" said Pam's mother.

"Yes, she sure is," said Pam.

"Then you don't need to worry, darling. So long as she's happy, everything will be just fine."

"I'm sure you're right," Pam agreed with a sigh. However, she continued to frown as she watched her little daughter. "I feel so blessed. It was a miracle that a newborn baby girl should be available at the very moment we arrived in Dublin. Sister Agatha was so kind to let us take her. You know, she said it was breaking every rule but Larry can be very persuasive."

"Once he'd promised to embellish their dreary little chapel with the biggest golden cross Ireland has ever seen she was ready to give you as many babies as your heart desired," said Pam's mother archly. "I really don't think luck, or God, had anything to do with it."

THE CHILD GAVE up trying to catch the nature spirit. She raised her eyes to the kind woman with red hair who was Adeline Deverill. "Hello, Grandma," she said and smiled.

BANTRY BAY

As I'm sitting all alone in the gloaming,
It might have been but yesterday.
That we watched the fisher's sails all homing,
Till the little herring fleet at anchor lay.
Then the fisher girls with baskets swinging,
Came running down the old stone way.
Every lassie to her sailor lad was singing,
Ah welcome back to Bantry Bay.

Then we heard the pipers sweet note tuning,
And all the lassies turned to hear.
As they mingled with a soft voice crooning,
Till the music floated down the wooden pier.
"Save you kindly, colleens all," said the piper.
"Hands across and trip it while I play."
And the tender sound of song and merry dancing,
Stole softly over Bantry Bay.

As I'm sitting all alone in the gloaming,
The shadows of the past draw near.
And I see the lovely faces round me
That used to glad the old front pier.
Some have gone upon their last logged homing,
Some are left, but they are old and gray.
And we're waiting for the tide in the gloaming,
To sail upon the great highway.
To an isle of rest unending.
Called peacefully from Bantry Bay.

Acknowledgments

How I have adored writing this book! It's been such a challenge but so invigorating—and it fills me with immense joy to know that I'll follow the characters I have created here into two more novels!

I really have to thank the angels first, because by some wonderful magic a man called Tim Kelly was inspired to e-mail me about one of my novels just as I was thinking about writing this one. After some fabulously funny correspondence, because really, Tim is just so witty, it transpired that he was born and raised in Co. Cork, the place I had started researching for my novel. Tim is a deep well of knowledge and wisdom; he has an eye for the absurd, an almost photographic memory for detail and a sharp understanding of human nature. He soon became my mentor, my adviser and most important, my friend. I genuinely could not have even considered writing this book without him. Therefore I have dedicated the novel to him, with my love and gratitude. I am so lucky to have found him!

I would like to thank my Irish friends Emer Melody and Frank Lyons for inviting me to their home in Bandon, Co. Cork, and for driving me around the wild and beautiful countryside so that I could get inspired. We visited the most compelling ruined castles, burned down by the rebels during the Troubles, and went for long walks up and down vast white beaches accompanied only by seabirds and the wind. I returned to London full of excitement and itching to start writing about a country that has taken hold of my heart.

I would also like to thank my Anglo-Irish friend Bill Montgomery for his invaluable advice and fascinating anecdotes. We enjoyed a long lunch at Sotheby's Café in London and I wrote pages of notes and a lengthy reading list of books that would help me research Irish history. I have always loved Bill and his wonderfully flamboyant wife, Daphne, because when I was a child they were grown-ups who always had time for us. Daphne would play the piano and encourage us to sing along and Bill would talk to us as if we were adults. They were fun and eccentric and memories of the magical summer holiday we spent with them in their house in Connemara have never left me. They are two of life's treasures and I thank them both.

My parents are always on the end of the telephone ready to answer questions about anything from gardening and farming to helping me find the right word or simply to give an honest opinion on something I've written. They seem to have all the answers! My mother is the first to read the manuscript and her pen is the first to grace the pages with corrections and suggestions. It really is a labor of love, and I'm so grateful that she finds the time to do it. The older I get, the more I understand

and appreciate the value of their love. They have made me the person that I am and therefore, because my writing is an extension of who I am, I owe them everything.

My mother-in-law, April Sebag-Montefiore, was a prolific and successful writer herself when she was younger. She manages to read my husband Sebag's books, which are massive, so she deserves a huge thank-you for making time for mine! Her encouragement and wisdom are invaluable.

I'd also like to thank Nora May Cremin and Noel Coakley for their Celtic translation of the curse, Stuart Squire for the Latin translation of the family motto, Peter Nyhan for his friendship and support, Nicky de Monfort for her advice on the Anglo-Irish and Mary Tomlinson for her thorough and sensitive copyediting.

Writing is one of my greatest pleasures—the fact that I earn my living from it is all thanks to my agent and publisher. Therefore, I would like to extend my most heartfelt gratitude to Sheila Crowley at Curtis Brown—she's completely brilliant and I'm so fortunate to be one of her authors—and to the other hardworking people at Curtis Brown who make up a really unbeatable team: Katie McGowan, Sophie Harris and Rebecca Ritchie. Thank you to Ian Chapman and my editor, Suzanne Baboneau, at Simon & Schuster UK for believing in me. Together with their colleagues Clare Hey, James Horobin, Dawn Burnett, Hannah Corbett, Sara-Jade Virtue, Melissa Four, Ally Grant, Nico Poilblanc, Gill Richardson, Rumana Haider and Dominic Brendon they have turned a hobby into a greater success than I ever dreamed. Thank you!

Finally, I would like to acknowledge the three people whose love is more precious to me than anything else on earth: Sebag,

Lily and Sasha—and to give a very special thank-you to my husband for taking the time and trouble when he was so busy writing *The Romanovs* to work on the various twists and turns that have made this book such fun to write. We are great collaborators.

Insights,
Interviews
& More . . .

Meet Santa Montefiore

Eliane Fattal

SANTA MONTEFIORE was born in England. She went to Sherborne School for Girls in Dorset and studied Spanish and Italian at Exeter University. She has written sixteen bestselling novels, which have been translated into thirty different languages and have sold more than two million copies worldwide. ∾

Q&A with Santa Montefiore

Q: Santa, The Girl in the Castle *is your fifteenth novel and it is the first in a trilogy. Why did you decide to write a trilogy, and how did you set about it?*

A: After having written so many novels that stand alone I needed a challenge. There's nothing worse for a writer than boredom! If I'm bored with my work the reader will be too! So I have to constantly find ways to entertain myself because I am the person I'm writing for. I love it. I do it because I adore telling stories, but it's very easy to get into a rut of writing the same thing over and over again. I didn't want to fall into that rut. So I signed a three-book deal with Simon & Schuster and decided to write three books whose story spans about sixty years. I was a little scared at the prospect of writing such a large story. I'm so used to a book being a certain size, with the beginning, middle and end all contained within about 120,000 words, I was a little daunted about following a family over three books. But I rather enjoyed plotting it, and once I got going it all came out rather easily! ▶

Q&A with Santa Montefiore *(continued)*

Q: *The novel is set in Ireland primarily and America secondarily, and the trilogy will span the breadth of the twentieth century. What drew you to that setting and that period?*

A: Before I start writing a novel I always ask myself where I'd like to go, as I'm going to be "there" for six to eight months! It needs to be a place I know well because I don't have the time to go and live in a new country–like Spain, for example. I'd love to set a book in Spain but I haven't lived there, and although I studied Spanish at university I spent all the time I could in Argentina! It also needs to be a place that inspires me. Having written fifteen novels set in mainly Latin America, Italy and France, I wanted a different feel. Different flora and fauna, different tone, different people. I'd based *Secrets of the Lighthouse* in Connemara and adored the deep mystical feel of Ireland, so I decided to set the trilogy in County Cork. I started the book with three girls of different backgrounds all born in the year 1900. The history of Ireland is so gripping, I knew I'd made the right choice when I started researching. To write a trilogy I felt the whole story had to have its root in something dramatic. The War of Independence gave me that drama. In fact, I think it's true to say that this novel is the first book where I didn't have to invent the drama–it was already there and I just dropped my character in! As for the castle, the whole story centers on it. It's like the main character–the most dominant character–pulling everyone into its orbit.

Q: *The history of this period is complex and troubled. Did you see this as an advantage or disadvantage when you sat down to write? How did you go about researching the history?*

A: A huge advantage! But I didn't want the book to be a history lesson. The characters are living at this time and of course the events shape them, set them against each other, move them to do things they might otherwise not have done. But ultimately it's about love. I read lots of books about that time and watched movies, which were all very informative, but I was lucky, just as I started to research, a man called Tim Kelly emailed me about one of my other books that he had enjoyed and we started a regular correspondence. It turned out he was from County Cork. Not only that, he knew so much about the history that we ended up meeting, plotting the trilogy together and have become great friends. I couldn't have done it without him!

Q: *Did you learn anything that particularly surprised you during the writing of the novel?*

A: I learned too many things to write down here. I really knew so little about that time, but I think I learned more ▶

about how the Irish lived from Tim. He has so many wonderful stories of characters he grew up with, some of which are in the book, but many are waiting to go into part three somehow, that I would have to say that the Doyle family surprised me the most. I couldn't have begun to write about them without Tim on the other end of the line!

Q: *Kitty and Bridie are wonderful characters. They are from different worlds, though their lives play out under the same roof. You write about the world behind the "green baize door"—can you tell us a bit about that world and what it is that fascinates you about it as a writer?*

A: I'm interested in people full stop. People from all walks of life. I thought it would be interesting to write a book about three women from different backgrounds. The Anglo-Irish daughter of the castle, the Irish daughter of the cook and the posh flighty first cousin who lives in London. Although we never had a green baize door growing up, I spent a lot of time in houses that did. Behind it was the staff's domain. But I'm no more fascinated by them as by those on the other side. I suppose the spice of life is in the variety—for my reader as well as for myself!

Q: Bridie travels to America and escapes her life in Ireland. How important is that idea of escape to you as a writer? Do you travel to the locations in your novels to get a sense of them in real life?

A: Much more interesting to me than escape is longing for home once you've gone! My characters all long for Castle Deverill before the Great War when everything was golden. They look back on that time as an era of harmony and happiness. When Bridie is sent to America she longs for home and her whole life is really a journey back and a yearning for things to be the way they were, which, of course, can never be, because *she* is no longer that girl. When Kitty goes to London she is consumed by homesickness. Her heart is in Ireland and she is miserable away from it. Celia endures great hardship in the second book and suffers the same longing for those golden summers before everything went wrong. I find that longing for the past and for home very evocative because I've felt like that so many times in my life. As for locations, I know them all already. I only ever choose to write about places that I'm familiar with, otherwise I don't feel confident about bringing them to life.

Q&A with Santa Montefiore *(continued)*

Q: How would the landscape around Castle Deverill have changed since 1925? Would your characters recognize it if they were to see it today?

A: I think the places I write about, rural towns and villages, have changed little and yes, they would recognize them, but of course there has been change. We all hate change! They'd have a good bitch and say that things were better in their day!

Q: Most of us find escapism in books. What novels did you read as inspiration for this trilogy?

A: I read *Troubles* by J. G. Farrell, Leon Uris's *Trinity*, *Walled Gardens* by Annabel Davis-Goff, *Star of the Sea* by Joseph O'Connor and another I'll have to look up when I get home!

Q: You have finished writing the second novel in the trilogy, and at the time of this interview you are working on the third novel. Can you give us a little hint about where the trilogy will finish?

A: In the third book everyone returns to County Cork for the final scenes. The characters (who are still living) are faced with their pasts but also with the great change that has taken place to them and Castle Deverill. The ghosts, well, all I can really say about them is that the ending will be surprising. It's not what you think! ∽

The Girl in the Castle Playlist

"ARWEN AND ARAGORN"

David Arkenstone from the movie *The Lord of the Rings*

"BELLA'S TRUCK/FLORIDA"

Howard Shore from the Twilight movie *Eclipse*

"BRAVEHEART–FOR THE LOVE OF A PRINCESS"

The City of Prague Philharmonic Orchestra from *The Symphonic Celtic Album*

"CASPAR: CASPAR'S LULLABY"

Joel McNeely and the Royal Scottish National Orchestra and Chorus from *Titanic and Other Film Scores of James Horner*

"CELTIC SUNSET"

Fridrik Karlsson from the album *Celtic Sunset*

"COMPROMISE/BELLA'S THEME"

Howard Shore from the Twilight movie *Eclipse*

"DANTE'S PRAYER"

Loreena McKennitt from the album *The Book of Secrets*

"ELANOR"

Howard Shore from the movie *The Lord of the Rings: The Return of the King*

The Girl in the Castle Playlist *(continued)*

"EOWYN'S DREAM"

Howard Shore from the movie *The Lord of the Rings: The Return of the King*

"EVENSTAR"

Howard Shore from the movie The *Lord of the Rings: The Two Towers*

"THE FELLOWSHIP OF THE RING: MAY IT BE"

Crouch End Festival Chorus and the City of Prague Philharmonic Orchestra from the movie *The Lord of the Rings*

"FLIGHT FROM EDORAS"

Howard Shore from the movie *The Lord of the Rings The Return of the King*

"FOUNDATIONS OF STONE"

Howard Shore from the movie *The Lord of the Rings: The Two Towers*

"THE GRACE OF UNDÓMIEL"

Howard Shore from the movie *The Lord of the Rings: The Return of the King*

"HIGHLANDER"

The City of Prague Philharmonic Orchestra from *The Symphonic Celtic Album*

"THE HIGHWAYMAN"

Loreena McKennitt from the album *The Book of Secrets*

"HONOR HIM"

Bruce Fowler, Elizabeth Finch, Gavin Greenaway, Hans Zimmer, Jack Smalley, Ladd McIntosh, Lisa Gerrard and The Lyndhurst Orchestra, and Walt Fowler and Yvonne S. Moriarty from the movie *Gladiator*

"THE HOUSE OF HEALING"

Howard Shore from the movie *The Lord of the Rings: The Return of the King*

"JACOB BLACK"

Howard Shore from the Twilight movie *Eclipse*

"JASPER"

Howard Shore from the Twilight movie *Eclipse*

"JOURNEY TO THE CROSS"

Howard Shore from the movie *The Lord of the Rings: The Return of the King*

"THE JOURNEY TO THE GREY HEAVENS"

Howard Shore from the movie *The Lord of the Rings: The Return of the King*

"LA SERENISSIMA"

Loreena McKennitt from the album *The Book of Secrets*

"MILLER'S CROSSING"

The City of Prague Philharmonic Orchestra from *The Symphonic Celtic Album*

The Girl in the Castle Playlist *(continued)*

"THE ROAD TO ISENGARD"

Howard Shore from the movie *The Lord of the Rings*: *The Return of the King*

"ROB ROY"

The City of Prague Philharmonic Orchestra from *The Symphonic Celtic Album*

"THE SHAWSHANK REDEMPTION"

The City of Prague Philharmonic Orchestra from *The Symphonic Celtic Album*

"SKELLIG"

Loreena McKennitt from the album *The Book of Secrets*

"TWILIGHT"

The Twilight Orchestra

"WATERMARK"

Enya from the album *Watermark*

"NOW WE ARE FREE"

The City of Prague Philharmonic Orchestra from *The Symphonic Celtic Album*

"BARRY LYNDON"

The City of Prague Philharmonic Orchestra from *The Symphonic Celtic Album* ∾

Recommended Reading

Walled Gardens by Annabel Davis-Goff
Troubles by J. G. Farrell
A Long Long Way by Sebastian Barry
Trinity by Leon Uris
The Children of Castletown House by
    Sarah Conolly-Carew
A Long Way to Go by Marigold Armitage
Picnic in a Foreign Land by Ann Morrow
Society's Queen by Anne de Courcy
Forever Amber by Kathleen Winsor ✑

A Sneak Peek from the Next Book in the Deverill Chronicles

Ballinakelly,
1925

Kitty Trench kissed the little boy's soft cheek. As the child returned her smile, her heart flooded with an aching tenderness. "Be good for Miss Elsie, Little Jack," she said softly. She patted his red hair, which was exactly the same shade as hers.

"I won't be long." She turned to the nanny, the gentleness in her expression giving way to purpose. "Keep a close eye on him, Elsie. Don't let him out of your sight."

Miss Elsie frowned and wondered whether the anxiety on Mrs. Trench's face had something to do with the strange Irishwoman who had turned up at the house the day before. She had stood on the lawn staring at the child, her expression a mixture of sorrow and longing, as if the sight of Little Jack had caused her great anguish. Miss Elsie had approached her and asked if she could help, but the woman had mumbled an excuse and hurriedly bolted for the gate. It was such a peculiar encounter that Miss Elsie had thought to mention it to Mrs. Trench at once. The ferocity of her mistress's reaction had unnerved the nanny. Mrs. Trench had paled and her eyes had filled with fear as if she had, for a long time, dreaded this woman's arrival. She had wrung her hands, not knowing what to do, and she had looked out of the window with her brow drawn into anxious creases. Then, with a sudden burst of resolve, she had run down the garden and disappeared through the gate at the bottom. Miss Elsie didn't know what had passed between the two women, but when Mrs. Trench had returned half an hour later her eyes were red from crying and she was trembling. She had swept the boy into her arms and held him so tightly that Miss Elsie had worried she might smother him. After that, she had taken him upstairs to her bedroom and closed the door behind her, leaving Miss Elsie more curious than ever.

Now the nanny gave her mistress a reassuring smile. "I won't let him out of my sight, Mrs. Trench. I promise," she said, taking the child's hand. "Come, Master Jack, let's go and play with your train."

Kitty went around to the stables and saddled her mare. As she brusquely pulled on the girth and buckled it tightly, she clenched her jaw, replaying the scene from the day before that had kept her up half the night in fevered arguments and the other half in tormented dreams. The woman was Bridie Doyle, Little Jack's natural mother from a brief and scandalous affair with Kitty's father, Lord Deverill, when she had been Kitty's lady's maid, but she had chosen to abandon the baby boy in a convent in Dublin and run off to America. He had then been taken by someone from the convent and left on Kitty's doorstep with a note requesting that she look after him. What else was she to have done? Kitty argued as she mounted the horse. As far as she could see she had done Bridie a great favor for which Bridie should be eternally grateful. Kitty's father had eventually come to recognize his son, and, together with her husband, Robert, Kitty had raised her half brother as if he were her own child—and loved him just as dearly. There was nothing on earth that could separate her from Little Jack now. Nothing. But Bridie was back and she wanted her son. *I had to leave him once, but I won't do it a second time,* she had said, and the cold hand of fear had squeezed Kitty's heart.

Kitty stifled a sob as she rode out of the stable yard. It wasn't so long ago that she and Bridie had been as close as sisters. When Kitty reflected on everything she had lost, she realized that her friendship with Bridie was one of the most precious. But with the unsolvable problem of Little Jack between them she knew that reconciliation was impossible. She had to accept that the Bridie she had loved was long gone.

Kitty galloped across the fields toward the remains of her once glorious home, now a charred and crumbling ruin inhabited only by rooks and the spirits of the dead. Before the fire four years prior, Castle Deverill had stood proud and timeless with its tall windows reflecting the clouds sweeping in over the sea like bright eyes full of dreams. She recalled her grandmother Adeline's little sitting room that smelled of turf ▶

fire and lilac and her grandfather Hubert's penchant for firing his gun at Catholics from his dressing room window. She remembered the musty smell of the library where they'd eat porter cake and play bridge and the small cupboard at the bottom of the servants' staircase where she and Bridie had met secretly as little girls. She smiled at the memory of stealing away from her home in the Hunting Lodge close by to seek entertainment in the affectionate company of her grandparents. In those days the castle had represented a refuge from her uncaring mother and spiteful governess, but now it signified only sorrow and loss and a bygone era that seemed so much more enchanting than the present.

As she galloped across the fields, memories of Castle Deverill in its glory days filled her heart with an intense longing because her father had seen fit to sell it and soon it would belong to somebody else. She thought of Barton Deverill, the first Lord Deverill of Ballinakelly, who had built the castle, and her throat constricted with emotion—nearly three hundred years of family history reduced to ash, and all the male heirs imprisoned within the castle walls for eternity as restless spirits cursed never to find peace. What would become of *them*? It would have been better for her father to have given the ruins to an O'Leary, thus setting them all free and saving himself, but Bertie Deverill didn't believe in curses. Only Kitty and Adeline had had the gift of sight and the misfortune of knowing Bertie's fate. As a child Kitty had found the ghosts amusing; now they just made her sad.

At last the castle came into view. The western tower where her grandmother had set up residence until her death was intact, but the rest of it resembled the bones of a great beast gradually decaying into the forest. Ivy and bindweed pulled on the remaining walls, crept in through the empty windows and endeavored to claim every last stone. And yet, for Kitty, the castle still held a mesmeric allure.

She trotted across the ground that had once been the croquet lawn but was now covered in long grasses and weeds. She dismounted and led her horse around to the front, where her cousin was waiting for her beside a shiny black car. Celia Mayberry stood alone, dressed in an elegant cloche hat, beneath which her blond hair was tied into a neat chignon, and a long black coat that almost reached the ground. When she saw Kitty her face broke into a wide, excited smile.

"Oh, my darling Kitty!' she gushed, striding up and throwing her arms around her. She smelled strongly of tuberose and money and Kitty embraced her fiercely.

"This is a lovely surprise," Kitty exclaimed truthfully, for Celia loved Castle Deverill almost as much as *she* did, having spent every summer of her childhood there with the rest of the "London Deverills" as their English cousins had been known. Kitty felt the need to cling to her with the same ferocity with which she clung to her memories, for Celia was one of the few people in her life who hadn't changed, and as she grew older and further away from the past, Kitty felt ever more grateful for that. "Why didn't you tell me you were coming? You could have stayed with us."

"I wanted to surprise you," said Celia, who looked like a child about to burst with a secret.

"Well, you certainly did that." Kitty looked up at the facade. "It's like a ghost, isn't it? A ghost of our childhood."

"But it will be rebuilt," said Celia firmly.

Kitty looked anxiously at her cousin. "Do you know who bought it? I'm not sure I can bear to know."

Celia laughed. "Me!" she exclaimed. "*I* have bought it. Isn't that wonderful? I'm going to bring back the ghosts of the past and you and I can relive the glorious moments all over again through our children."

"*You*, Celia?" Kitty gasped in astonishment. "*You* bought Castle Deverill?"

"Well, technically Archie bought it. What a generous husband he is!" She beamed with happiness. "Isn't it a riot, Kitty? Well, I'm a Deverill too! I have just as much right as anyone else in the family. Say you're happy, do!"

"Of course I'm happy. I'm relieved it's you and not a stranger, but I admit I'm a little jealous too," Kitty admitted sheepishly.

Celia flung her arms around her cousin again. "Please don't hate me. I did it for *us*. For the family. The castle couldn't possibly go to a stranger. It would be like giving away one's own child. I couldn't bear to think of someone else building over our memories. This way we can all enjoy it. You can continue to live ▶

in the White House, Uncle Bertie in the Hunting Lodge if he so wishes and we can all be terribly happy again. After everything we've suffered we deserve to find happiness, don't you think?"

Kitty laughed affectionately at her cousin's fondness of the dramatic. "You're so right, Celia. It will be wonderful to see the castle brought back to life and by a Deverill no less. It's the way it should be. I only wish it were me."

Celia put a gloved hand on her stomach. "I'm going to have a baby, Kitty," she announced, smiling.

"Goodness, Celia, how many more surprises have you in store for me?"

"Just that and the castle. How about you? Do hurry up. I pray we are both blessed with girls so that they can grow up here at Castle Deverill just like we did." And Kitty realized then that Celia had rewritten her past, placing herself here within these castle walls for more than merely the annual month of August. She was one of those people who revise their own history and then believe in the absolute truth of their own version. "Come on," Celia continued, taking Kitty's hand and pulling her through the doorframe into the space where once the great hall had been. "Let's explore. I have grand plans, you know. I want it to be just the same as it was when we were girls, but better. Do you remember the last Summer Ball? Wasn't it marvelous?"

Kitty and Celia waded through the weeds that grew up to their knees, gazing at the small trees that had seeded themselves among the thistles and thorns and stretched their spindly branches toward the light. The ground was soft against their boots as they moved from room to room, disturbing the odd rook and magpie that flew indignantly into the air. Celia chattered on, reliving the past in colorful anecdotes and fond reminiscences, while Kitty was unable to stop the desolation of her ruined home falling upon her like a heavy black veil. With a leaden heart she remembered her grandfather Hubert, killed in the fire, and her grandmother Adeline, who had died alone in the western tower only a month ago. She thought of Bridie's brother, Michael Doyle, who had set the castle ablaze, and her own foolish thirst for recrimination, which had only led to her shame in his farmhouse, where no one had heard her cries. Her thoughts drifted to her lover, Jack O'Leary, and their meeting at the wall where he had held her tightly and begged her to flee with him to America, then later, on the station platform, when he had been arrested and dragged away. Her head began to spin. Her heart contracted with fear as the monsters of the past were roused from sleep. She left Celia in the remains of the dining room and fled into the library to seek refuge among the more gentle memories of bridge and whist and porter cake.

Kitty leaned back against the wall and closed her eyes with a deep sigh. She realized she was ambivalent about this canary, chattering away about a house whose past she barely understood. Celia's chatter receded, overwhelmed by the autumn wind that moaned about the castle walls. But as Kitty shut off her sight, her sixth sense at once became sensitive to the ghosts now gathering around her. The air, already chilly, grew colder still. There was no surer feeling than this to drag her back to her childhood. Gingerly, she opened her eyes. There, standing before her, was her grandmother, as real as if she were made of flesh and blood, only younger than she had been when she had died and dazzlingly bright, as if she were standing in a spotlight. Behind her stood Kitty's grandfather Hubert, Barton Deverill, the first Lord Deverill of Ballinakelly, and other unfortunate Deverill heirs who were bound by Maggie O'Leary's curse to an eternity in limbo, shifting in and out of her vision like faces in the prism of a precious stone.

Kitty blinked as Adeline smiled on her tenderly. "You know I'm never far away, my dear," Adeline said, and Kitty was so moved by her presence that she barely noticed the hot tears spilling down her cheeks.

"I miss you, Grandma," she whispered.

"Come now, Kitty. You know better than anyone that we are only separated by the boundaries of perception. Love binds us together for eternity. You'll understand eternity when it's your turn. Right now there are more earthly things to discuss."

Kitty wiped her cheeks with her leather glove. "What things?"

"The past," said Adeline, and Kitty knew she meant the prison of the long dead. "The curse *must* be lifted. Perhaps you have the strength to do it; perhaps *only* you."

"But Celia's bought the castle, Grandma." ▶

"Jack O'Leary is the key that will unlock the gates and let them all fly out."

"But I can't have Jack and I don't have the castle." The words gripped her throat like barbed wire. "With all the will in the world I can't make that happen."

"Who are you talking to?" It was Celia. She swept her eyes over the empty room suspiciously and frowned. "You're not speaking to those ghosts of yours, are you? I hope they all go away before Archie and I move in." She laughed nervously. "I was just thinking, I might start a literary salon. I do find literary people so attractive, don't you? Or maybe we'll hire a fashionable spiritualist from London and hold séances. Gosh, that would be amusing. Oliver Cromwell might show up and scare the living daylights out of us all! I've got so many capital ideas. Wouldn't it be a riot to bring back the Summer Ball?" She linked her arm through Kitty's. "Come, let's leave the car here and walk with your horse to the Hunting Lodge. I left Archie to tell Uncle Bertie about us buying the castle. What do you think he'll say?"

Kitty took a deep breath to regain her composure. Those who have suffered develop patience and she had always been good at hiding her pain. "I think he'll be as happy as I am," she said, making her way back through the hall at her cousin's side. "Blood is thicker than water. That's something we Deverills all agree on."

Bridget Lockwood sat at the wooden table in the farmhouse where she had been raised as Bridie Doyle and felt awkwardly out of place. She was too big for the room, as if she had outgrown the furniture, low ceilings and meager windows from where she had once gazed upon the stars and dreamed of a better life. Her clothes were too elegant, her kid gloves and fine hat as incongruous in this house as a circus pony in a cowshed. As Mrs. Lockwood she had become too refined to derive any pleasure from her old simple way of life. Yet the girl in her who had suffered years of clawing homesickness in America longed to savor the familiar comfort of the home for which she had pined. How often had she dreamed of sitting in this very chair, drinking buttermilk, tasting the smoke from the turf fire and inhaling the sweet smell of cows from the barn next door? How many times had she craved her feather bed, her father's tread on the stair, her mother's good-night kiss and her grandmother's quiet mumbling of the rosary? Too many to count and yet here she was in the middle of all that she had missed. So why did she feel so sad? Because she was no longer that girl. Not a trace of her remained except Little Jack.

The farmhouse had filled with locals keen to welcome Bridie back from America, and everyone had commented on her pretty blue tea dress with its beads and tassels and her matching blue T-bar shoes, and the women had rubbed the fabric of her skirt between rough fingers, for only in their dreams would they ever possess such luxuries. There had been dancing, laughter and their neighbor Badger Hanratty's illegal poteen, but Bridie had felt as if she were watching it all from behind a pane of smoked glass, unable to connect with any of the people she had once known and loved so well. She had outgrown them. She had watched Rosetta, her Italian maid and companion whom she had brought back from America, and envied her. The girl had been swung about the room by Bridie's brother Sean, who had clearly lost his heart to her, and by the look on her face she had felt more at home than Bridie had. How Bridie had wished she could kick off her shoes and dance as they did, and yet she couldn't. Her heart was too heavy with grief for her son—and hatred for Kitty Deverill.

Bridie yearned to slip back into the skin she had shed when she had left as a twenty-one-year-old, pregnant and terrified, to hide her secret in Dublin. But the trauma of childbirth, and the wrench of leaving Ireland and her son, had changed Bridie Doyle forever. She had been expecting *one* baby, and was astonished when another, a little girl the nuns had later told her, had arrived, tiny and barely alive, in his wake. They had taken her away to try and revive her, but returned soon after to inform Bridie that the baby had not lived. It was better, they had said, that she nurture the living twin and leave the other to God. Bridie hadn't even been allowed to kiss her daughter's face and say good-bye. Her baby had vanished as if she had never been. Then Lady Rowan-Hampton had persuaded Bridie to leave her son in the care of the nuns and she had been sent off to start a new life in America.

No one who has given away a child can know the bitter ▶

desolation and burning guilt of that act. She had already lived more roles than most do in their entire lifetime, and yet to Sean, her mother and her grandmother, she was still their Bridie. They knew nothing of the sorrows she had suffered in America or the anguish she suffered now as she realized her son would never know his mother or the wealth she had, by accident and guile, amassed. They believed she was their Bridie still. She didn't have the heart to tell them that their Bridie was gone.

She reflected on her attempt to buy Castle Deverill, and wondered, if it had succeeded, would she have been willing to stay? Had she tried to buy it as an act of revenge for the wrongs inflicted on her by Bertie and Kitty Deverill, or because of a purer sense of nostalgia? After all, her mother had been the castle's cook and she had grown up running up and down its corridors with Kitty. How would they have reacted on discovering that poor, shoeless Bridie Doyle had become doyenne of Castle Deverill? The smile that crept across her face confirmed that her intention had been born out of resentment and motivated by a desire to wound. If the opportunity ever arose again, she would take it.

When Sean, Rosetta, Mrs. Doyle and Bridie's grandmother, Old Mrs. Nagle, appeared in the parlor ready for Mass, Bridie asked them all to sit down. She took a deep breath and knitted her fingers. The faces stared anxiously at her. Bridie looked from her mother to her grandmother, then to Rosetta, who sat beside Sean, her face flushed with the blossoming of love. "When I was in America I got married," she declared.

Mrs. Doyle and Old Mrs. Nagle looked at her in astonishment. "You're a married woman, Bridie?" said Mrs. Doyle quietly.

"I'm a widow, Mam," Bridie corrected her.

Her grandmother crossed herself. "Married and widowed at twenty-five, God save us! And not chick or child to comfort." Bridie winced but her grandmother did not know the hurt her words had caused.

Mrs. Doyle ran her eyes over her daughter's blue dress and crossed herself as well. "Why aren't you in mourning, Bridie? Any decent widow would wear black to honor her husband."

"I am done with black," Bridie retorted. "Believe me, I have mourned my husband enough."

"Be thankful that your brother Michael isn't here to witness your shame." Mrs. Doyle pressed a handkerchief to her mouth to stifle a sob. "I have worn black since the day your father was taken from us, God rest him, and I will wear it until I join him, God help me."

"Bridie is too young to give up on life, Mam," said Sean gently. "And Michael is in no position to stand in judgment over anybody. I'm sorry, Bridie," he said to his sister and his voice was heavy with sympathy. "How did he die?"

"A heart attack," Bridie replied.

"Surely he was too young for a heart attack?" said Mrs. Doyle.

Bridie's eyes flicked to Rosetta. She wasn't about to reveal that Mr. Lockwood had been old enough to be her father.

"Indeed, it was most unfortunate that he died in his prime. I was planning on bringing him here so that Father Quinn could give us his blessing and you could all meet him . . . but . . ."

"God's will," said Mrs. Doyle tightly, affronted that Bridie hadn't bothered to write and tell them of her marriage. "What was his name?"

"Walter Lockwood and he was a fine man."

"Mrs. Lockwood," said Old Mrs. Nagle thoughtfully. She clearly liked the sound of it.

"We met at Mass," Bridie told them with emphasis, feeling the sudden warmth of approval at the mention of the Church.

"He courted me after Mass every Sunday and we grew fond of each other. We were married only seven months, but in those seven months I can honestly say that I have never been so happy. I have much to be grateful for. Although my grief is deep, I am in a position to share my good fortune with my family. He left me broken-hearted but very rich."

"Nothing is more important than your faith, Bridie Doyle," said Old Mrs. Nagle, crossing herself again. "But I'm old enough to remember the Great Famine. Money cannot buy happiness but it can surely save us from starvation and hardship and help us to be miserable in comfort, God help us." Her wrinkled old eyes, as small as raisins, shone in the gloomy ▶

light of the room. "The road to sin is paved with gold. But tell me, Bridie, how much are we talking?"

"A cross in this life, a crown in the next," said Mrs. Doyle gravely. "God has seen fit to help us in these hard times, for *that* our hearts must be full of gratitude," she added, suddenly forgetting her daughter's shameful blue dress and the fact that she never wrote to tell them about her marriage. "God bless you, Bridie. I will exchange the washboard for a mangle and thank the Lord for his goodness. Now, to Mass. Let us not forget your brother Michael at Mount Melleray Abbey, Bridie. Let us do another novena to St. Jude that he will be saved from the drink and delivered back to us sober and repentant. Sean, hurry up now, let us not be late."

Bridie sat in the cart in an elegant green coat with fur trimming, alongside her mother and grandmother, wrapped in heavy woolen shawls, and poor Rosetta who was practically falling out of the back, for it was not made for so many. Sean sat above in his Sunday best, driving the donkey who struggled with the weight, until they reached the hill, at which point Bridie and Rosetta walked with Sean to lighten the animal's load. A cold wind blew in off the sea, playfully seeking to grab Bridie's hat and carry it away. She held it in place with a firm hand, dismayed to see her fine leather boots sinking into the mud. She resolved to buy her brother a car so that he could drive to Mass, but somehow she knew her grandmother would object to what she considered *éirí in airde* "airs and graces." There would be no ostentatious show of wealth in this family as long as she was alive.

Father Quinn had heard of Bridie's triumphant return to Ballinakelly and his greedy eyes settled on her expensive coat and hat and the soft leather gloves on her hands, and knew that she would give generously to the church; after all, there was no family in Ballinakelly more devout than the Doyles. He decided that today's sermon would be about charity and smiled warmly on Bridie Doyle.

Bridie walked down the aisle with her chin up and her shoulders back. She could feel every eye upon her and knew what they were thinking. How far she had come from the ragged and barefoot child she had once been, terrified of Father Quinn's hellfire visions, critical finger-wagging and bullying sermons. She thought of Kitty Deverill with her pretty dresses and silk ribbons in her hair and that fool Celia Deverill who had asked her, "How do you survive in winter without any shoes?" and then the girls at school who had called her a tinker for wearing the dancing shoes Lady Deverill had given her after her father's death, and the seed of resentment that had rooted itself in her heart sprouted yet another shoot to stifle the sweetness there. Her great wealth gave her a heady sense of power. *No one will dare call me a tinker again,* she told herself as she took the place beside her brother, *for I am a lady now and I command their respect.*

It wasn't until she was lighting a candle at the end of Mass that she was struck with a daring yet brilliant idea. If Kitty didn't allow her to see her child she would simply take him. It wouldn't be stealing because you couldn't steal what already belonged to you. *She* was his mother; it was right and natural that he should be with *her.* She would take him to America and start a new life. It was so obvious she couldn't imagine why she hadn't thought of it before. She smiled, blowing out the little flame at the end of the taper. Of course such inspiration had come directly from God. She had been given it at the very moment she had lit the candle for her son. *That* was no coincidence; it was divine intervention, for sure. She silently crossed herself and thanked the Lord for his compassion.

Outside, the locals gathered together on the wet grass as they always did, to greet one another and share the gossip, but today they stood in a semicircle like a herd of timid cows, curious eyes trained on the church door, eagerly awaiting the extravagantly dressed Bridie Doyle to flounce out in her newly acquired finery. In hushed tones they could talk of nothing else: "They say she married a rich old man." "But he died, God rest his soul, and left her a fortune." "He was eighty." "He was ninety, for shame.'" "She always had ideas above her station, did she not?'" "Ah ha, she'll be after another husband now, God save us." "But none of our sons will be good enough for her now." The old people crossed themselves and saw no virtue in her prosperity, for wasn't it written in Matthew that it is easier for a camel to go through the eye of a needle than for a rich man to enter the Kingdom ▶

of God? But the young were both resentful and admiring in equal measure and longed with all their hearts to sail as Bridie had done to this land of opportunity and plenty and make fortunes for themselves.

When Bridie stepped out she was startled to find the people of Ballinakelly huddled in a jumble, waiting to see her as if she were royalty. A hush fell about them and no one made a move to meet her. They simply stared and muttered to each other under their breaths. Bridie swept her eyes over the familiar faces of those she had grown up with and found in them a surprising shyness. For a moment she was self-conscious and anxiously looked around for a friend. That was when she saw Jack O'Leary.

He was pushing through the throng, smiling at her reassuringly. His dark brown hair fell over his forehead as it always had, and his pale wintry eyes shone out blue and twinkling with their habitual humor. His lips were curled and Bridie's heart gave a little start at the intimacy in his smile. It took her back to the days when they had been friends. "Jack!" she uttered when he reached her.

He took her arm and walked her across the graveyard to a place far from the crowd, where they could speak alone. "Well, would you look at you, Bridie Doyle," he said, shaking his head and rubbing the long bristles on his jaw. "Don't you look like a lady now!"

Bridie basked in his admiration. "I *am* a lady, I'll have you know," she replied, and Jack noticed how her Irish vowels had been worn thin in America. "I'm a widow. My husband died," she added and crossed herself. "God rest my husband's soul."

"I'm sorry to hear that, Bridie. You're too young to mourn a husband." He ran his eyes over her coat. "I've got to say that you look grand," he added, and as he grinned Bridie noticed that one of his teeth was missing. He looked older too. The lines were deeper around his eyes and mouth, his skin dark and weathered, his gaze deep and full of shadows. Even though his smile remained undimmed, Bridie sensed that he had suffered. He was no longer the insouciant young man with the arrogant gaze, a hawk on his arm, a dog at his heel. There was something touching about him now and she wanted to reach out and run her fingers across his brow.

"Are you back for good?" he asked.

"I don't know, Jack." She turned into the gale and placed her hand on top of her hat to stop it from blowing away. Fighting her growing sense of alienation, she added, "I don't know where I belong now. I came back expecting everything to be the same, but it is *I* who have changed and that makes everything different." Then, aware of sounding vulnerable, she turned back to him and her voice hardened. "I can hardly live the way I used to. I'm accustomed to finer things, you see." Jack arched an eyebrow and Bridie wished she hadn't put on airs in front of him. If there was a man who knew her for what she really was, it was Jack. "Did you marry?" she asked.

"No," he replied. A long silence followed. A silence that resonated with the name Kitty Deverill, as if it came in a whisper on the wind and lingered there between them. "Well, I hope it all turns out well for you, Bridie. It's good to see you home again," he said at last. Bridie was unable to return his smile. Her loathing for her old friend wound around her heart in a twine of thorns. She watched him walk away with that familiar jaunty gait she knew so well and had loved so deeply. It was obvious that, after all these years, he still held out for Kitty Deverill. ◠